MW00574686

HALL OF MIRRORS

also by john copenhaver

Dodging and Burning

The Savage Kind

HALL
OF
MIRRORS

BOOK TWO OF THE NIGHTINGALE TRILOGY

JOHN COPENHAVER

PEGASUS CRIME
NEW YORK LONDON

HALL OF MIRRORS

Pegasus Crime is an imprint of
Pegasus Books, Ltd.
148 West 37th Street, 13th Floor
New York, NY 10018

First Pegasus Books edition June 2024

Interior design by Maria Fernandez

Library of Congress Cataloging-in-Publication Data is available.

ISBN: 978-1-63936-650-7

10 9 8 7 6 5 4 3 2 1

Printed in the United States of America
Distributed by Simon & Schuster
www.pegasusbooks.com

Dedicated to the memory of Margaret and Elizabeth Hull
for their flair for life, independent spirit, and love of DC

"What are friends for, if not to help bear our sins?"

—Nella Larson from *Passing*

CHAPTER 1

MAY 1, 1954, LIONEL

I'm aware of the clear dusk sky beyond the smoke. I'm aware of cherry blossoms hanging in the breeze weeks past their peak. I'm aware of our building's Spanish Colonial Revival facade, its tiers and molded ledges and balconies sweeping upward, its demonic grotesques perched on the cornice, looming in vain, having failed to ward off evil spirits.

Firefighters rush past me, wearing wide-brimmed helmets, gas masks with trunk-like noses, bulky coats marred with the residue of past fires, and tall boots like fishermen's waders. They grip fire extinguishers and haul limp extra hoses over their shoulders. The polished nozzles glint in the light from the building's lobby entrance. They call out commands and move with extraordinary purpose, giving some order to the chaos. A hook and ladder truck, its wheel up over the curb and crushing a fledgling redbud tree, buzzes with commotion. The long expandable ladder shifts and begins to angle up. The clean-faced firefighter at its helm is so intent on his job that he briefly (and bizarrely) charms me. Not far behind me, distraught neighbors and nosey, babbling pedestrians gather. Parting the sea, the ambulance crew appear, searching for direction.

When I first visited the building, Roger stopped near this spot on the sidewalk, slid his hand across my shoulder, a gesture both thrilling and unsettling in a public space, and pointed to windows along the ninth floor. "We'll live up there forever, darling," he said, leaning in, his voice soft, conspiratorial. "We'll throw parties. We'll sip martinis and watch DC blink to life in the evenings. Just you and me." I cracked those windows at his request this morning to let in the mellow spring air. Now, a ribbon of black smoke seeps from those raised sashes, and I'm sure I spot a flame flicker behind the glass. A line of poetry surfaces: "His eyes darkened by too great a light." It's from Ovid, I think. A god riding a chariot too close to the sun, blinded by its rays. Perhaps that's it—Roger and I have flown too close and got burned, *are* burning.

Philippa is standing beside me, her hand gently touching the back of my arm, an awkward but tender attempt to console me. Judy, not the consoling type, stands a few feet from me, her arms crossed, her chin up, her dark eyes like twin camera lenses, recording it all.

Maybe Judy or Philippa mentioned Ovid? They tend to go on about cultural tidbits: "Gloria Grahame is just glorious in *The Big Heat.*" Or "Did you see *South Pacific* at the National? Those songs stuck to me like glue." Or "Hand over Kinsey's new book! I can't wait to read what he has to say about women." Or maybe the poet's words echo from my grade school days, something I was made to memorize but forgot, something buried deep, dislodged as I watch my life turn to ash.

I should be screaming; I should be crying.

Maybe it's shock. How did this happen? Was it my fault? Did I forget to turn off the stove? Did Roger fail to unplug the toaster? He can be forgetful. What about the bathroom heater? The towels dangle too close to it. I've noted it before. Maybe it wasn't our fault, but carelessness from another of the building's residents—a janitor ashing his cigarette in an oily bucket or a housewife neglecting her curling iron? Or maybe it's a defect in the fuse box, old mouse-eaten wiring, or a spark from colliding elevator cables?

It's a chilly evening, but I'm sweating, drenched.

Roger isn't inside, of course. Sure, he said he'd be home this afternoon, but he would've stopped the fire if he were inside. He would've used his strong runner's legs, dashed into the hall, yanked the extinguisher from the wall, and choked the flames with sodium bicarbonate. His naval training during the war, and his ability to stay cool under pressure, would've served him well. No. He's not there. There's no way. Maybe he's out securing work. We need him to find a new job, a damn good job. Or maybe he ran to the store for dinner fixings.

Just in case, as a cosmic barter, I lean into the horror. "Take my things," I say to God, to the universe, "but just don't take Roger!" In my mind, I fly up nine stories and turn time back an hour. I'm standing in the middle of the room we created by knocking down the non-load-bearing wall between the dining and main living areas. It's spacious, contemporary, and furnished with low-slung Herman Miller pieces in rosewood, upholstered in fabrics with bold geometric patterns. Against the back wall stands my gift to Roger last Christmas—a record player cabinet filled with Sinatra, Miller, Cole, Gillespie, Davis, and Peggy Lee—and beside it, a brass bar cart stocked with gin, martini glasses with delicate stems, and a big glass shaker that weighs a goddamn ton. The wine-red oriental rug, a bequest from his grandmother's estate, stretches over the wood floor, its weave flecked with golds, pinks, and an unusual tangerine. An ornate Victorian settee, a family heirloom I tolerate, rests under the window, a place to sip coffee, stare out, and daydream.

We papered the far wall in a bold poppy print, modern and a tad garish—absolutely a statement. It's there, amid the poppies, that I imagine the first flame emerging, as if the bright red-orange petals, inspired by their color, transmute into fire. The thick paper bubbles and hisses and begins to peel off; strips float to the floor, igniting the thin layer of linseed oil polish and sending a ripple of bluish fire across the wood. The glass on the starburst clock, now circled with flame, cracks and pops out. The hands stop. 7:24.

In a blast of heat, the upright piano makes a strange sound, like ghostly fingers swiping its strings. The photos Roger displayed on its top waver and topple over. They are black-and-whites of his dead grandparents, his mild mother and hard-visaged father, his grim aunt and uncle, his myopic sister, Rose Ellen, him looking handsome in his lieutenant's uniform, and the two of us on a hike in Shenandoah National Park, pressing close, laughing, soon to be tugging at each other's clothes behind a boulder, giggling like damn idiots, aroused, and happy, so happy. When the photo of us crashes to the floor, my heart lurches. Having gathered immense and uncontrollable energy, my imaginary blaze suddenly roars at me, bringing me back.

Roger and I are good at imagining the worst—an occupational hazard.

I remember a scene in our third Ray Kane novel, *Seeing Red*: "McKey paused at the door, heat radiating out, inky smoke blooming from its keyhole, its doorknob a branding iron. What was inside was more than some maniac arson's delight, but a demonic force, sentient and vicious, poised to consume."

Had Roger written the passage, or had I? I couldn't remember.

Then I smell it. The actual fire. It's a greasy odor, like an old furnace, and then something sulfurous and nauseating: the scent of death, burning hair. How could I smell it so far away? Am I inventing it? Oh, God. The wall of numbness cracks, and pain floods in. It's a sharp physical pang that knocks the breath out of me. My knees wobble, and I lean into Philippa, who, at a svelte twenty-two, is fifty pounds lighter than me. She catches me, her grip assured as if she were bracing for this, my collapse, and steadies me. Judy steps close, gazing at me, her eyes concerned and quiet, even a little cold. As the tremor dissipates, tears well up, and I sob.

Somehow, I know that Roger is dead.

CHAPTER 2

MARCH 1954, JUDY

Philippa flung open the apartment door. "You're here!" she cried, her loose curls bouncing and her light blue tea dress swaying. "I have something *amazing* to show you." She tugged off her gloves. I never knew what to say to her when she was in one of her exuberant manias: all that cheer rushing at me like water breaking through a dam. And me, after another exhausting day at my new job, trying to unwind on the sofa, a pile of sticks with busted springs we bought last weekend at a church rummage sale. I'm not an ogre, I want you to know, so I forced a smile.

She flounced beside me, the couch's brittle legs groaning underneath us, plopped her purse on the coffee table, popped the clasp—it was a trim leather bag with a bamboo handle (we spent more on clothes than decor!)—and produced a folded piece of paper. I eyed the half-consumed bottle of Claret on our sad little cracked Formica kitchenette counter, strategizing how to nab a drink before she gushed her news. She turned to me, beaming, and paused. She sensed my exasperation, even though I did my best to conceal it. She pressed her lips together and worried them, removing the last traces of her coral lipstick. "I'm so sorry," she said, lowering her hand to my knee. "I'm just . . . well."

"I'm used to it," I said, winking at her.

She leaned in for a kiss. The residue of her eau de toilette mingled with the faint odor of her sweat. I returned the kiss, glad to feel her so close.

She's a beautiful woman, even more striking than she was when we first met in high school. Her layer of baby fat has melted away, and her fleshy schoolgirl femininity, which once offered a striking counterpoint to my rail-thin body, barbed elbows, and razorblade knees, has transformed into something finer. Her cheekbones are more prominent, and her chin narrower, heightening her silvery blue eyes and the wide curl of her hair. Her hourglass figure has no need for a girdle, and she walks with a model's measured gait. When men gawk at her, which they always do, panic bubbles up in me: fear that they might try something. If they do, watch out! She's mine, and I bite. My greater fear is that one day she'll lose her restlessness and become the thing she often pretends to be: a nice young lady. I worry that she'll mute her dark shine under a shroud of pastels, floral prints, and tailored quarter-sleeve jackets. But, when we touch, whether it's a brief kiss or something demonstrative and carnal, I'm reassured. Her restlessness is still intact; she's still mine.

She withdrew and handed me the slip of paper. I unfolded it. It was the flyer for a lecture:

THE ART OF WRITING THE PERFECT MYSTERY

Author of the P. I. Calvin McKey mystery series, Mr. Ray Kane, explains all the tricks to create spellbinding twists and turns and unforgettable characters.

His most popular titles include
Love's Last Move and *The Broken Thread.*

Spend your April Fools with us!
Stop by for a delightful evening . . .
of murder and mayhem.

Book signing to follow!

April 1, 7:00 P.M.
Brentano's on F Street

"Can you believe it!" she gasped, wide-eyed. "I saw the flyer at school."
Philippa was churning through her first year of a master's in literature at
GW. She still dreamed of being a writer—a Daphne du Maurier or Anya
Seton—all dark, swooning, and psychological. She'd retained that dreamy
Romanticism from her high school days. Together and in our time apart,
we'd devoured all of Ray Kane's detective novels over the years but had
never attended a lecture or a signing. As popular as he was, he didn't
make public appearances, which was unusual. Mystery writers, I've found,
love to get up in front of polite audiences and talk about things like
strychnine poisoning and vivisection and the electric chair. The little old
ladies and mild businessmen eat it up—and buy books. But Kane hadn't
stepped out of the shadows, not until now.

"Let's splurge," she said. "We'll have an early dinner downtown, maybe
oysters at Harvey's, and go to the lecture. Would Iris want to join us?"

"She doesn't want to tempt fate at Harvey's. Times are changing,
but . . ."

Philippa sighed and, failing to conceal her irritation, said, "Maybe we
could eat somewhere on U Street? Maybe the restaurant at the Dunbar
Hotel? Then we could make our way down."

Going out was always a puzzle to solve. How would we appear to others? Who did we seem to be from one location to the next? If Philippa and I were out at a place like Harvey's, we were two white women sipping gimlets and gossiping. Perhaps a few leering men would read me as "exotic"—from the Mideast, from the Far East, oh my!—but the default was white. It was easy for me to pass, as I had, unknowingly, my entire childhood. My olive skin and straight black bob, and let's be honest, the texture of my upbringing by the Peabodys embellished the veneer further. As their adopted "white" daughter, it served me well to play into people's assumptions. Their blindness was my advantage; it still is.

On the other hand, if we went to a Negro-owned establishment, the patrons would gaze at us, narrow their eyes, and gently shake their heads. I imagined them saying, "Girls, are you sure you have the right place?" When Iris joined us for a night out—as rare as that was—we could only be read one way, and the restaurant options were decidedly fewer. With her, any veneer failed. She was who she was: a graduate of Howard Medical School, a take-no-prisoners bridge player, a daughter, a sister, and, in these settings, a Negro woman. In a restaurant together, her presence summoned our kinship to the surface; our skin, hair, physicality, and hand gestures, when offered for comparison, suggested our connection by race, by blood. It was more profound than that, of course. We were sisters, and that truth endlessly echoed between us, a kinetic energy identifiable at a glance.

"What do you think?" Philippa said, urging a response, perhaps a touch guilty for being annoyed at having to revise her plans.

"Sounds fine," I said stiffly. "But I doubt Iris will join us for the lecture. She doesn't like mystery novels now that she works at the medical examiner's office. Their inaccuracies frustrate her."

This news deflated her. "Well," she said, sighing again. "As always, she's entirely welcome."

Now I was annoyed: "*Of course,* Iris is welcome." I knew it, and Philippa knew it. "I get it," I said. "You and Iris aren't best friends, but we live here, in this apartment with cracked plaster and above-average square footage, because of her."

Iris lived in the unit below us and helped me snag the apartment by flirting with her lovestruck landlord and vouching for me. I didn't say, "We can be together because of her." I didn't need to.

Philippa grimaced, making unlovely her lovely features. "I know." She stood. "You don't need to remind me."

Iris had been slow to accept us as a couple. As time passed, she warmed a little to the idea that women could be romantically involved, but she didn't warm to Philippa. She would often raise an eyebrow at something she said or shoot her a skeptical glance. She winced at Philippa's doubleness: that special blend of blithe naïveté and impulsiveness that I loved about her. She thought Philippa was bad news, dangerous even. Once, when Philippa and I had fallen out of touch for a time, she told me: "White girls like her, they sashay through your life, unaware of the destruction they cause, because they don't have to be. You're better off without her."

Philippa walked across the room, snatched the Claret from the counter, plucked a clean wine glass from the drying rack, and poured herself a little. "Want some?" she asked. She didn't want to barrel into an argument, thank God.

"Um, yes," I said. "I've been staring down that bottle and waiting to pounce."

She gave me the glass in her hand and selected another from the shelf, inspecting it for dust.

She flopped beside me, her pale blue dress falling over my knees, leaned into me, and sipped the ruby-colored liquid. The creaky couch was the safest spot for us to be. We yearned for places where we could be a couple. The segregated gay bars downtown made me uneasy. Too well acquainted with flimsy facades, their patrons were talented at sniffing out a pretender like me. So, we usually ended up at Croc's, a gloomy lounge in the basement of a hardware store, where we could be ourselves amid the dim lights and sticky floors.

Philippa took another sip and set down her glass. "Can you believe it," she said, her tone softer, more reflective. "We'll see Ray Kane and maybe even talk to him. He's been with us from the beginning." The cover art of the first of Kane's novels we read, *Love's Last Move*, came to mind. It was a pulpy still life: a smoking gun surrounded by artfully arranged rose petals, an invitation to the allure of murder.

"If we do get to meet him," I cautioned, "remember we can't tell him—"

"I know, I know," she said, waving it off.

"We can't tell him what we sent him last summer."

"I'm not an idiot," she said. "I'm sure it never made it to him, anyway."

"Maybe," I said, recalling the packet of information we'd carefully collated, annotated, and mailed out—talk about an invitation to the allure of murder. We'd waited all fall and winter, twiddling our thumbs, but he never responded. None of the recipients had. Be more positive, Judy: None had *yet*.

◦──◦──◦

When Philippa and I arrived at Brentano's, it was teeming with people. Our tiff about Iris and dinner plans was for naught. She couldn't join us after all—an influx of bodies at the morgue. Spring fever had a body count.

The store was clean and well organized, one of our favorites, but it lacked the dingy charm of the bookstore we visited as teenagers, Somerset's, with its velvet-curtained backroom full of dirty trash and delicious banned books.

Philippa drifted over to a display and began flipping through the new Anya Seton novel. I lingered over March's much-buzzed-about *The Bad*

Seed. We already owned Kane's latest novel, *The Broken Thread*—one of his best—loosely based on the murder of a socialite in 1920s Baltimore and the young maid accused of the crime. We borrowed it from the library last year when it was first released and, after reading it repeatedly, added it to our collection. It was wedged in Philippa's purse beside *Love's Last Move*, the inscribed copy that had flung us headlong into an adventure years ago and held the key to the murder of our classmate, Cleve Closs. We wanted Kane to sign it.

An officious clerk in a pencil skirt and wire-framed glasses strolled into the center of the room and invited us to take our seats; the lecture would begin soon. Patrons abandoned browsing and moved to the rear of the store, where chairs were lined up, and a podium stood sentinel, waiting for Kane.

We grabbed seats in the front row.

The audience was primarily middle-aged women and a smattering of businessmen dropping in after work. Most of them were clutching Kane's newer novels. After a delay, during which the audience's hushed sideways chitchat grew louder, the clerk and Kane emerged from the backroom. The woman approached the podium and, reading from notecards, introduced Kane—a writer of popular detective novels, well known for his protagonist P. I. Calvin McKey and "a splendid practitioner of contemporary mystery fiction"—and reminded us to purchase his books and then, at last, relinquished the podium.

Kane was tall, wide-shouldered, and slender-waisted. Above his high forehead, his lick of chestnut hair was parted to the side and close-cropped. His striking facial features, which I'd noted on the cover flap, were diminished, grooved with worry lines at his eyes and the corners of his mouth. He was pushing forty. He wore a fine wool double-breasted suit tailored to hug his thin hips. He grabbed the sides of the podium and scanned the room without smiling, squinting at us as if he were short-sighted and had forgotten his glasses. Rousing a little, he greeted us, thanked the store, slipped a folded piece of paper from his pocket, flattened it out on the podium, and began reading: "At their core, crime novels embrace duality. Two stories are being told: the story of the present, the investigation, and the story of the past, that storyline which has been concealed by misinterpretation, manufactured untruths, and even the patchy fog of memory. In the case of a crime novel, the story, at first glance, might be about a legal transgression—the breaking of law—but any crime novelist worth his salt should be writing about morals, not laws." He paused and glanced up. His pale forehead was damp with sweat. He patted it with a handkerchief and returned to his lecture: "While in a perfect world legality and morality should align, it's often true that they are at odds, so crime novels, such as the books that bear the name Ray Kane, aren't telling neat stories about how a criminal breaks the rules and gets his just deserts for his transgression. At times, they are about how blindly following the rules can be more reprehensible than breaking them; at times, breaking the law is the right thing to do." Someone huffed behind me and shifted in their seat. Where was this talk headed? Sure, Kane's novels covered all matters of moral terrain, but this felt different. Something in his voice, some underlying distress, was bleeding through. Was it anger? "For instance, take the new novel, *The Broken Thread*, which was based on the case of Margery Smith, a young black woman falsely accused of robbing and bludgeoning to death the Baltimorean socialite Agnes Linden Abell in 1923."

As the lecture rolled on, Kane craned over the podium, gripping its sides, stabilizing himself. Even though the room wasn't especially warm, a sheen of sweat covered his features and dampened his collar. Was he ill? Or drunk? His explanation of the writing process behind *The Broken Thread* surged forward with intensity, his investment in the real Margery Smith's innocence clear, his disdain for the Abell family's snobbery and racial biases unmistakable. Still, his sentences were halting, becoming, like the title of his novel, a broken thread. I tried to follow his points but eventually gave up, lapsing into a daydream. Not all authors were adept at public speaking—the inner eloquence that flowed from the mind to the page didn't always flow from mind to lips—but this was something else; Kane seemed physically off-kilter like he might collapse at any moment. After his closing remarks, instead of asking for questions, he released the sides of the podium and stumbled backward, catching the arm of a chair against the back wall and guiding himself into it with a clumsy thud. Something was seriously wrong.

I popped up from my seat, shot a hot glare at the store clerk, grabbed the glass of water on the table beside the podium, and handed it to Kane, who stared up at me, confused. He whispered to me, "So dizzy. No lunch," creating an immediate, if odd, intimacy between us. He took the glass and swiftly gulped it down. Miss Officious was behind me, cooing concern. Philippa hovered nearby as well. The audience was on their feet, murmuring. Over my shoulder, I told Philippa: "Run next door to the bakery and grab a roll or something. He needs food."

An impatient audience member asked the clerk: "Is he still going to sign books?" The woman glanced at Kane through her wire-rimmed glasses, and he raised a finger as if to say, "Give me a minute."

"Jesus," I blurted, and Kane cracked a knowing smile.

Miss Officious refilled his glass and handed it to him. While Kane was preoccupied and the clerk calmed and corralled the patrons, I noticed that, in Kane's awkward tumble into the chair, his wallet had escaped and fallen, its flaps making a little brown tent on the floor. I scooped it up, and on the inside of a flap, I briefly glimpsed a photo before snapping it closed and handing it to him. Still dazed, he took it, nodded, and slipped it into his coat. From what I could tell, the photo was taken in a booth. In it, a younger version of Kane embraced a handsome, clean-shaven, short-haired, light-skinned Negro looking at the camera, squinting gleefully. Kane was looking away, and both men were laughing.

Finally, Philippa returned with an elaborate sticky bun wrapped in wax paper. Gathering his energy, Kane took a bite. "Damn," he said, "that's good." Philippa glanced at me, pleased with herself.

Most of the audience, irked by the situation, had fled, but after a few more minutes of eating, Kane revived enough to sign books.

We let the other fans go first, not wanting them breathing down our necks. Before approaching him, I whispered to Philippa, "Remember not to mention the morbid care package we sent him."

She glared at me. "I'm not a child, Judy. I don't need reminding."

Color had returned to his cheeks, and as she handed him *The Broken Thread* and *Love's Last Move*, he smiled at us. "Your names?"

"I'm Philippa, and this is Judy."

"Which book belongs to whom?"

Recalling the photo from his wallet, I said, "Sign each to both of us. We share *everything*." He perked up, eyebrow cocked, clearly detecting my emphasis on "everything." He must be wondering: girl *friends* or girlfriends?

He scrawled something on the title page and said, "Philippa, that's an unusual name. You don't hear it that often," and handed it back to her. She reverently opened the novel to inspect his John Hancock as if it were the final sacrament of a holy ritual.

"Roger?" she asked, perplexed.

"Oh no," he said, his shoulders drooping. "That's my real name. I'm so sorry."

"*Real* name?" I asked. Now I was the one with an eyebrow cocked.

"My name is Roger Raymond."

Philippa beamed. "Ray Kane is a nom de plume."

"That's right," he said, bewildered. "I've been out of my mind today. This isn't my usual modus operandi."

I shrugged, and Philippa said, "It makes the book more valuable, I imagine."

He offered a weary smirk. "If only that were true. If things keep going as they have, before too long, you may be burning it."

What was he talking about? Something weighed on him, but despite my instinct, I wouldn't pry. I detected a guarded nature in him, like my own. After a childhood of ordeals, my battlements were as thick as the Great Wall, and as high. I could spot the same quality in others. But all hard surfaces show cracks when light strikes them at just the right angle. I wondered about the photo in his wallet. Was the other man a lost lover?

"Let me say thanks by buying you a coffee—or maybe a drink?" He scanned us, perhaps noticing how close we stood to each other, our arms touching, at ease in one another's personal space. If he'd had a thought bubble, it would've read: "Girlfriends. Definitely, girlfriends." "I know a cozy place around the corner."

Philippa and I had gobbled oysters at Harvey's but held off on drinks. A Scotch on the rocks sounded good about now.

"Perfect," Philippa said, stealing the word from my lips.

⊙━┿━⊙

Roger's "cozy place around the corner" wasn't around the corner but blocks away, on 9th Street, and it was a gay bar called Cary's. He must've known what kind of place it was; the man who wrote the P. I. Calvin McKey novels wasn't naïve. In a closeted world, establishing a connection between people like us was often a slow unfurling, clues being dropped and picked up, the complete picture gradually emerging. It was dangerous to be vulnerable, especially in a town like this. But maybe he felt comfortable with us because he'd intuited that we were a couple, or because we'd run to his aid, or because he was in a reckless mood. Considering what I'd gleaned from his wallet, I reassured him by endorsing Cary's as a "swell watering hole." When I said this, Philippa gave me an odd look but played along, not quibbling in front of him. The bar was a run-of-the-mill luncheonette by day, serving businessmen, politicians, and their staff. At night, it transformed into a meeting place for closeted military men. We knew it by reputation—a *bad* reputation for late-night fights among drunk soldiers.

As we walked, Philippa gushed: "Did you know that *Love's Last Move* was the first detective novel I ever read—like that, I was hooked! Your sleight of hand in *The Gemini Case* left me speechless. The twins weren't twins at all. How *did* you come up with it? And *Seeing Red*—well, that's when I realized detective novels could be high literature. I mean, passages like prose poems!" Despite his aloof demeanor, she was melting him with her effusiveness. A smile crept onto his lips.

We pushed through the bar's entrance and spilled into a cramped but not unpleasant room. Men in sports coats leaned on a polished wood counter, sipping beer and chatting with men in uniform. Army and navy officers were arm to arm in the green leather booths, smoking dreamily and sipping cocktails. The jukebox faintly murmured Eartha Kit's "C'est si Bon." After lingering briefly, a booth freed up, and we slid into it, the two of us across from Roger. We drew quizzical looks from the men around us; they weren't used to seeing women in Cary's. We ordered—Philippa, a glass of wine; Roger, a bourbon neat; me, a Scotch on the rocks—and, after smoothing down a stray hair, Roger said, "This isn't my usual place. Too damned conspicuous." He glanced around, a fresh ripple of gloom passing through his features. "But who the hell cares now?"

Philippa cocked her head, and I asked, "What do you mean?"

The wrinkles across his forehead deepened, and he adjusted his position in the booth, bringing his hands to the table then dropping them in his lap again. Something was eating at him.

"As of today, I'm no longer working for dear ol' Uncle Sam," he said, chuckling bitterly. "You see, the job supported our writing habit." His cheeks flushed. "It will be over when the news spreads." Despair tugged at his jaw muscles. "How will I tell him? *How?*" He glanced hotly at the bar. "I wish they'd hurry up with those damn drinks."

"What do you mean '*our* writing habit'?" I asked.

He studied us, trying to determine how much he trusted us, it seemed. "Oh, what the hell," he said, loosening his shoulders. "Ray Kane is more than a pseudonym. It's a collaboration. The 'Ray' comes from my name, Roger Raymond, and the 'Kane' comes from my partner, Lionel Kane."

Philippa's eyes grew wide.

It was news to us. I recalled the man he was embracing in the photo. Was *he* Lionel? "What kind of partner?" I pressed.

His brown eyes quieted. "A writing partner."

I narrowed my gaze. He wasn't getting away with a half-truth.

"And a lover," he added gently.

With the truth just dawning on her, Philippa exclaimed, "The Ray Kane books are co-authored?"

"That's right," Roger said. "Lionel and I met in '41 when I moved here after law school in New York."

Drinks came. Roger took a swig of bourbon, and Philippa sipped her wine primly as if worried about seeming overindulgent. I pondered my Scotch before letting it warm my throat. Philippa ran her finger around the top of her glass and asked, "What made you want to write *together*?" She believed in the romance of being a writer, so it was difficult for her to imagine sharing artistic ownership with anyone. I often kidded her that she needed to chuck the typewriter and pick up a quill and ink.

He offered a feeble smile. "At first, it was for fun. We'd read detective fiction to each other. I'm a big Christie and Sayers fan, and he likes the Americans, Chandler and Cain. We'd dream up stories together, like a game. One day, Lyle—that's what I call him—wrote a story down. He's a trained journalist, so he knows a thing or two about how a narrative should unfold. It was excellent, a real winner, and I gave him an idea for a final turn, a clue that would make it pop, a word with two opposite meanings." He gazed up at the ceiling, trying to retrieve the word. "God, what was it? It's been ages—Got it! Cleave. It means to cut in half *and* fuse together. Anyway, he worked on it more and sent it away. It was published in *Street and Smith's Detective Story Magazine*, which was our start." Sadness appeared to swell in him, which he chased away with a gulp of bourbon. "One of us needed to make money to fund our hobby, so I stayed the course and landed a job writing for the press office of the Bureau of Public Affairs under the assistant secretary." His features tightened as if he were wincing at an acute pain. "Shit, I loved that job." He took another swig of his drink, leaned forward, and, his voice harsh and low, said, "Scotty McLeod's stooges in the Miscellaneous M Unit, those assholes, hooked me up to a polygraph and asked about my sexual history . . ." He faltered and rubbed his temple as if to quell a surging headache. "Goddamn humiliating."

I'd read about McLeod in the *Post*. He was big chums with Joseph McCarthy, and Secretary of State Dulles placed him in charge of ferreting out "security risks" from the State Department. He was rounding up closeted homosexual government employees, branding them "perverts," and casting them out, claiming they were threats to national security because Communist sympathizers could blackmail them. They might as well have pinned big lavender Ps on their lapels and publicly shamed them in Lafayette Square. In truth, it had nothing to do with national security. It was just something these opportunistic jerks could rally around like a bonfire on a cold winter's night. Give the people someone to hate, and they'll follow you into the flames. It ruined good government employees, and as a result, many of them were taking their lives. Is that what Roger was telling us? They'd done *that* to him. Jesus.

"Does Lionel, Lyle, have a job?" Philippa asked, focusing on the practical.

As we pulled back the curtain on Ray Kane, I wondered how much she was rethinking her aspiration of being a professional writer. It wasn't a piece of cake.

"No," he replied dismally. "He had an incident working for his newspaper—he was jumped and beaten badly—and afterward, he didn't return to work. I was making enough for both of us, so there was no need. Although we brainstormed together, he took on the bulk of the writing. I edited his work and, of course, became the face of Kane."

"Why?" I asked, spinning the cubes in my glass.

His brow crinkled with confusion.

"Why are you the face of Ray Kane? Why not Lionel?" I asked again to clarify.

Roger paused, his gears spinning. "It's mostly about the photo on the book flap. I rarely make appearances in person."

"I'd say," Philippa remarked with a huff. "We didn't realize Ray Kane was a local until now. All your biographical details say you're from New York. Even your publisher is in New York." She was thinking of what we mailed to them anonymously in August and where we mailed it. I beamed at her as if I could communicate telepathically: *"Don't say more, Philippa. Don't even hint. It's dangerous."*

"We like our privacy," he said coolly.

I recalled the photo in his wallet. I imagined he and the handsome Negro cramming into the photo booth, drawing the curtain, paying fifteen cents, and the flash bursting, capturing them as they collided into one another, laughing. The man *was* Lionel. He must be. Resolved, I said, "You didn't answer my question: Why are *you* the face of Ray Kane?"

"Look," he said, withdrawing, his defenses going up, "don't take this the wrong way, but I don't know either of you that well. You seem like nice, educated girls. Clearly, you have good taste." He chuckled. "I'm grateful to you for rushing in and scooping me up off the floor of Brentano's. You saved the day. But I've blathered on too long and need to—"

"Why won't you answer my question?" I asked, not letting him off the hook. I wanted to verify what I thought I knew—that he and Lionel are a mixed-race couple, and together, they were Ray Kane. I wanted him to say it. His stalling churned my stomach. Was he ashamed of Lionel? If Philippa and I were co-authors, would she be ashamed of me? Would she dodge the truth like Roger?

He studied me warily. "You *really* want to know?"

"Yes," I said, not concealing my exasperation.

"It may change how you feel about him—and *us*."

"It won't," I said, the flesh on my arms, legs, and back alive and prickling. My polished white facade had fooled a great mystery writer, who now sat in dread, waiting for us to judge him. I was invisible to him. What if, through a strange alteration in body chemistry, I could will my skin to grow dark, to shade from olive to umber to espresso? Would he notice the metamorphosis? The molting of skin cells? Would it set him at ease—or alarm him?

He glanced at Philippa and asked, "You, too?"

Philippa smiled. "Nothing will change how much we love your books."

Did she mean it?

His lips twisted into a skeptical smirk. "Let's put it this way," he said, exhaling. "If readers saw Lyle's face on the jacket, we wouldn't sell nearly as many books."

Just say it, Roger, I thought and said, "Because he's ugly?"

Roger laughed. "God, no. He's beautiful."

"Judy," Philippa said, "I think he's—"

"He's Negro." Roger cut her off. "Well, partly, anyway."

Philippa checked my reaction, but I offered her nothing. Even though I'd guessed the truth, the weight of it being said out loud flattened me. Our world was absurd, insane. As we read Kane's novels, it never occurred to us that the author, or, for that matter, his creation, Calvin McKey, was anything other than white.

"We don't care," Philippa said, punching cheer into her voice. "It doesn't matter."

"Of course, it doesn't matter," I snapped, irritated by her peppy reply. "*Why* would it matter? Ever?"

She shot me a look. I deserved it.

Roger took a swig of bourbon, coughed, and chuckled bitterly. "Well, at least we'll still have two readers!" Anguish burned in his eyes, and I understood: being booted from the State Department was just the beginning. They took everything from you—your given name and, worse, your invented one.

CHAPTER 3

MAY 1, 1954, LIONEL

When the policeman asks, I tell him Roger was my roommate. Because of who I am—by that, I mean because of my skin color—the cop, Sergeant Williams, a bulldog with rosacea-marred cheeks and a band of flesh bulging from his collar, eyes me with profound suspicion. His thick lips pucker. I sense his disgust and catch his thought bubble: *"Why are a white ex-State Department employee and an unemployed Negro journalist playing house in Kalorama?"* His eyes narrow. *"Faggots."*

I straighten my back, righteous anger shoring up my sprawling grief. Yes, I want to say, lobbing my pride at his disgust. We are lovers.

His next question flickers into view: *"Commies, too?"* The ultimate transgression!

Of course, we aren't. But there'd be no point in denying it. These days being a homosexual and working in the State Department, like Roger, is the same as being a Communist or at least a Communist puppet. If you're like me, without question, you're deemed a threat—a threat to the "American way of life." Whatever that means.

When he speaks, it doesn't surprise me that he relishes what he says: "Your roommate was in the oven." He imbues the word "roommate" with a degree of scorn.

"What?" I say, keeping my voice level, trying to conceal my shock. I don't want to give this bigot an inch. My heart is pounding, shaking my sternum.

"His head was in your oven, sir."

"What do you mean?" I murmur, still baffled. He couldn't be referring to Roger. He wasn't suicidal. That's not who he was; that's not like him. Maybe this is all a crazy mistake. I feel a stab of hope. Minutes before, I watched the firemen transport his body to a hearse, sheathed in a black bag and bound to a stretcher. Philippa held me, and Judy, warming a little, put her arm around me. "Hold on," she whispered. "Just hold on."

"Yes, sir," the bulldog says with a twinkle of amusement. "He checked himself out, if you know what I mean."

"No, I don't know," I growl under my breath, the urge to swing at him, to feel the impact of my fist on his fleshy nose or oily jowl, is almost irresistible. Times were tough, very tough, sure, but that's not Roger in the oven, not ever. I ball up my fingers, and my body lurches forward on its own accord. Judy's grip tightens around my elbow.

"It's too early to tell for sure," Williams says with a puffed-up authority as if he were the investigating detective, "but it looks like the oven is the source of the fire. The sprinkler system saved the building. Well, except your place." He's enjoying himself.

I can't breathe, but I refuse to let this asshole see me gasp.

"Look on the bright side," he says, sneering, "at least your 'roommate's' suicide didn't cost anyone else their lives."

I lunge toward him, but Judy holds me in place with Philippa's help. They're surprisingly strong, forceful even. Williams backs off, his face flushed and

horrified. I'm through with his bullshit, and he knows it. But he recovers and
spreads out his fat chest, straining the buttons on his uniform. He knows I
can't do a damn thing. I'm shifting and tugging between the girls, helpless.
Despite my best effort to keep them at bay, tears well up.

Judy releases me and tells Williams to "fuck off."

He arches his brow. "Watch yourself, miss." His derisive glee fades. He
seems unsettled by her. "We'll need to do an official investigation, of course.
We haven't ruled out foul play."

"When will you know something?" Philippa says, removing her hands
from my arm. Despite the radiant pink-gold of her strawberry blonde hair in
the streetlight, her face is dark, and her eyes alert and intelligent. She stands
beside Judy now, shoulder to shoulder. I wonder if Williams senses that they
are a couple. "My cousin, Quincy Berg, is a detective," she says, cocking her
chin. "Do you know him?"

He glares at her, nonplussed, unsure what to say. "No, miss, I don't."

"He'll have something to say about your treatment of us."

He shrugs it off—just another silly skirt—and looks at me: "The detective
assigned to the case will have questions for Mr. Kane."

"We have questions, too," Judy says, staring at him, unblinking.

He glances from her to Philippa to me and turns away.

CHAPTER 4

JANUARY 1949, JUDY

Revelations we prepare for are inevitably disappointing. We build up an idea about the best, worst, most earth-shattering reveal, so when the time comes to learn the truth, we're shielded from the impact; we don't want the awesomeness of Truth with a capital T to crash over us—which is why, when I saw my father, Ellis Baker, for the first time, sitting beside his radio in his small but well-appointed living room, I couldn't feel what I was supposed to feel.

He lifted his head and smiled at me. He was in his early forties with a band of prematurely gray hair at his temples and a distinguished English mustache. His sleeves were rolled up, and he wore a green-and-gold tie loosened at his neck. The moody, swirling saxophone from his radio flowed around us, catching us in an eddy of sound. We paused, each wondering who should make the first move. He knew I was coming, of course.

Iris had told him, but he seemed surprised to see me. Maybe he thought I'd back out, or maybe, his guilt taking over, he wished I had.

He stood from the chair. He was over six feet tall, rangy, and precise in his movements. It's clear where Iris got her poise. I detected the origins of my long-boned lankiness in him. It was an observation that should've stirred up a pang of emotion, but it didn't—or at least not one I could identify. What was I supposed to feel about meeting him? Elation? Relief? Anger, perhaps. Yes, anger. Why did you leave me to be raised in an orphanage? I wanted to ask. And what about my scars—the half-inch-to-an-inch marks that crisscross my forearms, the bottom of my neck, and my clavicle? Where were you when cats tore me apart? If I even remember what happened clearly? My childhood memories are so splintered. He crossed to the radio, switched it off, and I exhaled deeply in the absence of the music. Had I been holding my breath?

"Wow," he said, smiling, showing his wide teeth. "Wow."

"I'm Judy." I thrust my hand out to him.

As we shook, I felt the size of his expansive palm, his pianist's fingers. Iris had told me he'd played the piano for years before opening a pool hall on U Street. His spidery grip and soft skin texture nudged me past resentment and toward curiosity. I wondered about the moment he met my mother, about the strangeness of the pairing. The last time I saw her, she was crumpled at my feet. After taking responsibility for killing her sister, my aunt Charlene, she poisoned herself with a concoction of lye. Her desperation and fury led to madness, which led to a permanent room at St. Elizabeth's Hospital. She was an ugly part of me that had broken off and was writhing on the floor, gasping its last breath. Here, in contrast, was a mild man, the other half of me. What did my mother see in him? Maybe there was a clue in the music's ability to melt petty bigotries and unlock something in us. Perhaps she heard him playing the piano, watched his fingers glide over the keys, and fell for his talent. Maybe she dared herself to seduce him, a revolt against the suffocating primness of her world. I understood that impulse. But what did he see in her? Why would he cheat on his wife with her? I didn't understand it.

He released my hand and said, "You're such a beautiful girl." He looked at Iris, hovering behind me, having returned from hanging our coats. "Isn't she, Iris?"

"Yes, Papa," she said, moving beside me. "She looks like Grandma."

"My God, you're right." He gestured to the sofa. "Have a seat." He looked over his shoulder and said, "Alice, they're here!"

She appeared in the doorway. She must've heard the commotion. She was so much smaller than I remembered, just under five feet, and slender, almost slight. She wore a flower-print dress with short sleeves and a crisp white apron. Although in her forties, she had changed very little. Her deep-set brown eyes were kind and a little skeptical. When she saw me, she hesitated, scrunched up her nose, and, breaking into a smile, said, "Little Judy!" She crossed the room, and as I rose, she stretched her arms around me. She smelled of baby powder and fresh bread and faintly of mothballs. She was remarkable and implausible: I was the result of her husband's unfaithfulness, but she began working at Crestwood Orphanage to look over me, to be my guardian angel. No one, not even Philippa, had been that selfless toward me.

When she pulled away, the gold cross around her neck caught the light, and I remembered her smiling and looking down on me as a little girl at Crestwood. We were in the laundry room, where children were usually forbidden. She swiped my bangs out of my eyes with her finger and handed me her melt-in-your-mouth peanut brittle wrapped in wax paper. Her gold cross glittered on her breastbone. Sadness rippled through me. Alice had known me in a time that, to me, was still shrouded by darkness. But she was a link to the past, a living clue, something I could navigate toward. Maybe she knew something about my scars? I felt calmer and clearer. I leaned forward, wanting to be near her, to have another embrace, but we were already finding our seats.

Alice drove the conversation, peppering me with questions: Did I want anything to eat or drink? Tea, maybe? "No, no, I'm good." Was I comfortable? She could turn up the heat. "I'm fine." What classes did I like in school? "Literature, journalism, and at times, drama." Who's my favorite writer? "Impossible to answer. Maybe D. H. Lawrence or Nathanael West. The mystery author Ray Kane." Did I plan to go to college? "I'm not sure. I'd like to, if it was the right sort of place. Not a finishing school." What did I do for fun? "Read, listen to music, go to the movies, sip malts at Horsfields." (I wanted to add: "Smoke, drink, and solve mysteries.") Did the Peabodys, my adoptive parents, treat me well? I paused. "They feed me well. Their house is large, grand even. I want for nothing, as they say."

"Mama," Iris broke in gently. "Give her room to breathe. Golly."

Ellis grunted in agreement.

Alice looked at her lap and straightened her starched apron. "Isn't all this just so strange?" she said, peering up again and smiling sadly.

I nodded. "Very."

"So, how old are you now?"

"Eighteen. A discovery I just made."

"How's that?"

"I learned my birthday had been fudged on my Crestwood papers. I thought I was seventeen, but now like magic, I'm eighteen. I'm going to change my name."

"Oh really?" Her eyes twinkled. "When I knew you, you were Judy X."

"I'm saying goodbye to Judy X and Judy Peabody and hello to Judy Nightingale."

I glanced at Ellis, a little annoyed by his silence. His eyes were warm, tender even. He was absorbing the moment, it seemed, trying to get a handle on it. We all were. Alice needed to pelt me with questions to get through it, and he needed to soak it up quietly. All the same, I wanted him to say something, to engage.

"Do you remember those days in Crestwood?" Alice asked, her voice losing some of its levity.

"I remember you," I said, feeling drawn to her again. The desire to touch her strong. "I remember your baking," I said, "and your kindness." I reached out to place my hand on her hands, which were folded in her lap, nestled in her apron. The gesture was awkward and out of character for me but, in the moment, necessary.

"Well, it has won awards," she said, straightening her back and smiling proudly.

"It's true," Iris said to me. "Her snickerdoodles have taken first place at the church bazaar three years in a row."

Alice waved the comment away in a show of false modesty and, beaming warmth back at me, said, "I'm just glad I could be there for you for a few years."

"Before they framed and fired you," Ellis broke in.

"Let it be," Alice said calmly. "It was a long time ago."

He shifted in his seat. "Back when I was a fool. Those damn people."

"By 'damn people,' you mean Moira Closs," Iris said bitterly. "That entire family is rotten to the core."

"That woman and all her wealth and haughty bullshit," he said, hanging his head. "She had me under her thumb. What could I do?"

The thought of Moira, the Closs family matriarch who, chinchilla-trimmed cape flowing, was the architect of all my suffering, made me shiver. I saw her eyes—bulging, blue, and spiteful—and wrapped my arms around my body. She'd been my archenemy since I was born. Her son, Howard, that tarnished golden boy, was cuckolded by his crazy wife, and I was the result—a mixed-race child who Moira, fearing a scandal (oh, the horror!), had to "see to." She'd intimidated Ellis into declaring me an orphan. She'd had me placed in Crestwood and eventually adopted by the Peabodys. To hear her tell it, he'd let me go without a fight. Was his remark about being a fool referring to his giving me up? Was guilt weighing on him, or was he letting himself off the hook? The note of resignation in his voice reminded me of Aunt Charlene, who was privy to all these events and didn't protect me either. She chronicled all this and much more in her journal, which contained truths that got her and Moira's grandson, Cleve, killed—and which I swiped and keep close like some blasphemous relic hidden from the world.

"What could I do?" he asked again, rhetorically. Well, maybe more than he claimed. I needed to know. I wanted him to elaborate, to be remorseful. Before I could muster the courage to say something, he shifted in his seat, leaned over the arm of his chair, and retrieved a small black portfolio from the floor beside him. He handed it to me, his fingers shaking a little. I opened it.

Inside, neatly arranged, were newspaper clippings from last fall. I scanned the headlines: MISSING BOY FOUND DEAD, FOUL PLAY SUSPECTED. It referred to the discovery of Cleve's body by the Anacostia River. PRIME SUSPECT IN CLOSS CASE ARRESTED. That was Adrian Bogdan. He was a killer, for sure—he was also a spy for the federal government, a fact I still couldn't stomach, and was entangled with Moira's ambition to influence the political elite—but he didn't kill Cleve. BOGDAN RELEASED, ALIBI WATER-TIGHT. The monster was uncaged because Moira's son, Howard, was impli-cated in Cleve's death and Aunt Charlene's murder. Sorry, wrong number, police. Like Bogdan, he didn't do it. SUSPECT IN BOY'S MURDER PLUMMETS TO DEATH. Ah, and this was the *official* end of the story. Out of his mind, Howard chased Philippa and me and fell . . . accidently? I still think Philippa gave him a little (justified) push, although she claims otherwise. But, as far as the police were concerned and much to Moira's woe, Cleve's case was closed: death at the hands of his crazy father. How little they knew! Last fall, when Philippa and I set out to solve a classmate's murder, we didn't know the crime would lead to me discovering who my true mother and father were. We began solving the mystery of me. There's still so much to unravel, but I'm here now, facing a part of the truth.

I closed the portfolio and gently handed it back to Ellis. He took it into his lap, his hands folding around it, and said, "Iris told us when your aunt approached her about you." I knew this already; I also knew that for many years the Bakers wouldn't talk to Iris about my existence. "Since she told us she was going to watch over you, like Alice had at Crestwood, we've been collecting these clippings. Somehow, I guess, it made us feel like we were a part of your life. That sounds odd, I know."

I didn't know how to respond. It was odd and incredibly unhelpful but somehow understandable. I couldn't make sense of it.

Alice suddenly asked me, "Are you sunburned?" Ever the breaker of tension, the redirector. She was looking at my crossed arms.

"What?" I said, a little dazed. I'd been unconsciously fiddling with the dead skin on my wrist and forearm.

"In January, no less," she said.

I suddenly was aware of my skin, its whiteness and its blackness—my in-betweenness. My nervous habit felt like a symbolic gesture, a sloughing off, and it made me self-conscious. I uncrossed my arms and grasped my hands in my lap.

"Make sure to coat it with fresh aloe," she added.

I explained that I'd just returned from a trip with the Peabodys to the Caribbean, where I'd lingered too long on the beach. I didn't tell them we'd left town because they wanted to separate me from Philippa. We'd "become too *entangled*," they'd said, being aggressively euphemistic. And because they thought staying was dangerous; I knew too much about the murders and Moira's messy dealings with Bogdan. We needed to allow time for the dust to settle. That was a story for another day, perhaps. I told them I was heading to boarding school the next day to finish high school. I was in between everything, it seemed.

Iris jumped in: "The Peabodys want her away from all the drama."

"And Philippa," I said before thinking it through.

"Philippa?" Alice asked.

"She's a friend," Iris said quickly, cutting off any room for speculation. Did she sense that Philippa and I were involved, or was it just that she didn't like her? I wasn't sure. Philippa's obliviousness—or seeming obliviousness—rubbed her the wrong way. She knew how close we'd grown and that we were inseparable. I was not going to explain Philippa to them now or maybe ever. I had no idea how they'd react. It wasn't worth the risk. But the idea of hiding yet another part of myself made my gut churn. After everything, I still couldn't peel off all the layers.

"What's that across your arms?" Ellis said, gesturing with a long finger. His tone was surprisingly curious and open. "Was it caused by the sunburn?"

"Now, Ellis," Alice said, giving him a stern look. She seemed worried that he was overstepping.

He was noticing my scars. The sun had deepened my olive skin and brought the thin ridges into relief—another reason the choice of a tour of the Caribbean infuriated me. Bart and Edith Peabody wanted to create distance between me and the mayhem of the past few months, so what did they decide? Let's take Judy to a beach and plop her in the sun; it will burn the trouble away. Ironic, then, that its rays highlighted my scars.

I held out my arms and turned them over. "I don't know how they got there. It happened when I was young. Feral cats attacked me, I think, but I'm not sure. I only remember flashes."

Alice scrunched her brow with concern. From his dreary expression, Ellis seemed to understand the scars' weight on me and said, "I'm so sorry, Judy." I liked hearing him say it. "Sorry" was a word I deserved to hear more often. I softened to him a little. It then occurred to me: Alice and Ellis were puzzled by the scars, which meant they didn't recognize them. I asked Alice, "So I didn't have these when I was at Crestwood?"

"No, honey," she said. "You didn't."

Soon the conversation steered away from a jittery get-to-know-you inter-
view to chitchat about movie stars (Alice had just seen Ingrid Bergman
as Joan of Arc), politics (Truman's presidential inauguration was on the
horizon. For the most part, they approved of him), music (Ellis was a
Bud Powell and Charlie Parker fan), and business (Ellis's pool hall, called
"Baker's Billiards," had flourished during the war, but the high unemploy-
ment rate was steering the economy into a slump, and his patrons had
thinned out). Eventually, I accepted Alice's offer for refreshments—coffee
and fresh pound cake—and then, as evening approached, Iris and I had
to go. She had studying to do. I needed to begin packing for school. A
semester at Agnes March School for Girls loomed.

We hugged—which was bizarre. I never hug. Maybe I am changing and
becoming—what? Mushy? Judy Nightingale, a sentimental drip? I promised to write as soon as I was settled, and Iris and I began the walk toward
the bus stop in the chilly dusk.

After a period of silence, she asked if I wanted a cigarette; she was
having one. We smoked, relieved to give the task our attention. The
nicotine soothed me, slowing the spin of my feelings toward the Bakers:
relief and anger and what? . . . familial affinity? So often, strong emotions
brought clarity, even certainty: I want this. I don't want that. I love this.
I hate that. But this potent mix offered no clear direction. Finally, I said,
"How do you think it went? Was it okay?"

Iris glanced at me, tapping the ash from her cigarette with a slim finger.
She smiled wryly and said, "I was about to ask you the same thing."

I laughed. "I have no idea. None!"

"Did you like them?" she said.

"No, not at all," I said. "They're a *complete* nightmare." I groaned,
leaning into the joke.

She raised her eyebrows. "Be honest now."

"Look," I said, sadness bubbling to the surface. "Seeing your mom, seeing Alice again . . . You have to understand she's the closest to a mother, a real mother, I've ever had. So, yes, I liked her. No question."

"And Papa?" she asked, not letting me off the hook.

I took a drag on my Chesterfield and thought about his portfolio of news clippings. "He's more complicated."

"If you're angry, it's okay. He expects you to be."

I fiddled with my cigarette, nearly dropping it. "Okay, yes. If you want me to say it, I was—I am—angry or something. I'm also relieved—and very curious. I'm all those things at once, and they've bottlenecked in me, and I don't like it."

"Fair enough."

Spilling all that made me raw. I wasn't prepared to pick it apart. My messy feelings churned again, and I asked, "Why did you tell them that Philippa was my *friend*?"

"Well, she is, isn't she?" Iris said, puzzled.

"I mean, why did you speak for me? I could've told them, but you jumped in."

Her eyes fell dark. "Okay." She shrugged lightly. "I apologize."

I didn't believe she was sorry, which bothered me. I wanted to ask her: Did she know that Philippa and I were closer than friends, that we were a pair, that we were bonded to each other, that we had matching moon-shaped pins, a club of two, sisters who were more than sisters, and that no matter how much distance you set between us, we were inseparable? One heart, two heads. I wanted to ask her, but something held me back. Fear of her judgment, fear of hearing my voice asking the question, making it real. Being so closely aligned with someone else felt dangerous. All the same, my gut told me she sensed our closeness, our connection, and I could tell it troubled her.

"How does Miss Strawberry feel about you heading to boarding school for six months?" Iris's nickname for Philippa hadn't bothered me before today. Her thick, curly strawberry blonde hair made her who she was, which was Iris's point.

"As happy as I am about it."

"I see," she said, gesturing toward Kenilworth Avenue to the bus stop as if I'd already forgotten the way.

"You don't like Philippa," I said.

Iris stopped in her tracks. "I don't know her well enough to dislike her." She looked at me. "She's not going to understand who you are now."

Annoyed, I said, "I'm who I've always been," which, of course, was dishonest. I could feel myself changing but into what, into who? "She knows who I am *now*," I added with an edge. "She attended the 'grand unveiling' and didn't bat an eye." I'd been terrified she would. I was *sure* she would. But she drew me in when I expected her to push me away. She knew more about me than anyone else and hadn't rejected any of it. At times, it seemed, she even liked to pluck the dark chords stretched across my heart.

"You don't get it," Iris said coolly and began walking again. "She's fine with the idea of you being mixed, but is she going to embrace the day-to-day of you living that way?" She shook her head. "I don't think so. Hell, Judy, does she know what you were doing today? Did you tell her?"

I didn't respond at first. Street noise rushed in, cars whizzing by, horns blaring in the distance. She was right. I didn't tell Philippa. I didn't tell anyone. I wasn't ready to. I needed to figure it out first, to stick a pin in it. "No, I didn't," I said, and she offered no reply. I studied her profile—her long coffee-colored neck, her upturned chin, her intelligent eyes, and the trace of a smug expression on her lips. Anger surged through me. She's just assuming I'm going to . . . what? Live as a Negro or mixed? She's assuming that's the choice I'll make—the obvious choice. Or has she chosen for me? To hell with that, to hell with her! I was raised as a white girl and tormented as a white girl, and now that I know the truth, I'm not going to give up what little leverage was given to me. I've earned it.

Down the block, a small group of locals waited at the bus stop, wrapped in heavy coats, caps, and scarves. They were chatting and laughing, their collective breath visible in the cold air. So that, there, is what Iris means by day-to-day; you're either a part of them or apart from them. That's what she wants me to understand. I stopped and said, "Let's wait here."

Iris halted without a word, but I glanced at her and detected a glitter of annoyance. My anger deepened. Alice, sweet and kind Alice, now seemed weak, a simp, mopping up her husband's mess, and Ellis seemed selfish, impulsive, and irresponsible. I could even hear myself agreeing with Moira's assessment of him: a philanderer. And now Iris was haughty and judgmental, unaware of her petty blindnesses. I wanted to tell her, to shout it at her, that Philippa and I are lovers—goddamned soulmates, you hear! I wanted to say: Do you think those people huddled around the bus stop, those day-to-day folks chitchatting about the weather and the bus schedule, would ever open their arms to me? To who I really am?

Instead, I remained silent until the bus arrived, scooped us up, and carried me back to the Peabodys.

CHAPTER 5

SUMMER OF 1949, JUDY

After our six-month separation, Philippa and I met again on the rooftop of
Hill Estates Apartments, like criminals returning to the scene of a crime
(which, I suppose, is what we were). Since it was the site of Howard Closs's
deadly plunge from the board we used to cross from this building to its
neighbor last fall, we had steered clear of our old hideout, the only place
we'd had a little privacy, just down the block from the Peabodys.

I'd hoisted a new plank up the fire escape to bridge the gap, and
Philippa crossed the four-story abyss unscathed, and there we were,
staring at each other, completely mute. She was beautiful. Her cheeks
were flushed, and her lips were bright red and carefully shaped. She was
wearing green slacks and a black-and-white horizontal-striped blouse,
and her hair, flat against her head, was captured in a tight ponytail. She
looked older, more mature. Over the months, we'd forgotten how to be

in the same space together, making us tense. Sure, we'd written to each other, but still, once you're in the presence of someone you've missed, someone you've thought of constantly, it's difficult to find the right words, or maybe there are so many right words that they clog in your throat.

She made a crack about having to walk the plank again for me and stepped closer. She was breathing heavily from climbing the fire escape, and a jasmine scent, mingled with a rich tobacco odor, wafted from her. I imagined her smoking on the street corner, soothing her nerves before seeing me. Lines from our letters suddenly floated through me with no memory of who wrote what: *God, I miss you . . . We're inseparable even when separated . . . No one understands me but you . . . It's horrible here without you. Everyone stares at me like I've just kicked a kitten . . . I'm telling you, I live for these letters . . . Break out of that school, and come and see me. If anyone could jailbreak, it'd be you . . . You're a gorgeous idiot, and I wish you were here, next to me, bothering me, quoting some nonsense . . . We're silly Romantics . . . Oh, I sound tragic, but that's for effect . . . I want to feel you. I dream of touching you . . . I don't think we're two people, just one with two bodies.*

Over the past month, we'd shaped each other out of words, and now we were confronted with the reality, and as we stood there, it was more potent than I had anticipated. She was more confident than I recalled, and I was terrified by what she saw when she looked at me. I'd dropped the baggy sweaters and flapper pearls, put on makeup, curled the ends of my bob, and wore a simple white top and dark denim playsuit, taking pains to cover my scars, as if she didn't know they were there. Was I too boyish? Too plain? I noticed the crescent moon pin I gave her. It was attached to her collar; its mate, the waxing to her waning, was just above my heart.

"Seriously," she said, "how are you?" She leaned beside me, against the inside lip of the cornice, shoulder to shoulder. I mumbled something trite and unmemorable. She tilted her head back. She'd been working on her movie star moves. A surge of lust shot up through me and, like a shower of metal beads, shimmered through my limbs. My body hummed inside, and my heart clattered in my chest. I crossed my legs, focusing on the maddening and exhilarating heat between them. My eyes flicked over Philippa's body: the curve of her breasts in her blouse, the button at her clavicle undone with calculated carelessness, exposing her pale, freckled skin as it slipped into shadow.

Her legs, slimmer than I remembered, were stretched out, and her exposed ankles were crossed, delicate veins running down to the edge of her gray-green Mary Janes. I had the bizarre impulse to kneel and run my hand over her shoe and up her ankle. Although I couldn't say she wanted me to touch her, her body called me, demanding I do *something*.

So, awkwardly, I dropped my hand on hers, and she jumped a little, pulling away. Immediately, all the churning heat in my body sank around me like a low fog, threatening to dissipate. She shoved off the wall, moved away from me, and turned. Her blue-gray eyes blinked slowly, and her lips shifted as if they were trying to form a word. And then, and *then*, she stepped toward me. No, she stepped *into* me, her leg parting mine, her body, so fleshy and warm, pressed against mine, summoning the blood from my feet into my legs and groin. I embraced her, pulling her close, jamming my lips against hers, pushing her beautiful mouth open with mine as if to acknowledge the stupidity of words, their failure to express what our bodies already knew. I ran my hand along the waistband of her slacks, found their top buttons, and unhitched them. I expected her to shove me away, but she didn't. Instead, she arched slightly, opening her hips and widening her legs. I unzipped her pants, sliding them down a little, aware that, although we had privacy on the roof, we were still out in the open. A light breeze shook a nearby tree, car horns blared, and street noise rose to us, growing more intense, like water cresting a dam. We were exposed, vulnerable, and undaunted. As my fingers moved beyond her underwear and into her, she gripped me tightly, burying her face into my neck, her soft cheek against me.

When it was over, we slumped as one to the roof's surface, sheltering in the shadow of the inside edge of the cornice. She was disheveled, her makeup smeared, and sweat pooled in my armpits and trickled down my back. With the blue sky above us, she rested now, her head against my shoulder, breathing deeply and steadily. Her bright perfume encased us in an impenetrable fairy bubble, sealing us off from the outside world. She didn't return the pleasure I'd given her, but there was no need. The tension between us had been shattered, like smashing fine crystal, and I felt good, spent, and reflective.

I'd fooled around with the son of the history department chair this spring at Agnes March. Unlike my first time with a boy in high school, he'd shown interest in me, in my body. He lingered at my scars, touched one along my clavicle, and muttered something vaguely admiring. He wasn't gentle or particularly skillful, but he paid attention to what I was feeling—or it seemed important to him that I was enjoying it.

With Philippa, it was different. I felt exhilarated for taking what I wanted, not for being tended to like someone's pet. I wondered if this was how a man feels, if this was what they don't want us to feel, if that's what they're afraid we'll discover. I liked that I might know what they fear.

"Philippa," I said, "that was . . . unexpected. Wow."

A change came over her: the glow from the exertion dimmed, and a chill fell across her. Her lips drooped, and her mussed lipstick made her look clownish. Was she about to cry? I reached out to her, but she withdrew with a flinch. "I'm not sure what we're doing," she said. Her body curled inward, tightening like a fist. "I feel—I feel out of control."

"Don't do this," I said, aware of the shame cascading through her; I'd seen it before. In the past, she'd clung to a traditional notion of how the world was supposed to be, baked into her when young: men and women paired up, not women and women or men and men. On some level, she knew better but couldn't quite step out of the shadow of those ideas.

Maybe it was because she was still trying to please her father or step-mother or even her dead mother—the always-watching, always-judging matriarch—or maybe she was just frightened.

Self-reproof of this sort wasn't a problem for me, perhaps because I'd never been mistaken for normal and, early on, embraced my role as an outcast. At Agnes March, I kept my distance from the other girls, who were there to be finished, which was like being taxidermied—stuffed, glued, and on display for prospective husbands. A fate worse than death. If Philippa had gone instead, she would've felt their gaze, their stifling appraisal. "Wake up!" I wanted to scream at her. "Your good-girl persona is a trap."

Philippa stood up and gathered herself. As she wiped the wetness from her eyes, I said. "Check your lips before you go out on the street." I was trying to tamper down my emotions.

"I have my compact," she said, agitated, and added coolly, "Thanks."

"Don't feel bad, okay?" I said, climbing to my feet. "What just happened—it's nothing to feel bad about."

She paused and peered deep into me with her pearlescent eyes. "This—you and me—it doesn't make sense. I can't make sense of it."

"What do you mean?"

She scowled. "I want to stop feeling *this way*." She shook her arms as if she were trying to shake the feeling in question out of her fingertips.

"What *way* is that?" I asked, my tone hot.

She regarded me, her eyes growing watery, fearful. "I don't want to see you for a while, okay?"

"*How* do you feel, Philippa?" I asked, anger simmering over. "Explain it to me."

"Oh, Judy."

"Go ahead. I want to understand it."

"I mean . . ." She sniffed and wiped her nose. "I mean, this isn't healthy, is it? We're not *healthy*. Jesus."

I glared at her, my sympathy evaporating. Our letters over the last months were *love* letters, weren't they? Was she turning her back on all that, on me, on us, because I touched her, and she liked it? "Fuck 'healthy,'" I snapped. "Who cares what's 'healthy'? And when did you start caring?"

She shot me a searing look, said, "I'm going now," and turned away. As I watched her cross the plank, she seemed fragile, a wobbly-kneed tightrope walker about to plunge into a crowd of gawkers.

When she reached the other side, a fury rose in me, and I shouted at her: "I hate you! Do you hear me? I goddamn hate you!" She paused. "You'll be boring!" I yelled, desperation cracking my voice. "God, Philippa, you'll be dull. You'll be . . . like everybody else." It was the worst thing I could say to her, the most terrifying condemnation I could hurl at her. But she didn't turn. She just began moving forward again, winding her way through an obstacle course of grimy chimneys and stove pipes to the fire escape. Before mounting the first step of the ladder, she spun and looked at me, her face too far for me to read, but I felt her eyes, and a chill passed through me. She was going. After all that, she was going. The sheen of her strawberry blonde hair caught the afternoon light before she disappeared down the ladder.

⚬══⚬

I thought I'd hear from her soon. Our intense connection and abrupt break seemed unreal minutes after it had happened. At first, I blamed her and cursed her silliness and immaturity, but then gradually felt responsible: Why did I come on so strong? I'd frightened her—her body reacting to my touch, then the overwhelming flood of emotion that followed. As the days became weeks, though, I realized something terrible had happened.

As I replayed the scene, I recalled the strangeness of encountering one another after we'd spent the spring apart. Out of the raw materials of our letter writing, we'd shaped each other into flawed semblances of the truth. I understood, then, that the "something terrible" had been happening all along. Having cleverly managed our separation, our parents had won. We no longer knew each other. We only knew the fantasies in our heads, and the two, like an advertisement and the thing advertised, didn't line up. When I touched her, I was touching someone new, and my touch, to her, was shocking and disorienting.

After weeks of phoning her home, her stepmother, Bonnie, told me that Philippa had left town and was filing documents for a lawyer in Charlottesville for the summer. "I'm sorry," she said, sensing my distress. "Philippa seems distant from us, too, if that's any consolation." On the other hand, the Peabodys showed no sympathy: "It's for the best, Judy," Edith said, frustrated. "Can't you see that?" Infuriated and resigned, I set out to do what I'd intended to do since the previous fall: change my name from Judy Peabody to my chosen name, Judy Nightingale, and move out on my own.

CHAPTER 6

MAY 1, 1954, LIONEL

I'm sitting in front of a desk at the police department of the 2nd precinct, and a baby-faced uniformed cop has just offered me a cup of coffee, which I refused. Philippa and Judy have come with me, insisting on being my moral support. They were asked to remain in the waiting area. I watch them across the station's bustling workroom. Their concerned eyes shift from me to one another. They lean in and exchange words. Our friendship is new and strangely intense. They are such emphatic fans of the "great" Ray Kane, but they feel like peers, even though Roger and I are a decade older. None of it makes sense, but I'm glad they're here.

A burst of laughter from a cluster of uniformed officers startles me. I'm on edge after my confrontation with that bigot Sergeant Williams. It seems impossible Roger's dead, or at least improbable, like a poorly executed twist from one of our novels. I keep waiting for him to enter from stage right, a spotlight exposing him as alive, his smile shining and the audience swooning. In a mystery plot, the dead can rise from their graves.

The desk in front of me is worn with age but neat and clean. The shiny nameplate reads "Detective Quincy Berg." I imagine this detective, who apparently is Philippa's cousin, as if he were a character from a Ray Kane book. I sketch him as uptight, dim-eyed, and droll, with a shirt starched to the stiffness of cardboard. But before I can complete the picture, he says my name.

One of my gifts is my susceptibility to beauty. Seeing a beautiful work of art or hearing a seductive tune will transfix me and blot out everything and everyone around me, vanquishing even my darkest thoughts. It doesn't last, but the momentary relief has saved me many times. Quincy Berg, far from my unflattering rendition of him, is gorgeous. He's wide-shouldered, square-jawed, and dark-eyed. A mound of thick black hair swoops across his forehead, delightfully unkempt but not shapeless. After greeting me, he sits, and as he gathers his notebook and pin, his blazer strains against his muscular shoulders. A twinge in my groin startles me. The body's command: life goes on. After the horror of the past hour, though, I flood with guilt. I don't want his beauty to intrude now. Fuck off.

"I'm so sorry about Mr. Raymond," he says, smiling ruefully. "And your apartment. I can't imagine."

I don't respond.

"You must be devastated."

My silence is unnerving him, making him self-conscious.

"I am," I say, offering him relief, but I can't conjure this devastation he seems to want me to feel. I'm numb and pissed and watchful, waiting for the next punch to land.

He smiles again. It's a dreamy, tender smile. I sense an authenticity to him, a genuine friendliness. He asks for assorted personal information, including my full name, "Lionel Arthur Kane"; my birthday, "May 6, 1920"; my address, "2101 Connecticut Ave"; and my occupation, "writer," which feels like admitting to a dirty secret. He also requests Roger's family's phone number and address, which I give him. Eventually, he asks, "What is the nature of your relationship with Mr. Raymond?" Of course, I won't tell him that he is my lover. We can't tell the police the truth, even this beautiful specimen of manhood before me. *Especially* him. He's too innocent. He imagines himself to be a good guy, a lover of his fellow man, Negro or otherwise. But the kind ones, or those who have imagined themselves to be kind, are the worst because, when they twist your arm or break your jaw, they convince themselves they are caressing you. So, I tell him "roommate" and indiscreetly add "and friend." It's a stupid move. He raises an eyebrow and smiles again. God, that smile! It's like being interviewed by Monty Clift. I know he senses the truth, but he goes on with more questions: "How long have you lived in the apartment?"

"Six years."

"Do you have property insurance?"

"Yes, for my belongings." Roger's family will get the insurance settlement from the fire because my name wasn't permitted on the deed. The board of 2101 wouldn't have let a Negro own an apartment in the building, or at least we assumed that was the case. My personal property insurance as a "renter" will cover only a fraction of what I'd lost.

"And life insurance?" he asks.

"What? For me?"

"To benefit you, yes."

"I don't know."

I do know, but for now, it's best to play dumb.

His dark eyes settle on me, probing.

Because the property wasn't in my name and I couldn't have homeowner's insurance, Roger started funding an insurance policy and named me the beneficiary. It's not that nickel insurance the companies peddled to most Negros; it has a thirty-thousand-dollar payout. He wanted me to have security. I don't know if Roger's death being self-inflicted will complicate things. It might. But I must find a way to spin it for the police and the insurance fools. Maybe they'll believe we're roommates and the best of friends. After all, that's not fiction, just not the entire truth.

I meet his gaze and lie: "Roger never mentioned a policy to me."

He continues scribbling notes. Eventually, he looks up: "Do you know who called in the fire?"

"No," I say. "Maybe a neighbor? The firemen knew about it before I did."

"Think back. Can you recall any suspicious activity in your building recently?"

This question catches me off-guard. "Sergeant Williams seemed to think this was an open and closed suicide case," I say. "He told me so with the bed-side manner of a rabid dog."

"He was being hasty." His expression softens. "I apologize for Williams. He's old school and insensitive."

By "old school," he means a goddamn racist, but I don't say anything.

His handsome face grows narrow, interested. "I hate to ask this, but where were you this afternoon before you returned home?"

"At the Library of Congress doing research." I frown at him and anticipate his follow-up: "I'm sure the librarians who helped me will confirm my alibi."

I don't share the subject of my research: the murders of young girls in eastern and central Virginia—a topic Judy and Philippa are on fire about and, likely, the subject of our next true crime–based venture after the success of *The Broken Thread*. I wouldn't say I liked the idea, but Roger was very keen on it, and he was blue as hell, so I didn't fight him. I didn't discover anything new today, though. Frankly, I'm not sure why he insisted I read a bunch of old newspapers we'd pored over before. "Just to double-check," he said. "We might've missed something." What did it matter, I thought, we're writing fiction.

While Berg is jotting information in his notebook, I glance at my moral support team, who are still arm to arm. They offer me encouraging nods, curious about what's being said, I imagine, and I nod in return.

"Did you know Roger's plans for the afternoon?" Berg asks.

"Yes." My heart sinks, recalling my wishful thinking that he'd changed his plans. "He told me he was going to write. He said he was feeling inspired and needed some quiet."

"So, I have to ask . . ." The creases at the sides of his mouth deepen. "Was he down in his spirits recently?"

Down in his spirits. What a euphemism! He was terrified. He'd been humiliated by the State Department and sent packing. It was only a matter of time before the government goons or some rag exposed us as the homo duo behind the macho mystery writer Ray Kane and destroyed that revenue stream. Hot off the presses: SHOCKING DISCOVERY: NAVY FAG AND COLORED FAIRY INVENT MYSTERY AUTHOR RAY KANE. I can see it now: "How did they do it, folks? It's unbelievable that two homosexuals wrote such gritty detective fiction. It's a shocker that everyman P. I. Calvin McKey, confidant to men and lover of women, sprang from the imagination of two inverts." If the news got out—*when* the news got out—we'd be lynched, if not literally, then socially. Maybe that's why he was so impatient to write the next book. Lord knows straight folks hate a fag, but they really hate a fag who holds up a mirror to them: *"We know how to dress up as 'macho men.' We know it's drag by a different name."*

"Not especially," I answer the detective. "He was always an upbeat person."

His eyes drift down to his notebook. When he looks up again, his lips are shut grimly, and his eyes are mellow and sad. He swallows and says, "Mr. Raymond's body was burned badly, and it's difficult to identify. Do you know of any dental records? Does he have a regular dentist?"

The image Sergeant Williams forced on me of Raymond with his head in our oven rises before me, his long, graceful limbs splayed out at awkward angles. It's absurd. A wave of nausea passes through me. "He hated the dentist. Had a phobia of them," I say, the room quivering. "He must've had one at some point, though. He had good teeth." A beat later, I realize it's more intimate knowledge than a roommate usually shares. Everything around me seems liquid and unstable. The floor is swallowing me slowly like a tide:

first my toes, then my feet, then ankles. Maybe this is the devastation Berg wants me to feel.

"Can you think of anything to help us verify his identity? Past injuries, for instance."

All this time, my hands have been tightly clasped in my lap, but it's only now that I've become aware of the hardness of the gold band around my ring finger. On its inside edge, it reads, "R & L FOREVER, 1948." Roger wore one corresponding to it on his right pinky with the same inscription. I gently spin it on my finger as if doing so would unlock its power and offer me guidance. Should I mention it to Berg? Does it expose us? Do I trust this handsome cop? *Tell me, Roger, what do I do?* And then, with no answer from beyond, only an urge in my gut, I say, "Roger wore a ring like mine on his right pinky." I slip it off and hold it out to him. He takes it, holds it up to his desk light, the gold gleaming briefly, and reads the inscription. He returns it to me, jots down a few notes, and says, "Are you certain he wore it on his *right* pinky finger?"

"Yes."

"You're positive?"

"I'm certain. Why?"

He frowns and shakes his head.

"What?" I say, the liquid floor lapping at my knees.

"It's like your ring, but it wasn't on his right hand or pinky."

"Where was it?"

He looked at me sadly and said, "I'm sorry, I can't say."

Shortly after we'd moved into the apartment, Roger surprised me with a candlelit dinner on our anniversary. We'd been together eight years. He made beef Wellington, green beans, potatoes, and coconut cream pie. After dessert, he said, "We're practically an old married couple, so you may think this is silly, but I thought we should make it official." He whipped his napkin off the table to reveal two ring boxes. As he handed me my felt box, he said, "I want you to be able to look down at it and remember that you'll always have me." Of course, it wasn't silly. We soon discovered that the jeweler made the rings the same size. Roger has thicker fingers, so he wore his on his pinky, which to the casual observer, further obscured our connection.

I slip my ring back on. "So, you don't *actually* know if the man in our apartment is Roger." The rising tide of terror begins to recede. I glance at Judy and Philippa, who seem to sense my change in mood. Their expressions quizzical.

"We'll just say"—he clears his throat—"that we haven't verified it."

"Indeed, you haven't," I say, feeling a tug of hope.

⌐━━✦━━⌐

I drop onto Philippa and Judy's creaky couch, limp as a noodle. For a few minutes, they dart around me, bringing me a whiskey and water. They curl a throw blanket around my shoulders like I'm someone's nana. I can't focus on their nervous chatter, glancing condolences, and earnest attempts to soothe. For a moment, I hate them, or rather, their intrusiveness—or is it my intrusiveness? After all, I'm on their couch. From what I gather, I'm their guest, which is a first for them. The whiskey revives me; its heat stings my throat.

"Ladies," I say, "sit down and be quiet. I'm fine. I'll be fine."

Philippa stops, sucks in her breath, and blushes.

Judy turns and smiles. Her smile is something I haven't gotten used to. It's a blend of chill and delight, scrutiny and mirth. I like it. I like *her*. But somehow, I feel I shouldn't trust her. I never know what to do with someone who can—and does—pass. I can't blame her. I've passed in my way before. I can butch it up if the situation calls for it.

"We're sorry," Philippa says, obeying my instructions and sitting across from me in a mismatched armchair. Judy stands beside her. "We don't know what we're doing," she says, brushing a curl of reddish-blonde hair from her cheek. "We're just—we're so horrified this happened to you."

I take another sip of whiskey. "They haven't identified his body."

Judy rests on the arm of Philippa's chair, her pencil skirt sliding up a little to reveal her long tawny legs. She has a self-confidence that Philippa doesn't, but Philippa has a warmth Judy lacks. I get their attraction to one another. A yin and yang thing. "Wow. Is that so?" Judy says. She also has a whiskey. She raises her tumbler to her lips.

"His ring—the one that matches mine." I hold it up for them. "Wasn't on his right pinky where it should be, which is damn odd. He would never take off that ring. It should be there."

They exchange glances and shrug. I'm not sure if they think I'm grief-mad or if they have no explanation to offer. An awkwardness falls among us, and I feel pressure to break the tension: "Look," I say. "You know Roger well enough. Do you think he'd kill himself?"

"He was depressed about his job," Judy says, then sighs and adds, "No, I don't think he would."

"I don't either," Philippa says softly, almost shyly.

There's a knock on the door—a knock to alert, not a request for entrance. A tall Negro woman in a taupe overcoat steps in. She's gripping her bonnet in her gloved hand. Her hair is cropped short and curled. Everything about her is long and trim and elegant, even if what she's wearing is a little plain. Her eyes fall on me, and she advances.

"I'm so sorry, Lionel." She doesn't offer me a pitying look but rather something sterner, more sincere. She seems to intuit my anger. "I'm Iris Baker." She holds out her hand, and I catch a whiff of something foul and vaguely sweet as I shake it. She steps away, hovering near the door. She looks at Philippa and Judy and, as a sort of explanation, adds, "I'm family."

I'm not sure what this means. Is she a lesbian? Or is she *actually* family? Then, through the fog in my brain, it clicks: she's Judy's half-sister. The girls have spoken of her.

"Iris!" Philippa says. "We're so glad you're here." Her tone is bright, false.

Judy grimaces. "You didn't change? I can smell you from here."

"Shit, shit," Iris says, stepping back. "You can smell it through the overcoat?"

And I remember: she works for the medical examiner at the city morgue. The off odor is decomposing flesh. It clings to clothing. I recall the horrible smell of the fire. Ash mingling with the cherry blossoms. I take another swig of my whiskey to chase away the odor.

"I'm horrified." Iris pulls her overcoat around her. "I'll change."

"Good idea." Judy's eyes widen a little.

But I say, "So, you work for the medical examiner?"

She nods and offers a gentle smile.

"And you went to medical school at Howard."

"That's right." She looks at the girls. "I should get out of these clothes. I don't know what I was thinking. My God."

"Impressive," I say. "A woman and a doctor."

Her face takes on a stern cast. I wonder if I've insulted her. "Well, *they* won't trust me with the living, so I assist the medical examiner."

By "they," I imagine she means all the white men in the medical field, but she could also mean the Negro community—I don't know if they'd take to a woman doctor. As a mystery writer, I've done my fair share of research about corpses, so I'm intrigued by her job—about what she's witnessed, about who she sees pass through the medical examiner's office, both the living and the dead.

"More on that later." Her dark eyes smile at me. "I need to change—and have a cigarette. Be back in a minute." She slips out the door.

"You'll stay with her," Judy says. "She lives downstairs and has a proper guest bedroom."

This news releases something in me, a tremor of grief, and I sigh and suddenly feel I could sleep for days.

"You must be exhausted," Philippa says, noticing me.

"You can't imagine," I say, attempting a smile.

CHAPTER 7

JUNE 1952, JUDY

News about Bart Peabody came to me during a beautiful day in Paris.

After my botched attempt to seduce Philippa failed, I fled the country. I'd like to say I was fleeing to France, not away from Philippa, but that would be a lie. I had my new name; money to spend from the Peabodys, who were relieved I was putting an ocean between Philippa and me; and the idea that Europe, and particularly Paris, which I'd always swooned over in magazines and movies, would be the right place to reinvent myself and wear my new name like a fancy hat. In the wake of the war, Paris was, well, a bit grubby, and I was very alone, but it wasn't the loneliness of Agnes March or the Peabodys' palatial row home. This loneliness was forgiving; it gave me space to breathe, to feel a degree of freedom. Sure, Paris was scarred by the war, but like any place remaking itself, there was a sense of the possible rustling the leaves of the trees and stirring up the dust in the streets.

I rented a flat in the Latin Quarter and studied French and literature at the Sorbonne. Yes, as revolting as it is, I embraced the rich debutante in Paris stereotype, using Wilde's epigram, "When good Americans die, they go to Paris," to justify this new mode as "revolutionary." Judy Peabody was dead, I told myself, and now, Judy Nightingale would live. Since I'd stopped styling myself like a half-baked flapper, as much as I could afford, I adopted the new look of Paris: pillbox hats and mushroom cloches, wide-collared coats, fitted blouses, and sculpted two-piece suits. I drank a lot of briny martinis and ate a lot of bread and cheese. I made quick and shallow friends and took equally quick and shallow lovers, both men and women—Lucy, David, Juliette, Camille, and Alain—which was like trying on shoes that didn't quite fit. Philippa's sharp rejection had left me spinning, and I couldn't shake the vertigo. I searched for her in these lovers, which made sleeping with them clumsy and embarrassing. On Saturday nights, though, we'd gather on the terrace of the Café de Flore or at the Deux-Magots and then dance or listen to jazz at the clubs. We'd whirl through the nights, sleep until lunch, and despite the haze of alcohol (and the ache of hangovers), hit the books in the afternoons, and then, we'd repeat the glorious fervor. For a year or so, it was hedonistic bliss, hovering somewhere between serendipity and oblivion.

Eventually, the Peabodys, convinced my bond with Philippa had been severed by distance and time, began pelting me with firmly worded letters about my need to curb my spending and, perhaps, consider returning home. Eventually, they threatened to shut off the tap, and I became worried that my generous stay-away allowance would dry up. I came across a notice in Le Monde for a position as an office manager at a local radio station. I'd purchased a radio to improve my French and began listening to Paris Inter. Le français est une belle langue! Radio was state-controlled and lacked variety, but still, it sufficed. I kept up with the news about the Korean War, notably France's contribution, an infantry battalion of over three thousand soldiers, who fought in romantic-sounding confrontations like the Battle of the Twin Tunnels and the Battle of Heartbreak Ridge, which I was sure weren't the slightest bit romantic. Over time I became a fan of its storytelling format and was thrilled by the occasional performance by Édith Piaf or Josephine Baker. Somehow, I convinced the station to take me on and began to earn my own money. I quickly learned that gainful employment and a vigorous nightlife weren't compatible. The work was interesting, at least tangentially—I was not allowed on the radio—but the more I saw Paris in the daylight, the less I liked it.

When the telegram came announcing Bart's death, I didn't flinch. It was time to return to DC. After reading Edith's message, I stepped into the light-filled street, took in the glistening cobblestone and sun-warmed buildings, and suddenly felt that Paris had been a missed opportunity. I recalled a Sacha Guitry quotation that someone flung at me during those first weeks in Paris: *"Être parisien, ce n'est pas être né à Paris, c'est y renaître."* To be Parisian is not to be born in Paris; it is to be reborn there. But I hadn't been reborn. I'd changed my name, friends, and clothes, but I'd never left home behind. How could I? That's where Philippa was, and that's where my demons were.

If nothing else, I was my demons.

⚬━⚬

So, that's how I found myself on Edith's love seat holding a cup of strong punch and staring at the post-funeral gawkers pantomiming their sympathies. At one point, the Peabodys had played an active part in the Washington social scene. The wealth they accrued through their local drugstore franchise gave them access to the upper echelons of society, but over the years, their grief distracted them from the rhythms of luncheon, fête, fundraiser, repeat. The murder of their daughter, nine-year-old Jackie, had changed them—warped them, really. In an act of supreme grotesquerie, they'd adopted me to replace her. *La fausse fille.* And their failed attempt

to lock up the murderer and the simmering outrage that had followed
made them curiosities. "Poor Bart and Edith," these mourners whispered,
"they could never move on from little Jackie, even after they adopted
that girl who gave them so much trouble. Yes, the one over there on the
settee, looking surprisingly chic."

I sipped the tangy punch and observed Edith, stout and elegant in black
chiffon, making her rounds. She kept her posture rigid, shook hands with
guests, and smiled stiffly. But her broad shoulders and imposing frame
seemed diminished, fragile. Although I couldn't hear her conversations, I
guessed they began with her navigating an obligatory condolence. Then,
with well-practiced poise, she'd redirect the conversation to empty
chitchat and away from Bart. She was embarrassed by him because of
his drinking, because it had fallen on her to keep up the household, and
because she was the one who had made the call to sell Peabody Drug
not long after I fled. At times, though—usually as she listened to a guest
yap—a nervous vibration rippled through her. It was difficult to put a finger
on it, but I wondered if behind the humiliation, behind all the turmoil she
and Bart had weathered, she had loved him. I'd never thought of them
that way—a couple in love. Sure, they'd been united in grief and bitterly
angry that justice was never served, but what had they been before?

When Philippa entered the parlor, I tossed my sympathies to the side.
She wore a dark gray suit with pale gray gloves. Her hair was up and
glowed like a flame under her fascinator. I'd forgotten how beautiful she
was. She'd grown taller, and the curve of her body was more gradual, less
voluptuous—a body made for tailored outfits and slim-heeled pumps.
Her fascinator jerked this way and that. She was searching for me, which
gave me time to take her in and be astonished she'd shown up at the
reception—which, I'm sure, she wasn't invited to. Her gall amazed me.
Her level blue-gray eyes finally met mine, and she smiled broadly, quickly
downshifting to a bemused smirk. It was a solemn occasion, after all. I
detected none of the shame and worry that had consumed her when

I last saw her. I wanted to laugh. I did. She made her way to me and said, "Hello, Judy. I'm so sorry. My—"

"If you say 'condolences,' I'll vomit." She blinked, a little stunned. "Right here, on the floor, in front of God and everyone."

She pursed her lips, concealing her amusement. "It's good to see you."

I glared at her. She seemed so confident, forthright. I barely contained my happiness. "Sit down, will you?" I shifted over and patted the cushion beside me. She joined me. "Here," I said, handing her my cup of punch. "Drink up."

To feel her body's weight on the cushion beside me, its warmth, its whirling energy, was a salve for the rawness in my heart, for the failure of Paris to transform me into whatever I was supposed to become. Something worldly and refined? Ha! It drove me mad she had that power over me, but she did. Can you imagine a vicious creature like me, all thorns, barbs, and hard looks, being in love?

"Where's that dog of yours? Where's Roosevelt?" she asked after a sip of punch. Her eyes darted around. "Little Rosie?"

"He's locked in an upstairs room to keep him from tripping mourners." Since I'd left the country, Edith, who complained endlessly about my Frenchie pup's behavior, had made him her fast companion, her emotional support while Bart was in decline. "Rosie is no longer *my* dog," I said. "He and Edith are thick as thieves."

Philippa smiled. "Well, that's what you get for deserting him."

A pang of guilt shot through me. "You're right, I suppose."

After a moment, she broke the tension, and we began chatting about the guests, sizing them up, as we had years ago at Bart and Edith's Halloween shindig. Of course, we didn't have costumes to riff on, but we did chew up some of our fellow mourners.

"Her hat is the size of a butler's tray," Philippa quipped.

"That one over there, she's had three ham sandwiches. Grief does wonders for the appetite," I said.

"Oh God, who wears fox fur to a summer funeral?"

"She didn't want Bart to be the only taxidermied thing here."

"In the corner of the room . . ."

"The man shoving a petit four in his mouth?"

"Yes, that one. Do you see it?"

I gasped. "His fly is undone."

Philippa laughed. "Splendid."

The rhythm of our back and forth was familiar and comfortable, but still, I was curious what was on her mind. Why was she here? Had anything changed since I saw her three years ago, or was she here out of a sense of duty or, worse, nostalgia? "Look," I said, "it's great you've come. Believe me. But I—"

"It's been too long," she said, cutting me off and touching my leg gently. "I take full responsibility." She patted me and removed her hand. Her energy was odd, both warm and contained. "There's a lot to say, but perhaps not just now." She smiled and nodded at the room. "What would the guests think?"

"Damn the guests!" I said too loudly.

She was about to respond when she stopped; her eyes landed on someone across the room, and blood drained from her face. "Moira Closs," she whispered. It had been years since I'd seen Moira, but the fear and anger flooded back: The Wicked Witch of Washington. Queen of Capitol City Hardware. Consort of conservatives. Party-thrower for political fixers. Dabbler in espionage. Abettor of evil. Orchestrator of my fate. She wore a dark blue Chanel suit piped in white, leather gloves, a sculpted felt hat, and an impressive diamond brooch, glittering like a dying star. Although in her late sixties, she moved with force, a mist of L'Air du Temps trailing her. Her movements were decisive, even aggressive, but greased with good manners, her voice buttery, her posture open. Her stern crystal-blue gaze gave her away, though; it'd been honed by years of repressed rage and grief over the loss of her grandson and son.

I remember her bending over me four years ago, her eyes bulging like a goat's, and her growling, "I know more about you than you know about yourself." At the time, it was true; not now, though.

Moira spotted Edith, split the room like an arrow, and flung out her arms. She cooed her grief loudly. She was on stage. Once again, my heart ached for Edith. Jesus, I *was* growing soft. Bart and Edith didn't know that Moira had been the reason Jackie's murderer was never brought to justice. Philippa and I made that discovery in '48 before we were separated. My anger at the Peabodys kept me from telling them the truth. I wanted them to suffer in payment for how they made me suffer. Over time, my fury mellowed, but I was abroad and refused to put it in a letter. What would I have written: "Dear Bart and Edith, although Adrian Bogdan was absolved of Cleve Closs's murder and, by dull-witted extension, Jackie's murder, the authorities were only half right. Sure, he didn't kill Cleve, but your earliest suspicions were correct: he's a monster and Jackie's killer. It can't be proved, but I know, and Philippa knows. Hope that makes you feel better! Love, Judy"?

Philippa shifted nervously beside me and straightened her dress. We glanced at each other. I leaned toward her and said, "I can't believe she would show up here."

"Does Edith know . . . about everything?" Philippa asked.

My eyes told her no.

"She's frightened of her," she said. "Look at her body language."

"Animal instinct."

We watched as Moira and Edith pulled back from their embrace, Moira's gloved hands still gripping Edith's arms. They exchanged a few more words, and then Moira looked in our direction as if she sensed us watching her. "Shit," I said under my breath. She smiled and strode our way.

"Hello, girls," she said, her attempt at friendliness falling flat. "You look well." Her icy gaze drifted over us. We didn't stand up. To do so would've implied respect or even deference. We weren't budging for her.

"Moira," I said, offering nothing else.

Her face lifted, and I detected a trace of amusement in her lips. "I wanted to tell you how sorry I am about Barton."

"Edith is crushed."

"Is she?" Moira returned.

"Of course she is," Philippa said, incensed.

She paused. "I don't believe it. Sad, sure, but 'crushed,' no. She's now free to be her own woman, to move on."

"We haven't forgotten," Philippa said, throwing her shoulders back as if to say, I'm not afraid of you.

"I didn't think you had," Moira said, smirking. "Neither have I." Her eyes glistened. "Both of you are always in my thoughts."

Philippa's gray gaze narrowed, and in a low tone, she said, "We're not going to move on." Moira's polished veneer rolled back, revealing traces of her hostility underneath. They studied each other, and Philippa added, "He's been killing again."

"What?" I said, shocked. "What are you talking about?" She seemed proud to possess knowledge I didn't. She always treasured the power of secrets, even secrets kept from me. I found this quality in her tolerable only because I admired her for grasping a little power of her own. I could imagine this news about Bogdan being accurate, but I couldn't imagine how Philippa knew this or why.

Moira waved a gloved hand. "Pshaw!"

"He's killing girls again," Philippa said, keeping her voice low. "I don't think he ever stopped."

We'd hoped his brush with the police and his handlers at the FBI would keep him in check. We'd *hoped* they'd make him vanish.

"You have a fertile imagination," Moira said feebly.

"Betty Hicks, Carol Combs, Maggie Osborne." Philippa paused briefly after each name, allowing it to echo in our minds. "And there are more."

Moira's face burned with embarrassment, and her eyes, usually so fixed and piercing, were blinking and unfocused. The wrinkles at her mouth deepened, and concern darkened her features. She'd slipped into the shadowy world of state secrets, fashioning herself as the queen of the Washington social scene. Her glittering parties, we suspected, served as smoke screens for the passing of secrets and the connecting of spooks. But I remembered how much Adrian Bogdan frightened her. In her dealings with us, she'd been unwavering and assertive, never revealing the slightest chink in her designer-label armor. Still, Bogdan had unsettled her, and I sensed she felt conflicted about working with her FBI pals to shield their precious asset. Perhaps the part of her that was a mother couldn't help but find a child killer repugnant, no matter his "value" to national security.

She suddenly shook off her gloom like a chill, and her haughty glow returned. She twisted her upper lip at Philippa, but Philippa just glared and said, "He's still out there, killing girls, and you and those government goons are still protecting him."

"Don't be stupid, dear," she snapped and then exhaled, probably thinking it unwise to go to battle in a crowded room. "That man, he's long gone, no longer a part of our history or anyone else's. You and Judy need to get on with your lives." She wavered, undercutting the certainty of her statement. "Goodbye, girls." She forced a smile and traveled to another group of mourners.

❦

Philippa slid a long flat crate out from under her bed. It was full of her journals, which she'd dated, labeled, and lined up neatly. I thought of my aunt's journal, which I'd taken with me to France and now stowed again under my bed, but unlike Philippa's catalog of memorabilia, it was a talisman against evil. I asked her if she'd organized her writings by the

Dewey decimal system, and she gave me a half-withering, half-amused smile. Across the top of them lay a large rectangular photo album, conspicuously dust-free. Embossed in its black leather at the lower right corner was "Memories" in a loopy script. She gestured for me to sit on the narrow rocking chair across from her bed, which required me to move her scrawny stuffed bear. I looked at her sad excuse for a child's toy, said, "I'm sorry, Mr. Fred," and tossed him to her. She caught him and gently dropped him at the head of her bed. Her room had retained much of its girlishness, even though she'd tried to disguise it with muted colors and a tailored bedspread. We'd changed so much since the last time I'd been in this room four years ago. I felt like a giant monster stomping through a miniature landscape of her past.

"It's all in there," she said, handing me the album. She sat on her small bed, its springs squeaking. "Go on," she said, "open it."

After we'd shooed Moira away, Philippa understood that I needed an explanation for why she thought that Adrian Bogdan was killing girls again, so she brought me here. In our last showdown with Moira and friends in December '48, she'd exposed us to the truth about Bogdan to scare us into silence. She had secrets to hide, and she used his potential viciousness to threaten us, even if, in the end, she knew she was out of her depth. I'm still shocked we didn't end up in the river that night like Jackie. Those horrible memories of him still arose: his chiseled features, his thick black hair, his full, bow-shaped lips, and his dead eyes. His smell, the mingling of sweat, booze, and rancid breath, would occasionally swirl in my nostrils. Most of all, I remembered his smile. His eyes would sparkle an unholy blue, and his lips would pull back, revealing his twisted and rotten teeth. It shattered his looks. The monster revealed.

I opened the album. Inside, Philippa had pasted newspaper articles and photos. It reminded me of Ellis's collection of clippings. Headlines from local newspapers flashed by as I flipped pages:

COMBS GIRL FOUND DEAD, FOUL PLAY SUSPECTED,
Winchester Star, Winchester, VA, October 1, 1949.

TRAIL GROWS COLD IN JONES GIRL DISAPPEARANCE,
The Daily News-Record, Harrisonburg, VA, May 14, 1950.

TWELVE-YEAR-OLD CULPEPER GIRL MISSING,
Virginia Star, Culpeper, VA, August 17, 1950.

'WE WANT JUSTICE!' CRIES MOTHER OF SLAIN CULPEPER GIRL, ELIZABETH HICKS,
Virginia Star, Culpeper, VA, August 28, 1950.

STILL MISSING: ELEVEN-YEAR-OLD NORFOLK GIRL, SUSANNAH LEE,
Daily Press, Newport News, VA, June 30, 1951.

FAMILY OF MURDERED ASHLAND GIRL SEARCH FOR CLUES,
Richmond Times-Dispatch, Richmond, VA, August 20, 1951.

GRISLY DISCOVERY IN JAMES RIVER,
Richmond Times-Dispatch, Richmond, VA, October 29, 1951.

NO CLEAR LEADS IN OSBORNE MURDER,
Richmond Times-Dispatch, Richmond, VA, November 12, 1951.

Philippa also included photographs. Several were snapshots of river-banks during different times of the year, some picturesque and dappled with sunshine and others scattered with debris. Other photos were of the fronts of buildings: a townhouse, a bungalow, a farmhouse, and an apartment complex. Another was the front of a Culpeper County elementary school, another of the Winchester police department, and another of a brick church. I looked at her and asked, "What is this, exactly?"

"Well," she said, taking a deep breath. "It's a murder book, or that's what the police call it."

"A murder book?"

"During my first semester at college, a girl went missing in Ashland, down the road from Briarfield."

"Edith said something about you attending a small school near Richmond, but she didn't say which one." I shook my head. "Jesus, we have been out of touch."

"Briarfield is an MRS degree factory. It was my only choice. During the spring of my senior year at Eastern High, my poor grades disadvantaged me. It also didn't help I decided to attend a college at the last minute."

I recalled her fleeing from me after our encounter on the roof of Hill Estates, her strawberry hair vanishing below the roofline. Was that when she decided to enroll? Was she running away from me? From us?

"After two years, I transferred to UVA. I had to prove myself with good grades at BF first. Not a difficult thing to do."

The glint in her eyes told me she sought my approval, but the memory of Hill Estates left me raw. I couldn't muster a kind word, so I said, "What about the girl?"

"I heard about twelve-year-old Maggie Osborne's disappearance in my second year. It was in the local newspaper. I was bored with my classes, so I followed the case intensely. On her way home from her youth group at the local Methodist church in August, Maggie was abducted. Two months later, her remains were found on the south bank of the James River in Richmond. Maggie had beautiful chestnut curls, and she had no clothes on. The police were—and still are—stumped. Initially, they thought her father did it, but his alibi was solid."

"Bogdan," I said.

"Yes," she said, her eyes flashing. "And then I began to do research. Two other girls, Carol Combs of Winchester and Betty Hicks of Culpeper, were kidnapped and murdered. Carol in October 1949 and Betty in

August 1950. Both girls were found in a river or at a river's edge—Carol in the Shenandoah and Betty beside the Rapidan. Carol was nine and had light brown hair. Betty was a young-looking twelve and had dirty blonde, almost brown hair. That's when I enlisted Quincy's help. He contacted a cop friend, Piers Richardson, who works for the Harrisonburg Police. He told us about eight-year-old Nancy Jones, who disappeared in April 1950. She vanished on her walk home from school. She had dark brown hair. Richardson also shared information on Susannah Lee, an eleven-year-old with darkish wavy hair, who vanished in May 1951 from Norfolk, Virginia. Like me, Richardson thought there was a connection. He told Quincy he'd learned that Betty's body had been written on. She was found only ten days after she was kidnapped, so her body wasn't far gone."

"Well, damn." I was amazed at her tenacity. "And then you made this book?"

"I started collecting newspaper articles and needed to organize them, but I wanted to get a sense of the places where the crimes happened, so I borrowed my roommate's car and drove around photographing these towns with my Brownie, especially any location mentioned in news stories, including where the bodies were found." She paused, her eyes distant, pained. "Although I was sure this trail of nightmares was Bogdan's doing, it wasn't until I visited the place where Betty was found on the bank of the Rapidan that I became certain. I didn't have information on the exact spot of the discovery, but it wasn't far from a bridge named in the *Virginia Star*, so I went exploring. Bring the book over here."

I rose from the chair and sat beside her, the bedsprings crying out again. She flipped several pages, paused, and pointed at a photo. It was a black-and-white of a rock-strewn riverbank, shaded by a dense cluster of trees. The river was narrow, but it surged with whitewater like a storm had just passed through. The photo had a distinct mood about it, a palpable gloom. "Call it intuition," she said, "but I stood on that rock and knew Adrian Bogdan had been there. I even imagined him musing about the Rapidan being like the River Styx and rowing dead girls over to the other side or something equally ridiculous."

How could I forget Bogdan's absurd rationalization: He had cast himself as an Orpheus figure, a conduit to the underworld of ancient myth, who wasn't killing girls but transporting them to the underworld for safe keeping along with his dead sister, Anna, who his father had savagely murdered. He marked his victims with the name Эвридика, Eurydice in Russian. Like Orpheus's descent into hell to retrieve Eurydice, he would eventually journey into the afterlife and bring his sister and the other dead girls back from the dead like an army of child goddesses or something. It was an insane story, but Bogdan wasn't insane. He needed a narrative that excused his vile appetite, so he borrowed one.

Philippa looked at me, her expression grave. "While listening to the water rush by, I got bitterly angry. I picked up a big river stone and heaved it at the water and screamed, 'Fuck!'"

"Throwing stones and yelling 'fuck' at nature," I said, nudging her side, "I wish I'd been there."

A hint of a smile crept into her lips. "I couldn't shake the idea that he was out there killing girls and that those government goons were still turning a blind eye for the sake of their precious state secrets."

I played the devil's advocate: "The FBI would say that Bogdan's intelligence gathering is vital to national security, that protecting the nation outweighs protecting a few girls."

She twisted toward me, the bed springs screaming. Mr. Fred toppled over. "That's a false dichotomy! Find another spy. There's another way."

I put up my hands and grinned. "Okay, okay! Don't throw a big rock at me."

"I shouldn't have told you that story." She sighed. "I knew you'd use it against me."

I leaned into her, allowing my shoulder to touch hers, wanting to linger there. "I'm glad you told me," I said softly.

She pulled back and looked at me. "I want to get him. I want to stop him."

Footfalls echoed up from the floor below. Her father and stepmother were home.

"Shoot," she said, frowning.

The Watsons didn't like me, particularly Carl, her father. He'd judged me a bad seed. Perhaps I am. Anyway, I would've preferred to have avoided them, but the only way out was through, so she hid the murder book, and we headed downstairs, bracing for the impact.

Bonnie, the stepmother, burst into a greeting of maniacal cheerfulness. She grabbed me by the arms: "Wow, Judy, it's been ages. You're all grown up. What a beautiful young woman you've become!" Her expression fluctuated between bafflement and strained delight. With her springy curls flattened tightly against her scalp, she struck me as a pretty woman in a delicate, mousy way. She was a pale substitute for the glamour of Philippa's dead mother, though. I recalled her photograph on Philippa's dresser, a jaunty wedding snapshot, one eye peeking out from a wide-brimmed hat, glaring giddily. Philippa worshipped her. She'd been a writer and an intellectual and died giving birth to her. My heart went out to Bonnie, who lived in her long shadow but never seemed to mind.

Bonnie released me so I could greet Carl, whose stony countenance remained fixed. He was tall, clean-shaven, and seemed older than I remembered. His eyes darted over me, evaluating the situation and determining his next tactical move. He was very much the military man, the JAG. I sensed his distrust of me, but I wasn't sure if it was because of the craziness of the fall of '48 or if, on some level, he detected my romantic feelings for his daughter. Whatever the case, I wanted to be away from him. Philippa sensed this, told them she was escorting me home, and swept me toward the door.

As we strolled, we ran through Philippa's discoveries again, and for the first time in a long while, I felt excited about something. After my adventures in Paris, after all the worldliness I indulged in, what electrified my skin and sparked my nerve endings was the thought of ferreting out Bogdan and punishing him. I imagined Philippa at the edge of the Rapidan River, crouching in her plaid skirt or slacks to scoop up a smooth river stone the size of a dinosaur egg, heaving it high above her head, her arm muscles quaking, yowling like a prehistoric man—Fuuuck!—and bringing the boulder down, not on the bubbly waters of the Rapidan, but on Bogdan's smarmy good looks, his piercing blue eyes, his vile grin. Splat!—like a tomato. His jawbone flying off in one direction, his eyes in another, making little splashing noises downstream.

Philippa escorted me as far as the Emancipation Statue in Lincoln Park and, as if spooked by the grim, condescending president presiding over a freed slave, she stopped and fanned herself. The summer air swam around us; beads of sweat had formed on our foreheads, the backs of our necks, and our underarms. "It's a thick day," she said, turning to me and stepping into the statue's shadow. "Let's sit for a minute." We found a shaded bench.

Philippa had shed her gloves, hat, and quarter-length suit jacket at her house. Underneath, she wore a light scoop-necked blouse, showing off her shape. Sweat dampened the fine edge of the crepe de chine, and the dewy skin that rose from her breasts to her clavicle sent a wave of lust through me. I wasn't particularly proud of my gawking, but something about finding out that, on her own, she'd been trying to track down our villain, our nemesis, the man whose actions had rippled outward to touch—and destroy—so many excited me. When I met her four years ago, I had no idea she'd be an avenging angel. Jesus, I thought she was a namby-pamby strawberry blonde with a penchant for saddle oxfords. There's no better aphrodisiac than being wrong.

"Look," she said, flashing a nervous smile. "I need to tell you something."

"Yes," I said, feeling strange palpitations in my chest.

"In Charlottesville . . ." she said, letting it hang in the air.

"Yes?" I pressed, drawing out the word.

"I met someone."

My heart sank—no, my entire body sank. The boards of the bench underneath me seemed to press upward against my legs. I took a deep breath.

"His name is Stan Wickham."

"*His* name," I said, unable to disguise my disgust.

"We've been seeing each other for about a year, and it's going well."

"It's going well?"

The humidity was closing in on me, wrapping its tentacles around my legs and arms. My throat. I stood up.

She peered up at me, her face inscrutable. She wanted to present me with glossy confidence, a veneer of maturity, not the boldness of a woman hurling a rock at her greatest fear. Instead, I saw ripples of pain, a crushing murk of emotion so bewildering that I had to turn from her. I wanted to scream: "You know, *you know*, that's not your nature. You're being a fool. It will end in disaster. I promise." But I held my tongue. I didn't possess the strength to drag her out of the undertow of her shame.

"I'm sorry if . . ." she said, sighing heavily. "If I surprised you with that news."

"Well," I said, facing her again. "You did."

I was stupid to give in to the pressure to go to Agnes March. I should've fought Bart and Edith. I was foolish to let Philippa leave me after our encounter at Hill Estates. I was an idiot to go to Paris. I should've ignored my bruised heart and held on to her. I might have driven the shame away. But I didn't. I let it all happen. *Ça ne va pas du tout.* Now, it was too late.

"That doesn't mean we can't still hunt down Bogdan," she said. "We're good at this."

Her strained hope irritated me. "How?" I said. "You live in Charlottesville, and I'm . . . here for now, I guess."

"We can meet up. We can find a way." Now she was pleading with me.

"Philippa," I said, heat creeping into my voice. "It's unrealistic, and I will have to get a job. I don't want to be tethered to Edith and her money."

"He's going to keep doing it."

"Yes," I said, glaring at her, and, like an accusation, added, "He is."

She wilted and fanned herself. "You're angry with me."

"I'm trying to understand you." I shifted my weight from my right foot to my left and back again, unable to sit down and unable to leave. "I really am."

She ruminated for a moment. "Maybe if you met Stan—"

"Thanks, but no," I said sharply.

She flinched, stung. She dropped her chin. "I was lonely, Judy." A loose reddish-blonde curl fell from behind her ear.

I sighed, gave in, and sat beside her, still unable to say it: *Please don't go with a man. Please don't do that to me.* Instead, I said, "I had to flee. I couldn't stay here and watch you run away from me every time I tried to touch you."

She glanced over at me. "I can't be that way."

"What do you mean?"

"The way you want me to be."

"You *are* that way."

After a heavy pause, she sucked in her breath and said, "Yes, I know who—what—I am, but I don't see what it leads to. Do you understand?"

"You want to play a role," I said, "because it's easier."

She thought about it, biting her lip. "We all play roles, and I've been cast for this role. I'm an actress doing my job." Gloom entered her eyes. "At the end of the day, you—everyone—must be practical. *I'm* being practical. Stan *is* practical."

"Fuck being practical," I said, standing with a jolt. "You're the one who wants to go after Bogdan. You're the one with a goddamn murder book." I was wagging my finger at her. "What does Stan think about all of this? Do you two cuddle up and talk about little dead girls for kicks?" She sucked in her breath. I'd struck a nerve. "Have you told him about me?"

She shifted on the bench, rubbing a hand across her lap. "So, I guess you are angry."

Leveling my tone, I asked again, "Have you told him about me?"

Her expression hardened. That was a "no."

"Have you told him how you feel about women?"

Her calm eyes were like windows reflecting bright sunlight—dazzling, brilliant, but opaque. I couldn't see inside them. She wasn't going to let me in. I was too dangerous.

She broke away and rose to her feet, smoothing out the wrinkles on her skirt. She peered at the Emancipation Memorial. "Well, it's time to go," she said, her tone flat, remote. "I told Stan I'd drive back to Charlottesville this evening." She looked at me with a measured gaze and held out a slim, freckled hand. A rose gold bracelet dangled from her wrist, perhaps a gift from Stan. Where was her crescent moon pin? It was a symbol of our friendship, our *relationship*. She was wearing it the last time I saw her. Did she throw it away? A shimmer of anger rose through me, but it flew beyond me like the rush of birds alighting. I took her hand; its delicate warmth was soothing. "If you want to stop Bogdan," she said, offering me an enigmatic smile. "You know where to find me."

As she walked away, more beautiful than ever, I was weak, drained, and collapsed on the bench, too stunned to cry.

Days later, restless and seething, I wrote her a letter: "You love women, you love *me*," I scribbled savagely. "You only want to team up to find Bogdan because you miss me. You don't care about those dead girls. You miss me, your *living* girl."

She didn't write back.

CHAPTER 8

MAY 3, 1954, LIONEL

We take the elevator to the eighth floor of 2101 Connecticut Ave and the stairs to the ninth floor. Although the smoke is sharp in the air, the ninth-floor hall, at first glance, appears undamaged. On closer inspection, I detect a film of water-streaked grime on its cream-colored wallpaper. Where the sprinkler spray seeped through, the smooth fabric bubbled up, boil-like.

Handsome Detective Berg and an investigator from the fire marshal's office, Dan Green, escort me, making small talk: the weather this, the Washington Senators that. How do these men find air temperature and baseball so entertaining? As we move down the hall, I want them to shut up, so I can prepare for what I'm about to see: an apocalyptic landscape of cinders and ash, the scorched outline of my former life. I hold my tongue, though, not wanting to irk the fire investigator. Berg seems placated by my alibi, which he's verified, but Green has implied that he suspects me of arson and killing Roger for the life insurance. I should've told Berg about the policy, but I was so worried about falling under suspicion because of my skin color that I held it back. Oh, the irony.

The door isn't closed. It's flung wide, barely on its hinges. The firemen had forced it open. Our beautiful living room, although not a hellscape, is a mess. Our lovely Danish modern pieces are overturned, shoved aside by the frantic firefighters, hauling their hoses through the room. Paintings and other wall decor are askew. The hardwood floors and Roger's grandmother's oriental rug are marred with boot prints. Shards of glass from the broken window are everywhere. The sprinklers have doused everything. A copy of *The Broken Thread* lies on the coffee table, its cover warped and its pages plump with moisture. Aside from the water, the record player cabinet and the bar cart against the back wall are untouched. The fragile stemware and decanters of liquor glitter in the morning light.

I don't see the shaker, though, which is hard to miss. The upright piano is intact but, I imagine, inoperable. A Cole Porter songbook has crinkled and fanned out in its stand. Most of the photos across its top are still in place and, perhaps, salvageable, but the picture of us hiking in Shenandoah is missing. I glance around and spot it on the floor near a toppled chair, shattered, his bright smile glowing through the fractured glass. I badly want to see him, feel his arms around me, and hear his firm voice grow soft with boyish wonder when I tell him a bit of good news or about a discovery I made while writing that day. My impulse is to rush to the photo, pick it up, and protect it from further damage. But I can't, not yet. The police haven't officially released the scene.

"The fire started in the kitchen," Green says, mainly to Berg. Unlike me, they're focused on the evidence of a crime, not the evidence of my life.

My eyes drift toward the kitchen, compelled to look at the horror despite the pain it brings. The smoke damage begins on the living room ceiling, a grayish stain that gradually dissolves into a dark smudge that fans out and coats the entire dining area, shadow-like. Unlike the living room, this space is a total loss: The table, chairs, and cabinet are blanketed in damp soot and debris and in complete disarray. The firemen had thrust the table out of the way to get to the kitchen, knocking over several of the chairs and the now-desiccated bunch of yellow roses I'd bought for the centerpiece. It's hard to believe that the flowers didn't catch fire.

Through the archway, the kitchen itself is unrecognizable. How it was: clean linoleum, pale blue cabinets, dark counters flecked with mica, the stainless-steel sink, and the white-enameled range and fridge. How it is: charred from corner to corner, from floor to ceiling, drained of all color—a photo negative. The wallpaper is curled, the linoleum melted and blistered, and the cabinet doors brittle and burnt. The fridge is sheathed in grime. The stove door droops open, broken, touching the floor. It's impossible to imagine Roger, on all fours, collapsed into it. He wouldn't have done such a stupid, humiliating thing. No way.

"Do they know how it started?" Berg asks Green.

"Not exactly," he responds. "The gas valve in the oven was open. Not uncommon for a suicide." Green studies me. He's older than Berg, perhaps in his mid-forties, and has bland good looks. His face is slender, and his irises are hazel and snake-like. "What ignited the fire didn't come from the oven." He nods toward the electrical outlet nearest the range. An incredibly dark blast of char blooms up the wall from the socket. "The sprinkler in the kitchen didn't work—a mechanical failure. Could've been accidental or the result of tampering. Difficult to tell. The gas exploded like a fireball and cooked the room and Mr. Raymond."

The word "cooked" cuts into me. "Mr. Green," I say firmly, "choose your words carefully." I stay calm, although a blend of anger and grief tumble through me. "Roger was in the service. A navy man. Not a Christmas turkey."

His hazel eyes blink, but he doesn't seem surprised or annoyed by my comment. "Of course. My apologies," he says, and then I understand. It's a test. I'm being tested. That's why I'm here. I glance at Berg, who seems vaguely troubled by Green's thoughtlessness, but maybe it's an act. Good cop, bad cop. I want to trust him, but I don't. I feel observed, as if they're gauging my every facial expression. What do they want from me? Should I collapse on the floor and wail for my destroyed apartment and dead lover—if he *is* the man in the oven? Or should I remain stoic, controlled, and show no weakness? In truth, I feel neither melodramatic nor cold, just bewildered. Cops like this want to cast a prime suspect, as if gut instinct were more important than evidence, then work backward to a solution. For Christ's sake, I want to shout, I have an alibi!

Green sighs and asks me, "What do you think happened here?"

"I don't know," I say. "I hoped you'd have a theory." I'm not biting.

He swipes a hand through his thin brown hair. "Look," he says, "To be honest, I don't know either. It seems like Mr. Raymond—Roger—chose to take his own life by asphyxiating himself with gas, but a spark in the electrical socket, perhaps a short circuit, ignited the gas. The result was an unintentional fire. It's happened before, but . . ." He twists up the corner of his mouth.

I look at Berg, who is standing very still. "Roger wasn't suicidal. It's just not something he would do," I say and add forcefully, "You don't even know it's Roger."

"It's true," Berg says. "We're still tracking down dental records. And there's the ring.

"Ring?" Green's eyes lift.

Berg looks at me like he's trying to decide if he trusts me, then explains, "His ring—a ring he always wore—was on the wrong finger."

"It doesn't make sense," I say, scanning the dark shell of a room. "None of this makes sense."

I leave them and walk back through the house to our bedroom, the least damaged portion of the apartment. I stand at the end of our bed, still neatly made. The layer of wet grime on its pale coverlet strikes me as particularly offensive. I run my fingertip across it, holding the soggy soot up, absurdly, to sniff it—smoldering campfire. I feel hopeless and sick—then, as if an antidote to my despair, I remember sliding my body against Roger's long, sinewy form in the bed. The springs creak. The sheet covering us falls away. The heat from making love is still burning off. I run my hand up his leg and across his torso. My fingers brush his wiry pubic hairs before I settle my palm on his sternum.

We begin talking about when we first met. We'd often talk about that afternoon, each with our interpretation: It's a Sunday, and I'm at a little Negro-owned café near the corner of M Street and Wisconsin Ave in Georgetown, reading Agatha Christie's latest, *Sad Cypress*, and Roger sits at a table beside me. In Roger's version, I'm reading *The ABC Murders*, and he asks to sit with me because all the other tables are taken. We strike up a conversation about Christie. I tell him my thoughts about *Sad Cypress*: "So far, there's a lot of lovers' angst." In his version, he explains why the twist in *The ABC Murders* is his favorite to date. Our conversation tumbles into a lively discussion about mysteries. He's a fan of Patrick Quentin and his *Puzzle for* books, and I like hard-boiled writers like Cain. As we lay there in bed, I tell him that what I remember most about that first meeting is how easy he was to talk to and how, through some sixth sense, I knew he was like me. "There's nothing you said. You made no overtures. I just knew."

He smiles, and we kiss, and the memory evaporates.

Sad Cypress, indeed.

Across the bedroom, our closet door is ajar, and a rumpled piece of fabric spills out of it. Inside, Roger's clothing has been rifled through. Some hangers are bare and twisted as if suit jackets and shirts were ripped from them in haste. My clothes hang neatly, untouched. Something's off. Roger wouldn't tear through his things like that, and the firemen wouldn't have had reason to go in the closet. I spot empty spaces in his shoe rack, and his dark gray Stetson fedora with a green band I bought for him, a favorite, is missing, as is his leather duffel bag. The shoebox that held his service weapon, a Navy issue M1911 purchased through the government surplus program, is on the ground, the pistol missing. Did someone steal his clothes and his firearm? Or was this collected as evidence?

Berg and Green are closing in. I hear them in the living room. More weather, more sports. I pick up my pace and head to our office, just off the bedroom. Light streams through the only window, making the buttery wood paneling glow. Sprinkler water has glued a scatter of papers to the desk's surface. Our meticulous research has been flung across the floor, now a jumble of notes and scraps of primary source material. It'll take days—weeks!—to make sense of it again. I remind myself that until this morning, I thought it was a total loss. Chin up, Lionel. I crouch to the floor and peel back some drier pages to inspect the damage. Although the ink has been blurred by moisture, it's still legible. I tug at another delicate, water-warped piece of research. And another. I look up, and Berg and Green are standing at the office door, watchdogging me.

"There'll be time to do that later," Green says, jittery. Does he think he made a mistake by bringing me here? Does he consider Roger's and my research evidence?

Ignoring him, I pick up one of the leather-bound notebooks where we record our novel ideas. Stuck slimily to its back, a six-by-four photograph peels away and drifts to the floor. I've never seen it before. It's black-and-white, yellowed with age, and slightly out of focus. In it, a scrawny teenage boy has his arm around a pretty girl with dark blonde, perhaps brown, hair. They're sitting on a wooden bench in an open space lined with cobblestone, like a courtyard. She's younger, five or six. The boy is wearing suspenders and a sloppy cap, and the girl has on a crudely made dress. Their faces press against the surface of the photo. Unsmiling. Their eyes are hollow and intense. Yearning. I flip it over, and on the back, it reads, "Адриан и Анна, 1918." Is it Russian? I quickly tuck it in my coat pocket. Berg and Green, distracted by a noise in the other room, fail to notice.

CHAPTER 9

FALL OF 1952, JUDY

My brief stint in French radio landed me a job as a secretary at WSDC-FM, a CBS station on 14th Street. My duties: type, file, schedule, and greet visitors. I wasn't thrilled about it, but it was a job.

After Bart's death, Edith had become needy, ordering me around like a servant. She'd stare at me, blink rapidly, wring her hands, and invent something for me to do: "Judy, sweep out the front hall." "Judy, polish the silver." "Judy, beat the curtains." But she'd soften during cocktail hour or over coffee in the morning: "I don't know what I'd do without you." Some days, she'd ignore me; others, she'd fly at me with directives. Occasionally, she'd squint at me as if she were trying to work out how I was to blame for everything—or maybe she was just wondering if she still knew me. When I was a girl, she and Bart had tried to force me into the mold of little dead Jackie, a memory solid and unyielding in their minds, so it must've been puzzling for her to watch me become a woman. I was not—would never be—her Jackie, so perhaps she was also grieving that loss. With some distance from that ordeal, I'd come to balance my anger at them with appreciation that they'd provided for me and given me a home. It could've been so much worse. So, I lingered, helping her lick the wound torn open by Bart's death, but after a few months, I'd had enough. It was time to carve out a new life.

WSDC was on the top floor of a five-story building, not far from Thomas Circle. The station was constructed in the 1930s during the height of live radio and contained four studios and a small art deco auditorium for live shows. The station had thrived during the war, especially in broadcasting national news. With television on the rise, it now focused on local news, weather, and popular music. They still broadcast syndicated radio shows like *Jack Benny* and *Amos 'n' Andy*, which were transitioning to television, and produced one scripted show called *Dark Secrets*, a horror series like *Inner Sanctum Mysteries* or *Suspense*. My bosses, Rich Brockman and Ed Davies, grumbled about television and cursed *I Love Lucy*: "We've all been undone by a silly redhead!"—who, I'm sure, they secretly admired.

Rich managed the station, and Ed announced the news and wrote *Dark Secrets*. Ed was a wiry and sharp forty-something who wore black square-framed glasses and was graying at the temples. Rich was fat, friendly, avuncular, and, I suspected, often drunk. When they slowed down to notice me, they seemed to like me.

I typed up Ed's scripts for *Dark Secrets*. He liked to give traditional scary stories a fresh twist, weaving in social and political commentary. One of the first scripts I typed was a version of Nathaniel Hawthorne's "Young Goodman Brown" called "The Dream." In it, Goodman Brown becomes Mr. Brown Goodman, an anti-Communist zealot who follows his all-American blonde-haired, blue-eyed young wife to a party that turns out to be a clandestine gathering of Communists. It was smart and satirical, but Rich refused to produce it: "The world can't joke about this yet." He bit off the end of his cigar and spit it in the trash. "We don't want McCarthy's cronies breathing down our necks."

I was hovering at the threshold to Ed's office, visible to Ed but not Rich. He removed his glasses and rubbed the bridge of his nose. "We've got to begin somewhere," he said to Rich. "We need to critique this witch-hunt nonsense, or we're not being responsible journalists."

Rich shifted toward Ed, his bulk swaying, and snatched up a match from Ed's desk and struck it. "This isn't journalism. It's a spooky story. For *entertainment*, not political rhetoric." He lit his cigar.

"If it's just entertainment—"

"Nothing is *just* entertainment." He pointed at Ed with a fleshy finger. "We can't afford controversy. TV is already fucking us. Sorry, my friend, but no." That's when Rich spotted me. "Do you always creep around like that?"

I clutched the manuscript pages to my body. "I wasn't creeping—"

"Do you agree?" he asked me.

"About?" I was confused. I wasn't used to them asking my opinion.

"About Ed's little twist on a classic?" He took a puff on his cigar. Its smoky and sweet aroma filled the office. "About it being a problem? Surely, you read it while you were typing it up."

"It was funny."

"You *are* an odd one." He smirked.

"We have a responsibility," Ed said wearily. "We can't just sit around and hand the microphone to the Walter Winchells of the world. He's spewing lies that prop up that fool McCarthy."

Rich waved his hand at Ed. "Winchell knows how to make lies feel like the truth, but you can't reverse engineer his technique."

Feeling bold, I said, "But you can." I clutched the typed pages close to me, their thickness protective.

"How's that?" Ed asked.

"I mean . . ." I glanced from Ed to Rich and back to Ed. "Fiction disarms you and, well, makes you more susceptible to the truth."

Ed smiled and addressed Rich. "See, she gets it."

"Susceptible to the truth," Rich said, shaking his head. "Folks don't want to feel 'susceptible.' They want to feel certain."

"Even if it's a lie?" Ed asked. His eyebrows arched with genuine interest.

"Especially if it's a lie." He tapped his cigar over the ashtray on Ed's desk.

"You have less faith in humanity than I do," Ed said.

"I have faith that humanity rarely behaves in its best interest."

Ed glanced at me, a faint smile on his lips. He was enjoying the debate. "What do you think of that, Miss Nightingale?"

I considered it for a beat. "I don't like to feel certain. I like to be certain. If I can't be certain, I'd rather feel. . . open to a range of possibilities."

"Bah! You sound like Ed," Rich said. "You must be an artistic sort."

I shook my head, but he wasn't convinced.

"Most of our listeners aren't artistic sorts."

I didn't know what to say, so I offered a little shrug.

"I've got things to do." He glanced from me to Ed. "We're not doing that script." He was pointing his finger again. "Maybe later, when things have settled down."

He left the office.

Ed gave me a gloomy glare. "What do you have for me?"

I handed him my stack of typing, most of which was the updated script for "The Dream" and some news items. He took it, glanced at the first page, and dropped it on his desk with a thud.

"Too bad Mr. Brockman won't produce it," I said. "It's clever."

His chair squeaked as he leaned back. "Don't worry. We'll get it on the air."

I was glad that he said "we." He knew I wasn't an airheaded secretary. I'd even wondered if I shouldn't try my hand at a radio play.

"Is anything that McCarthy says true?" I asked. Although not a fan of communism or the Soviets, I doubted McCarthy and HUAC's feverish claims that nefarious Commies lurked around every corner in government buildings and Hollywood soundstages, plotting to destroy the American way of life. It was too farfetched, like a pulp novel, but many Americans bought it. Of course, Bogdan—the only "Commie" I knew (and he was an ex-Commie)—seemed greedy, violent, and politically indifferent. Self-interest, it seemed, was the thing to watch out for.

Ed smiled coolly. "Never listen to what someone says. Watch what they do."

Annoyed, I said, "But that's not what I asked."

"An effective liar builds lies on truths," he said. "They hold up better that way. There are spies. Sure. Klaus Fuchs and Julius and Ethel Rosenberg. But not everyone interested in Communist political philosophy is a spy. McCarthy's fearmongering is political showmanship."

"It's dangerous."

"Yes, it is."

He studied me, twitching his lips back and forth as if he were mulling something over. His eyes drifted to a scrap of paper on his desk. "If you will," he said, handing it to me. "Read a line or two."

I took it and read:

Washington, D. C.—Polio is cutting a grim path through 1952. The prediction is at least 50,000 cases will flood the US, surpassing the 1949–1951 record of 42,366. Twenty-one states have reached epidemic rates.

"Stop," he said. "Never mind. Girls can't read the news." He shook his head. "It sounds like you're reading a recipe from a cookbook. No authority."

His words stung, and I thrust the transcript page back at him. "Then why did you ask me to read it?" Newspaper images of polio-infected children in iron lungs swam through me, their smiling faces sprouting out of the metal tubes as if being trapped in one of those horrible things was playtime.

"I like your shrewdness," he said, "and I was curious."

"But I'm a woman, so . . ." I didn't hide my irritation.

Behind his thick glass frames, his eyes flickered. "It's not what people want, Miss Nightingale. Maybe you can play a character in a radio play."

"So, *now* you care about what people expect."

He squinted at me like he was confused. Office "girls" don't talk back to their employers. "That's all, Judy." And like that, I was dismissed.

I accepted his slight as a challenge and began studying him when he read the news. I would take a coffee break and watch him at the sound booth window as he hovered close to the mic and rattled off the news. Despite his anathema to Winchell, he seemed to emulate the announcer's famous staccato blast. He didn't editorialize, though. Well, not as egregiously. Eventually, he noticed me and seemed pleased.

Ed called in sick one day, and the usual fill-in, Burt, was running late. Rich couldn't reach the other subs. I watched the blood rush to his doughy face. He loved the radio, but he wasn't a performer. He didn't want to do it, and he didn't want to run old material. Channeling Philippa's pluckiness, I said, "Mr. Brockman, let me have a crack at it."

He gazed at me like I'd spoken to him in a foreign language. *Vous me comprenez?* I nudged him: "I've been practicing."

His bafflement turned to skepticism, then suddenly, he said, "Fine, fine. A segment or two won't hurt, I suppose."

I gave it my all, keeping my voice sharp and confident, and delivered each story with a controlled blast of energy. I even offered the slightest editorial flourish. Rich was impressed, and even though Ed still objected to women news announcers, he let me read several local news segments a week, giving me feedback afterward.

I won't lie: it felt good to be a part of something. I wondered if Philippa was listening. I'd continued to write to her, but she didn't respond. I imagined her scanning stations and happening on my segment. She'd perk up, then gasp with recognition. Maybe it'd inspire her to write me or pick up the phone.

In mid-October, as I was preparing to go live, Rich burst into the booth and dropped a news story in front of me. "Start with this," he ordered. "Not your usual petty crime. Listeners will remember you telling them about this one." I glanced over it, and my first thought was *shit*.

Ed announced me: "Here's Miss Judy Nightingale with the local news and weather."

I paused briefly, collected myself, and said, "Good morning, Ed. This tragic news just in: McLean, Virginia—The body of eleven-year-old Candice Conklin of Falls Church, Virginia, was found in an eddy of the Potomac River in Great Falls Park late Sunday by a pair of hikers. Candice, known as Candy by friends and family, went missing three days ago on her way home from Cherrydale Elementary School. Candy's mother and father, Meredith and William Conklin, haven't released a statement. Foul play is suspected. Fairfax County and Montgomery County Police request information on Candy's whereabouts from October 17, at 3:20 P.M., until her discovery yesterday or any other pertinent information. Such sad and terrible news."

After the segment, I gripped the sink's edge in the ladies' room. My anger flung itself at the tile walls, fixtures, and the grimy toilet. I silently cursed Philippa. I cursed myself. Most of all, I cursed Bogdan. I knew he was responsible for Candy, another one of his Eurydices. He wouldn't stop unless we did something. No matter what I did, I couldn't escape the shadow of these dead girls. First, Jackie Peabody. Then, Carol Combs, Nancy Jones, Betty Hicks, Susannah Lee, and Maggie Osborne. Now Candy Conklin. Jesus. I glared at myself in the mirror: my bob mussed and my eyes damp. I wanted to claw at my image, mess her up, and teach her not to be a fool. I let out a stupid little cry, gulped some water, and straightened my hair. I knew what I had to do: that weekend, I would borrow Edith's car and drive to Charlottesville.

Philippa's apartment was on the first floor of a large, weather-worn Victorian, not far from UVA's medical school. The neighborhood bustled with students and hospital employees. I didn't see the attraction of a college town. Everyone was so damn idealistic and bright-eyed. I couldn't imagine wading through dull classes and moth-eaten professors to earn a degree. Besides, the world was my textbook, and its lessons decidedly less gilded.

I checked myself in the rearview mirror to make sure my face didn't go to hell on the trip down: eyebrows still finely drawn, hair still smooth and glossy, lipstick still a deep fuchsia bow. I wore a fitted blue dress, a light wool box coat, heels, and a semi-ridiculous saucer-shaped fascinator. I hated all the trimming, but I wanted to make an impression on Philippa. I was there to tell her the news about Bogdan, but also, I hoped to offer contrast to her current love interest, this Stan person.

I stepped out of Edith's Dodge coupe, approached Philippa's door, took a deep breath, and knocked. No one answered. I waited and knocked again. Still, no answer. I returned to the car to bide my time, mulling over what I'd say to her. I watched the dead leaves scrape across the pavement until my eyelids grew heavy.

I spotted her strolling up the sidewalk. She was dressed in a knee-length gray coat and slacks, and was clutching a heavy satchel. Perhaps she was coming home from classes at the university or her part-time job at the lawyer's office where she'd worked before Briarfield. Even in the dimming light, her hair glowed like copper threads. I imagined I could smell her perfume. Something spicy and bright. I left the car, calling to her as she reached the door. She spun around. "Judy?"

"Hi, Philippa," I said, smiling.

"What are you doing here?" Her eyebrows were knitted together. She didn't seem happy to see me.

"May I come in?"

She scanned the street, unsettled by my surprise visit. "I suppose so. Stan won't be home for a few minutes."

Fuck Stan, I thought, not allowing a trace of annoyance to show.

Her apartment was spacious but sparsely decorated. After casting off her satchel and coat, she led me to the den, which was dominated by a secondhand brown plaid sofa and a cable rug; neither were her tastes. On the wall above a defunct fireplace hung Stanley J. Wickham's framed degree from the University of Virginia like the head of a dead animal. I'd noted his dirty boots by the door. She caught me looking at it and said, "Stan wants to be a cardiologist."

"How nice for him," I said, sarcasm slipping through.

"Okay, Judy," she said wearily. "Did you come here to fight? If that's the case, I can't do it." Her eyes were blurry as if impinged by a headache, and a tight wrinkle had formed on her forehead. I didn't want to cause her pain. "May I," I said, gesturing to the couch, and she nodded. As I sat, its springs bit into my rear. She positioned herself on an uncomfortable-looking armchair across from me.

"So, why are you here?" she asked impatiently.

I rubbed a hand across the scratchy wool upholstery on the sofa's arm and looked at her. "He's killed another girl."

She inhaled and straightened her posture. "He's not going to stop." She began to focus on me for the first time since I arrived. "I told you he wouldn't."

"We need to do something."

She squinted doubtfully. "What about your job?"

I didn't understand her at first, then remembered that needing a job was my excuse for not partnering with her when she suggested it months ago. "Don't worry about that. We can meet up on the weekends."

"Where are you working?"

"At a radio station. WSDC."

She brightened. "Didn't you do that in Paris?"

"It's secretarial work for the most part. Lots of typing. Scripts and such. But now I announce the news several times a week. That's how I learned about the murder."

The tension between us abated a little. "What's her name? The girl."

"Candice Conklin. She was found in the Potomac River near Great Falls. She was eleven."

She stood and went to the window, peering out, checking for Stan again. "I don't know what I can do," she said. "I mean, what can either of us do?" She leaned against the broad windowsill, her profile falling into a gentle chiaroscuro against the afternoon light. "It's no mistake that the press hasn't connected the crimes, and the police haven't built a case."

"J. Edgar and company will protect Bogdan," I said. "They'll never let that monster surface."

"No question," she said, her expression more activated with thought. "If his behavior the last time we confronted him is any indication, he'd take them down with him."

The scene in Moira's study that snowy night arose: the FBI agents, Moira, and Bogdan standing in the dim room, the firelight luridly warping everyone's features. We were all frozen at the threshold of hell, waiting to be sucked in. It was when Philippa learned that Iris was my half-sister and that I was not lily white, and shortly after, Bogdan threatened to kill us and struck Philippa. We made it out alive, but the chill of it persisted. Bogdan was unambiguously evil. He seemed somehow superhuman, unassailable.

"I wonder if he's still valuable to them," I said. "Still a pipeline for intelligence about nuclear arms."

"Maybe, or maybe they just don't know how to stop him."

"Maybe they don't even give a damn."

Philippa rose from her half-seated perch on the windowsill. "Stan's going to be home soon." She glanced out the window again.

It was an invitation for me to leave, but I ignored it. "We should talk to Moira again. She must *know* something."

"Look, Judy," she said, moving close to me. "You better go."

I caught her eyes. "What's going on?"

She crossed her arms. "Stan's due home and it would be awkward for you to be here."

"Why?" I glared at her. She wasn't telling me something.

"You won't like him, and you don't hide your dislike for others well."

I sat back on the scratchy sofa. "The puzzle is why *you* like him."

Her cheeks flushed red, a sign of deep annoyance. "I've told you—"

"That's right," I said. "Loving a woman isn't in the cards for you."

She hung her head, her dusty pink curls spilling over her shoulders. "Judy, please go," she muttered to the floor. Something was wrong, more wrong than when she told me about Stan in DC. My anger melted, and I rose and went to her, touching her arm, painfully close to her. Her fragrance haloed her hair, a delicate floral scent, not spicy at all.

"What's wrong?" I asked.

"Stan found my book with all the clippings. All my notes." She showed me her face. "He demanded I throw it out. He said it was inappropriate and morbid."

I pulled back from her. "Don't tell me—"

"No," she said. "I hid it."

I shook my head. "Why are you with this asshole? Did you tell him about me, or would that ruffle his feathers too much? Or maybe *I'm* too morbid?"

"Judy!" she snapped and suddenly walked toward the door—her second unsubtle invitation to leave. "You need to go. Now."

I stared at her eyes, more gray than blue in this light, and considered my next move. I didn't want to leave with her seething, but I didn't want her to think I was all right with this Stanley J. Wickham situation. Her agitation was intensifying as we regarded each other, so I started toward the door, then stopped. I had an idea: "Give it to me."

"The book?" she asked.

"Yes, the book."

She bit her lip. "I don't know—"

"I'll keep it safe until we can work on it." I was extending a hand. I didn't want to lose contact with her. I also knew she'd hate herself if she let him destroy her hard work.

She mulled it over, and, without saying a word, she dashed into the next room—a bedroom, I believe—and returned with a little blue faux-leather suitcase. "It's in here," she said. "Take it and go before he comes home."

I took it by its handle; it was heavy. "Will he miss the suitcase?"

"I'll make up an excuse."

She walked me to the door. I leaned toward her for a kiss, just a peck on the cheek, but she was too distracted and impatient to notice. Before she closed the door, though, she said, "Thank you, Judy."

"I'll ring you," I said.

She blinked. "Okay," she said, "but if he answers, say you're . . . you're . . ."

"A friend from high school."

She smiled. "That will do."

And she closed the door.

⚊⚬⚊

"Come on in, sis," Iris said as she stepped back, and I trudged through the entryway, dragging my bags. The room smelled of Murphy's oil and the faint residue of fried food. Light was streaming through her bay window, making the bare floorboards shine. On the opposite wall hung a large, framed black-and-white poster from an Ella Fitzgerald concert at the Savoy Ballroom in 1940 and a collection of family photos in mismatched frames. Iris had furnished the living room with a large, braided rug, a small coffee table, on which sprang an arrangement of fresh, colorful dahlias, and a couch draped with a worn patchwork quilt. I left my luggage in the center of the room, collapsed on the sofa, and groaned with relief. For the first time in the last twenty-four hours, I could breathe.

"Need something to eat?" she asked, moving behind me and resting a large, slender hand on my shoulder. "Or some coffee?"

"Coffee. *Please.*"

Because of her new position assisting DC's chief medical examiner, she'd moved out of the Bakers' home three months ago to Le Droit Park, not far from her alma mater, Howard University. I'd always envisioned her working with the living, not the dead. But she seemed content with this new turn in her medical career. "I'm still helping people," she'd said. "Just indirectly." She also reminded me that, as a Negro, she was lucky to get such a well-paid position. "I'm a first of sorts."

Soon a cup of steaming coffee materialized in my hands. After blowing on it, I nursed it for a few minutes.

"Okay," Iris said, sitting beside me, her long arms elegantly folded over her lap. "Tell me what happened?"

"Edith's moods have been cycling more rapidly. The peaks are higher, and the valleys lower," I said, clutching the warm mug tighter. "I've been spending more time out of the house, mostly at work. But she's become more suspicious of me."

Iris pursed her lips with concern.

"So, she decided to rifle through my things, searching for . . . well, who the hell knows? Perhaps some evidence I was a complete failure as a surrogate daughter."

Iris grimaced with disapproval. "She invaded your privacy." She was furious for me, and I loved her for it.

"Damn right." I sipped the coffee, and not wanting to cause a ring on the coffee table, I sat the mug by my feet on the carpet. "Anyway, she found Philippa's murder book, an album full of clippings, notes, photos about an unsolved spate of child murders occurring in eastern Virginia, all similar to Jackie's murder." Besides a slight shift in her eyes, Iris's expression remained fixed. Although she knew Adrian Bogdan's name—after all, his arrest for Jackie's murder and quick release had been in the news—she didn't know that we'd had direct interaction with him or that the FBI was involved. Philippa and I knew we couldn't share the details with anyone. It was too dangerous. "Edith flew into a rage. She didn't want to be confronted with evidence that Jackie's killer was still alive and killing. She began ripping out pages, and I grabbed the book from her, which threw her off balance. She stumbled backward over a small ottoman and fell to the floor." Iris's eyes grew wide. "I tried to help her up, but she spat vitriol at me—more of that you-were-a-mistake, we-should've-never-adopted-you nastiness. Then, she stopped speaking to me. Edith can freeze you out like no other."

"And now you're here," Iris said, her tone warm but edged lightly with criticism.

"Thank you for taking me in." I smiled at her. "I couldn't stay in that house another minute, or I was going to do something I regretted."

"Like what?" She arched her left eyebrow.

"Like push her down the staircase."

Iris laughed and gave me a dismissive wave. Suddenly, her face darkened, growing thoughtful. "Why don't you ever visit Mama and Papa?" she said, suggesting a contrast between parental figures. "They wonder about you, you know? Mama says she gets the odd note or two from you, but she worries they offended you somehow."

Guilt stabbed the pit of my stomach. I couldn't tell Iris that it frightened me to see them, that being in their house felt shameful. I thought of Ellis handing me that portfolio of clippings; he felt shameful, too. I knew my thinking was wrong, even horrible, but I couldn't shake it, so I steered clear of them, sending jolly and superficial letters to disguise my reticence. Clearly, they'd seen through it.

The heaviness in Iris's face changed, lifted a little, and her eyes flashed with clarity. "Judy, why don't you just tell Edith?"

"Tell her what?" I said, reaching for my mug.

"Tell her who you are. That I'm your half-sister."

My heart skipped, and I turned to her. "I can't tell her."

"Why?" Iris asked. She wasn't letting me off the hook easily.

I swallowed. "It's just—"

"If you can't stand her, why do you care?"

I didn't want Iris to be angry with me, but I didn't want to explain my reasons for not telling Edith about Ellis Baker—that I didn't want to see the horrible blank look on her face and hear her special blend of grief and invective that would follow. When I found her in my room in a rage, I first thought she'd discovered my precious and perverse talisman, Charlene's journal, under my mattress. Its pages were my unintentional inheritance, and they made clear that my olive skin wasn't evidence of a mysterious Mediterranean heritage as Edith desperately wanted to believe. She nurtured the delusion that, although I was adopted, I may share her Greek roots. I shouldn't care what she thinks, and I should've told her and Bart to go to hell years ago, but somehow, I'm linked to them, as much as I'm linked to my past, as much as I'm linked to Philippa. Like the scars on my chest and arms, those carefully woven threads, the Fates' intricately knotted tangle, isn't something I can snip and be free from. My name may now be Judy Nightingale, but I was once Judy Peabody, just as I was once little orphan Judy X.

"I'm trying to find the right time," I said meekly. "When Edith is in a state, it's not the right time."

"Shit, Judy, it's never going to be the right time."

Shifting into a defensive posture, I said, "If you don't want me here—"

"Oh, stop it!" she said. "I want you here, but I want you to understand something: you can't hide forever." She gripped my hand on the quilt and flipped it over as if she were about to read my palm. With the fingers of her opposite hand, she touched the flesh of my forearm between my latticework of scars. "In the right light, you're as black as me. In the shadows, you're as white as the Peabodys and Philippa Watson." She released my hand. "The question is: Will you live in the light or the shadows?"

I almost answered: "the shadows." After all, that's where I was born, and so much of my childhood memory is still lost in the shadows. But I held my tongue. I knew her disapproval of me came from love. Edith's disapproval also came from love—but not of me, of Jackie.

As I unpacked my things in Iris's guest bedroom, I extracted my aunt's journal from the suitcase's side flap, unwinding the handkerchief I'd quickly flung around it to protect it. The diary was my insurance that Moira would leave Philippa, Iris, and me alone. She was afraid that it contained details about her political entanglements, incriminating information Charlene might've had access to before she died. In truth, while it exposed Moira's vile treatment of me, it offered little of her dubious dance with clandestine governmental affairs. She didn't know it, though, which was to my advantage.

Holding its leather-bound cover in my hands, I thought of my aunt, her elegance and poise, the fleeting tenderness she showed me, her broken nature, her negligence, her demise, and her tortured relationship with my mother.

To stave off a downward spiral, I flipped through its pages, wondering if Kismet would guide me to a revealing passage, some bright fragment in her buttery voice, some answer to the confusion inside me. After scanning pages for my name, I landed on lines from late summer 1948:

> Judy is a splendid young woman, so intelligent, brilliant really,
> but my heart shatters at the thought that she might ever know
> about her parentage, that she's tainted with colored blood. It
> would be an unspeakable cruelty to tell her the truth of her
> race, an act of savagery—

I slammed it closed, and tears welled up. "Damn you," I whispered more to myself than to her. Of course, I knew what it contained—a mixture of failed love and vicious pity. If I'd been thinking clearly, I knew it would stir up bitterness and anger. I'd read it in its entirety once, and it changed everything. So why did I open it again, hoping for another truth? Hoping that, in the years since I'd first read it, the words would have rearranged themselves into something useful instead of a wounding account of my birth, rejection, and the ensuing cover-up. I needed a compass to my future, a guide, not the swirling murk of the past.

I wiped away the tears, wrapped it again in the handkerchief, and shoved it under my mattress.

CHAPTER 10

SPRING OF 1953, JUDY

After months of bunking with Iris, I began to itch for my own place. The renter in the unit above hers unexpectedly vacated, so Iris sweet-talked her landlord, who she'd already been flirting with, into letting me have the apartment for $40 a month. I gathered my things and hauled them to the new apartment. The space was shabby, but a fresh layer of paint, secondhand furniture, curtains, and a few wall hangings made it present-able. Before long, it began to look like a home. I updated Philippa about my changes, and we continued to phone each other irregularly. I repaired the murder book where Edith had damaged it. I didn't want Philippa to think I was a lousy steward of her hard work. But the hunt for Bogdan fell to the side. After all, what was there to do? We only had theories, and no one wanted to hear them. If we'd told the police about our encounter with Bogdan, Moira, and the FBI, no one would believe us.

One evening, a knock rattled my door. It was late, so I gazed through the peephole. On the other side, pale-faced and bedraggled, was Philippa. She had come to *me*.

I opened the door, and we didn't say anything for a moment. I was overwhelmed and brimming with questions. Why was she here? Why wasn't she in Charlottesville? Where was Stan? She was always attractive to me, but I'd never cared for the sad sack Philippa, who occasionally emerged during our teenage adventures. Arguably the Philippa before me was behaving like a sad sack, but in this case, I found her intensely appealing. Perhaps it was because, despite her drooping shoulders and messily ponytailed pinkish blonde locks, the delicate blue in her eyes twinkled. My gut told me she had news—news I'd like. "Well," I said, "are you coming in? Or do I have to invite you in like a vampire."

She smiled, just a flicker, and muttered, "Jesus, Judy." She didn't usually curse; it was a good sign.

She stepped over the threshold, slipped out of her winter coat, and flung it and her purse on my coatrack. "So, this is your new place," she said, wandering into the living room and scanning the decor, still a work in progress. "Nice."

"It'll be better than nice," I said. "I need more art. I loathe even a single bare wall."

"Stan didn't like me chipping the plaster, so we didn't hang much—well, you remember."

As she looked around, I studied the curve of her arm, her poise, the fine layer of peach fuzz on her cheek, and her perfect nose in profile. I would've snapped a photo of her if I'd had my camera. The light in the room was soft, diffused, and her beauty had a stillness, a vulnerability. But like a work of art, she remained closed off, unwilling to say whatever she'd come to say. I understood: she needed me to pry it out of her.

"How is Dr. Stan?" I leaned into the sarcasm. Perhaps unwisely.

She turned to me abruptly, offered a blank, tight-lipped expression, and said, "Well, he's asked me to marry him."

My chest heaved. I tried to conceal my reaction, but she detected my alarm. "Don't worry. I'm not marrying him."

"Fuck," I gasped, "you had me worried." I tore across the room, gestured at one of the two parlor chairs I'd scavenged from Edith's attic, and plopped down in the other. "What happened?"

As if she were moving through water, Philippa found her seat. She smoothed out her skirt and adjusted her hair, tucking a stray curl behind an ear. I couldn't grasp her mood. If she wasn't marrying Stan, what had transpired? Had he been angry? Did he hurt her? A surge of fury spiked in me. "Philippa," I said soberly, "what did he do to you?"

She gave me a perplexed stare. "He didn't do anything to me."

"You're just . . . You're behaving strangely."

Her eyes softened. "I'm sad, Judy."

"Because of Stan?"

"Yes."

"Because he asked you to marry him?"

"Yes."

I sniffed, leaned back, and folded my arms across my lap. If she said no, what did she have to be sad about? She must've realized that it wouldn't work. "I don't understand you."

She sighed. "I broke his heart. He was in love with me."

"But you weren't in love with him."

She looked down. "No," she said and raised her gaze to meet mine. "How could I be?" Her eyes were wet; a tear leaked down her cheek. I rose and went to her. I wanted to bend to her and kiss her. I wanted to slip my fingers between the buttons of her blouse. I wanted her to shiver under my cool touch. But I hesitated, crouched, and lay my hand on her knee. My desire ran deep; it was elemental and indivisible from my understanding of myself. I needed Philippa like I needed food, water, and air—like I needed my apartment, my freedom. But if I pushed myself on her now, if I pulled off her clothes and ran my lanky fingers through her mess of curls, if I pressed my lips against hers, against her cheeks, against her breasts, her sex, if I did as I liked at that moment, I'd obliterate her—and us. I couldn't crash into her as I had on the top of Hill Estates. It was a mistake. We couldn't just fling our bodies together; we were too volatile, too explosive. Our desire for one another, our love, if not handled with care, would destroy us.

So, I kneeled beside her until my kneecaps hurt and her tears dried, and she slipped out of the chair, looked into my eyes, leaned toward me, swaying, and connected her lips with mine. At first, the kiss was timid and tight, but something gave away in her; a border was breached, and she sank into it—into me. I returned the kiss, but I held myself back, not fully believing that she was here to stay, that Stan, an idea more than a man (at least to me), had been vanquished, not because I went on the offensive, not because of anything I did, but because Philippa couldn't betray herself, at least not with him. We separated, and I said, "So what are you going to do now?"

"I don't know." She lowered her chin. "I'll graduate and move back home, I guess."

"Have you told your parents?"

"Yes." Her chest lifted, ballooning with emotion. "Dad was disappointed. Bonnie was kind, but I could tell I'd let her down."

"You can't live at home."

"I can't?"

"No, you can't."

⚬━⬦━⚬

Within a month, she moved in with me. As long as she visited her parents for Sunday dinner, they didn't question her living situation. She distracted them with a vivid portrait of her plucky single-girl-in-the-city existence, weaving in details of the fictional girls' boarding house she claimed as her home. She applied to the master's in literature program at George Washington and was admitted for the fall. To help with rent and tuition, she found part-time secretarial work through a temp agency.

Iris wasn't pleased with Philippa's arrival, but she bit her tongue. To her, she was an impediment to my embracing the Negro in me, whatever that meant, and a boost to my lesbian "lifestyle." Although Iris had eschewed her religious upbringing, her unease with homosexual behavior lingered. Her involvement in the medical community didn't help, who, by and large, branded it abnormal. If it was an illness, then, damn it, I was happy to be sick.

I didn't doubt Philippa had chosen me over Stan; her love hadn't wavered. But we circled each other sexually. We'd hold, stroke, and kiss each other, but when I tried to consummate the attraction, she'd retreat to her room. At first, I enjoyed the tension and sweetness of our chaste existence, but soon I became impatient. I fought against my urges, scolding myself to give her time and remember her relationship with Stan had wounded her. She needed time to heal.

Soon after the move, we revived our hunt for Bogdan. I didn't investigate solo when she was in Charlottesville; the thought of it was too dismal. She, on the other hand, hadn't stopped researching. She squirreled away news clippings on Candy Conklin's murder and, now that she was reunited with the murder book, added them to its pages.

In the fall, police had quickly ruled out Candy's parents, and for a few weeks in December, they focused their energy on a new suspect—a local man with a history of "bothering" girls—but they'd cleared him, as we knew they would. Then, like the other murders, the trail dried up. Some details about the crime were released. Like Jackie, she was discovered with no clothes on. She'd also been strangled and violated, but they didn't mention writing on the body.

We needed a car to continue our research. One of the Watsons' cars was in the shop, and Bonnie needed the other. So, I swallowed my pride and made up with Edith. Surprisingly, she met me halfway, admitting she'd been overwrought and shouldn't have torn up "that morbid book" despite her feelings about its contents. The tension between us thawed, but neither of us was unhappy I'd moved out. It was time.

Philippa and I drove out to Great Falls Park in the Dodge. We didn't know the precise spot Candy had been found, so we wandered around, stared into the post-rainstorm whitewater, and snapped photos of the rocky landscape dotted with daffodils. Imagining her pale body slipping through the rapids, obscured by debris and foam from the churning river, sent a chill through me. Bogdan must've dumped her upstream, and she floated down. We took a few artful photographs of the terrain but discovered nothing new.

On the way back to the car, Philippa paused at a heap of withered flowers, tattered bows, and cards left in memory of Candice Conklin, which must've been refreshed earlier in the spring. She turned to me and said, "I know the Conklins' address."

"How?"

A flicker of guilt passed through her. "I went to her memorial service and followed the family back to their house."

"Jesus, Philippa."

"I borrowed Stan's car to do it. He wasn't happy about it."

"Did you go in?"

"I lost my nerve." She knelt at the makeshift memorial, cleared away dead flowers, and positioned a few fresh daffodils in their place. "I wanted to get a sense of them and how they were after losing their girl. I'm not sure why, but somehow, I thought it'd help."

"Did it?"

"No." A card she was propping up read, "May the angels be with you, Candy Bear." "But I didn't speak to anyone. I just observed from afar."

"Okay?"

She rose, dusting off her knees. "We should try again. Together."

And so, we drove to Falls Church and located the Conklin home in a suburban neighborhood called Dominion Heights, not far from Cherrydale, Candy's school. It was a simple brick bungalow with a three-quarters bay window, a well-groomed lawn, and a station wagon with polished chrome bumpers. It was midday, so we weren't surprised to find Meredith Conklin alone when she opened the front door. She greeted us brightly— "Hello? How may I help you?"—but it was a facade. Her eyes seemed remote, disengaged, but she was put-together: hair curled, makeup applied, housedress steamed. She hadn't cracked up. I wondered if the house—and all its demands on her—were welcome in the face of her loss. Something to do, *anything* to do, to avoid the pain.

We introduced ourselves, and Philippa said, "We're so sorry to surprise you like this. We're here about your daughter." Mrs. Conklin winced, and a veil of gloom fell over her features. She was hoping we weren't here about her daughter. It was probably the last thing she wanted to discuss.

I broke in: "We may know something that could help find her killer." I wanted her to understand immediately that we weren't ghoulish gawkers or the press.

"What?" she remarked, astonished. "*Who* are you again?"

More softly, Philippa added, "We may have some information."

Mrs. Conklin gripped the edge of her door. On a hall table behind her, I glimpsed a line of neatly displayed family photos, the most prominent of which was an eight-by-ten of Candy, her light brown sausage curls spilling over her shoulders—the image from the newspapers. I thought of the portrait of Jackie that Edith displayed in the townhouse on Tennessee Avenue. When you entered either home, the girls' faces greeted you. Their mothers wanted you to understand that nothing defined them more than the loss of their child. It's who they were—that absence. For a long time, I hated Edith because she placed her dead daughter before me, but now, it seemed unavoidable. We were in the clutches of fate.

"I'm sorry," Mrs. Conklin said, beginning to shut the door, "but I have a cake in the oven. I appreciate your concern, but honestly, I've had enough of folks trying to help." She offered us a flat smile. The red herrings the police had pursued must've exhausted her.

"Wait," I said, stepping forward. "I go by Judy Nightingale now, but I used to be Judy Peabody, the adopted daughter of Edith and Bart Peabody. Their first child, Jackie, was murdered by the same man we believe murdered Candice."

She paused, the lines at her mouth and eyes deepening. "That so?" she said. "I've never heard of a Jackie Peabody."

"There are other girls who've been murdered," Philippa said and rattled off their names. We should've brought the murder book with us.

Mrs. Conklin dropped her hand. "I know about some of the other girls, but it's all just talk."

"According to who?"

Her eyes moved warily from me to Philippa and back again. "The police."

"They don't want you to make a connection," I said, treading carefully. If I began talking about the FBI or spies, she'd balk at the idea.

"Why is that?"

"They're embarrassed."

Philippa glanced at me. "Because they failed to protect children from a monster."

"From a man named Adrian Bogdan."

Mrs. Conklin's expression shifted from wary to skeptical. "So, you're telling me you have all the answers? Two women? Seriously?" Her hand returned to the door.

Fearing losing her, I asked, "Did he write on her body?"

She gasped a little. "What?"

"When your daughter's body was found, had the murderer written something on her skin? A word?"

She tried to speak, but nothing came. She was pained by the thought of her child being defiled. Her troubled eyes dipped away from us. "Not that I know."

"We're sorry," Philippa said. "Other girls had writing on them. Jackie Peabody, too."

"I must get back to my baking." She began to close the door.

"Ask the police about the word," I said, holding my hand against the door. "Ask them about Eurydice. And ask them about Adrian Bogdan."

She paused briefly, regarding us. "Leave me alone." Her bottom lip was trembling. Her eyes watery. "I've had enough for today."

"He's not going to stop," Philippa said, her frustration surfacing.

"That's enough." I felt pressure from the door. "Go away."

"He'll kill more like your Candice," I launched back, but she shut the door, its dry hinges squeaking like a little far-off scream.

CHAPTER 11

MAY 4, 1954, LIONEL

Detective Berg calls me first thing and asks me to come to the station. He assures me I'm not in trouble, but I'm not jazzed about returning to a room full of cops. When I arrive, I'm greeted by Berg, still chiseled and dreamy but now on edge, and escorted to the Detective Sergeant's office where I meet two men: Detective Sergeant Dell Colby, who is lean, bald, well over six feet, and wears a serious expression like a Halloween mask, and the chief medical examiner, Dr. Tate Shipley, who is in his sixties, has a trim gray beard, narrow ferrety features, shrewd eyes, and, if his snug three-piece is an indicator, a good tailor. I can't imagine why I'm here or why the medical examiner is here.

Sergeant Colby circles behind his desk and extends his long arm toward a chair. I take a seat, scanning the office. The venetian blinds across the wide window to our left allow in ribbons of bright morning light. On the desk sits a glum black-and-white portrait of Colby's family. On the wall hangs an impressive stuffed fish, perhaps a bass, and beside the fish, a collection of commendations for bravery in the line of duty. There's a golf bag in the corner. Dr. Shipley sits beside me, and Berg stands behind us as if waiting to be dismissed. He's not, which is a relief. Although I don't trust him, I trust him more than these men.

"Thank you for coming in, Mr. Kane," Colby says, the corners of his mouth curling up into a brief, cheerless smile. "You've been through a great deal in the past few days."

"My condolences," Dr. Shipley mutters, bringing his fingers together like he's offering a prayer. His fingers are small and delicate, perfect for pushing into corpses and slipping around organs.

"I appreciate your sympathies," I say, failing to conceal my irritation, "but why am I here? Do you have an update on Roger?"

Colby glances at Shipley and straightens his posture; his desk chair squeaks. "Although it's unfair to ask this, we need your help." Berg stirs behind me.

"How's that?"

Colby narrows his thin lips as if about to say something but looks to Shipley, who speaks. "Well, we've had a mishap." He shakes his head. "No, I'm not going to diminish our responsibility. It's not a mishap. It's a serious error and not one that's reparable."

My stomach churned. What *is* this about?

"There's no easy way to say this," he continues. "It concerns your room-mate's body. After the autopsy, instead of being stored as he should've been, a clerical error was made, and he was processed and sent to the crematorium." He softens his voice. "We discovered the mistake too late.

"A clerical error?" I glance at Colby, whose expression is focused as a hawk's, his eyes like polished steel. They seem to be bracing for a dramatic reaction. "I don't understand."

"The body was mislabeled," Colby says, glaring at Shipley, who clearly, he blames for this "mishap."

"It's happened before, but it's rare," Shipley says, mounting a weak defense.

"So, what *exactly* are you telling me?" I'm still dumbfounded.

"He's gone," Shipley says, embarrassed. "His body is ash."

A wave of grief begins to build in me. "And his dental records?" I ask, fearing that they'd positively identified his body, that that's the reaction from me they're bracing for. I didn't care about the cremation. He wanted to be burned, despite his family's tradition of burial. "Just build a pyre and float me out on the ocean," he once told me, half-joking. "A Viking funeral!" Please. Don't tell me it's him. Don't tell me he ended himself and left me alone.

"We have the records." Shipley's eyes shift, a subtle change. "But we didn't get a chance to do a comparison."

My swell of sorrow dissipates, and hope emerges, but it's a torturous hope because I don't know it's him, and I don't know it's not him. A sudden anger blazes through me. Sergeant Williams's casual cruelty the night of the incident rings in my ears: "He checked himself out, if you know what I mean." I glare at Shipley, then Colby, and picture Berg's handsome face hovering behind me, and say, "You're telling me we don't know who died in my kitchen, and we won't know."

"Yes," Colby says, "which is why it makes it even harder for us to ask a favor of you, but we're compelled to ask."

"A favor?" I seethe. "What favor?"

There's a moment of eye contact between Colby and Shipley. Then Shipley pipes up. "As you might imagine, Mr. Raymond's immediate family has been informed about the fire and the discovery of a body."

His family. Of course, they were going to contact his family. I'd met them a handful of times as his roommate, and they were put off by my skin color. They were all very Catholic. His pious mother, a limp dishrag, adored Roger and was sweet enough, but his father, a patriarch with a capital P, refused to make eye contact. He would talk past me as if I were invisible. I wondered if he sensed the true nature of my relationship with his son. Perhaps he had a touch of the homo, too. Rose Ellen, his sister, with her chubby little girl cheeks and stupid cow's eyes, lived at home even though she was well over thirty. She was a total drip and overtly racist. When she met me, she said, "I'm surprised a Negro can afford to live in such a nice part of town." Fuck you, Rose Ellen.

"Okay, what about his family?" I ask.

There's another uncomfortable pause. They're exhausting me.

Shipley says in a kind of purr, "We want your support when we tell them that the body we removed from the oven is their son."

I sit up. "What?!"

"Look," he says, "we're ninety-five percent sure Roger killed himself in your apartment. The circumstantial evidence suggests that interpretation."

I'm on my feet. "Jesus," I cry. "You want me to lie for you?" Anger—no, *rage*—buzzes through me like an electrical current. "No, sir. No damn way." I swivel to Berg, who is as white as a sheet, as white as a white boy can get. I regard Colby and Shipley again, both standing, staring at me. They're icy calm, eyes hawkish, determined. I know what's coming before they say it. Surely, they guessed that Roger and I were more than roommates. After all, we only own one bed, and our clothes hang together in the same closet. I recall Roger's plundered clothes and his missing gun. They must've taken them. Was this why? They'll use my love for Roger to force me to do their bidding, to cover up their bungling, just like it was used to boot him from the State Department.

"The Raymonds hate me," I say. "Their son and a mixed-race fool penning mystery novels . . ." My voice is high, squeaky with anxiety. They didn't know we wrote together; they thought it was all Roger. These men don't know that, though. "They won't believe me." I chuckle.

"Don't worry," Shipley says. "They'll believe us for the most part. But they'll be upset about the mishap with the body. They'll need confirmation."

"So, we're back to calling it a 'mishap'?" I say bitterly.

"Error," he states, gripping the arm of his chair. "We don't want to tell them we cremated their son before confirming the identity of the body." His facial features narrow; his small, coal-black pupils pierce me. "Especially when we're certain it is your *lover*, Roger, not some stranger."

"Lover" shoots through me like a bullet. My knees weaken, my head swirls, and my mouth goes bone dry. I glance at Detective Berg, standing with his arms by his sides and his face trance-like. He's not revolted by this realization; he's frightened. For me, perhaps, or for himself.

Shipley steps around his chair, approaches me, and adds, "Think of it as a kindness. You're allowing them to grieve. Bringing them peace."

"You just don't want a scandal," I say. "You don't want a lawsuit or a public fuss."

Shipley's ferret eyes glitter in acknowledgment.

"Good," Colby says. "We understand each other." He seems impatient, like this is just one of the many blackmailing meetings he has lined up this morning. "If you help us, we'll keep your situation with Roger Raymond out of the papers. A fair trade."

My chest tightens. I don't have a choice, not a fair one anyway.

Showing nerve, Berg asks, "What about the ring?"

"The ring?" Colby asks, miffed.

"Raymond's ring was on the wrong finger when we found him," Berg squeaks out, still pale as a ghost. "We don't know why. We don't have a satisfactory explanation."

"And the missing clothes and the gun," I blurt, bolstered by Berg's guts. "How do you explain that?"

"Only you can attest to the ring being on the wrong finger, Mr. Kane." Colby clinches his jaw muscles. "We can't confirm it."

"Yes, we can," Berg asserts, his voice sterner, more confident. "We have other witnesses who can confirm that detail." He's thinking of Philippa and Judy, I imagine. There might be others. "And the missing clothes and gun speak for themselves."

So, the police don't have Roger's things—or at least Berg doesn't think so.

Shipley shifts his glare to Berg. "Good work, Detective." His voice once again slides into a purr. "You've given us a great deal of information, and we appreciate it."

"Detective Berg," Colby says, "perhaps you have other work to attend to?"

There it is—the dismissal.

"My schedule is open all morning—"

"Find something to do."

Berg and I make eye contact as he's leaving. A mixture of apology and trepidation beam from him. I have another ally.

Colby emerges from behind his desk and stretches out a hand. I study his wide mitt but refuse to shake it. Why the hell should I? "If you don't support us," he grumbles, "we'll throw you to the fucking wolves."

Fear leaps up in my throat, but I don't show it. "Goodbye, Sergeant," I say flatly. "Goodbye, Doctor." I walk to the door, pause, and turn to them. "You realize that telling a Catholic family their son ended his life won't bring them peace."

Colby doesn't respond. Shipley clears his throat. Are these men really that worried about saving face? About a lawsuit? Or is it something else—or *someone* else? Maybe that someone is pulling strings to erase the inconsistencies in Roger's alleged suicide. I'm missing something: a link, a detail. I consider the old photo of a young man and a girl I lifted from the smoky grime of the apartment floor. It's something I have that they don't, and it gives me hope, real hope. I need to figure out who's in the picture, what the Russian inscription says, and who left it and why. Like our detective, Calvin McKey, I have a lead to follow.

To keep the wolves at bay, I tell them: "I'll support you. I'll do it."

But I don't mean it. At all.

CHAPTER 12

SPRING OF 1953, JUDY

Meredith Conklin's response left us at a loss. Perhaps if we'd foisted the murder book under her nose, we would've shocked her into action, but it would've been an ugly violation of her grief. In truth, we didn't have the authority to convince the victim's families of a damn thing. Pursuing them, it seemed, would only create confusion. Instead, we decided to pump Quincy, Philippa's cousin, for information. On the pretext of planning her father's birthday party, Philippa asked him to meet us at Horsfields, our old stomping ground.

It was late morning, and the diner, usually overrun with high school students, was empty, aside from a few suits taking a mid-morning break. Not much had changed since we haunted its booths as teenagers and Iris slung milkshakes. We ordered coffee, and Quincy, who arrived after us, ordered eggs and bacon.

After we chatted about the stalemate in Korea, the Baton Rouge bus boycott, and Quincy's new television, we slid into a discussion of party ideas. I was certain Carl Watson wouldn't respond well to a surprise party, but I kept my mouth shut. After a tedious back and forth about themes—"Hawaiian or Mexican? . . . Or maybe his favorite musical, *Guys and Dolls*."—I asked him about Candy Conklin.

"Oh no," he said, chuckling warily. "You're not going to get that out of me."

"Doesn't it bother you that Bogdan is out there killing girls?"

"That's a theory," he said, waving his fork at us. Bits of scrambled egg were tangled in its tines. "There's no proof."

"Was Candy written on like some of the others? Like Jackie?" I asked.

"How would I know?"

I glared at him: He was as handsome as ever. His shoulders were broader, and his face leaner and tanned. His thick hair rose from his proportional features like a dark wave. Still, his sharp looks clashed with his dull wit, and I hated him a little. "Aren't you curious enough to ask?"

"It's not my case. It's not my business. Literally."

"There's a pattern, Quincy, and you know it," Philippa said with a flash of irritation. "Your pal Detective Richardson believes there's a connection. He wants to work with other counties, right?"

Quincy's statuesque features drooped, and after a lingering pause, he said, "He's not made much headway. No one wants there to be a connection. No one wants to believe we have a crazy man stalking children."

"But you believe there's a connection." I narrowed my eyes at him. "You must."

"It's just a theory." He picked up his napkin and wiped his lips. "And theories are useless without a tapestry of factual evidence, and we can't weave the facts together because no one wants to believe the theory—no one wants that mess on their hands."

I scoffed at his verbiage. "'Tapestry of factual evidence.' Gee."

"Even the press hasn't linked the murders in a meaningful way," Philippa said, stepping in to redirect.

"They've mentioned an uptick in the suspicious deaths of children," Quincy said, "but they've never suggested that these girls were connected by a single killer."

"They're circling the story but never landing on it," I said. "Why?"

Quincy stared at us, his black eyelashes flicking. "It's more than an administrative resistance to cross-jurisdictional partnerships." He was almost whispering. "It's like they don't want us talking to each other, like they're jamming their fingers in their ears, shutting their eyes, and hoping the boogeyman isn't real."

"He is," Philippa said. "He's very real."

———

In Edith's Dodge, we drove to the small, whitewashed brick police station in downtown Harrisonburg. Although we knew Quincy would squirm at the idea of us marching into the station and demanding an audience with Piers Richardson, we needed to do something. He wasn't there when we arrived, so we bided time by reading the local newspaper, doing the crossword, playing tic-tac-toe and hangman, and watching the sunlight creep across the checkered linoleum floor. Eventually, a lean, lantern-jawed man in a gray suit darted through the waiting area, blinders on. The desk clerk greeted him as Piers, and Philippa leaped to her feet, calling out, "Detective Richardson!"

He stopped and turned. His thin hair was slicked back, and his eyes were close set. He was roughly thirty.

"I'm Philippa Watson, Quincy Berg's first cousin."

He broke into a smile and offered her his hand. She introduced me. His eyes roamed between us, curious and guarded. "What are you two doing in Harrisonburg?" he asked.

"We have something that might help a case of yours." Philippa said and unconsciously lifted the murder book to her chest. We'd remembered to bring it this time.

"Like what?" he asked, offering us an all-too-familiar skepticism. Our being women, to men like this, invalidated our point of view, even our work. "What could we seriously offer?" echoed the refrain. I thought of Meredith Conklin closing the door on us, of Quincy's lack of encouragement. They seemed to acquiesce to forces greater than them, an attitude I neither endorsed nor fully understood. I had too much fight in me. "Could we go somewhere to talk?" I asked, my tone firm and professional.

Philippa smiled and added, "It will be easier to explain."

Richardson's office was in a gloomy back corner of the building. Smoke from his last cigarette still hung in the air. He sat behind his metal desk, cluttered with stacks of papers, a butt-filled ashtray, and an old typewriter. We positioned ourselves across from him in two hard-backed chairs designed, it seemed, to be uncomfortable. Philippa rested the murder book on her lap. "We have important information about Nancy Jones's disappearance and Betty Hicks's murder." Both girls were local: Nancy in Luray and Betty in Culpeper. "And others, including the most recent murdered girl, Candy Conklin."

"Okay." His eyes lit up. "What do you have?"

Philippa rose and handed him the book. "What's this?" he asked, perplexed. "A photo album?"

"It's a scrapbook," she said. "We've been tracking the murders and disappearances of these girls. There are at least seven. The same man is responsible."

Again, that skeptical look, this time with a touch of weariness.

He cleared space on his desk and opened it. For several minutes, he flipped through it, his features frustratingly unreadable. He'd perfected his poker face at the Police Academy. Eventually, he closed it and grunted. "It's just a bunch of photos and clippings." He rose and handed it to

Philippa. "There's no evidence here." He leaned on the front of his desk, peering down at us.

"But what it implies—" she began. He held up his hand to silence her.

"I know what it implies, and I'm not disagreeing, but there's nothing to act on."

"What do you mean 'there's nothing'?" I was furious. "Shouldn't you be talking to police departments in Winchester, Ashland, Norfolk, or DC? Isn't that your job?"

Philippa glared at me. Her eyes pleaded, "Take it down a notch, will you?"

He shook his head. "I've tried. It's not that easy. Not everyone sees what we see."

"Do you know the name Adrian Bogdan?" Philippa said softly.

"Your cousin mentioned it, and I've looked into the Jackie Peabody case."

"And?" I said, crossing my arms, refusing to hide my displeasure.

He studied me for a moment. It was an odd, knowing appraisal, the look you might give a potential suspect. "There's not enough to connect them."

"Why doesn't anyone want to stop these murders?" I asked, flinging my skepticism back at him. "What's stopping you? Are you afraid of catching Bogdan?"

"Afraid?" he said, scowling.

"Maybe someone told you to leave it alone, to look the other way."

"*Judy,*" Philippa cautioned.

"No one can intimidate me into dropping a case." Now *he* was furious. "Frankly, I don't care if you're Quincy's cousins, friends, or whoever. Your suggestion is offensive."

His hazel eyes trembled; my words had shaken him. He cared after all, it seemed. Still, he wasn't pushing hard enough. None of these policemen were. It was obvious. Maybe they didn't have a method for productively working across counties and state lines. Or maybe, just maybe, the FBI had instructed them to stay in their jurisdictions.

"You'll excuse me," he said. "I'm swamped with work. These cold cases aren't priorities."

We were on our feet about to exit when Philippa spun and said, "Explain to me why it's a cold case." Her voice was hot, accusatory. "Tell me: If another girl dies, will it cease to be a cold case?"

He regarded her gloomily. "Say hello to Quincy for me. Good day."

⚬━━⚬

On our trip home from Harrisonburg, Philippa continued to express her outrage at Richardson and the police in general, even slapping the dashboard in an almost comic burst of frustration: "Fools!" I shared her anger, of course, but her fury aroused me—its passion infiltrated me, and I wanted her—her frenzy of hair, her full breasts, her muscled calves, her tapered ankles, the blue veins that ran under the surface of her pale forearms. I reached for her leg and squeezed her thigh, and she pulled away. Anger flashed through me, but I quelled it. I told myself: Not now. Not yet. She needs time.

That night, she flopped across my bed in her robe and began reading an article in *Life* magazine to me, written by the anti-Communist fanatic Whittaker Chambers. As she read, I fiddled with Silly Putty I'd picked up on impulse at the local market. Its red, egg-shaped casing lay cracked open on my night table. Chambers accused Alger Hiss of being a spy several years ago, and Chambers's book *Witness* fanned the flames of McCarthy's cause célèbre last year. Good ol' Ike signed an executive order in April forcing *every* federal agency to ferret out employees who could be blackmailed by the enemy for alcoholism, addiction, mental illness, or, of course, having "relations" with someone of the same sex. She held the magazine up; a blonde in a cap and gown peered out from the cover as if to say, "Even girls graduate college now." As she read, she made her voice gruff and faux-manly in a mockery of Chambers's righteousness. She slowly scissored her suspended bare feet back and forth. Swish. Swish.

As I listened, I fiddled with the Silly Putty. I squished it flat and stretched it out over and over. Suddenly, I'd had enough. I balled it up and threw it at her, knocking the magazine out of her hands. "Hey," she cried, her face bright with shock. "What's the big idea!" The magazine fluttered to the floor, and the putty bounced into a dark corner.

"Jesus Christ, I can't take it."

"Take what?" she asked, annoyed. "My rendition of Whittaker Chambers?"

"No," I said. "You keeping me at arm's length."

Her face was scrawled with confusion.

"You're lying there reading why we're a national threat and should be shunned, etcetera, like Whittaker and McCarthy and the lot of them, and their bullshit doesn't apply to us when I think it does—then again, well, maybe it *doesn't*. After all, every time I reach for you, you shrink away. I mean, what does 'us' even mean?"

She rose to her knees. "I don't 'shrink away' from you."

"You do."

She started to make her way off the bed, but I reached out and grabbed her arm, pressing hard into her flesh. She tried to pull away, but I didn't let her go. "Do you get it?" I growled. "Do you understand?"

She glared at me.

"Not a bit."

To clarify, I said, "I don't want just pecks on the cheek and cuddling, the schoolgirl nonsense." I softened my voice. "I want all of you."

She tore away from me and launched off the bed, but before she reached the door, she paused, breathed deeply, and turned to me. She swept a loose hair out of her face and said, "I know you do."

For a long moment—it could've been hours, it could've been years—she stood there, staring at me, her blue-gray irises trembling, as if she were viewing various newsreels of her future, trying to decide what to do. The endlessly dividing of paths had locked her in place, unable to choose a way forward. In that instance, she became the frozen princess, the sleeping beauty. Part of me wanted to grab a heavy book from my bed stand, fling it at her, and watch her shatter. Part of me wanted to approach her softly, slide my arm around her, and whisper that I was sorry. But I did neither. I rose from the bed and approached her. I wasn't her goddamn Prince Charming, but I would wake her from her spell, the hex Wicked Witch Stan cast. I lifted my hand, touched her cheek, and drew it slowly down her robe's lapel, nudging the folds open, revealing a sliver of her naked body. She allowed this, but she was shaking, afraid of what my touching her this way would mean, a line she was stepping over, irrevocably. No, I thought, I wouldn't ravish her like some creep, like fucking Stan. I took her hand and guided it gently under my loose blouse and to my left breast, pressing it against my heart. Her pinky strained to graze my nipple, an unmistakable yearning. An electric shock rippled through me, and I drew her into a kiss, more intense and unfettered than I'd ever allowed of myself or anyone else. All the passion we'd experienced on Hill Estates was in us, but we were in control of it, not the other way around.

With that, the spell was broken, the specter of Stan banished.

CHAPTER 13

SUMMER OF 1953, JUDY

After striking out with Richardson, we realized the murder book wasn't enough. We needed a different approach. So, we decided to arrange our clippings, photos, knowledge, and experiences into a straightforward story. Philippa borrowed a typewriter from her father, and over the July Fourth weekend, we wrote down everything we knew about the murders. We began with Bogdan's violent upbringing in Ukraine, particularly his father's alleged murder of his sister, Anna, whose death he supplies as an excuse for killing girls, to his evolution from a soldier in the Red Army to a double agent and prized asset for the US government in the arms race. We only had a glancing knowledge of Bogdan's ties to the intelligence community, a trace of smoke from a roaring fire. Still, it seemed essential to understanding the scope of the situation. We discussed the murder of Jackie Peabody in 1941, and the disappearances and murders that had happened in the years since, pointing the arrow at Bogdan.

Doing this had a strange effect on us. It was satisfying and affirming. We knew we weren't wrong. But it also unsettled us: Were we summoning Bogdan to us like witches casting a spell we didn't understand?

After we read it over, an idea struck me: "What if we edit this down, and I slip it into the news segment on Monday? We could broadcast it over the airwaves. That would smoke him out."

Philippa scrunched her nose. "You'll get fired."

"I will," I said, fanning myself with a page. "I can always get another job."

We chewed on the idea, listening to the distant crackle of fireworks coming in through the open window.

"You like Ed and Rich, don't you?" Philippa asked.

I knew what she was implying. "Shit," I said.

"They could get in trouble, right?"

"Yes," I said, thinking of McCarthy's attack on Hollywood and the entertainment industry. "Big trouble." I couldn't do that to them. After all, they trusted me to announce the news and represent the station. I would be betraying them. Still, girls were being murdered. What else could we do?

Philippa stood and started walking in circles around the room. Eventually, she stopped and asked me, "Do you have anything to drink?"

"So, we're drinking now?"

She rolled her eyes. "It *is* the Fourth of July."

"I thought Ike declared it a 'national day of penance and prayer.'"

She gave me a withering look.

"We're fresh out of booze. The corner store has wine if they're open, which I doubt."

"I could use some air." Philippa grabbed her purse. "Want to come along?"

"I'd prefer to stay here and cultivate my despair."

"Suit yourself."

"Grab me a pack of Chesterfields."

"Sure thing," she said and was out the door.

While she was running her errand, I fished the last crumpled cigarette out of my black hole of a purse, reshaped it, and lit it. I leaned on the inside ledge of the window, smoked, and watched the fireworks as they popped and flashed against the humid night sky, raining down streamers of light. The tip of the Washington Monument loomed over the city, illuminated briefly and then gone in the hazy dark. It's odd, I thought, that we used explosions to celebrate independence. I considered Korea and the hydrogen bomb. Perhaps it wasn't so odd.

The apartment door opened with a bang, and Philippa dashed through, clutching a brown paper bag. She was drenched with sweat and panting. She closed the door and slid the bolt in place. Her face was bright red, and her eyes wide with fear.

"What is it?"

She caught her breath. "After I bought the wine and your cigarettes, someone started following me."

"What?"

She thrust the bag at me and collapsed in a chair. "As soon as I stepped out of the market, I sensed a presence behind me. At first, I ignored it, but then I remembered how we'd been followed when digging up all the dirt on the Closses years ago. The hair on my neck stood up. When I glanced over my shoulder, there he was, a tall man in an ivy cap, dark clothes, and boots, walking ten yards behind me. I started moving faster to put space between us, but he kept pace with me. When I looked back again, he was even closer. I couldn't see his face, but I imagined it was Bogdan—his icy eyes and rotten teeth. My heart was slamming in my chest. Then he said something crude. Just vile. And I broke into a run."

"At least you didn't drop the booze," I said, lifting a bottle of Chianti out of the bag.

"Don't joke," she snapped.

"I doubt it was Bogdan. I'm sure it was just a garden variety creep."

She glanced at the typewriter, stack of paper, and open murder book. "We've been at this too long."

"We have."

"And he's still a shadow."

I rose to my feet and walked behind her, resting my hands on her shoulders. Have we conjured him after all? Have we summoned the boogeyman to our doorstep? I craned over her. "On the bright side," I said, "you're beautiful when you sweat." I kissed her damp forehead, absorbing the bright floral scent of her perfume.

"Open the bottle," she ordered. "If ever I needed a drink."

⚬──┼──⚬

While Philippa visited her parents the next day for Sunday dinner, I rewrote our account of Bogdan, molding it into a brief news story focusing on the murdered girls beginning with Jackie. Although it necessitated mentioning the Peabodys, I didn't discuss Philippa's and my role, which meant I didn't draw a connection between Bogdan and the FBI or mention the FBI. It was the least credible part of the story, so perhaps it was for the best. Regardless, there were still enough details to get people talking.

Philippa approved my changes. I decided not to surprise Ed with it during a segment. It would get me fired and perhaps the station in hot water. Instead, I'd bring it to him and ask him for feedback. Maybe, just maybe, he'd be impressed. He knew me as Judy Nightingale, not Judy Peabody, so he wouldn't connect me to the Peabodys in the story. When I handed it to him, he raised his eyebrows and asked, "What's this?"

"A story I've been investigating."

"Investigating?" He slipped on his readers and glared down at it. "So now you're an investigative journalist?"

Ignoring his sarcasm, I said, "I'd like to read it in today's segment."

"The hell you will."

But he didn't look up; he was engrossed.

When he finished, he removed his glasses and said, "Hmm, interesting," and asked me to explain how I researched the story. I told him as much as I wanted him to know.

"It's a compelling pattern," he said. "Why hasn't anyone else put this together?"

I was about to tell him I didn't know, but inspiration struck: "Because I'm a woman," I said, which was dodging the question and also accurate. "Men don't understand predators like Bogdan." I recalled Philippa's experience being followed on July Fourth and added, "Women have a sixth sense about this sort of thing."

"I remember the story about the Peabody girl's murder years ago," he said. "They found her killer years later, but it wasn't this fellow."

"The police aren't always right."

"No, they aren't." He frowned. "If you're on to something, this will upset many people."

He didn't know the half of it. We had to do something, however risky, no matter the consequences to Philippa, me, or the station. Girls would continue dying if we didn't get Bogdan to step out of the shadows.

"So, you're not going to read it," he said.

"But it's important," I said, my temper heating up. "These girls—"

He held up his hand. "I'll read it."

"What?" I said, startled.

"Not to steal your thunder." He smiled grimly. "But to protect you."

He was telling the truth. "Okay," I said, deflated. "Read it."

⚬━✦━⚬

After running the story by Rich, Ed broadcast it the morning of July 6. When I came in on the 7th, they fired me.

Baffled, I wanted to know why. Precisely. But I didn't ask. I sat in a chair in Ed's office. Ed was behind his desk, eyes cast down, and Rich leaned uncomfortably against the wall to Ed's right. I focused on Rich. Although he concealed his emotions beneath a thick layer of flesh, I could read the agitation in his dark pupils. He was fighting with himself. I appreciated his concern for me.

"I'm sorry about this, kid," he said. "We wanted to find a way to keep you, but we need to cut back. It's purely a fiscal concern, you understand."

Sure, right. I didn't want to lose my job, but, more than either of them, I knew the risk of airing the story. A job is just a job, and there are other radio stations. They seemed surprised at my calm and, perhaps, relieved. They promised good references and, surprisingly, professional guidance if I wanted to continue my career in radio. As I rose to leave, I said, "I know this is about the murdered girls." They glared at each other, tension taut between them, but didn't respond.

I gathered my things, which they'd already shoved into a cardboard box. Before I left, Ed sprang out of his office. His glasses were tucked into his messy hair, and his eyes were bloodshot, a detail I'd missed earlier. He checked that the hall was empty and asked me to follow him into the theater. Because of its lack of use, it was the most secluded room in the station.

"You need to be careful, Judy," he whispered, his breath reeked of coffee and booze. Had he slept? "This story—it upset some serious people." He scanned the empty stage behind me, everything draped with sheets like a scene from a haunted house chiller. "People with power." I imagined FBI agents in suits showing up, flashing their credentials, and speaking in threatening innuendos. We had poked the bear, after all.

Ed studied me with his tired eyes. "There's more to this story, isn't there?" What had these "people with power" said to him? I recalled his radio play, "The Dream," that Rich had nixed because it critiqued, even indirectly, the government's Communist witch hunt. They had no idea how dangerous this story was, how it was a thread in a much larger, stickier web. I felt bad for using them, but Philippa and I had to do something.

"Forget it," he said, waving the question away. "I don't want to know."

No, you don't, I thought.

"We're firing you to protect you. Aside from Rich and me, no one knows you wrote the article." He swallowed. "Stop pursuing this. If you don't, it will ruin lives."

I wanted to say to him, "If Philippa and I don't pursue this, lives won't just be ruined, they'll be taken." But I didn't. He'd done enough for me; I appreciated his kindness.

"It's okay," I said, touching his arm. "Thank you for looking out for me."

He tried to smile. "Now, go. The less we talk, the better."

I left WSDC, already mulling over our next move.

⚬━━⚬

When I told Philippa the news, her eyes lit up, and she said, "We need to be a blunderbuss!"

This Philippa—the activated, purposeful Philippa—I loved the most. I didn't even mind that she forgot to express sympathy for me losing my job.

"Blunderbuss?" I asked, needing her to elaborate further.

"We should blast news establishments," she said, pacing the living room. "We'll send anonymous packets of information to all the local newspapers and radio stations detailing the facts of the case. The police, too. We can type it up and use the mimeograph machine at the library at GW to make duplicates. WSDC is only the beginning. We have a spark that we need to turn into a blaze."

"It's going to take a lot of work."

She smiled at me. "Do you have anything better to do?"

"Look for a job?"

She gasped and darted to me, throwing her arms around me. "You must be so disappointed. I know you liked it there."

In the blink of an eye, she went from purposeful to hyperbolic. "I'm okay," I said, stepping out of her embrace. "I'm just wondering how we're going to pay rent and, you know, eat."

"I have enough saved up for several months. We'll be fine. When did you become a worrywart?"

I wondered the same thing.

We set our plan in motion. After expanding the WSDC story to include more supporting details and documentation, we made copies. Our apartment was strewn with paper for a few days and reeked of drying print fluid. We stuffed envelopes and addressed them to every local radio station and newspaper, including the *Washington Post* and the *Richmond Times-Dispatch,* as well as police departments in counties and precincts where the crimes occurred. We mailed them, then scanned the news and the radio for a sign. Weeks went by, and nothing.

"Why don't you think anyone is reporting on it?" Philippa said as we gobbled up fried chicken at our favorite diner on 18th Street.

"In most cases," I said, wiping my mouth, "it's probably not getting into the hands of someone who would take it seriously, and if it does, it's probably not enough to report on, especially since we sent it all anonymously. They don't have a name of a source or any trail back to us. We've drawn them a map, but they must corroborate it."

"Do you think the FBI has gotten to them?"

"Maybe, but I doubt it."

Philippa exhaled a heavy sigh and pushed her plate away from her. "Please tell me we didn't do all that work for nothing."

"We might have," I said. "But give it time."

And we did.

But by the end of August, we were on the cusp of giving up, and I began searching for a job, everything from secretarial work to store clerking.

On an insufferably humid day, Philippa arrived home, pale as a sheet and soaked in sweat. She was slouching, a posture of defeat, and her eyes were shaded, gloomy. I was on the sofa in shorts and a thin cotton top, legs spread wide and arms flung out, trying to stay cool. "We failed," she said coarsely and tossed a rolled newspaper in my lap. It was the *Times-Dispatch*. "Look on page three."

I did, and I knew why she was upset. At the top, a headline read: LOCAL MISSING GIRL FOUND MURDERED. The story was familiar: "Tuckahoe, Virginia, August 24. The body of thirteen-year-old Melody Harris of Glenn Allen, Virginia, was discovered this morning in the James River off Tuckahoe Island after being missing for forty-eight hours." It was the work of Bogdan. I flung the newspaper across the room, and it smacked the wall wetly and fell to the floor.

After wallowing in our frustration for a day, we decided that the best we could do, the *only* thing we could do, was to send out another round of packets, mentioning Bogdan's latest addition to his Eurydices, Melody. Maybe, since the news of her murder was fresh, they'd pay attention. Despite violent thunderstorms in the forecast, Philippa returned to the library to make copies. I went to buy stamps and envelopes at the post office.

We converged at the apartment mid-afternoon before the sky opened in a deluge. I'd left the window cracked to keep the room cool; I shut it just as raindrops splashed against the panes. When I turned, Philippa was standing, holding a book. "Look what I picked up at the library from the new novel shelf," she spouted with levity. "After we stuff all these envelopes and send them off, we should read it as a reward." She handed it to me. It was a new Ray Kane novel, *The Broken Thread*. A pattern of golden threads crisscrossed the black cover, and a gloved hand gripped a pair of scissors, poised to snip a glistening thread. On the nose but effective. I flipped it open and read the jacket blurb.

"Hey!" I called to Philippa, who was already crouched on the floor laying out the copies to make short order of assembling the packets. We didn't have a table big enough for the process.

She glanced up. "What is it?"

"This book is based on a true story."

"Yeah, it's not a P. I. Calvin McKey novel."

"A *true* story," I repeated.

"A murder in Baltimore," she said over her shoulder as she collated pages. She didn't notice that I'd read the flap. "Something about a bludgeoned socialite and a falsely accused woman. Sounds intriguing." She stopped, turned to me, and wiped her forehead with the back of her arm. "God, anything to get my mind off this."

"You're missing the point." I gave her an impatient look, and her face suddenly bloomed with understanding.

"We should send a packet to Ray Kane," she said, and, as if on cue, a flash of lightning filled the window beside us.

We braced ourselves for the thunder, but nothing. Just more rain.

She continued, "It's easy enough to find the address of his publishers."

"He might really be interested," I said, my excitement building. "Hell, if the truth won't be published in the news, maybe it will be in fiction. It's worth a shot."

She shrugged and smiled. "It can't hurt, right?"

"No," I said, "it can't."

And with that, thunder finally boomed in the distance.

CHAPTER 14

MAY 4, 1954, LIONEL

After my jolly chat with the detective sergeant and the chief medical examiner, I wander downtown, untangling my emotions on a long walk. In minutes, these men offered me a fake apology, blackmailed me into agreeing to lie to the Raymonds, and confirmed that there was more to Roger's death than the official narrative implied. I don't dare believe Roger is alive—it's too dangerous, too painful—but hope is beginning to edge in.

I jam my hands in my coat pockets, my fingers grazing the old photo from the apartment. I remove it, unfolding it carefully. The teenage boy's intense stare challenges the cameraman. On closer inspection, his pale face strikes me as oddly familiar. The little girl beside him isn't looking directly at the camera, but a little to the right, distracted by something, her dark blonde curls rimmed with sunlight. I flip it over and again read "Адриан и Анна, 1918" in Cyrillic script. I'm only blocks from Brentano's. Maybe I can breeze into the store without drawing too much attention from the white staff and locate a Russian-to-English dictionary. We'll see. Despite the abolishment of segregation, many of the clerks in DC hadn't desegregated their attitudes.

As I push through Brentano's front door, the soothing smell of fresh paper and ink wafts over me. The store clerk, a young woman in cat-eye glasses and a Kelly-green sweater set, spots me, smiles politely, and returns to sorting new arrivals. Relief washes over me. A few other store patrons raise their eyes, and one in particular, a man in his sixties wearing tweed, squints murderously at me and grunts displeasure, snaps up a book—some tome on military history—and marches past me. My nerves buzz a little, but I go on.

I pass the mysteries as I make my way through the large store. A store clerk has artfully stacked copies of *The Broken Thread* on a table and neatly printed "Signed by the Author!" on a placard. I pick up a copy, open it, and run my finger across Roger's rendition of Ray Kane's signature. What a flourish! Seeing his penmanship, his loopy R and bold K, cuts through me. Tears fill my eyes. I close the book, shooing them away, and stare at the cover with its semi-abstract design of crisscrossing threads and the ridiculous gloved hand gripping a pair of shears, a designer's on-the-nose visual metaphor.

"May I help you, sir?" a voice asks.

I turn, and it's the woman in Kelly green blinking at me with concern. "Yes," I say. "This book"—I hold up our novel—"is it any good?"

"Oh my! Yes!" she says. "Mr. Kane is a superb writer. This story is a bit different from his others. It's based on a crime that happened in Baltimore. I blazed through it in a single evening."

Ha! I like her, Miss Kelly green. But it stings bitterly that I can't claim the novel as mine or say, "You know, I'm Ray Kane—at least half of him." I smile and say, "Well, I'm sold!"

As I say it, an unexpected blast of resentment rolls through me, and I falter, bringing my hand to my mouth. Although Roger played Ray Kane in public, I never witnessed it. It always happened off stage—well, off *my* stage. But there's been a shift since Judy and Philippa entered our lives. I've become aware of how different it is for him, how there's a glow he gets to bask in that I don't, that I never will. Early on, Judy and Philippa learned we were both Kane, so their fandom wasn't a problem; it was a pleasure. They were accepting of me. But over the past month, they started spending more time with Roger and cutting me out, almost as if they preferred his company to mine. Gradually, subtly, I began feeling like the lesser of the pair. Of course, this could be my imagination. Lord knows I can get blue and blow things out of proportion. But the feeling is undeniably there, pecking at my heart.

The store clerk seems to detect none of this rattling around in me. Her expression tells me she is genuinely pleased I want to buy a book and is patiently waiting for my next move, so I drop my hand from my lips and ask, "Can you point me in the direction of the foreign language section?"

She leads me to it and leaves me to peruse. I find a Russian-to-English dictionary. With little effort, I translate "Адриан и Анна" into Adrian and Anna, and I realize why the teenage boy's face is familiar to me. It's Adrian Bogdan. The only other photo I've seen of him is in the information someone anonymously mailed us detailing his alleged crimes. He's much older in it, perhaps in his fifties, and it's from an old newspaper and grainy, making it difficult for me to draw the connection. Anna, who the letter in the packet also mentions, is his sister. The odd thing is that I am sure the photo wasn't in the materials. Where did it come from?

I pay for the signed copy of *The Broken Thread*, thank the clerk, and go. Despite my rumbling feelings toward Judy and Philippa, I'm curious about what they'll make of the photo. Maybe Roger said something to them. Maybe together, we have all the pieces to this puzzle.

CHAPTER 15

APRIL 1954, JUDY

After our evening at Brentano's and then Cary's, we didn't expect to hear from Roger Raymond, a.k.a. the "Ray" in Ray Kane, again. We'd exchanged information after drinks, each party scribbling their address and numbers on cocktail napkins, but at the time, it felt like a formality. Our curiosity was piqued, of course. We were in deep mourning over the idea that Ray Kane, our favorite mystery author—correction, *authors*—might be no more thanks to the absurd purges at the State Department, and we wanted to know more about the situation. But Roger was so despondent, so flattened, about being fired that we were sure he wouldn't reach out; his mind was focused elsewhere. And who were we, two fan girls, to ring him up? So, it was a surprise to hear his voice on the other end of the line two days later, inviting us to dinner. "Lyle wants to meet you," he said. "You're his heroes, he tells me. He insists we offer you a more gracious 'thank you' than the hurried drink I bought you the other night."

The temptation to meet Lionel Kane and spend another (but less chaotic) evening with Roger was irresistible. When I told Philippa, she grinned and threw her hands together like a little girl. Her eyes glimmered; the gears were turning. I reminded her: "We still need to avoid mentioning that we mailed them our write-up on the dead girls."

After we mailed the Bogdan murder-spree packets to Ray Kane and to every local media establishment and police station again, we'd become neurotic about checking the news. Weeks and months passed, and zip. No one was interested in the pattern of murders we described, or they were too frightened to write a report about them, or maybe it was because we didn't give our names. Perhaps their anonymity undercut their validity? Who knows?

Occasionally, I'd find Philippa sitting with the murder book in her lap, slowly flipping through its pages like she was taking a trip down memory lane. Here and there, we'd think of another newspaper, magazine, or radio station to send the story. Over the winter, we mourned our defeat and decided to move on, still watchful for news but no longer obsessive. As the spring emerged, the murder book and the box of packet pages began gathering dust under the bed.

"Their publishers probably dumped them in the trash," Philippa said and sighed.

"Since we're becoming friends with them, or whatever we're becoming, maybe it's for the best."

"Why can't we tell them about it?" She set her jaw, determined. "We could mention it casually, like a bit of gossip, but leave out our connection to Jackie and Bogdan."

"What if they did get the packet?" I posed. "What if they're already pursuing it?"

Her eyes flashed, a begrudging acknowledgment of my good point.

"Hinting at it is too risky. If they connect us to Bogdan, it might be dangerous for us. We don't know how they'd use the information. Maybe they'd write about it and leave us out, but the temptation to include us might be too great. If that happened, who do you think Bogdan would come for first? That is, if the FBI didn't beat him to it."

"What if the creep already knows about it, about us?"

I didn't answer.

She went on. "It's not impossible, especially if the press contacted the FBI. He might already know that an amateur has mapped his crimes." Her eyes narrowed. "What if he's already taken an educated guess? What if he's looking for us?"

I remembered her being followed on the Fourth of July and shivered. I didn't know how to respond to her. I shared her bewilderment, her fear, but what could we do? I was out of ideas. We had to keep moving forward cautiously.

"What if, what if, what if!" I cried, threw my hands up, then quickly tempered my reaction. "Maybe we should just go to dinner and get to know them better."

She blinked at me, a little astonished. "You're right. I'm getting ahead of myself." She reached out, pulled me into an embrace, and kissed me. When she withdrew, we locked eyes. Her beautiful features dimmed. "I'll shatter if another girl gets murdered, Judy."

"I doubt you'll ever shatter," I said, brushing a strand of rose-gold hair away from her forehead. "But I know how you feel."

<hr />

Lionel opened the door when we rang, and Roger was right; he was a beautiful man. Beautiful, not handsome, because in his bronze eyes and lightly pursed lips, I detected a bashfulness—or aloofness?—that undercut his stocky frame, golden brown skin, strong cheekbones, and close-cropped hair. He was shorter than Roger but thicker, heartier, and perhaps tougher. The scar that interrupted his left eyebrow and ran up his high forehead somehow completed him. This detail seemed to confirm that P. I. Calvin McKey was primarily his creation, that he, not Roger, was the beating heart of the Ray Kane novels.

Behind Lionel, Roger appeared much keener and cheerier than when we saw him last. We all greeted each other. Roger took our coats—it was a chilly spring evening—and excused himself to attend to the rib roast. The rich, welcoming odor of cooking meat permeated the hall. Lionel led us into the living room, which despite the modest size of the apartment, was large and open. It was elegantly decorated with low-profile modern pieces in light wood and an accent wall of bright orange poppy wallpaper. A bank of windows ran along the far wall, inviting a spectacular view of DC. Lights twinkled, and behind the silhouette of the Washington Monument rising out of the skyline, mellow twilight glowed. Philippa drifted to the windows. Her crêpe de chine dress nearly matched the purplish hues in the evening sky. Lionel asked us if we wanted martinis, to which we responded, "Yes!" and "Yes!" After switching on the record player, he began making the drinks in a bulky glass mixer. A smooth and amorphous Thelonious Monk tune floated across the room. I wandered over to a bookshelf and began perusing their stash of first-edition Ray Kane novels. I also noted a copy of The Broken Thread on the coffee table.

Lionel handed us martini glasses; the glorious, chilled gin was garnished with a ribbon of lemon peel. I took a sip and smiled at him, hoping to set him at ease. Despite what Roger claimed on the phone, I wondered if he wanted us there. He seemed gracious but uncertain of us. Regardless, he returned the smile, glanced at my feet, and said, "I love your shoes." I wore black-sequined pumps that I'd purchased at a sidewalk sale. They sparkled tastefully and showed off my feet, one of my better attributes, and they went with all my black dresses. Although I'd long ago cast off the ghoulish flapper look, I still had a penchant for the glamour of the 1920s.

"Thank you, but squint when you're looking at them," I said. "They're missing a sequin—or ten."

He laughed. "Have a seat."

We found our places on the couch, more stylish looking than comfortable. He grabbed his drink and sat across from us, the poppy wallpaper ablaze behind him.

After taking solace in her martini, Philippa beamed. "We told Roger this, but we're immense fans of your Calvin McKey series, and *The Broken Thread* blew us away."

"I appreciate you saying so," he said, crossing his legs. "Calvin McKey has been a blast to write, but *The Broken Thread* was something else. The journalist in me will always be drawn to true stories, especially stories of injustice."

Behind us, Roger emerged from the kitchen. "Well, I'm very proud of myself," he announced to the group. "I've timed the roast perfectly." He moved to the drink cart and poured himself a martini. "We have about fifteen minutes to chat; then the curtain goes up on the show."

"Roger has long pursued the culinary arts," Lionel said with an amused twitch on his lips. "But the culinary arts have remained at large."

Roger gasped dramatically. "Your job is to be supportive, Lyle." He looked at us. "*Their* job is to be critical."

"If I must," he said and, to us, with thick sarcasm, "Prepare to be amazed!"

Roger positioned his long, elegantly dressed body on the arm of Lionel's chair. His tailored slacks and blue dress shirt were clean and crisply ironed. He bent toward him, kissing the top of his head. "Lyle likes to test my love, but I always pass."

Lionel squeezed Roger's thigh tenderly. "It's true." He smiled. "He always passes."

They seemed so natural together, so comfortable. The Roger we met at Brentano's was in shambles compared to the man before us. Of course, nothing had changed. He was still jobless, humiliated, and rejected by a government he'd served well. But I understood his good mood. They were at home with each other. Philippa and I experienced the same feeling: within our four walls, in front of each other, we could truly be us. You never felt that way at work, eating out, or even walking down the street. A sword of Damocles loomed over your head, about to drop, especially these days. Now all four of us were together, safe in each other's company. I touched the edge of Philippa's hand, which was close to mine. I expected her to move it away, but she didn't. Was she ready to be demonstrative with our love? In response, her pinky brushed tenderly against mine. She felt safe, too. "This is a gorgeous apartment," she said, delighted. "Your décor is so contemporary."

"We're proud of it," Roger said. "Purchasing it and remodeling it nearly killed us."

"The fruits of Ray Kane," Lionel said. "It's nearly perfect, aside from that piece in the corner."

Roger rolled his eyes. "He means the Victorian settee near the window. It's been in my family for ages."

"Since the Dark Ages." Lionel chuckled.

I'd noticed it earlier, but it didn't seem too out of place. Our apartment was a collection of mismatched pieces, so maybe I was used to a patchwork of décor.

"Was it difficult to remodel?" Philippa said, reaching for her martini.

Lionel's eyebrows raised. "Everything about it was difficult."

Roger sipped his drink and explained, "For the longest time, we rented separate apartments, and Lyle would shimmy up the fire escape at night like a cat burglar."

"My place was tiny," Lionel said. "A room, a kitchenette, and a toilet."

"It was an absurd existence," Roger continued, "but we couldn't find anyone to rent to us. We searched all over the city. They didn't like the idea of a white man and a Negro bunking together. The responses were either blatantly bigoted or the more indirect sorry-everything's-rented approach. If they only knew the truth!" He laughed. "We lived this split existence for years until I started working at the State Department, and the Ray Kane books were selling well. We saved up and bought this place. Voilà!"

"Keep in mind," Lionel said. "By 'we,' he means himself. My name's nowhere on the deed. It had a covenant prohibiting the sale of this property to colored people. These covenants stain many a deed in this supposedly 'enlightened' city." He stretched out his arm suddenly, addressing us like he would an audience from a stage. "My dear guests," he cried in a melodramatic tone, his eyes glimmering, "I've infiltrated the hallowed halls of white America. The Fortress of Solitude. Roger, here, is my Trojan horse. My big, beautiful, and *very* white Trojan horse!"

"Once we moved in," Roger added, amused, "some of the neighbors complained to the building manager, but since I owned the apartment, they couldn't do a damn thing."

"Cheers to that!" Lionel raised his glass to Roger's. The crystal chimed, and they drank.

We did, too.

"After a year or two," he continued, "those neighbors quieted down and began greeting me as we passed in the halls. Can you imagine? White people being polite to a Negro neighbor!" His scar rippled with the muscles in his forehead as he spoke, cocoon-like and alive. Everything about him seemed on the verge of something new, something powerful and brilliant. "I guess they realized I wasn't going to ruin their building. No, I wasn't going to ruin *our* building." He paused, looked at me, and a thought seemed to enter him. His expression sharpened, his eyes brightened, and he said to me, "Never let them shame you, hear? Never let *anyone* shame you."

His words jolted me: He knew I was mixed-race, but how? I hadn't mentioned it to Roger. He just *knew*.

Philippa and Roger continued discussing remodeling and decorating, and Lionel rose to flip the record. A tad unhinged by his advice, I grew distant, moody. I thought about the Bakers. Ellis was far from being the father I'd cast for myself in my childhood daydreams. He was flawed, a rash and foolish cheater, but not bad. Not now, anyway. And Alice, sweet Alice, she'd been kind to me all those years ago at Crestwood when no one else had. She alone kept my heart from freezing over. But she also seemed soft. Was a woman who tended to her husband's illegitimate child exceedingly generous or self-negating? Where was her self-respect? Perhaps that's why I avoided them; I feared their weaknesses would rub off. And then there was Iris. Her words rang in my ears: *"In the right light, you're as black as me. In the shadows, you're as white as the Peabodys and Philippa Watson. Will you live in the light or the shadows?"* Was she shaming me for passing or challenging me to be true to myself? And how could she demand that of me but wince at my desire for women? Was her dislike of Philippa a dislike of that part of me? Her message was muddled.

But Lionel, he'd seen right through me, and his message was clear: Don't let them shame you. Don't allow it. Outwit them. Outsmart them. Strike back. Trojan-horse them. A phrase emerged in me like a bright creature surfacing from the murk: I will not pretend to be anything for anyone anymore. Not for Edith. Not for the Bakers. Not for Iris. Not even for Philippa. As Thelonious Monk spilled out of the record player, that thought, which had felt so certain, so bold, wavered and doubt intruded. I wondered, "Is it possible to be yourself around other people, or was there something about other people that made it impossible?"

Roger vanished into the other room, then dinner was on, and he summoned us to the dining room. It was a smaller but equally stylish space with gleaming modern rosewood chairs, a table, and simple place settings. Over the sideboard hung a large Cubist oil painting of calming blue, green, and yellow rectangular blotches. Candles in tapered brass holders flickered above assorted side dishes, including collard greens, red potatoes, and a cheesy pasta casserole. It smelled rich and delicious. Our hosts invited us to sit catty-cornered from one another and offered us wine—Burgundy or a white Bordeaux. Once all the fussing and pouring was over, we settled into eating our salads, little works of art Roger had already delivered to our places.

As we ate, the conversation rolled on. Tipsy now, Philippa launched in with questions about each of their novels. She wanted to know about the *Macbeth* influences in *Love's Last Move*, the complex motivations of the crazed arsonist in *Seeing Red*, and their spin on the locked room mystery in *Cry of the Dead*. "You completely flipped the convention," she gushed, her cheeks pink and eyes bright. "You locked all the suspects in a room and had the murder happen *outside* the room—or seem to! It was brilliant." She moved on to *The Broken Thread*, which she complimented as their most emotionally sophisticated and moving novel. "You were commenting on racial issues," she said, "and the prejudice in our legal system."

Roger and Lionel volleyed back thoughtful and indulgent responses, often finishing each other's sentences, making me wonder if they did the same when they wrote. I expanded on Philippa's observations while she sliced her juicy slab of rib roast or sipped her wine but couldn't conjure my own questions. I was having a lovely time, but I was distracted—what Lionel had said to me still stirred in the periphery of my thoughts.

Once we were satiated, Roger began clearing our plates. Despite the heavy meal, which had drawn all the blood to my stomach, Philippa hopped up full of energy and began helping him. They were chatting about films now and debating the best crime thriller of all time. Philippa argued for *The Lady from Shanghai* and Roger for *The Third Man*. Philippa had had too much to drink, and perhaps I had, too. They disappeared, and Lionel turned his keen eyes on me. "I didn't mean to be so direct with you earlier," he said, his tone gentle, smooth even, "and I didn't mean to assume that you were—"

"I am," I said softly. "My father is Negro, and my mother, she's white."

"Well then," he said. "My pa was white, and my ma was Negro." He smiled broadly. "Look at us, two fruity mixed-race people ripping through some rib roast and having a ball." He raised his glass.

I lifted my Burgundy to him. "May I ask you a question?"

His eyes twinkled. "Philippa hasn't held back a bit, but you, my friend, have been shy."

"She's had too much to drink."

"Oh, don't apologize."

I set my glass down, my thoughts spinning with my ruby-colored wine, and asked, "Why do you write under a pseudonym?"

His face grew serious. His brow wrinkled, and he leaned back. "What you're asking me, I think, is why I hide behind a white face?"

Although I don't think he intended it, his response landed on me like a criticism: Was *I* hiding behind a white face?

"It's a fair question," he said, mulling it over, "and I'm not especially proud of the deception, but you must understand that if I hadn't, it's unlikely that we would've been able to make enough money to afford this place. Hell, it's possible I wouldn't have been able to publish at all."

"So, it was a strategy?"

"You make it sound so calculated." He chuckled to himself. "But I guess you're right. For obvious reasons, Roger had to be the face on the cover flap, but he didn't want to use his name, so we created the almighty Ray Kane. The name sounds masculine and authoritative and evokes Raymond Chandler and *Citizen Kane*. It's drag, honey, but instead of a dress and wig, Kane wears 'muscular prose' and 'witty, hard-boiled metaphors.' Like most straight white men, he's an invention."

"But he's *you*," I said in a whisper, glancing at the door to the kitchen. Dishes were clinking, water was running, and Philippa and Roger were still laughing and debating. "You're the real writer. I knew it the moment I saw you. It was just there, on your face." His scar, I thought, I could tell by the scar.

The tendons in his neck tightened, and his posture stiffened. Fear—or was it anger?—surfaced in him. "Roger is essential to Ray Kane," he said, suppressing his emotion. "As essential as I am."

Sure, I thought, but you're not denying it. "It's like when you bought the apartment. Roger is your Trojan horse." What was I saying?! Wow, I'd overdone it with the wine, too.

He sighed. "It's more complicated than that, Judy." His voice was low, gentle. "Roger is more than a mask I wear and call Ray Kane. He's much more to me. Yes, I do most of the writing, but he edits and gives me the time and space to write. Our love for one another has made Ray Kane; our love will see us through whatever is coming." A darkness came over him, and his eyes tarnished a little. "But all of that is neither here nor there. With torches raised, the witch hunters are on the way, and Ray Kane may have penned his last book." He reached for his glass.

The kitchen door opened, and Roger came through carrying a tray with chocolate mousse in crystal dessert glasses. Philippa followed with coffee. Dessert was served, and coffee was poured, and my thoughts shifted away from the grim possibility of Ray Kane's demise to Philippa's flushed, happy face. Her silvery eyes sparkled. She'd had a wonderful evening befriending her heroes, who, from her point of view (from what I could tell), were made more intriguing, more daring by their unusual partnership. I was sure that she'd be appalled at the suggestion that being a writer was anything other than a solitary and deeply romantic activity. For her, Ray Kane was increased, not diminished, by the truth. I loved this openness in her but couldn't quite rise out of the unease of being in Lionel's and Roger's presence. It wasn't about who they were or how they treated me, but something else, something harder to pin down.

"Well," Philippa said, motioning with her dessert spoon. "I won the argument!"

"Is that so?" Lionel said, smiling at Philippa's tipsy-on-the-verge-of-smashed behavior.

"Yes!" she exclaimed. "*Lady of Shanghai* is the winner!" She swung her gaze to meet mine, her dessert spoon still dancing in the air. "First, Rita Hayworth is completely ravishing, blonde hair and all, and then that climactic sequence in the fun house . . ."

"The hall of mirrors," Lionel said. "You're right. It's extraordinary." Philippa spun toward him, jostling the table.

Roger shrugged. "I tried to convince her that the Ferris wheel scene from *The Third Man* was superior."

"No," Lionel said, smiling. "I agree with Philippa, at least about the scene. Filming it must've been a feat. Where do you hide the camera in a hall of mirrors?"

A hall of mirrors.

In a flash, I understood why I'd never relaxed into the evening, why all the booze failed to mellow me. Lionel and Roger were *us*, a reflection of us, a vision of our future. Through wit, cunning, and love for one another, they'd conceived of Ray Kane, and now Kane's existence, however artificial, was threatened, if not doomed. Eventually, the world would know that the author was two authors, that they were homosexuals, and that one of them wasn't white. Did Philippa and I have a chance? Or were all the Joseph McCarthys of this world coming for us?

"May I ask you something?" I said to Lionel. "How did you get your scar?"

A gloom fell across him again, but he didn't flinch. He responded frankly, "Three foolish white men beat me out of spite." Of course. Roger had mentioned the incident to us at Cary's.

"He was on assignment for the *Washington Afro-American*," Roger added, squeezing Lionel's arm. "He was walking home from interviewing folks at the sit-in at the Little Palace cafeteria near 14th and U streets, and these goons jumped out of an alley and beat him within an inch of his life and stole his wallet."

"It was never about my money, though," he said. "It was because I was a Negro reporting on Negro news. Because I was a witness." He raised his hand to his scar and rubbed it. "I'm almost certain that I interviewed one of those fools while they were loitering outside that damn cafeteria. But I can't remember much of that day."

Roger leaned toward us, his slender and handsome face uncannily sober. "If you want the real Ray Kane backstory, the reason we started writing in the first place . . ." He glanced at Lionel. "Well, it was because of that attack. Born from the ashes, as it were."

"Nothing like having a crime committed against you to make you want to write about crimes," Lionel said with renewed levity. "The tough guy Ray Kane who wrote tough guy P. I. Calvin McKey helped me heal. If not, I might be in the nuthouse by now."

We were mirrored again: Writing saved him; books saved me. We shared scars; we even shared memory loss.

"Is that why you based *The Broken Thread* on a historical crime?" Philippa asked after swallowing a bite of mousse. "Is that why you were drawn to a real murder?"

"I think so," Roger said, "and it's probably why we're basing the novel we're researching now on true crimes—unsolved crimes."

Lionel laughed bitterly. "Not that it will ever get published."

"Have hope!" Roger demanded unconvincingly. "If we're permitted to write it, it will be a great book."

"Our most difficult book."

"How so?" Philippa asked, suddenly alert. "If you don't mind me prying." I was beginning to believe that she'd never tire of writerly chitchat.

"We have a title," Roger said, waving a hand through the air like a ring-master's dramatic presentation: "*The Tattoo Artist!*"

"What's it about?" I asked, scooping up a spoonful of the creamy mousse.

"Last fall, our publisher sent us a letter that a fan had mailed to their offices and requested that they pass it on to us. It was a detailed account of missing and murdered girls in DC, Maryland, and eastern Virginia, beginning with the Peabody girl back in 1941." I glanced at Philippa, who flared her eyes at me. She remained still, but she was breathing heavily. I was, too. "The theory was that these crimes were connected, that there was a killer of young girls roaming the countryside. It was well-researched. The writer even gave a name: Adrian Bogdan."

"I remembered the Peabody case from years ago," Lionel said, "and that Bogdan was a suspect in another crime in '48, a boy's death, Cleveland Closs. But he was ruled out. The authorities concluded that someone else had committed both crimes. His father—who died, I believe." I felt an urge to tell them the police had come to the wrong conclusion, but why muddy the waters. It had nothing to do with Bogdan's killings.

"We dismissed the theory at first," Roger continued, energized. "We receive a lot of fan mail, so you can't take letters from readers too seriously. But then, last September, Lyle stumbled across an article about the funeral of a thirteen-year-old girl from Glenn Allen, Virginia, Melody Harris, and her parents' horrible grief, and we began digging into the case. That's when we decided to write fiction about it. It was dark material, so we aged up the victims. The publisher would ask us to, anyway. And instead of writing on the bodies, as was done in the actual crimes, the murderer tattoos clues on their flesh before dumping them. Hence, *The Tattoo Artist.*"

"We considered writing nonfiction about it," Lionel added, making eye contact with Roger. "But I wasn't ready to head back into journalism."

"A mystery novel 'based on true events' might cause a stir, and of course, our publisher liked the idea of buzz around the novel." Roger wiggled his eyebrows. "And if it would get people talking, it might help the case. Who knows."

"Now, it's anybody's guess." Lionel shrugged. "Maybe we shouldn't have pursued a story about child murders."

It was Roger's turn to slip into a gloom. "I don't know if our editor will hear from Scotty McLeod's men at the State Department. McCarthy and the FBI have targeted other artists and writers, so I wouldn't be surprised if they try to stop us from being published. Not that we're big shots, like those writers and actors being blacklisted in Hollywood, but because it's easy for them to destroy us. It would just take a phone call." His eyes fell to his empty dessert bowl. "Everything's hanging by a thread."

Philippa stared at me with wide, urgent eyes. She wanted me to tell them that we'd sent the envelope, that we set them on this path, that I was once Judy *Peabody*. But I glared back at her: "No," I hoped my eyes communicated. "Don't say anything. Not yet."

"Hell," Lionel said, resting his elbows on the table, "Roger even did the legwork."

"Legwork?" I asked.

"He chatted up the police in DC, Harrisonburg, Richmond, and Culpeper." He smiled wearily. "They'll take a meeting with Ray Kane."

My throat went suddenly dry, and my heart was pounding. I confirmed with Roger, "You talked to the police?" I wondered if he'd spoken to Piers Richardson. We showed him Philippa's murder book, and he could've connected us to the anonymous packets, although it's doubtful he'd mention us to Kane.

"You know what?" he asked rhetorically, still in a mood, and rose from the table. "Most of them told me they'd received a packet, too. They even asked me if I'd sent it. Unbelievable."

Jesus, I thought. He didn't realize he was poking a grizzly bear. That's why he lost his job. It must be.

I don't know if it was the alcohol or her impatience, but Philippa blurted out, "We need to tell you—"

"That we should go," I said, glaring at her again, willing her to shut up. "We don't want to overstay our welcome." We needed to think this through. Roger and Lionel were more than jobless and possibly out of a publishing contract. They were in danger. If the FBI knew they were writing about the murders, then Bogdan knew, and he would come for them.

Philippa's mouth fell open, but she thought better of challenging me. "Yes," she said, deflated. "You're right. It's late."

◦━━◦

The elevator doors closed, and Philippa, woozy from all the booze, leaned her back on the polished wood paneling and drew her face into a silly frown. "Why wouldn't you let me tell them?" She caught her reflection in the mirror on the other side of the elevator and said, "God, I am totally stoned," and sighed.

Sure, she frustrated me, but there was something sweet and open about her when she was this drunk. I couldn't be angry. "Look," I said, after pressing the button for the lobby, "I'm not saying we shouldn't tell them, but we need to think about it first."

I was already mulling it over. While saying our goodbyes and clumsily slipping on our coats, I realized we needed to turn over one more stone before we told Lionel and Roger the entire story.

When the doors closed and the elevator began its descent, Philippa stood up straighter and, vacillating from wobbly petulance to sadness, said, "We're responsible. You realize that."

"We are, I know."

"They had no idea what they were walking into when they began waving around information about the murders and Bogdan." Her features quieted, and she turned inward. "We smashed things up for them." Pain was scrawled on her face, made even rawer by her intoxicated state. "We're why Roger lost his job. Why else did they drag him in and question him and polygraph him?" She leaned her dour, rosy-cheeked face into mine. "We're good at that. Smashing things up."

I steadied her so that she wouldn't topple over. "You've made your point."

"We must tell them who we are and our connection to that goddamn monster."

I was beside her now, hooking my arm in hers. Hailing a cab was going to be a blast. "We'll tell them everything, but first, we need to do something I never thought I'd suggest we do. The idea of which makes me want to vomit—more than all that wine."

She perked up.

"Talk to Moira Closs."

"Why?"

"Because, like us, she's a link between Bogdan and the murders. Queen Closs knows something. I'm sure of it."

"Isn't that dangerous?"

"Of course," I said, propping her up. "But we don't have a choice. It's not just about us now."

The doors opened, and standing before us was a tall, wide-shouldered man in a navy suit and a dusty black fedora. His face was as expressionless as a slab of stone. His small dark eyes didn't flicker at us. Philippa grabbed my arm and squeezed it. Through her alcoholic fog, she must've also felt the penetrating chill of his gaze. We moved briskly past him and into the expansive lobby with its ornate plaster ceiling. Philippa stumbled over the edge of a plush oriental rug and muttered that balancing would be easier without heels. As I bent down to help her,

I glanced back at the elevator just as the doors began closing. No one was inside the car, and no one was visible near the elevators. Had we seen a ghost? Or a spook? Mammoth pillars veneered in wood paneling, most likely structural support for the building, flanked both sides of the lobby. They could be blocking my view of him—or he could be hiding behind one of them. Although I wasn't as sloshed as Philippa, I'd kept pace with the others. So maybe I *was* seeing things.

Once I helped her off with her shoes, I ushered her toward the front entrance, looking over my shoulder, still unable to spot the man. I was relieved when the doorman stepped forward and opened the door for us. I wanted to ask him if he'd seen the ghost, but we needed to get home, so we stumbled on. Philippa moaned about her cold feet as I waved for a cab. I continued checking the building's entrance and U-shaped turn-in until a taxi pulled over. Nothing. Maybe we'd imagined the creep after all.

CHAPTER 16

MAY 4, 1954, LIONEL

To the casual observer, the alley in the back of Shaw Hardware on U Street was the perfect setting for a mugging. I wouldn't consider entering it if I wasn't familiar with it. But I did, even though it made my skin crawl. At the end of the trash-strewn passage between buildings, down a flight of narrow stairs, a small door opened to what was once a well-kept secret, a club called Crocodile Tears, Croc's for short. These days, when the mood strikes them, the police raid it, so the door, kicked in regularly by a thug's heel, pivots precariously on its hinges as I enter, more the suggestion of a door than an actual door.

Entering Croc's is like diving into a dark aquarium. No matter the time of day, the large basement is dim, suffused with smoke, and drenched in liquid reds and modulating blues. The cracked cement floors are dotted with café tables draped with gingham and lit with flickering red votives. Along the perimeter run booths upholstered with worn leather cushions and tables engraved by customers' pens and pocketknives—"Timmy and Will Forever," "Vern Is A Great Fuck," "Lucy + Diana" surrounded by a heart and pierced with an arrow, and even a dirty limerick or two—evidence of the desire of men and women who passed through these hallowed halls. On the east wall, like an altar in a grotto, stands the bar haloed by a green backlight and manned by a beefy Czech import named Kasper, who bulges from his shirtsleeves and pretends to know little English. At the back, threadbare velvet curtains present the stage, which on Thursdays, Fridays, and Saturdays features live entertainment, a medley of drag performances and musical numbers and, for good measure, a vaudeville act, often more inadvertently funny than *actually* funny.

As I step in, the Select-o-matic, a recent addition, switches to Eddie Fisher's "I'm Walking Behind You." Being a Tuesday, the room was mostly empty, except for several couples tittering at the tables and the flies sipping their drinks and ogling Kasper's biceps at the bar. Fisher's sappy croon swirls in the thick, dank air. I yearn for Eddie Boyd or Willie Mabon, tunes you feel from the heels up, not this sentimental shit. Maybe I'll put one of them on.

Judy and Philippa wave me down. After Brentano's, I phoned them and told them to grab Iris and meet me. It's important. They're all at a booth in the corner. Iris is sitting up very straight and swiveling around, making sharp movements, a flick of the hand here, a jut of the chin there. She's usually so cool, so put together, but I immediately recognize her discomfort. She's never been to the land of the fairies, has she? And Croc's, well, it's so different. My first time, I had the same reaction. Unlike most bars in town, the proprietor doesn't care about the color of his fruity fish. Negros and whites mingle, dance, and disappear to another back alley for sex. When Roger and I discovered it, it was a revelation—a glorious improbability—but it was also frightening, if for no other reason than its novelty.

"We made it before you," Philippa chirps. "How about that!"

I plop down beside Iris, who gives me a half-hearted smile.

"We just ordered drinks," Philippa continues quickly. "I'm sure our waiter . . . What's his name?" She seems jumpy, overcompensating with cheerfulness.

"Nick," Judy says, scanning the room behind me.

"Yes, Nick. Nick will return soon."

Judy's hand shoots up, and suddenly the waiter, a slender Negro in his early twenties, appears and delivers glasses of beer to the women. I recognize him. He takes my order—Bourbon neat. I smile at him and appreciate his quiet, vaguely bemused eyes. He seems like the only person in this place not humming with nervous energy. After my day, I need a little peace, a place to slow my swirling thoughts.

"Where is your boyfriend?" Nick asks, holding his smile dreamily. "You're usually together." He's flirting, checking to see if I'm still attached. If I explain why Roger isn't here, if I speak it out loud, tendrils of doubt will wrap around me and strangle my nascent hope that he's still alive. Judy clocks my unease and answers, "It's just the four of us."

Nick loses his smile and leaves.

"So," Judy says, her dark eyes probing. "What happened?" Unlike twitchy Iris or frenetic Philippa, Judy is cool, perhaps a little too cool.

I look at each of them, and then, rebelling against the fear that comes with daring to have hope, I speak it: "I don't think Roger is dead."

I explain to them about Roger's ring being on the wrong finger and how he'd never make that mistake, how he never took it off, and how his clothes and gun were missing. I tell them how his body was accidentally cremated, which makes Iris burst out furiously—"That should've never happened! Never! The morgue is disorganized, but lord, that's just something else."—then I tell them that Shipley and Colby are forcing me to lie to Roger's family by confirming that the body they turned to ash was his.

"I don't think he's dead," I say, liking the sound of it in my mouth, "or at least that the body they 'accidentally' cremated isn't his."

For a breath, Judy and Philippa glance at each other. A strange wavelength passes between them. Something I can't put my finger on. Iris shifts beside me.

Philippa brightens suddenly and says, "That's incredible. Do you really think he's alive?"

Judy adds drolly, "Never underestimate the police."

My bourbon arrives, and I knock it back. The burn flows down my throat and spreads through my chest. The drumbeat of desperate longing in my heart quiets, and I can feel hope ease into me, not the fragile denial I initially clung to. Roger could be alive, could be still himself, that beautiful long, muscular body of his could be leaning against a wall someplace; that smile could be creeping into his lips; those little neurotic habits of his, like rearranging the silverware drawer or straightening the bookshelf or reorganizing the liquor, could still be intact, little irritations that now would make me melt. God, where is he?

Remembering my other reason for summoning them, I retrieve the photo of Adrian and Anna from my coat and lay it in the center of the table. The group stirs, especially Philippa and Judy, who slide closer together. Their faces tighten, their shoulders rise and fall. Again, I detect an odd, subliminal communication between them. I can't be certain, but they seem to recognize it. The sting of being excluded, of Roger and the girls cutting me out, surfaces again, a little like being on the outside of an inside joke. "I found this when inspecting the damage to the apartment." I flip the photo over to show the writing on the back. "I did a little research. It translates to 'Adrian and Anna.' I've never seen it before and have no idea how it got mixed in with our research for *The Tattoo Artist*." Judy and Philippa aren't making eye contact.

Judy turns it over again and drags her forefinger across the surface of the image as if its crumpled texture holds a mysterious fascination for her. Philippa stares intensely at her beer, the amber liquid glowing in the light from the votive. I check on Iris, who seems as baffled as I feel or is doing a fine job pretending otherwise. "It's the same Adrian as Adrian Bogdan. It can't be a coincidence."

"You're right," Judy says, reaching out and flipping the photograph over. "It can't."

"Do you know anything about it?" I ask.

Philippa slowly lifts her eyes. Their silver-blue intensity unsettles me. Her lips tremble. She wants to tell me something but can't, or won't.

"We've never seen it," Judy says, "but it's interesting."

"Did Roger ever mention it to you?"

"No. I'm sorry." She smiles, but lingering in her expression is a touch of condescension.

"Odd," I say, "it seems like you recognize the photo."

"Like I said," she says firmly, "we've never seen it."

Philippa adjusts the cuffs of her blouse nervously. Iris sits very still. And my suspicion gels into anger. I pick up the photo, refold it, and slip it back into my pocket.

"When we first met"—I stare hard at Judy, then Philippa—"I thought you were cool, like you believed Roger and I being a team was something special. Then, something happened. It's like you got your hooks into him, and the three of you were pals, and I was out, no longer in the inner circle. I can't say when it happened or why, but I don't think I'm wrong."

"That's not true!" Philippa reaches across the table to reassure me, but I withdraw. "We didn't get our *hooks* into anyone. That's not—we would never."

I study her soft, freckled face and wonder if its pale skin, like many a white woman's, is a facade for all kinds of ugly. Maybe I'm being unfair—or maybe not. I knock back the last of my bourbon and throw down change. "And, since the fire, all of you—Iris, too—have been exceedingly helpful. I'm thankful, sure, but I don't get it. I don't understand why you give a damn. We hardly know each other." I scoot out of the booth.

Judy narrows her eyes at me, a trace of anger in them. "Because we're fans, because we *admire* you. Why else?"

"Maybe," I say, standing now. "Maybe not."

"Lionel," Iris says, offering me her big brown eyes. An unsteady blend of compassion and guilt vibrates behind them. "We're on your side."

"I don't know," I say, shaking my head, "but all of you are acting *very* strange."

Judy offers a guarded gaze, her angular features still shadowy and secretive. She knows something, somehow.

"I need a break from you. I'm sick of wandering around in the dark." To Iris, I say, "I'll be back late."

Not waiting for a response, I leave.

CHAPTER 17

APRIL 1954, JUDY

Using the direct approach, we rang Moira a few days later, doubtful she'd speak to us. We weren't her favorite people, to put it lightly. In a stroke of luck, her secretary, Agnes Streppo, answered. I seized the opportunity and pretended to be a beautician from Tres Beaux, Edith's fashionable beauty parlor downtown, and—I had a hunch—Moira's as well. "Was Mrs. Closs still planning on a shampoo and set today?" I asked primly. Then, with a slight lift in register, I added, "We've reserved a chair for her."

Flustered, Mrs. Streppo asked me to hold. In the background, I heard the flutter of diary pages. "I'm sorry," she said, "I have no record of the appointment. She's at lunch now, then peeping at cherry blossoms. We'll have to reschedule."

"Very well," I chirped and, thinking on my feet, fished a little. "I hear the blossoms are stunning this year, but I never know where to begin."

"The Tidal Basin near the Jefferson Memorial, for sure. Mrs. Closs insists on strolling through them at their height every spring."

"Well, I'll have to make time," I said. "Good day, then."

We knew where to find Moira and had the advantage of surprise.

Edith had barred our use of the Dodge. Her new housekeeper, who didn't own a car, needed it on hand to run errands. So, we hired a taxi to take us to the Jefferson Memorial. As we pulled up, the memorial's austere marble dome rose against a bank of dark clouds on the horizon. A storm was fast approaching, but the sun still shone brightly. Its rays intensified the otherworldly aura of the pink blossoms that clung like cotton candy to the trees circling the Tidal Basin. Stray petals stirred by the wind floated around us like something from a fairytale.

We spent thirty minutes or so scanning the memorial's grounds and the edge of the Basin. The blossom peepers were thinning out, the threat of a spring shower driving them away. We weren't daunted. We could always dash into the memorial and take shelter with Thomas Jefferson's massive likeness. I wondered, though: Would the looming bad weather keep Moira away? But, as if in response, Philippa said, "There she is."

Indeed, there she was, in a tailored robin's-egg blue suit with matching heels and a hat tastefully askew. Her silver bouffant swept up from the sides of her powdered face and disappeared under her hat.

As we approached her, she was studying the sky skeptically. She sensed us and leveled her gaze, lifting an eyebrow. Her thin nose and protuberant crystalline blue eyes gave her a fierce, raptor-like quality that never ceased to unsettle me. A striking woman for her age, her bitterness and contempt had sharpened her features, scraping the glamour down to the bone. If once she'd been lovely, she now was only intensity.

"Hello, girls," she said, seemingly unflappable. "I can't imagine this is a coincidence."

"We need to talk," I said bluntly.

"Let's stroll down to the Basin," she said, moving away from the buzz of the tourists. "You're not going to spoil my cherry blossoms." She glanced up again. "Who knows, this storm might roll through in a rage and blow them all away. Carpe diem."

At the Basin, blotches of shivering white from the blossoms and glints of sunshine reflected in the rippling black water.

"So," she said, turning to us, "why have you ambushed me?"

"You must have an idea," I said.

She addressed Philippa: "I imagine this has something to do with what you told me at the reception after Barton's funeral. Neither of you know how to let something go."

"We have evidence that Bogdan is still killing girls," I said, drawing her gaze. "He's killed two more since we last spoke."

"Candy Conklin and now Melody Harris," Philippa said urgently.

"It's not going away," I added. "You can't ignore it."

Moira's lips twitched as if in response to a sharp pain.

"All of them have similarities to Jackie's death," Philippa added. "Naked, abused, written on, and dumped in rivers. We studied newspapers and whatever we could get our hands on. There's a pattern."

Moira sniffed, unimpressed. "You need proof, something definitive. It doesn't sound like you have a damn thing."

Philippa wasn't frightened of her; she leaned in. "We've studied the case and woven together our observations into a narrative that—"

"He's not my monster to keep," Moira cut in.

"We put together packets and mailed them out," I said.

"Dossiers of the victims," Philippa jumped in. "We spelled it out in black and white for anyone who would listen."

Moira's eyes flashed with alarm. "*Did* anyone listen?"

"We sent our story to every police station, newspaper, and radio station in the area," I added. "We blasted it out to everyone we could think of."

"A blunderbuss!" Philippa blurted, showing an almost childish pride in our efforts.

"*And?* What happened?" As her question hung in the air unanswered, her mouth melted into an impatient sneer. "Did anyone listen?"

We couldn't mention Lionel and Roger, so we had to lie or admit defeat. Philippa's expression shifted, her confidence cracking. She needed to work on her poker face.

A nose for weakness, Moira homed in. "So, clearly, no one was interested," she said, propping her hand on her hip.

"No," Philippa admitted, her eyes flicking over at me. "Not yet."

I expected Moira to launch in with a blistering critique, but instead, she gazed out over the water. The breeze surged, and petals spun in the air like snow.

"It's beautiful here," she said wistfully. "Calm."

Bogdan was a kind of evil even she found difficult to stomach. Sure, she manipulated, connived, and deceived, but she drew the line at the murder of children. In '48, she kept Bogdan from harming us. After he hit Philippa, her maternal instinct kicked in, and she flung a protective arm around her. It was odd, even surprising.

She turned to us. "I can't help you." Pink petals dotted the front and sleeves of her suit jacket. "If you had evidence, real evidence, I might be able to do something, but even then, I don't know what would be possible."

"You're part of it," I said, jabbing my finger at her. "You protected him. You knew what he was years ago."

Philippa flushed with emotion. "Young girls are being murdered," she pleaded, grabbing Moira's arms. "You must do something. You must." Her voice squeaked. The waiting, the inaction, the dread of it all was taking its toll. Maybe that's why she over-imbibed the other night. "You have connections. You know, muckety-mucks. Big shots," she urged, her grip tightening. "Tell someone at the FBI that Bogdan will never stop. Make *them* do something."

Moira's eyes widened, and cord-like tendons stood out in her neck. "Shut up!" she snapped, jerking violently away, offended that Philippa had dared to touch her, as if to do so was sacrilege. "Don't mention the FBI to me ever again, or you'll be in the goddamn river with those girls."

There she was, the Moira I knew and loathed. Self-interested to the core. Philippa shrunk back, stung. Her eyes damp.

And then, as sudden as Moira's fury had erupted, it faded. She casually brushed petals from her lapel. Smiling a bloodless smile, she leaned into us. In a low voice, she said, "I know what you two have been up to. Making house together like man and wife. It's appalling." She shook her head. She wasn't disgusted out of moral righteousness; she was disappointed in our vulnerability, what she perceived as weakness. "Now you've decided to keep company with that pair of mismatched fairies. You know how to pick them."

The first splatter of rain hit my cheek.

Moira glanced at the sky. "Damn it, I don't want to get caught in the rain."

Shaking, Philippa groaned, "You've been *following* us? You've been spying on Roger and Lionel and us? I can't—" She bumped into me, thrown off-balance by the shock. I slid my arm around her to steady her. It had taken time for her to give herself to me, to accept us as a couple, and to banish Stan and what he represented. The thought of her love for me being flung out in the open for all to see was mortifying. It was a point of no return.

"I have photos of you—your friends, too," Moira said, eyeing us like prey. "Hard evidence. Something you lack."

"You're a monster," Philippa spat out.

She winced, stung by her remark, it seemed. "If I tell your parents or your school or your employer about what you and Judy are doing, I promise you, I won't be the one labeled a monster."

Philippa grimaced but didn't cry. Don't let her see tears, I thought. Don't give her that satisfaction. Blood pulsed in my neck, in my temples. My hands flexed, and my body lurched forward, muscles tight, activated. I wanted to grab Moira by the shoulders and shove her into the Basin. I wanted to watch her robin's-egg blue suit plunge into the watery mirror below us. I wanted to watch her thrash around, and her icy composure split open, then, succumbing, slip under the surface and vanish. I wanted to watch the quiet beauty of the water, a fusing of sky and sea, restore itself as if nothing had happened.

Raindrops began lightly pelting us through the tree branches.

As if nothing nasty had just occurred, Moira grumbled, "Well, it's time to go before we get soaked." She walked away from us, paused briefly, and over her shoulder, said, "Good luck, girls." Then she bustled away, raising a gloved hand to shield her makeup from the rain. On the drive near the memorial, her black Cadillac pulled up, and her uniformed chauffeur, a tall gray-skinned man with blond hair peeking out from his cap, popped out and opened the door for her.

We scampered up the steps of the rotunda as the skies opened. The mammoth bronze Jefferson greeted us stoically, along with clusters of chattering families, tour groups, and school groups taking shelter. Philippa and I huddled close, shaking the rain off our arms and adjusting our hair. "That woman!" she fumed, almost comically. "That cow."

I chuckled. "Cow?"

She flashed her eyes at me. "What?"

"She's much worse than a cow."

"Okay." She frowned, still engaged. "Hag, then."

"Worse than that."

She pinched the fabric of her wet blouse, pulled it away from her body, and shook it lightly to dry it. "Whatever you call her," she said. "I understand why she hates us, or at least wants to keep us in check, but for the life of me, I don't understand why she won't do anything to stop Bogdan from murdering girls."

Philippa's passionate plea to Moira had been so urgent, so genuine—even a little unhinged. Why—I wondered rather coldly—did she care so much about these girls? At first glance, the answer is obvious: it's right and noble to fight for justice, etcetera. I knew why I cared, and it was for more complex reasons. I'd spent years in the shadow of Jackie Peabody's murder. Edith had even attempted to fashion me in her image, which made me hate her and Jackie. When we'd confronted Bogdan years ago, I understood I'd gotten it wrong. Jackie was a shadow of myself, not my enemy. Bogdan and his enablers deserved my ire. Fate had crowned me their nemesis. Along the way, after we'd escaped Bogdan, Philippa took up my cause. I fled to Paris, but she continued to hunt him. Why?

"You're like a dog with a bone about these girls, aren't you?"

"I am, I guess." She was confused. "But—"

"It's a good thing. I don't understand your passion for it."

She was baffled, even on the verge of anger, but she softened. "I can't get the mothers out of my head," she said, her voice heavy. "Their sad faces in newspapers. Mrs. Conklin's despair. I even remember catching a glimpse of Edith's grief. I continue to think, what if Melody, Candy, or any of them were my daughter?"

Her daughter? Did she see herself being a mother? It hadn't occurred to me. I didn't want it and, I suspected, never would. Her mother had died in childbirth. Maybe she wanted what she never had. Maybe that was her attraction to Stan. Jesus. My heart sank. "Oh," I said, "that makes sense. Of course." I stood away from her, aware of a rush of cool air from the storm. For the first time, I understood she hadn't been frightened of us being a couple. She'd been afraid being a couple would limit her.

As the cab navigated the crowded, rain-slick streets, we discussed how we would break the news to Lionel and Roger. Now that we knew Moira was spying on all of us, they needed to know. We'd hashed out a strategy, which meant swinging by our apartment before heading to Connecticut Avenue, then fell quiet.

Philippa leaned her head back and closed her eyes. I studied her frizzed-out hair and pale profile, softened by the muted light. My love for her was keen, made keener by the thought that she might give up motherhood, that powerful imperative, to be with me—a woman who had had her procreative impulse stamped out by a series of damaged and damaging mother figures. If wolves had raised you, did you want to be a wolf mother? Not me.

I hung my head, my eyes falling on my lap. My coat sleeves were pushed up, exposing a few of the scars on my forearms. I remembered only fragments of how I'd received them: The dark basement—root cellar, really—where it happened. The intense, acrid smell of cat urine mingled with the damp soil's funky odor. The yawling and hissing of cats. The feeling of being overwhelmed and pushed outside of myself, the pain everywhere, and a yawning blackness, the missing piece of a puzzle about myself. Where did it happen? When? Why? So much from my childhood was still a dark smudge, like ink spilled across a page of prose; only a word or two remained legible. I reached for Philippa's hand, and she let me take it, opening her eyes. She frowned, her mind a million miles away, probably writing the script for our talk with Roger and Lionel, but she squeezed my hand. She made that gaping hole in my past manageable. She didn't fill it—that was impossible—but she shored up its edges.

Roger answered the door when we knocked. His shirtsleeves were rolled up, and his blue tie flecked with gold dangled from his loosened collar. A pair of tortoiseshell reading glasses crowned his chestnut hair.

"Are you back for more rib roast? Or Burgundy? I thought you'd had your fill," he said dryly. His eyes fell on the little blue faux-leather suitcase Philippa was carrying, "Or are you moving in?"

We strolled into the living room, and he followed us. "I'm sorry," he said. "Lyle is out. You just missed him." Roger gestured toward the coffee table. On it, situated among other stacks of documents, was the packet we sent their publishers. This spread was their research for *The Tattoo Artist*. "We thought we'd finish the book since we have the time. Even if no one wants to publish it, at least it's something to do, and, who knows, it could help in some way. And if it all goes to hell, we'll go out gloriously!"

"Oh, okay," Philippa said, straightening her back, preparing for impact, "we need to tell you something." Her tone was grave.

"The other night . . . you seemed like you had more to say," he said, looking at us like, "Go ahead, shoot."

I scooped up our packet from the piles of research.

He registered alarm and snapped, "Don't get that out of order!" and reached out to take it from me.

"Don't worry," I said, holding on to it. "We know what it says."

His face went blank. "What do you mean?" His incredulous gaze shifted between us.

Philippa stepped in. "We sent it to you. We're the ones who wrote it."

His mouth dropped open, and his reading glasses slipped down, landing on the bridge of his nose. His hand darted up to return them to their place just above his forehead. "Okay," he said slowly, stunned. "Sit down and explain." He gestured to the couch. I returned the packet to the table, my picking it up having had its intended effect, and took our seats. Philippa deposited her blue suitcase by the side of the couch. He remained standing, tightly gripping the back of one of the armchairs. Despite the flat light pouring in from the windows, the wall of orange poppy wallpaper glowed behind him. Philippa launched in, explaining her research process, beginning with her time at Briarfield's. He watched her intently, his face still, absorbing everything. I wondered if this angered or excited him, but he wasn't showing his cards. When she finished, he said, "Jesus," and circled the chair and dropped into it, crossing his legs, his loafered foot cocked at an angle. "And you sent it to us?"

"Yes, and newspapers, radio, and the police," Philippa answered. "We wanted someone to report on it. Since *The Broken Thread* was based on a true crime, we guessed you might be interested."

He chuckled. "You guessed right."

"Keep in mind, we thought Ray Kane was solo, not a writing team. We didn't know anything about you. We didn't imagine you worked for the State Department or were a couple."

His face dimmed. "Why didn't you tell us the other night?"

We needed time to consider the impact of this news, but I didn't want to say that to him, so instead, I said, "You've interviewed several police departments about the murders, right?"

"Yes," he said, blinking, annoyed I hadn't answered.

"Do you have a record of who you talked to?"

"Sure, I take thorough notes. Most of them told me they'd received an anonymous package like mine and shrugged it off as just another crackpot or crazy." He smiled. "They probably thought I was a crackpot, too, but they enjoyed basking in the glow of a notable author."

I paused, then asked, "Did any of them claim they didn't receive a package?"

"Yes," he said. "Paulson, Leo Paulson, Commander of the First District." Philippa sucked in her breath. We knew that name. He questioned us back in '48. He was also an old flame of Moira's. "We talked about the murdered and missing girls in the region. He didn't believe the crime added up to the work of a single man. We chatted more fully about Jackie Peabody's murder, Bogdan as a suspect, and then the Closs man, who died in an accident but was the likely culprit in the Peabody girl's death. Back then, Paulson was the lead detective on the case. I told him about the information mailed to our publisher, but he never mentioned his department receiving a packet."

"That's the connection," I said, grabbing Philippa's knee and quickly releasing it, not wanting to embarrass her. "He didn't mention it to you," I said to Roger, "because he participated in covering up the truth about Jackie's murderer. It hit too close to home. He knows Bogdan is still out there."

"By the time Ray Kane came knocking," Philippa added, also energized, "I bet he'd already told Moira, the FBI, or both."

Roger glared at us, perplexed. "I have no idea what you're talking about. Who's Moira? And what about the FBI?"

"Moira Closs," I said. "She's the owner of Capitol City Hardware."

His face spread wide. "The grande dame of hammer and nails. Her name is always in the society pages of the *Post*." His reading glasses began slipping again. He reached up, grabbed them, and tossed them on the table, making a show of his frustration. "And what about the FBI?" he demanded, his voice intense, even threatening—the soldier in him activated.

I checked with Philippa, and she nodded, and I started in. "Bogdan isn't just the murderer of girls. He was in the Red Army, defected, and eventually wound up in the clutches of the FBI." Roger shifted uncomfortably, his foot twitching. "He's a spy for our government—or was. We're not sure."

Roger burst into laughter and bolted to his feet. "You've lost me!" He waved it off. "I can't believe it, and if it's true, I don't want to know." He circled behind the chair as if to put it between himself and the idea that Adrian Bogdan was a spy.

"It's hard to believe," I said. "But it *is* true."

He began roaming the floor, agitated. "What kind of spying does he do?" He stopped and glared at us. "Never mind. I don't want to know." He resumed pacing.

"Nuclear arms, uranium trafficking," I said, ignoring him. "The one time we crossed paths, he implied as much, but he was also going on about why he murders. His Eurydice thing."

"What?" Roger looked at us, bewildered. "Eurydice?"

"The myth of Orpheus," I explained. "Orpheus descends into the under-world to retrieve his dead wife, Eurydice, after she was bitten and killed by a snake. Hades and Persephone grant his request on the condition that he doesn't look back as his wife follows him out of the underworld. Of course, he looks back because he's so smitten, or foolish, or something like that, and she vanishes. Poof."

"I know the myth," he grumbled, still wearing a path in the carpet, "but what does it have to do with Bogdan?"

"He's cast himself as a modern-day Orpheus." I rolled my eyes. "It's a nutty rationalization. He's sending them to the underworld, not killing them, you see, and when the time comes, he'll retrieve them. Unlike Orpheus, he won't look back."

Philippa piped up: "It's insanity."

"It's an excuse," I growled.

"We don't know much about him," she added. "But we do know he's so valuable to the FBI that they've decided to protect him even though he's a killer."

"We don't know if they are protecting him. They may be searching for him, too. But we do know that they don't want the world to discover they shielded that monster from prosecution. No one will believe that it was the right thing to do, national security be damned."

Roger started shaking his head. "No, no, no. You're making this up." He chuckled. "We don't know each other well enough for a practical joke."

"It's not a joke," Philippa said, reaching for her blue suitcase. She positioned it on her lap, opened it slowly, and retrieved the murder book.

"What's that?" he asked, coming close.

"It's our research. Our *complete* research."

She handed him the repurposed photo album. He returned to his seat, plucked his glasses from the table, slipped them on, and began flipping through the leather-bound book. As he did, his face drained of color. "You got me," he said. "If you are making it up, you've gone to extraordinary lengths for a terrible joke."

"We're sorry," Philippa said, understanding, I'm sure, his sinking feeling, the queasiness of realizing how vulnerable you are.

He looked up. "Where does Moira Closs fit in all of this?"

"She orchestrates social gatherings that double as opportunities for powerful men to meet," I said. "She's far from the first socialite to serve cocktails and canapés to senators and spooks and get tangled in their sticky web."

Moira's vicious disregard for us weighed heavily on me. Once again, I imagined her slipping under the surface of the Tidal Basin, her robin's-egg blue suit vanishing into the murk. "But I won't undersell her ability to cause suffering. She's one of them."

"We don't know exactly how she ended up rubbing elbows with the FBI and Bogdan," Philippa added, "but I'll wager it was the allure of power."

"Who knows?" I shrugged. "Maybe J. Edgar has something on her."

"That reminds me of the Peabody woman," he said. "When I interviewed her, as soon as I mentioned Moira Closs, she clammed up."

"Peabody woman?" I sat up. "Do you mean Edith Peabody?" Another piece was falling into place.

"Yes, she didn't appreciate me knocking on her door and asking about her dead daughter, but it seemed important research to do. She answered a few questions and shooed me away."

"That's Edith," I said, trying to imagine his conversation with her, especially after her violent response to finding the murder book. Roger pursed his lips as if to say: Is there more you haven't told me? Taking mercy on him, I explained, "Edith Peabody is my adoptive mother. After Jackie died, she and her late husband, Bart, adopted me as a surrogate. It didn't go well."

"Jesus," he said, closing the heavy book and resting his hands on it. "She didn't mention you to me." He returned the murder book to Philippa, and Philippa placed it in the suitcase.

"I'm not surprised." I shrugged. "I wasn't a good stand-in for Jackie. I don't behave, and Edith doesn't like girls who don't behave."

"Sounds like a peach."

Philippa nodded in affirmation, but I couldn't churn up any bile for Edith. "I understand her now," I said. "She's a very sad woman."

He tucked his hands under his arms, hugging his chest. He was visibly unnerved by all the revelations of the past few minutes. "You're in the middle of this. Both of you. Right in the middle."

I leveled my gaze at him. "You and Lionel are, too."

He held out his hands in an I'm-fresh-out-of-ideas gesture. "So, what do we do now?"

"Tell Lionel," Philippa said. "He should know."

"No," Roger said firmly, his expression becoming grave. "We can't tell him."

"Why?" Philippa and I asked, overlapping.

"Lyle has been through hell. The beating he took years ago after interviewing folks at the sit-in—it damaged more than his body."

"What do you mean?" I asked, trying not to imagine the elegant, self-assured Lionel we knew being pummeled by dirty fists.

"I mean, he worries." His eyes softened, his love for Lionel evident. "Sometimes he worries so much that he won't leave the apartment for days. It's been a long time since he's had one of these spells, but this is just the sort of thing to set him off, particularly on top of me being jettisoned from the State Department."

"Oh no," Philippa said sadly. "We didn't realize that . . ." She let her sentence die out. Nothing more needed to be said.

Lionel was emotionally wounded like the soldiers who returned from the war in Korea or the Second World War. I was furious for him and swarmed with guilt. We'd stupidly brought another threat to his door.

Philippa slumped and, more to me than Roger, muttered, "But he'll be in danger."

I touched her arm, and she turned to me. "I know what we'll do."

She squinted, unsure of my meaning.

"We'll have to return to Moira," I said softly. "She knows how to find Bogdan, and I may have something she wants."

Her eyes grew wide. She knew what I meant.

CHAPTER 18

APRIL 1954, JUDY

When we returned to our apartment after breaking the news to Roger, the phone was ringing. Edith was on the line, inviting me to lunch the next day at The Colony. Had we summoned her by talking about her? Had her ears been burning? The thought of Roger surprising her and asking her about Jackie bugged me. Essentially, we'd sent him to her door. Even though I found her haughty and remote, even though I'd always resent her—it had been woven into the fabric of my being—it bothered me that I'd failed to see her as a grieving mother. Sure, you could argue that it wasn't my responsibility to tend to her heartache, especially since she tried to squeeze me into Jackie's outline, but it kept me from loathing her. If I'm being honest, I didn't want to sever all connection with her. We'd experienced too much together, bound forever as cogs in Moira Closs's machinations.

On DeSales Street downtown, The Colony restaurant was a meeting place for politicos and the Washington elite. Faux portraits of famous Washingtonians lined the entryway, and the mixture of bright rose carpet, a coffered ceiling painted to match, and cream-tinted trimmings gave the room a warm, nostalgic glow, like stepping into a pink cloud. On the walls, plaster reliefs of mythological scenes alternated with wide mirrors, all the tables were draped with starched tablecloths, and polished place settings glittered in the mellow light. The maître d' showed me to Edith's table.

Edith gave a little half-hearted wave and rose to her feet. She wore a pale mauve suit with a wide gray collar and a gray felt crescent hat. A mist of brassy, rich perfume hung in the air around her. We hugged cordially and took our places on either side of the table, Edith falling heavily against the rose-tinted banquette cushion. Had she put on weight, or was she weakening with age, less able to control her body?

As we dove into small talk, a team of white-coated waiters approached with all manner of offers and demands—drink orders were taken, the amuse-bouche arrived, meal orders were requested, place settings vanished, and drinks appeared—Edith had a white Bordeaux and me, a French 75, garnished with a delicate curlicue of lemon peel. Edith told me about the lives of her friends, none of whom she liked, none of whom I cared about, while she sipped cream of asparagus soup and I stabbed my fork at a Caesar salad with salty anchovies that one of the waiters, a handsome French man named Édouard, had mixed table-side with great theatricality.

I had lamb chops with a cognac cream sauce for an entrée, and Edith had a duck breast in blackberry sauce. It was about this time Edith began grilling me: "What are you doing for money, dear? I hope you're having some sort of social life. Young women need to have a social life." I batted her questions away with expert precision: "Yes, I'm doing secretarial work for WSDC-FM." Of course, I didn't want her to know I'd lost that job. "And rest assured, I'm partying like a maniac. Steno pad in one hand and martini in the other. It's the life." She gave me a droll look, but to her credit, she didn't press me too hard. As her attention turned to her duck and she started sawing away at it, sadness crept in at the corners of her mouth and the edges of her eyes. Even her dainty diamond earring sparkling on her large earlobe seemed, somehow, full of woe.

I had planned to ask her why she never told me about Roger's visit—Ray Kane's visit, that is. But I couldn't figure out how to discuss Jackie with her. I'd never figured out how to broach that subject. Moreover, I didn't want to explain how I knew Roger. So, I held back every time it was on my lips, swallowing the impulse.

With the cheese course came talk of politics and the aftermath of war. Edith was a fan of Eisenhower's and sang high praises of his tough-minded handling of the conflict in Korea and the declaration of an armistice last summer. She shook her head at Truman's loss of nerve and his allowing "that horrible war of attrition to go on as long as he did," especially as news of the brutal torture and murder of American prisoners had been recently exposed in the war atrocities report, but her outrage rang hollow. "These days," she said, after nibbling on a piece of aged Gruyère, "there's much being said about Communists haunting the hallowed halls of our government buildings and now the military." She was referring, of course, to HUAC's investigation of the Army. "It all seems far-fetched. Certainly, there's one or two, but to hear McCarthy and this committee talk, you'd think every government institution was practically crawling with them." She smiled at me. "You don't hang out with any Communists, do you?"

"Jesus, Edith," I said, "I'm not a fool." I thought of Roger and Lionel. They weren't Communists, but they might as well be. McCarthy and company were using their witch hunt as a cover for reinforcing bigotry. They weren't hunting Commies; they were hunting artists, homosexuals, Negro civil rights leaders—outsiders.

"Smart girl," she said, reaching for her wine.

The restaurant was nearly full now, the height of lunch hour, and everyone around us was white and influential and glowing with smug self-assurance. I could never come here with Iris, even if legally they were forced to serve her. From the decor to the menu, it was designed to reinforce its clientele's delusion of themselves. Anyone who didn't fit neatly into that fantasy it repelled.

All this made me wonder (somewhat masochistically) how Edith would react if I told her the truth about me. I visualized her face as she received the news about my birth father: First, no detectable change, except that the muscles in her lips, along her jawline, and across her forehead would tighten. Her wide, heavily powdered cheeks—an attempt to subdue the Greek heritage evident in her olive skin—would try not to tremble. She wouldn't want to crack. Almost imperceptibly, her pupils would deepen, hinting at the despair roiling underneath. She would begin shifting uncomfortably in her seat, fiddling with the napkin in her lap.

When I mentioned my romance with Philippa, she would gasp, and, that revelation being the tipping point, anger would crash through her facade. I couldn't help who my blood parents were—a more difficult resentment for her to lean into—but my proclamation of love for Philippa would be me thumbing my nose at her, at all that she'd done for me, her plucking me out of Crestwood, her showering me with wealth and splendor. Quickly, all the pain she held inside, even suffering that had nothing to do with me—her persistent grief over Jackie's murder and her fresh grief over losing Bart—would explode like a shotgun blast. I imagined her, despite her sense of propriety, taking the cheese platter and hurling it at me. I imagined her tearing at the starched tablecloth. I imagined her screaming and writhing, her arms flailing, her hat slumping to the side, a diamond earring arcing through the air and landing on the plush red carpet, Édouard and the other waiters restraining her like mental hospital orderlies until she collapsed in a stupor.

No, I could never tell her.

Iris's voice echoed: "Will you live in the light or the shadows?"

In response: Charlene's journal entry, "It would be an unspeakable cruelty to tell her the truth of her race, an act of savagery."

But I knew the truth, and I was just fine. It was the world that wasn't.

"Dessert?" Edith asked, her eyes twinkling at the thought.

Overwhelmed by the rabid Edith I'd conjured, I acquiesced. "Sure."

We ordered: an apple tarte tatin à la mode for Edith and a crème brûlée for me. Coffee for both of us.

Edith smiled vaguely and then, remembering something, reached for her purse and extracted a pale pink envelope. "What do you think of this?"

I took it and slipped a piece of creamy high-quality card stock from the open envelope. It was an invitation for a luncheon next Thursday at the Mayflower Hotel across the street: "You are cordially invited to a luncheon in honor of donors to the Cherry Blossom Festival Fund. Special Guest, First Lady Mamie Eisenhower." Shaking her finger at it, she said, "I didn't give a cent." She cocked her head. "Do you know who leads the festival committee?"

I shrugged.

"Moira Closs."

"Why did she send you an invitation?" But as soon as I asked, I knew. It was a threat.

"I don't know, but I don't like it." She reached for her wine glass, but it was empty. "Moira is a snake. I still can't believe she showed up at the reception after Bart's funeral."

"I didn't know that bothered you."

She huffed, a little drunk, and gazed at me. Her eyes betrayed a vulnerability, a softer, more resigned grief. I considered saying something comforting to bring us closer but cutting into my thought, she griped, "Moira likes you to know who's in control. I keep my distance."

I waved the invitation back and forth, an idea forming. "Are you planning to go?"

"No," she said firmly.

"The First Lady will be there. She's going to crown a Cherry Blossom princess the queen of the Grand Ball. You might be able to get the inside scoop and place a bet."

"Sounds dreadful." She smirked. "And what is it with Mamie's obsession with pink?"

"Have you RSVP'd?"

"No."

"Do you mind if I keep this, then?"

"By all means." She studied me for a beat, bemused, and then with a bit of sadness, said, "You'll always be a mystery to me."

She was right; I would remain a mystery to her. But somehow, her comment neutralized the roaring woman I'd envisioned being subdued by waiters. A tremor of tenderness entered my heart, a reverberation of love for her. "I'm sorry," I said quietly, more quietly than I'd ever said anything to her.

"Don't be sorry," she said, shaking her head, her diamond earrings flashing. "Sorry isn't a good look on you." She smiled. "It never has been."

Before I could say anything else, dessert arrived.

CHAPTER 19

APRIL 1954, JUDY

Politicians, bigwigs, and movie stars frequented the Mayflower Hotel's grand cross-shaped lobby. Its polished marble floor, brass balustrades, and gilded trim glittered in the wash of sunlight from its translucent coffered ceiling. Its brand of glamour suggested that power, not commerce or culture, ran this town. Its marble-faced piers, a mezzanine on three sides, and a bustling cocktail bar tucked into the south transept added to this effect.

I wore a wide-collared double-breasted brown silk suit with tiger's eye buttons. Its waist was tight, giving my body the illusion of hips. I was far from the only woman dressed to the nines, but most of the others, who were undoubtedly destined for Moira's luncheon, wore pastels: an explosion of pale pinks, mint greens, and baby blues. I didn't wear spring colors. I'd branched out from the black and gray of my teenage years, but I'd be damned if I'd dress like an Easter egg.

I waded into the throng of chirping socialites and their daughters and nieces and cousins and friends. At the heart of the commotion, I imagined, the First Lady stood like an overstuffed cherry blossom centerpiece. They all pretended to know each other the way rich, influential people often do, bound by an unspoken unity of purpose: at all costs, stay on top.

I asked the concierge where I could find the Chinese Room, the location of the luncheon. He pointed across the lobby to the promenade. "Walk to the end," he said. "Mrs. Closs has asked us to remind attendees to have their invitations out." I shook my purse at him, signaling I had mine nearby.

As I passed a massive bronze torchère, Moira emerged around the corner. She'd swapped her robin's-egg blue suit for a belted lizard-green pencil dress adorned by an enormous diamond-and-pearl-encrusted brooch shaped like—what else?—a cherry blossom. As always, she was elegant and heartless, a spiked suit of armor under all that professional tailoring. She searched the crowd, intent on something, her peacock feather fascinator spinning back and forth like a weathervane in a windstorm. I imagined she was poised to leap into action and summon everyone to the banquet room. When she spotted me, her eyes widened, and she frowned. As I approached, her frown sunk into a scowl. "What in the hell are you doing here?" she growled under her breath. "Relentless, aren't you?"

"I have an invitation." I opened my purse and showed her.

"How?" Her face showed surprise, and then, she put it together. "Edith."

"Why did you invite her?"

"I thought she might like to have lunch and meet the First Lady. She's practically vanished from the social calendar. Poor thing."

"How thoughtful." My sarcasm sizzled.

"I know why I invited *her*." She looked over my shoulder, expecting, it seemed, for the other women to notice her any minute and stampede our way. "But I don't know why you showed up in her place." Her eyes narrowed. "We've said everything we need to one another—or did you come out of a self-destructive impulse, the proverbial moth to the flame?"

"I have something you've wanted for a long time, and I want to make a deal with you," I announced loudly, not caring if I embarrassed her. My anger toward her was strangely pleasurable. "Charlene's journal in exchange for Bogdan's coordinates."

Her gloved hand shot out and tugged me by the elbow. "Follow me." She whisked me down the promenade, her heels alternately clicking on the floor and muffled by carpet, holding her chin high and her eyes fixed at a point in the distance so as not to draw luncheon attendees' attention. She led me into the Grand Ballroom, a cavernous space with arched ceilings, an upper gallery on all sides, and a proscenium stage. I imagined men in tuxedos and women in jewel-toned ball gowns dancing to the jazz band on the stage and mingling in the galleries to each side, remnants of the '20s or '30s, perhaps friends of Coolidge, Hoover, or Roosevelt—the thought of which made the space more empty, more solemn, as if their ghosts were spinning through me.

A few paces in, Moira turned. "Why do you think I know anything about Adrian Bogdan or his whereabouts?"

"A hunch."

She laughed. "You think I'm horrible, don't you?"

"Yes."

Her gleeful expression snapped closed. "I'm not." She gave it thought, her large eyes growing still. "I'm a victim of Bogdan's, too."

"How's that?" I asked, genuinely wanting to know.

Secret knowledge writhed under her powdered skin, lined lips, and green-gold eye shadow. She was pushing seventy and disguised it well—or had a professional cover it up. I noted the deepening wrinkles, the cracks in her foundation, and the crumbs of mascara stuck in her eyelashes. "Tell me, Judy. Do you ever wonder if you're the problem?"

"What do you mean?"

"Maybe *you* are the monster."

"I don't want to hear it." To hell with her bigotry.

"I'm not talking about your parents or your sex life."

Didn't she want to return to those fawning pastel birds in the lobby? She didn't want to be right here now. But she emitted no sense of urgency. She seemed delighted to linger, carving more grooves into my heart. "Spit it out, Moira."

"You've done bad things, too, my dear." She waved her gloved finger at me. "You and your friend are responsible for my son's death. You don't have a right to judge me so harshly."

I didn't want to discuss the bad things she thought we'd done. Everyone is the hero of their own story. Moira was no different. "I'll give you the journal," I said. "I'll offer up that peace of mind for you, but only if you tell me where to find Bogdan." I stepped forward, pushing against my fear of her—a fear deeper and older than my hatred, a fear of the power she could wield over me, a power she'd used in the beginning when she orchestrated my adoption and ripped me from the Bakers' arms. I wondered if I'd seen her sneering, flame-blue eyes as an infant and burst into tears. "Whatever you think of me. Whatever I think of you. You must acknowledge that Bogdan is vicious and won't stop killing." She blinked, her brilliant glare still unsettling. It was as much acknowledgment as I was going to get.

"I'm not a monster," she said with an air of finality as if it was a fact I must accept.

I tried to muster something to say that would nudge the conversation forward and didn't betray my feelings. My hatred of her was keen as ever, and I wanted her to feel it, for it to burrow into her thin flesh and wriggle alongside her secrets. "If you're not a monster, then the hell if I am."

"Very well." She smirked. "That's fair."

I leaned into her, making her recoil a fraction. "For the last time, will you lead me to Bogdan?"

She didn't budge an inch, and her breath stank of gin, perhaps a pre-lunch warm-up martini. "I'm not going to help you, Judy. You've brought me nothing but pain. Why should I?"

My frustration boiled over. "If you don't help us," I said, my voice growing louder, echoing through the vast room, "we'll send copies of the journal—my aunt's recordkeeping skills were impeccable—to all the media establishments in the region. You'll be exposed and completely ruined."

Her glassy eyes trembled with fury, but before she could speak, I added, "I bet those FBI boobs you won't talk to will be upset about its contents, especially the passages about them."

In truth, the journal said little about her dealings with spooks and much about her treatment of me and the Bakers, which would be embarrassing, but not what she really feared. I was hoping she wouldn't call my bluff.

She ran her tongue across her upper lip. "Fine. You win. Do you have it now?"

"No," I said, a little startled by her sudden willingness to barter.

"Bring the journal to my house tomorrow at noon, and I'll point you in the right direction. That's the best I can do." She swiveled away from me. "I must go. You've held me up enough." She took several steps to the door, paused, and turned. "You're welcome to join us, even though you swiped that invitation from poor Edith. After all, you've dressed for the occasion." She scanned my outfit. "I like your ensemble."

"No, thank you."

"If you want to see a real monster rear its many heads, keep those ladies from their champagne flutes." She smiled. "Until tomorrow."

And with a ripple of lizard-green silk, she was gone. The hammering of my heart slowed, and the vastness of the ballroom flooded in. I nodded to its dim corners, bidding farewell to the ghosts eavesdropping on us, soaking in our muted rage.

CHAPTER 20

MAY 4, 1954, LIONEL

Leaving the mellow ambiance of Croc's behind, I blunder into the alley, distracted. My bourbon didn't have the intended effect. Instead of smoothing my nerves, it's unbalanced me, nudging my suspicions toward beliefs: Why are Judy, Philippa, and Iris lying to me? What do they know about the photo they're not telling me? Why be so damn cagey?

It's night, and the alley is draped in shadow. A pang of fear stops me. Since the beating I took after the sit-in at the Little Palace cafeteria, I steer clear of empty streets and back alleys, especially at night. Even if my head is in the game, my body usually says, "No, sir. You're not doing this. Turn back." I consider returning to Croc's, but the thought of staring into the eyes of those women and wondering what they know about Roger pushes me forward, past my aversion. The bourbon helps, too.

I kick through trash strewn on the ground, and an empty bottle clatters. I dodge several stacked crates, perhaps shipping materials for merchandise sold in the hardware store, and steer around a large dumpster rank with decomposing food. I set my eyes on a car parked at the end of this backstreet canyon. The gleam of the hood and chrome fender serves as a beacon, guiding me out of the alley's claustrophobic grip. But the pool of pale yellow from the streetlight doesn't cut the gloom as I emerge onto 11th Street.

Someone calls my name, and I spin.

Two men in suits, one from either side of the alley's opening, fly at me. I wonder if it's a hallucination, some reverberation from Little Palace, but it's not. I should've listened to my body. The first man, squat, thick-necked, and bald, punches me in the abdomen. My stomach molds around his fat fist, and I double over, gasping for air, pain shooting up through my chest and down to my groin. When I try to stand straight—*"Never let them see you flinch!"*—the other man, shaped like a V with sandy brown hair and eyes like black pebbles, smashes his fist into my jaw, knocking me off-balance and causing me to twist and stumble into the car, a cream-colored Buick Roadmaster. I smear blood across its glossy finish and, insanely, think how pretty the contrast is—abstract expressionism! I slide to the curb, confused and dizzy, my cheek throbbing, my brain buzzing in my skull. What's happening? Jesus, what *is* happening?

As if from the bottom of a murky pond, the faces of the three young men who attacked me after Little Palace surface. I see their hot, hateful eyes. Their gritted teeth. Their oily hair. Their raw acne. The tendons in their necks. The blood vessels in their foreheads. The stains on their T-shirts, on their jeans. I hear their slurs, their jeers. I feel a shower of their spit and sweat and their fucking relentless fists and boots.

I interviewed one of them. I know I did. I didn't imagine it. I remember now. How odd. When I asked him if he supported the sit-in, he said he did, that it was the right thing to do. He said it for the *Washington Afro-American*. He was a supporter of his Negro brother. Why say something like that and then beat me? It makes no sense. Why am I remembering it now?

Maybe it's the gift of insight before you die.

I'm going to die.

The bald man scoops me up, his massive hands gripping me under my arms—pain like a thousand needles blasts through me. As soon as I'm upright, he shoves me down again across the hood of the Buick. The metal pops against my body. I worry about the car, about denting it. He twists my arm violently behind my back, my shoulder screams like it's been dislocated. He's pressing my cheek into the cold steel. The weight of his thick body crushes me. I hear him grunting. I wonder if he's enjoying this—some man's man, bending me over a car. Does he want to have his way with me? I laugh—or is it just that I want to laugh? Then, like that, I hate him with burning intensity. He wrenches my arm, and I scream out. The V-shaped goon leans into me and—his voice soft, a purr—emits a stream of slurs. I hear them, but I don't hear them. They spill over me but bead up and dribble away. I'm thinking again about the boy who supported the sit-in and then beat the shit out of me and stole my wallet. When I interviewed him, he struck me as sincere, kind even. He was handsome but wet behind the ears. Had I flirted with him? Did that do it? Oh god, is that why?

Baldy twists my arm again, and I'm sure he wants to pop it out of its socket. He wants to dismember me. I sense that rage in him.

Is dismember the opposite of remember?

I'm going to die.

Mr. V slaps his hand over my outstretched arm as it flops helplessly on the slippery hood. With his other hand, he grabs my forefinger—which seems far away from me, somebody else's forefinger, an onlooker's forefinger, a memory of a forefinger.

I'm breaking apart. Eroding. Dis-remembering.

He yanks this forefinger back hard—and I know it's *my* forefinger; the pain is sharp and clarifying: They despise me, I know, but not for the reasons they give themselves. That boy despised me years ago because he thought I'd flirted with him, and he'd liked it. But *had* I flirted with him? Did I remember it right?

V leans in and pierces me with his dark eyes, little glittery pinpoints, and growls, "I'll bend all of your fingers back until I break them off. You'll never write again." He moves closer, his cigarette-soured breath pouring into my nostrils. "Stop asking about the dead girls, or we'll break every bone in your fucking body. Hear me?"

"What?" a small, confused voice murmurs deep inside me. *"He knows who I am? He knows about our novel."*

I hear a commotion behind me. Feet sliding against gravel. Glass shattering. Someone yelling. A woman.

V releases my finger and withdraws, the flap of his coat opening to reveal a revolver holstered to his hip. He moves out of my view. He's not going to kill me. He would've just shot me and skipped the walloping if he was planning to. The relief is merciful, but Baldy still holds me tight, my left arm wrenched behind my back, his bulk flattening me against the Buick.

V shouts at whoever is behind me: "I'll put fucking holes in all of you!"

"You're going to shoot *all* of us?" the woman challenges. "Really?"

I know the voice. Judy.

For a moment, the sound of traffic from U Street, half a block away, floods in. I'm aware of panting bodies, mental gears turning, and a call being made: Will it be bloodshed or discretion? I know now that these goons didn't attack me out of infantile hatred, not for the reasons the boys struck me, but with a colder purpose: to scare me away from our research, our book, to make sure *The Tattoo Artist* wouldn't be written. Since the fire, I'd been insulted, suspected, blackmailed, beaten, and threatened. What did we get ourselves into, Roger?

Baldy releases me. For a long time, I wait. Then, slowly, I prop myself up on my elbows, and with my uninjured left hand, I push my weight off the hood. My shoulder announces itself, but I need to be upright, so I ignore the pain and find my feet. The creamy metal is dented, blood smeared. My jaw aches, my guts are mush, and my finger sings a dreadful tune. I clutch it with my other hand to quiet the pain. Maybe it's broken. Too soon to tell.

As I turn, I see V and Baldy running down the sidewalk, flashing in the streetlight and vanishing into the darkness. Iris throws down a board she's clutching, perhaps a crossbar from one of the storage crates, a makeshift weapon, and rushes to me, asking me if I'm hurt, if I'm damaged. I mutter, "My finger," and show it to her.

She cups my hand in hers, inspecting it gently. "We need to tend to it and maybe get you to the hospital. It's swelling," she says. "Can you wiggle it?"

I can, but the pain screams.

"That's good," she says and scans my face. "What happened here?"

"I'm okay," I squeeze out. "I took one to the jaw."

She chuckles. "Like a prizefighter."

I give her wearied eyes. "I need a drink."

"Let's get you home."

Judy and Philippa come into view. Philippa is crouching, slowly depositing a brick on the ground, another impromptu weapon. Judy is still standing, gripping a broken wine bottle by its neck, her arm tensed, and her feet spread apart as if she's still prepared to leap into action and slash one of my attackers. Her face is hard, bright, angry, and a little terrified, but she's keeping it well hidden. I know that look. That struggle. She's keeping a lot well hidden. "You can put it down," I say, wincing at the pain in my jaw. As if out of a trance, she awakens, her eyes blinking. She tosses the bottle to the side, where it shatters, and we go.

CHAPTER 21

APRIL 1954, JUDY

Before leaving the apartment for Moira's, Philippa walked in on me using a straight edge and utility knife to excise several pages from my aunt's journal. I was removing them carefully so that when Moira flipped through the book, which she was sure to do, she wouldn't notice their absence. In reality, the pages contained passages I didn't want her or, frankly, anyone to see. Private matters between Charlene and me. But their removal served a dual purpose. Once she read the journal, she'd notice inconsistencies and, on closer inspection, the missing pages. We were buying time and maintaining the threat of what she might believe those pages contained. Her paranoia was our advantage.

When I explained to Philippa what I was doing, she griped I'd never allowed her to read the journal in its entirety. A complaint she'd registered before. "I don't have the right, I know," she said, "but I don't understand your resistance either."

Charlene was a beautiful and intelligent woman, a keen observer of the world, but selfish and bigoted. She'd become swept up in the Closses' chaos, which marked her for tragedy. The last time I saw her alive, she'd said, "Judy, I was a fool. I should've looked after you better, but I couldn't see beyond my desires." It was already too late, though. It was difficult for me to let Philippa read those pages. It was my story, but through another's eyes, colored with those layers and impressions. I wanted her to have the story from my point of view. I explained it to her, and despite her disappointment, she seemed to understand.

Redirecting with a non sequitur, I asked Philippa, "Do you know where we left the Silly Putty?" It had been floating around the apartment, appearing and disappearing, it seemed, at will. She gave me a puzzled look and shrugged. I asked her to search the kitchen and living room. "We may need it," I told her. She left me baffled but on a mission. I tucked the extracted journal pages in a safe hiding place.

Our taxi ascended Moira's steep driveway through a thicket of trees. By way of the Capitol City Hardware fortune, her dead husband had out-fitted her with a pretentious English manor–style home at the end of a secluded cul-de-sac in Chevy Chase, Maryland. With high-pitched gables, oversized chimneys, and clusters of small windows, the exterior had an unsettling face-like quality. Its reproduction leaded glass windows cast a penetrating glare. The weather-worn statues of mythological gods and beasts positioned at intervals in the gaps in the boxwood that lined its turnaround heightened the effect. Who knows? Perhaps we were being observed. I was beginning to get used to it. It was hard to believe we'd returned to this house by choice, a place we'd fled from through the snow five years ago, but here we were, prepared to duel at high noon. We paid our driver to wait. We didn't want to linger after swapping the journal for information on Bogdan.

Moira's mammoth iron knocker, a snarling Green Man gripping a vine-like ring between his teeth, stared back at us. The taxi's motor died behind us. We hesitated, a little afraid, but I said, "Go ahead. What choice do we have?" Philippa reached for the knocker, but I pointed to the doorbell.

She rang it, and after a few moments, a solemn woman in her forties opened the heavy door and said, "Hello," and smiled without her eyes. "You must be Judith Peabody and Philippa Watson."

"The last name is Nightingale," I said, more harshly than I should have. "But, yes, it's us."

"Miss Nightingale, then," she said lifelessly. Her mousy brown hair was cut short, and she wore a functional navy dress and tan cardigan. "I'm Agnes Streppo. Mrs. Closs's secretary." She was the woman I spoke to while pretending to be a beautician from Tres Beaux on the phone. "She's waiting for you on the veranda."

We followed her through Moira's manor house mock-up, complete with mahogany paneling, exposed rafters, vibrant and hectic floral wallpaper, oriental carpets, various Indian artifacts hung and pinned to the walls like spoils of the conquistadors, and her portrait of Queen Elizabeth—the First, not the newly crowned queen—which drew a conspicuous line between the owner and a monarch famous for her shrewd leadership. Both the front hall and the lounge we passed through strived for timeless-ness, sullied only by a television set in the corner of the room.

We'd been here before, of course, but the flash of déjà vu followed by the tremors of fear I was anticipating didn't surface. We were older now, more worldly, and Moira's lavish abode struck me as an even greater sham than it did in 1948. In Paris, I visited the Colonnade de Carmontelle at Parc Monceau, an artificial Roman structure inspired by an eighteenth-century trend in England, where the British aristocracy constructed fake ruins to lend an air of nostalgic decay to their gardens, suggesting a rich familial history, a prominent bloodline preserved in stone and mortar. Ah, the past—wasn't it glorious? All of this was, of course, pure fantasy. I wondered how self-invented Moira was. Were her swagger, hawkish demeanor, and tailored outfits an artifice, a show? Did it matter? After all, eventually, the masks we wear become indistinguishable from our skin.

We followed Miss Streppo through the conservatory, a glassed-in room at the back of the house, lined with vegetation and potted flowers, and through its door to the verandah, which I noted had a simple locking mechanism. I made eye contact with Philippa. We'd separated the Silly Putty between us in the cab ride and agreed that, if we had the chance, we'd use the rubbery substance to discreetly fill in the slot in a lock's strike plate to keep the retractable bolt from catching. We wanted to make it easy to slip back in le manoir de Moira, retrieve the journal, and locate the damning photos she had of Roger, Lionel, and us.

On a slate patio surrounding her still-winterized swimming pool, Moira was reclining in a lounge chair wearing slacks, a houndstooth wrap, and a straw hat. The sky was mostly clear, with only a wisp of a cloud in the distance. She was reading *Newsweek*. On its cover, two women were gleefully road-tripping in a convertible. Over them, in a slash of yellow, it read: THE BOMB: WHAT ODDS FOR SURVIVAL NOW? What a contrast, I thought, as she lowered the magazine. The sunlight glistened off the lenses of her tortoiseshell sunglasses, making it impossible to read her expression.

Miss Streppo announced us and asked if, since it was Friday, she could be excused for the afternoon. Moira nodded, and Miss Streppo left, her heels clacking on the stone.

For a long moment, Moira said nothing. The caw of a crow punctuated the silence. And then: "Well, do you have it? I'm not interested in being convivial today."

"You're never interested in being convivial," Philippa said.

Moira sat up and turned, flinging her magazine to the side. "Let's stop wasting time." Her lips tightened. She seemed irritated, not quite what I was expecting.

"I have the journal," I said, retrieving it from my coat pocket. "But before I give it to you, I want Bogdan's address. We want to know where he's hiding out."

Moira stood with surprising speed, her large straw hat casting a shadow over us, our own little solar eclipse. She removed her glasses, and her eyes, like her lips, seemed tight, distressed even. She moved her mouth as if it were difficult to form words and said, "It's dangerous for me to give you that information." She breathed out of her nose and lowered her voice. "It's dangerous for you, too."

I didn't know what to make of her warning. Did she really give a damn?

Philippa piped up: "It doesn't matter. We can't let him continue—"

"To murder girls," Moira finished for her. "Yes, I know. Dear God, I know." She gave us a little dismissive wave. "You two are up against someone who can crush you without a spike in his blood pressure."

"Give us the address," I demanded. Now I was the impatient one.

From her slacks pocket, she produced a small piece of paper. Holding it between her fingers, she said, "Here's his address. It's in the slums of Southwest DC." She waved it like a little flag of surrender. "It's not a safe place. There's a lot of condemned buildings, a result of the urban renewal program."

"Negro removal program," I said, remembering Iris referring to it that way.

"We'll be fine," Philippa said.

"Well, you were warned." She dangled the piece of paper in front of us. Now it was a lure. "So, I have the address. Now it's your turn."

I held out the red-brown leather journal, slightly cracked with age, and we made the exchange. I quickly glanced at the address, somewhere on G Street SW, not far from where Bogdan had moored his houseboat in 1948. Moira opened the journal and flipped through it, not noticing the pages I'd removed. "Is this everything?" she asked. "I hope you're playing fair."

"We're playing as fair as you are." I smirked.

I expected her to toss a sarcastic remark at us, but instead, she said, "Be careful." She uttered it with a strange tonelessness, making it difficult to interpret. Did she mean "Be careful" as in "Don't push it with me!" or "Be careful" as in "Watch out. Proceed with caution"? I couldn't tell. Maybe she was being ambiguous on purpose.

Sensing that I'd stalled out, Philippa cleared her throat.

"We should go," I said.

Moira slipped on her sunglasses. "Yes, you should."

On our way out, Philippa pantomimed tripping on a loose brick, grasped the edge of the conservatory doorframe to steady herself, and cleverly used her palm to cram the Silly Putty into its catch without, I hoped, drawing suspicion. Perhaps Moira would find it; perhaps she wouldn't. Even if she did, I'm sure there were other ways in.

⊙━━┼━━⊙

It seemed impossible I would be invited to Sunday dinner at the Watsons, but Philippa's stepmother made the gesture. Although we'd delayed the inevitable for nearly six months, we failed to keep our living situation a secret. Philippa's parents had been shockingly uncritical when she blundered into revealing we were roommates, the result of some blurt about how she was covering rent with my help. After she moved in with me, she'd reflected on how odd it was they hadn't interrogated or shamed her for living "in sin" with Stan. "Perhaps they were relieved," I told her. "Better to live in sin with a man than to live in sin with a woman." Philippa protested, "They can't imagine I like women. Completely oblivious." But I suspected that they worried in the backs of their minds, and Stan, I'm sure, relieved that brewing anxiety. Other than a phone call or two—that I knew of—Stan had faded fast, but he still camouflaged us from their suspicions.

Served in the early afternoon, dinner was glazed ham, green bean casserole, potatoes, and ambrosia salad. Conversation flowed uneasily. Bonnie chattered about nothing: the beautiful weather, a sale at Hecht's, and how difficult it was to get coffee stains out of her porcelain sink. Carl, on the other hand, went on about the news. He told us Ed Murrow's criticism of McCarthy on *See It Now* was "a brilliant move," and he called the senator "a sinking ship." He showed admiration for Eisenhower's speech on the domino effect theory. "McCarthy's a fool," he said, "but communism is a serious threat. If Vietnam falls, all its neighbors will." Shifting to a lighter mood, he asked us if we'd heard about Walt Disney's plan to build an amusement park in California called Disneylandia. We had, of course. When it opened, we'd save up and go.

Eventually, Philippa asked to use the convertible for a drive in the country. "We want to take in the spring bloom," she said too brightly. Of course, it was a lie, and Carl seemed to sense it. He studied her for a beat. Then he smiled and told her she could take the Bel Air, but she needed to fill it with gas. Bonnie rose from the table to begin cleaning up, and I joined her in the kitchen. When I returned for more plates, Carl had opened the Sunday paper, and Philippa had vanished.

After saying goodbye, we slid quickly into Carl's blue 1951 Bel Air. We left its top up, though. Where we were going, we didn't want to be exposed. Philippa exhaled as if she'd been holding her breath for the last two hours. She handed me her purse, which felt unusually heavy, and started the car, its engine roaring to life. As we pulled away, I reached into her purse, felt the cold shock of metal, and lifted out a silver snub-nosed revolver by its handle. "What's this?" I asked.

"A gun," she said, stating the obvious.

"So, that's where you were while I was scrubbing Bonnie's fine china."

"Yes," she said. "I thought we needed protection."

"Do you know how to shoot it?"

"Dad taught me." She shrugged and offered me a blasé frown. "I also shot his service pistol once, but it's too big and clunky."

"*Carl* taught you?"

"He's practical, remember." She mimicked a husky male tone, "A woman needs to learn how to protect herself."

"I'm impressed."

"Ugh," she said, "don't be. I hate guns, but we need it."

I returned it to her purse. Delicately.

"I'm a pretty good shot," she added, her left eyebrow lifting.

"I'm sure you are."

CHAPTER 22

MAY 4, 1954, LIONEL

After Iris carefully cleans up my face, I hold a kitchen towel full of ice on my wounded finger and sit in a chair with saggy springs, making me feel trapped, ensconced, as if gravity were more concentrated in this spot. Philippa and Judy are on Iris's couch, their faces like sad tragedian masks, limp and listless, but masks all the same. Finally, Iris arrives with a glass of whiskey, and I throw it back, the liquid burning down my throat and flooding me with warmth. I ask for another, and she retrieves it. I look at Judy and Philippa. "Who were those men?"

"Thugs," Judy says wearily.

"Nah," I mutter. "They weren't street thugs. They had holstered revolvers and shitty suits."

"Strange." Philippa squints like she's racking her brain. "What did they want with you?"

"Wanted me to stop writing about the murdered girls. To trash *The Tattoo Artist*. That licking was a threat. They're coming for me if I continue to poke around in that story."

Philippa glances at Judy, who returns a stern glare.

"Is there something you want to tell me?" I shift in the chair and groan aloud. The soreness is settling in and working its way to my core. My finger throbs despite the numbing cold of the ice.

Iris appears behind the other two, her long slender face and dark eyes soft with concern—and maybe a touch of exasperation. "Look," her hands fall to her hips, "enough with this. We need to—"

"We need to come clean," Judy breaks in. "We've seen one of those creeps before. The tall one."

Philippa begins to fiddle with the seam of her sweater.

"Where?" I sit up and, registering the deep ache in my body, clamp down my teeth.

"After having dinner with you and Roger at your apartment," Philippa says, rubbing the arm of the sofa with her palm, petting it like an animal. "He was lurking in your lobby."

"Lurking?"

"We bumped into him coming out of the elevator."

I mull over this new information. "Why didn't you mention it before?"

I get nothing from Judy, and, fidgeting, Philippa says, "We didn't think anything of it. He seemed out of place, but we had no idea he was there to snoop or hurt anyone."

"And you were drunk," Judy adds, smirking.

Ignoring her, Philippa continues. "Maybe these guys, whoever they are, know something about the girls, about their murderer."

Judy drops her hand on Philippa's leg.

"You think so?" I say, laying on the sarcasm.

Iris turns her back on the conversation and walks into the kitchen.

Exhausted, I let out a low moan as dull pain spreads through my body. Philippa springs to her feet, but I gesture for her to sit down. From the day of the fire, she and Judy have been by my side. Again tonight, they saved me. A detail I hadn't considered before pops into my mind, and I ask, "Why were you two already at the apartment building?"

They look puzzled.

"When I arrived, the apartment was ablaze, and you were already there?" I remember them flanking me, staring up at the flames and smoke. "Why?"

"Oh," Judy mutters, caught off guard, "we were in the neighborhood."

"So, it was just a coincidence," I say, again with sarcasm.

"Yes," Philippa says. "We've dropped by before, haven't we?"

I'm suddenly aware of a dampness on my leg. The ice has started to leak, soaking into my pants and the upholstery. I grab it with my good hand, set it aside, and reach for my whiskey. The amber liquid is the only thing giving me solace right now.

"Let us help you," Judy says.

"No!" I snap and, softening my response, add, "I'm fine." I drink up. As the burn eases through me, I wish Roger was here. He'd gently pry the truth from them.

Judy's expression is serene, impenetrable. How can she be so sealed off? When I first met her, her haughty remoteness was understandable, even charming. She was protecting herself, holding the truth of her identity close to her chest. The result, intended or not, was mesmerizing. She floated a little higher than most of us and, on occasion, would descend goddess-like and zap us with her sharp wit. Being within the circumference of a personality like hers is a pleasure because you're in on the joke, smirking alongside them. Now, though, I'm on the outside, on my own.

Despite needing rest, my desire to understand is stronger, drug-like. "When I showed you the photo of Adrian and Anna," I say to Judy, reaching into my coat pocket, "I saw a look of recognition in your eyes. You're holding back. Why?"

She frowns, bewildered. She's not going to tell me.

My hand searches one pocket and then another. "Shit," I say, pushing myself up and out of the chair. A sharp pain shoots through me, but I ignore it.

On my feet, I thoroughly inspect my coat and pants pockets. The photo of Bogdan and Anna is gone. I lost it, or V and Baldy took it. If that's true, then they knew what to look for. "Damn it!" I cry out, my frustration melting into hot anger. I stamp my foot—yes, like a child—and glare at Judy. Her calm black eyes are empty and inscrutable and utterly maddening. I say, also somewhat inscrutably, "You have no goddamn idea who you are, do you?"

She winces as if I'd just slapped her.

"You're still walking around like you're a white woman, but your skin—it isn't a white woman's skin, is it?" I take her by the arm and yank her to her feet. I hold my forearm against hers, elbow to elbow, wrist to wrist. Our skin tones are close in hue, somewhere between cocoa brown and olive. "We're the same!" I shout. "But you're wearing a white mask. You're hiding out, playing pretend." I step close to her and whisper, "I know you as plain as day, but you have *no* idea who you are." I'm being cruel, but I can't help myself. That confused boy from Little Palace, V, and Baldy—they're climbing up from my heart and out of my throat, swinging punches again.

Judy's eyes are damp, trembling, but her mouth is a fierce slit. She's not going to melt. She stares at me hard, then growls through her teeth, "Don't lecture me about hiding out, Ray Kane. You're no better."

I let her go and stumble backward, my heel knocking into the towel of ice, scattering half-dissolved cubes across the floorboards. I find the chair and lower my body into it, letting the agony shut out my hectic and spiraling thoughts.

"I'm sorry," I mumble, ashamed. "I'm not myself now."

CHAPTER 23

APRIL 1954, JUDY

Southwest DC was primarily a working-class Negro neighborhood. Bart and Edith—as well as, I imagine, Philippa's parents—considered it a blight on the city. Many wealthy Washingtonians did. In their view, the blocks of old brick row homes and storefronts standing between the Mall and the confluence of the Anacostia and Potomac Rivers marred great monoliths like the Washington Monument, the Capitol, and other gleaming marble and granite government buildings. Since the war, cities were getting funding from the Feds to renew the slums, but—as Iris had explained—in many cases, it'd become an excuse to force out Negro families and business owners, raze the old structures, and build new city blocks and neighborhoods, populated with white families and businessmen. We didn't know what to expect, but we knew the address Moira had given us wasn't near a streetcar or bus stop. Whatever we were heading into, we were happy to be in the protective cocoon of the Bel Air.

On Fourth Street, SW, we drove past grocery stores, restaurants, barber shops, and churches. The sidewalks were teeming with a mixture of Negros and whites who, in this part of town, mainly were Jews. This area didn't have the shine of downtown, the self-importance of Capitol Hill, or the pompous prestige of Chevy Chase, but it wasn't a wasteland. Sure, there were boarded-up storefronts and empty lots high with weeds, but it was clean and neat and mostly just people being people. As we turned onto G Street, I spotted a Negro woman about my age, leaning against the outside of a corner market next to a Pepsi-Cola sign, smoking a cigarette, chin tilted up, sunglasses on. Her thin, gangly frame, light skin tone, and short hair reminded me of my own. If things had been different, I could've been her. This neighborhood could've been my neighborhood, which was alarming. A rush of gratitude to the Peabodys ballooned in me—they'd saved me from this, from being ordinary, from poverty—but the feeling quickly deflated. The life I've had—the life I'm *having*—isn't my own. Edith and Bart adopted me to play the role of Jackie. I'd failed at it. Spectacularly and justifiably. But I'd slipped into another role: the anti-Jackie, a part defined purely by its opposite. My smoking doppelgänger haunted me. I knew she wasn't the sort who played roles, and that made her lucky—and free.

As we turned onto G Street, the pedestrians thinned out. After a few blocks, the homes on either side, with some exceptions, became rundown or uninhabited. Sure, there was one with newly painted trim. Another with flowers blooming in its window boxes. But mostly, it was squalid—the sight of which would've satisfied Edith's notion of this neighborhood as endless tracts of urban decay. Several blocks in, Philippa parked the car behind a black sedan that had seen better days and switched it off. I scanned the street. Not a soul in view. A bulldozer, construction equipment, and debris dominated a vacant lot on the corner. This entire block was probably slated for "renewal."

"There," Philippa said, nodding at the dreary two-story row house with boarded-up windows on the ground floor, a small strip of overgrown yard, and lush Virginia creeper vines crawling up its face, digging its tendrils into the mortar. The deepening shadows from the late afternoon sun didn't increase its appeal.

"Do you *really* think we'll find him here?" I asked, still staring at the building. My spine prickled with dread. This could easily be a trap or a wild goose chase. I was doubtful Moira had given us the correct information, but what else were we supposed to do? I was sick of being followed and feeling watched. Someone had to put an end to Bogdan, and it wasn't going to be the police.

"How should I know?" Philippa said. "But we're here."

The thought of staring Bogdan in the face, of confronting him, seemed abstract and still out of reach. For many years, he hovered phantom-like at the back of my mind, and now I had trouble imagining him as a flesh and blood man. "God," I said, almost under my breath. "What do we do if we find him?"

Philippa lifted the revolver from her purse by its grip. "We'll use this," she said, her eyes locking with mine. "We'll make him surrender to us and turn him in." Handling it delicately, she slowly loaded it with bullets from her slacks' pocket.

That didn't make sense to me. Who would we turn him over to? Quincy or that cop from Harrisonburg, Piers Richardson? He'd been so helpful before. No, I didn't see them listening to us or taking us seriously, so I said, "Or we'll just shoot him."

Philippa gulped silently. "You mean, *I'll* shoot him."

She had it in her. She was a killer if she allowed herself to be. We'd been avenging angels before, but that was during the wild throes of adolescence when impulsiveness was our default. Now, I wasn't so sure. Her frustrating "good sense" might reign.

Refusing to acknowledge her anxiety, not wanting to give it life, I opened the car door and said, "Let's go."

As we approached the house, I noticed footprints on the dusty stairs leading up to the small landing in front of the door. The doorknob also appeared functional and clean. Over my shoulder, I whispered, "Should we knock or just enter?"

"I don't know," Philippa murmured. She was frightened. I was, too.

"It was a stupid question."

I tried the knob, and to my surprise, it turned, and the latch gave.

"You ready, Annie Oakley?" I said, my voice low. She held the gun with its muzzle toward the ground. "Aim it forward, not at our feet." She raised it, her hand trembling. I almost snapped at her to hold it steady but stopped myself. I couldn't do much better.

With adrenaline surging and my shoulders tight, I pushed the door wide. Beyond it, a hallway vanished into shadows, and stairs rose to a hazy second floor. The pungent odor of rot hurled itself at us, and an animal scampered into some far corner of the house. We stepped in, breathing through our mouths to mitigate the stench. We crept into a living room just to the right of the hall. The room was dim, lighted only by the sun peeking through the boarded windows. It was covered in dust and cobwebs and void of furniture. Its only feature was a small fireplace with a cockeyed mantel. I tried the lights, but nothing. The property had been abandoned some time ago.

We worked our way back to the dining room, also vacant, save a single lounge chair in the corner, stuffing bursting from its seat cushion, the handiwork of rodents. I silently begged the universe: "Don't let it be a rat." The faint, frantic scrape of small, clawed feet passed close by, and my stomach churned. That sound shook awake something deep in me. I was again the girl in a shadowy basement, surrounded by mewling, hissing cats. My scars began to itch. Philippa remained close to my side, clutching the shiny revolver with two hands. The glint of its metal offered a strange kind of solace.

We entered the kitchen. Light poured in through a window exposing the film of grime on the counters, table, and cheap linoleum flooring, its tiles curling up at the corners. The sink was relatively clean, its faucet dripping slowly, creating a rusty streak across its surface. I thought of Bonnie complaining about how difficult it was to get stains out of porcelain. One of the cabinet doors was ajar, so I opened it. Cans of beans and vegetables were neatly lined up inside. They didn't appear dusty. Maybe Bogdan is here—or *was* here. We noted the cellar door, but neither of us wanted to go down there without a flashlight or some other illumination, so we passed it by and returned to the bottom of the stairs at the front of the house.

The staircase was narrow, so I gestured for Philippa to go first. She paused and gave me wide eyes. Pushing through her fear, she thrust the pistol out in front of her, gripping it tightly, the muzzle making little shaky circles. We began our ascent, stepping softly, but despite our efforts, the risers creaked and popped. Every few steps, we'd pause and listen. Nothing but the buzzing of flies. Shafts of afternoon sun from the upstairs windows sliced through the air, particles of dust floating like powdered gold, brightening the dingy purple-and-green wallpaper.

Once we reached the upstairs hall, the odor of rot overwhelmed me. I retched, but nothing came up. Philippa gagged and covered her nose with her loose sweater. Something—or someone—had died up here. Flies were circling above us, bouncing off the walls. A flicker of gray suddenly shot across the floor. Philippa spun, aiming at it.

"Jesus!" I blurted. "Fuck."

"It's a mouse," Philippa said after catching her breath. "Or a squirrel—or something."

We waited for more movement. I expected Bogdan to leap from the doorway of one of the four rooms that made up the second floor, swinging a big knife or a baseball bat or his fists. But nothing, just the distant groans of a house slowly crumbling around us—and the drone of flies.

We moved on, starting with the room at the back of the house.

The afternoon sun pooled on its floorboards. Other than a small pile of clutter in the south corner, it was bare. Its mellow pink wallpaper of dancing circus animals suggested a children's room. I gestured to Philippa to stay by the threshold as I walked over to the clutter and nudged it with the toe of my Oxford. Most of it was trash—scraps of paper, old rags, a toy truck, a single children's shoe—but I noticed a small, framed photograph toward the bottom. I gently retrieved it, blew off the layer of dust, and brought it to the window. Its glass was cracked, and it had an overexposed blur on one side, but its subject matter was still visible—a young Negro woman, an older woman, a man, and a young boy, sitting around a dinner table, the table in the kitchen. They were smiling. I imagined they were the property's original owners and were now gone—bought out, run out, or both. I slid the photo into my purse. I felt protective of them, these people I'd never know.

Back in the hall, we were again assaulted with the stink of decay. I shoved my nose into the crook of my elbow, trying to soak in the residual odor of laundry detergent. Philippa, her sweater still over her nose, resumed her stance as markswoman, and we glanced into the bathroom. Also empty, except for a toilet, sink, and a crud-covered clawfoot bathtub with a yellowed plastic curtain strung from a tarnished rod.

A single open window illuminated the next room, its shabby semi-transparent curtain rippling in the breeze. It was the freshest smelling of the upstairs rooms, which wasn't saying much. In the middle of the wall, farthest from the door, was a stained mattress with a tangled ball of blankets at its foot. Beside it, empty cans of food and beer bottles, a portable stove, and a stack of old *Life* magazines littered the floor. A photo cut-out of young Shirley Temple beamed luridly on the wall above it. Bogdan had a thing for the actress—she resembled his sister. He'd made a shrine to her in his last den. Moira hadn't lied. He'd been here.

Beside me, Philippa whispered through her sweater. "We gotta get out of here—the smell."

"One more room."

Before we reached it, we knew the front room was the source of the putrid odor. Behind its closed door, we could hear the hum of flies. I looked at Philippa, who raised the pistol and nodded to me. I gripped the knob and flung it open. As I did, a whoosh of flies escaped, and the stench of decaying flesh collided with us, causing me to retch dryly and brace myself against the doorframe. Philippa dropped her sweater from her nose and heaved, vomiting Bonnie's glazed ham and green bean casserole.

"Oh God," she muttered after wiping her mouth on her sleeve.

Dust and flies swirled in the murky room. Heavy curtains shielded the windows, only a few ribbons of light breaking in around their edges. Like the other rooms, it was stripped of character and disintegrating. But the details alluded us because our attention was drawn to its center, where under a blanket on the bare floorboards lay a body.

A pang of horror shot through me, and I choked out, "There's someone . . ."

"I can't . . . I can't . . ." She whimpered and turned away.

I wanted to leave right now and beeline for our apartment. I imagined sinking my jittery, nerve-taut body into a warm tub of water and unfurling, able to breathe again.

But we'd made it this far, and I had to confirm that what we were looking at was, in fact, a body. So, I crept forward into the thick, palpable wall of stench. Flies zigzagged around me, bouncing off the walls and ceiling and me, my heart slamming against my sternum, my nose still shoved in the crook of my elbow. A few feet from the shrouded form, I knew two things: it was a body, and it was a girl. She was only about five feet in height, the tips of her fingers protruded from the side of the dark wool blanket, and strands of golden-brown hair spilled out of the edge nearest me. I didn't know much about forensics, but Nancy Jones and Susannah Lee, the only girls not found, had disappeared years ago. Their bodies would've been bones by now. This was a new, unreported victim.

I knelt to grab the corner of the blanket and throw it back. It was important to see her face. Maybe I could identify her later. But the blanket's surface was alive with flies and other insects. I recoiled. If I pulled back the shroud, would I see a face or only the ruins of one?

I thought of Jackie, of her photograph Edith kept in the hall, enshrined in an expensive frame and flanked by lilies. In a tam and houndstooth coat, she peered out inscrutably. The dead in photos and paintings tease us with the mystery of the beyond, the well-kept secret of death, holding it just out of reach, but Jackie, wearing a bemused, impish expression, offered a different challenge: "Is it death you want to know about, or how it feels to die as I did?" For years, I hated her for gripping that knowledge tightly with her little hands and how the Peabodys would use it against me. "You have no idea the horrors she went through, the anguish," they would cry. "You should be grateful you're alive and loved." But now I understood her taunt: I didn't want to lift the blanket from the girl's face. I didn't want to know.

Behind me, Philippa cried out. I stood up with a jolt and spun. Standing at the threshold, with her back to me, she aimed her pistol at something in the hall and pressed the trigger—once, twice. The gunshots flashed in the dark room and echoed through the house, rattling the mortar between bricks, cracking the plaster, and stirring the thick dusty air into coils. Or so I imagined.

"What is it?" I yelled, dashing toward her. The hall was empty.

"I don't know," she said, her face scrawled with shock. "I saw something move, and I just—"

"Let's get the hell out of here," I said, tugging her sleeve.

We bounded into the hall and down the staircase, our footfalls waking up every fly, every bit of dust, every horrible odor. Philippa held on to the gun but didn't point it forward—no time for that. We needed to get out. Now. The air seemed to be gathering force, becoming solid, even sentient. For a brief, irrational moment, I wondered if everything here was somehow an extension of Bogdan, his dark soul had seeped into all the cracks and crevices. His face surfaced in my mind: his bright blue eyes, his hard jawline, his mangled, rotten teeth. He was close, so close. We swung the front door open violently, flung ourselves outside, and scrambled to the Bel Air. Philippa tossed the pistol at me, fished the keys out of her pocket, and started the car.

She shifted into first and pulled out, hands clamped around the steering wheel. She quickly shifted into second and gunned it down G Street, only to come to a screeching halt at busy South Capitol Street. I could still smell the rot in my nostrils. I wanted to wash it off. I wanted to burn these clothes.

"Who was that on the floor?" Philippa asked, glancing at me. "Did you recognize her?"

"I don't know," I said. "But it was a girl, one of his victims."

"You didn't look at her?"

Shame stabbed through me. I was supposed to be the tough one who could stare a decomposing corpse in the face and keep my cool. "Did you hit what you were shooting at in the hall?" I threw back at her.

"Something moved in the room with the mattress."

"Something or someone?"

"A shadow."

"A shadow?"

"Not a mouse."

"You were scared."

"Of course I was."

She checked the rearview mirror. An older-style black Pontiac sedan pulled in behind us. Rust marred its finish. It was the car we'd parked behind in front of the house. I couldn't see who was driving from the glare on the window, not to mention the grime. Suddenly, the driver revved its engine.

"Go!" I yelled. "It's him."

Philippa pressed the gas, and the Bel Air lurched into oncoming traffic. Horns blared, and drivers swerved and cursed us. She integrated the car into southbound traffic, but it wasn't the way home. After about half a block, the Pontiac was back, just two cars away. "Jesus Christ," I grumbled. "He's following us."

Philippa spotted an opening in oncoming traffic and swung quickly onto K Street, wheels squealing. Looking back, I watched as the Pontiac brazenly maneuvered out of traffic and sped diagonally across the north-bound lanes to keep up with us.

"Faster!" I commanded her. "He's still after us."

"I'm doing what I can!" she cried and twisted the steering wheel to the right, veering onto Half Street. The tires cried out again. I caught a whiff of scorched rubber. She sped forward through an intersection, nearly smashing into a seafood delivery truck. We barreled toward M Street, but as soon as we were there, she slammed the car to a halt. M was bustling with rush hour traffic. "Damn it!" she yelled and shook the steering wheel.

We hadn't lost our pursuer. He was a block away and closing in.

Cars, taxis, and delivery trucks whizzed past us, giving us no oppor-tunity to pull out. We wanted to go east, but that seemed impossible. West wasn't much better. "Come on, come on!" I begged the universe. My stomach ached, and cold sweat soaked into my blouse. "Give us a break."

Ten yards away, the black car slowed, its chrome grille like gritted teeth.

"What's he doing?" I thought out loud.

"I'm trying to turn," Philippa said, stating the obvious. Her nerves were shot.

He began creeping toward us. I stared at the driver's side, but the glare concealed his face. Was Bogdan really in there? Had he followed us from his den of despair? Had he been watching us the entire time?

"We *have* to do something, Philippa."

"I know, I know."

"Come on!" I said harshly. "Pick a goddamn direction and gun it."

"I'm trying!"

The Pontiac's grille was nearly touching us.

"He's going to smash up your dad's car," I said, absurdly believing this would motivate her to charge into traffic and away from this creep. Anything for Daddy!

The bumpers made contact, and the Bel Air pitched forward. Under the Pontiac's visor, I saw the outline of a square jaw and what I thought was a smile. Suddenly, he threw on the gas, his engine grinding loudly, gravel spitting out behind him, and we began sliding into M Street.

Philippa looked at me, confused.

"He's shoving us into traffic," I said, fluttering with panic.

She stomped on the brake pedal, but the tires failed to grip the slick asphalt, and we continued to drift out, soon to become rush hour casualties. Passing drivers honked and gave us dirty looks. But what could we do but pray they'd continue to swerve and maybe stop?

"The gun!" Philippa shouted. "Use it to shoot out his tires."

I rolled down the window and snatched it from the seat beside me. I leaned out, twisted my torso, and clutched the revolver with both hands as Philippa had done. Forget the tires. I aimed at the driver's side. Wanting to kill him wasn't an ambiguous feeling, but did I have the skill to do it? I tugged at the trigger, and a shot rang out, sending a jolt through me. The bullet glanced off the hood, making a mark. I pulled it again. It hit the Pontiac's windshield with a pop, spider-webbing the glass but not shattering it. My finger tensed on the trigger, prepared to fire again, and suddenly we lurched forward, careening into M Street across the westbound lanes and heading east. Oncoming traffic screeched to a halt, and a green pickup twisted out of our way, its front wheel popping up on the curb and rolling over an A-frame sidewalk sign advertising "Fresh Strawberries, 30¢." Horns blasted, and cursing was sure to follow. Disoriented, I dropped into the seat, still grasping the pistol, my finger perilously resting on the live trigger. "Jesus."

"There was an opening. I had to take it," Philippa said breathlessly. "Sorry, I didn't warn you."

I glanced over my shoulder. The Pontiac had shot out after us, but a delivery van blocked him. The van's driver was getting out, and Bogdan was backing up on Half Street, his car disappearing behind a building.

Once we were blocks away, relatively safe, cool spring air whipping through the open window, I released the gun and laid it beside me. I was stunned at having used it—and a little thrilled.

⊶

Philippa parked in a space near our apartment and removed the keys from the ignition. She lowered her shoulders, leaned her head back, and, to release tension, groaned at the inside of the roof. I reached across the seat and took her hand, rubbing its top with my thumb. I was so proud of her, proud to be *hers*. I hadn't made sense of what we'd just experienced, but I was surprised by her tenacity and bravery. Her urge to break out, to make a bold gesture, was something she'd suppressed in the past, fearing it violated some notion of herself. Today, she blew through that notion. For several minutes we sat, quietly letting the dust settle from the chaos.

Still staring at the roof, she said, "I got vomit on my new sweater."

I laughed. "Oh, the horror."

She laughed, too. "Wanna smooch?" She puckered her lips at me.

"Brush your teeth first."

She frowned in jest. "Is it strange that I'm hungry?" She began inspecting a small streak of dried vomit on her arm.

"Nothing seems strange now, but yeah, it's strange. I really want a bath."

"Did you shoot out his tire?"

She hadn't seen what I'd done. When would she have? "No," I said, "I hit the windshield."

Her face sharpened with concern. "Did you hit him?"

"I don't know. I don't think so."

She chuckled. "Jesus, we're practically Bonnie and Clyde."

"Bonnie and Clydette."

A silence fell between us. I continued to rub her hand as I listened to the murmurs of passersby on the sidewalk. I was relieved to be in a neighborhood teeming with people.

She pulled her hand away and began resecuring her ponytail. "What do we do now?" she asked, turning to me.

"We should tell the police about the body."

"Yes," she said. "Someone might be looking for her, whoever she is."

"Can you phone Quincy and give him the address?"

"I'll get lectured, but yeah, I'll tell him." She smiled. "He'll do it for me."

"How will you explain the address?"

She considered it. "I'll tell him I have to protect the person who gave me the information." She chuckled. "That's ironic."

I lifted the revolver off the seat and handed it to her, "Keep this. We may need it again."

She gingerly took it from me. "I don't like it," she said, "but you're right. We should hang on to it. Dad's not going to miss it anyway."

"Can you ask to keep the car a day or two longer?"

"Why?" she asked. "He won't like that." She returned the gun and the remaining bullets from the pocket of her trousers to her purse.

I inhaled deeply, allowing my brain to unwind. "I can't tell if Moira sent us into a trap."

"What do you mean?"

"Well, if it was a trap, it wasn't a very good trap." I shook my head. "If he was lying in wait, why didn't he pounce when we were inside?"

"Maybe he didn't expect us to have a gun."

"Maybe." The more I thought about it, the less sense it made. "What about the car chase?"

"That *was* terrifying."

"Sure," I said, turning to her. "But clumsy."

A wrinkle formed on her smooth forehead. "I don't understand."

"So, Bogdan lurks inside, keeping his distance, but then he follows us and tries to shove us into traffic. It's a terrible way to murder someone but a great way to scare someone."

"You're saying . . . Wait, *what* are you saying?"

"We don't even know if it was Bogdan in the car. I never got a good look. We don't know if he was in the house. After all, you shot at a shadow, not a person. It could've been anyone, even one of those government goons who keep popping up wherever we go."

"What about the body?"

"She was Bogdan's latest victim. I'm sure, although I don't know why we haven't heard about her in the news. I don't know why she wasn't dumped like the rest. That's not his usual pattern. Maybe he left in a hurry?"

Philippa sat with all this, then brushed a stray hair away from her forehead. Blue-gray eyes glittering a little, she said, "Moira sent us there to scare us, not to get us killed."

"It's possible."

"Maybe she didn't know the body was there."

"Or she did and wanted us to discover it, knowing it would spook us."

She sighed. "What now?"

"We need to break into the Closs manse when Moira isn't home and have a snoop. She's still lying to us, and I want the journal back and the photos she claims to have of us."

"How do we do that?"

"A distraction."

"What sort of distraction?"

"We need Ray Kane's help."

"Roger," she said, her face lighting up.

"A decoy, if he's willing."

After mustering what remained of our energy, we exited the Bel Air. I paused in the late afternoon sun, absorbing its muted rays and trying to calm my nerves. Before I stepped away from the car, Philippa muttered, "Oh God." I wondered if she'd just registered the damage to the back bumper, something she'd have to explain away: "Sorry, Dad, we were the victim of someone's vicious parallel parking!" But she wasn't looking at the bumper. She gestured for me to come and see the other side.

Drawn in the dust on the Bel Air's dark blue fender were the Russian letters Эвридика or Eurydice—each letter precise and clear. Bogdan wrote it on his victim's bodies like a signature. It was a pointed and dramatic attempt to frighten us, and it proved nothing; he wasn't the only one with that knowledge. It was time to gain the upper hand and do something they didn't expect.

CHAPTER 24

I lick my wounds for a day. Iris wraps up my finger, and it swells, but it's not broken. I can move it again—a little. My jaw aches and bruises purple, but I lay low. Sleep is difficult. The beatings—the goons in suits from days ago and the boys from years ago—spin through my head, their faces and fists superimposed and swirling like a kaleidoscope. After my outburst at Judy, she's kept her distance. It's understandable. I lashed out hard, and—she's right—I need to answer for my hypocrisy. Still, I don't understand why they're lying to me.

So, this morning a new approach: I ring Detective Berg. He tells me he's planning to be near Dupont Circle around noon and can meet at the fountain. He doesn't want me dropping in on him at the station. Fine by me.

The weather is clear and cool. Water from the large marble fountain splashes over the robed figures representing stars, sea, and wind that hold up its goblet-like upper basin. It's pretentious but oddly soothing, and I'm glad for the sunshine. Detective Berg spots me. We shake hands, and when he notices my bruised face and wrapped finger, he says, "What happened?"

"The result of a friendly conversation."

We find a bench. Although he has circles under his eyes, with his breeze-tousled black hair and Adonis-like chin, he's no less handsome. Something is eating at him, though. I want to believe it's how the police have treated me, but I'm careful not to assume his allegiances.

"Did someone do this to you?" He sits a pace away from me. He doesn't want to be spotted sitting too close and be mistaken for a pansy. I don't want our meetup interpreted that way, either. We don't know who's watching.

"Two men," I say, "a bald guy and a tall guy, not your usual street roughs. They wore suits and had what I think were government-issued holsters. They knew who I was and ordered me to stop researching our new novel based on the unsolved murders of young girls in the metro region."

He raises his dark eyebrows.

"Frankly, I wish we'd never gone down that path."

"And they did *this* to you?" He nods at my damage.

"They almost broke off my finger," I say, holding it up, which makes it smart, "but your cousin, Judy, and Iris showed up and shooed them away."

His face tightens with concern. "Really?"

My next impulse is to tell him about the men stealing the photograph of Adrian and Anna, but I stop myself. I'd be admitting to swiping evidence from the apartment. It'd raise unwanted suspicion. Instead, I ask, "Have you ever heard of Adrian Bogdan?"

He studies me for a beat. "Yes," he says, clearing his throat. "How did you come by his name?"

"In my research. Also, one of the men who attacked me mentioned him." I lie, hoping Berg might fill some of the missing gaps.

"You know he was a suspect in several child murders back in 1948 but was exonerated. Howard Closs, the scion of the Capital City Hardware Closses, was the perp, but he died before he could be prosecuted."

"Yeah, I know about it."

"I'm sure Judy and Philippa told you everything they know, too."

This comment surprises me. Why would Quincy assume Judy and Philippa have special knowledge of child murders from 1948 and Bogdan's connection to them? Sure, they're interested in the case, but as outsiders, right? As fans of our novels? "They haven't said much to me."

"Maybe they don't like to talk about it. It's understandable, but it doesn't sound like them."

"We've shared details about the research," I say, keeping my tone conversational, even though I'm vibrating on the inside.

"But they didn't mention their involvement?"

"Involvement?"

"That's odd." He shrugs. "They had a front-row seat to the ordeal."

I bite my lip to hide the shock and relief I feel at receiving an answer to the question gnawing at me. "That so?"

"It's not exactly a secret."

I urge him on. "I don't get it." I need the entire truth.

"Judy is Judy Peabody. The Peabodys adopted her after Jackie was murdered. She changed her name to Nightingale a few years ago."

"Judy is Jackie's adopted sister?"

"In a sense—although they never met, of course."

"Damn." I struggle to understand how I could've missed this connection. "I didn't come across Judy's name in my research. I vaguely remember reading about an adopted child, but it would've been a small detail, not central at all."

"That's understandable," Berg says. "During the whole Bogdan-Closs affair, the Peabodys worked their connections and kept Judy and Philippa out of the papers. My uncle Carl and aunt Bonnie were relieved."

I watched the fountain water spill into the ground-level pool, its droplets catching in the midday light. I let it all sink in: Judy and Philippa had firsthand knowledge of a case in which Adrian Bogdan was a suspect, and they never mentioned it to us. I remembered Roger and me going on about it at dinner that night, explaining a story to them they already knew. Their deceitfulness burns me. If they're such fans, why not say something? Even now, after the fire, they hold back. Why? Then it gels: the anonymous packet of information—they sent it. That must be it. But why? I don't understand it.

"Look," Berg says, rubbing his knees, "there's something you need to know." He sounds serious, grim even. "I'm going to be straight with you. You lied about not knowing if Roger had a life insurance policy." My heart falls to my stomach. I twitch my finger, and pain flashes up my arm. "You're the beneficiary."

We're looking at each other now, and I don't detect malice in him, only a faint disappointment and perhaps fear. "I did know," I say, glancing at my feet. "It was stupid to lie."

"Why did you?"

I raise my chin and meet his eyes. "You don't understand what it feels like to be a Negro man in a station full of white cops, do you?" He seems perplexed, so I spell it out. "I didn't want to add something to that suspicion already embedded in you—all of you."

"Well," he says, unimpressed. "We were always going to find out. You just made it harder on yourself."

"Realize that now."

"You've given Colby and Shipley even more leverage."

He stands up and peers down at me. His handsome face is now decidedly less handsome. "So, this is the deal. Come to the station tomorrow morning at nine. The Raymonds will be there. Back up the brass and confirm that Roger is dead, and they'll stamp Roger's death a suicide." The ugliness of all this bothers him. He hates being their messenger. "I don't know what the insurance company will decide. The suicide clause in the policy may preclude you from collecting, but at least you'll be out from under the Metro PD's suspicious gaze."

"What are they hiding?" I ask.

Berg looks away and says, "Their ineptitude."

CHAPTER 25

APRIL 1954, JUDY

"Ring her and convince her to meet you," I said to Roger, sitting across from us at a hole-in-a-wall bar in Woodley Park called Allies Lounge. Reprints of famous photos from the Second World War—Iwo Jima, D-Day, the sappy kiss in Times Square—cluttered its limited wall space. It was late afternoon; besides a couple of barflies, it was empty. "We need to get her out of the house."

"Why?" he asked, wrapping his hands around his beer but not drinking it.

"We want to break in and search it," Philippa said.

"Jesus," he said, gazing at the amber liquid like a crystal ball. "What are you looking for?"

Philippa and I exchanged glances.

"More information on her connection to Bogdan," I explained, then elaborated on our experience in Southwest DC, including our discovery of the corpse. "She sent us there," I added, "and we want to know if she knew what we'd find."

At first, his face tightened with shock; then, it gradually eased into a concerned frown. "This is dangerous," he said, not fearfully but factually. He had the practical training of a soldier and was assessing the situation—a quality I admired. So, I met his somberness with strategy.

"Plan to meet her on Friday afternoon," I said. "Her secretary, Miss Streppo, takes off Fridays." I recalled her asking to leave during our visit to Closs Manor.

He pursed his lips, mulling it over. "What will I say to this woman when I meet her?"

"Tell her the truth," I said. "Tell her you're researching the murders of girls in our area and their connection to Adrian Bogdan. She'll be interested. Trust me."

"Does she know who I am?" he said.

"Possibly," Philippa said, sipping her beer. "It doesn't matter. She'll want to speak with you. She'll want to size you up."

"Give her crumbs," I said. "Whatever will keep her away from her house for an hour."

"How will I explain this to Lyle?" he asked, the staunch soldier in him wilting.

"Come up with a good excuse," I said, annoyed. Wasn't he one-half of Ray Kane? He knew how to improvise. Of course, I understood that Lionel was his soft spot. Hell, we were meeting in a dive bar because he was still intent on keeping Lionel out of the loop. I was uncomfortable withholding from him much longer. Roger didn't want to worry him—I got it—but perhaps he *should* be worried.

⊶

We parked on the street below and wound our way through a dense perimeter of trees up to the back of the house. The weather was breezy and overcast, threatening a spring shower. We had done our best impression of cat burglars by camouflaging ourselves in green and gray tops, gabardine slacks, gloves, and berets. If nothing else, we'd blend into the vegetation.

We scanned the back of Moira's faux-Tudor manse for signs of movement within. Convinced we were alone, we skirted the pool and tried the exterior door on the glass conservatory, hoping the Silly Putty had prevented the latch from slipping into place. Unfortunately, it failed us, and the door didn't open. Jittery and breathless, Philippa glared at me and whispered, "What do we do now?"

On the north side of the house, a large oak tree shaded a detached two-car garage, not visible from the front. We could easily climb on its low-hanging roof, but the gap between it and the house was perilous. We noted an ivy-covered trellis on the back of the house we could scale to get to a cluster of second-floor windows, but it was the purview of cat burglars, not us. Frustrated, I pointlessly tugged on the locked door again. One of the small rectangular glass panes lining its casing rattled. Its soldering had corroded with age. It was approximately three-by-four inches and less than a forearm's length from the door handle. I tapped it with my finger, and it wobbled.

Underneath it, on the floor, sat a large fern. Although I couldn't pluck out the pane, I might be able to knock it in, and with a little luck, the fern would break its fall and keep it from shattering. We could replace it once inside and not alert Moira to the break-in. I gave it a forceful tap, the soldering popped loose, and the pane disappeared into the fern—no sound of breaking glass. Success! Philippa showed me surprised eyes and smiled. I reached through the opening and unlocked the door.

Roger had phoned Moira yesterday, introduced himself as Ray Kane, and told her he had information on Adrian Bogdan and his murder victims. They agreed to meet at a small coffee shop downtown at 3:00 P.M. For Roger's safety, it was a public space; for Moira's anonymity, it was a location rarely frequented by her set. We had an hour, but we would try to get in and out in thirty minutes. Philippa brought along the pistol, just in case.

We crept through the conservatory, which smelled of fertilizer-rich soil and chlorophyll, and into the lounge, peering around corners in case we were wrong about Miss Streppo being off on Fridays or if any of Moira's other staff members were lurking—she employed a large team to keep the grounds trimmed and the furniture polished.

The other times we'd passed through this house, we'd been in a state of anxiety. In that sense, this time was no different—every muscle in our bodies was taut, every nerve buzzing, every noise had us on alert—except that we were free to explore on our own. Moira wasn't holding a sword to our necks. If we could find just one bit of information, one detail about Bogdan that would link him to his crimes or tie together Moira, Bogdan, the FBI, and the murdered girls, we'd expose them or, at least, buy safety for Roger, Lionel, and us. I also wanted my aunt's journal and photos of Lionel, Roger, and us that Moira claimed to have as proof of our "prurient" lifestyle.

Before we set the plan in motion, Philippa and I decided we wouldn't have time to search the entire house. It was too big. So, we were going to focus our energy on the rooms where Moira would most likely hide evidence: her study and bedroom. We'd been in her office years ago. The only time we'd come face-to-face with Bogdan was in that room. We began there.

We took a long hall on the north side of the house that opened into the living room, back lounge, dining room, and kitchen, and ended at the study. Like the entry hall, the study was paneled in dark wood. Several built-in bookshelves displayed leather-bound volumes, mostly classics such as *Ivanhoe* and *The Last of the Mohicans*, and expensive bric-a-brac such as a porcelain bust of William Howard Taft, an intricate brass hourglass, and a stuffed hawk frozen mid-screech. A low-profile leather couch had once dominated the room, but she'd replaced it with two plush deep-green settees positioned across from one another and separated by a small coffee table, and above the fireplace still hung the portrait of Moira's late husband, Howard Closs Sr. His stiff, bow-tied, and bespectacled likeness was back-grounded with bucolic farmland, crisscrossing fences, and, in the distance, an absurd little hermit shack. There was nothing remotely pastoral about Mr. Closs. His gray, sloping flesh, alert eyes, and reproving sneer had no relationship to the romantic setting rolling out behind him. According to Iris, he horribly mistreated his Negro employees. I didn't doubt it. Wedged in a nook beside the fireplace was the chair that Bogdan had watched us from years ago, his blue eyes peering out, sizing us up, before stepping from the shadows and introducing himself.

We started our search with the large oak desk that dominated the east side of the room. I took the drawers on the left and Philippa on the right. We were careful to return papers and other items to their original posi-tions. We didn't want to leave a trace of our snoop. I flipped through old bank statements, creamy expensive stationery, and used check registers. Moira had roughly two hundred thousand in cash and another four in investments. She was wealthier than I imagined. So, if money wasn't her motivation, or at least, didn't seem to be, assuming her fortune came from the coffers of Capitol City Hardware, what was it? Power? Boredom?

Philippa tugged the handle of the bottom right drawer. It was locked. We combed the office for a key. It wasn't in the desk, slipped under the blotter, or high on a bookshelf. I tried to conjure from memory how to open a lock with paper clips, a trick I'd learned from a detective maga-zine years ago. After several tries, I gave up. Why didn't I come better prepared?

Philippa nodded toward Mr. Closs. "He looks like he's guarding some-thing, doesn't he?" She pulled the painting gently away from the wall and peered behind it. "No wall safe," she said, then her eyes grew wide, "Wait." She fussed with its edge, then produced a small key. "It was wedged between the canvas and the frame. He *was* protecting something." She darted past me and tried the key in the drawer, and, voilà, it opened.

Inside, we found birth certificates—her son's, her husband's, and her own—she was born Moira Lutz in Bluefield, West Virginia, not exactly a breeding ground for royalty. There were also death certificates for her husband, son, and grandson. She'd lost everything except, of course, wealth and status and power. Still, the certificates were sobering. We also uncovered insurance policies and deeds to various properties, including this house, several original hardware buildings in DC, and Elysium Farm in Loudoun County, about forty miles outside of DC. In the folder with the deed were several black-and-whites of the farm, mostly open fields edged by forest and anchored by an old clapboard farmhouse. We kept searching. We found a sealed envelope titled "Moira L. Closs, Last Will and Testament." My impulse to rip it open was almost unbearable, but I didn't know how to reseal it, so I returned it to its place.

In another folder, we discovered correspondence on plain but expensive stationery from someone named John. I wondered if he was the same John—one of J. Edgar Hoover's close associates, we'd surmised—who had threatened us into silence years ago in this very room. We scanned several recent letters, but most of what was written was dull chitchat about social events, scheduling a White House tour, or general inquiries about friends and family.

"Maybe all this isn't as boring as it seems," Philippa said. "Maybe it's in code." At first, I was skeptical, but then I read a paragraph from a note dated April 9:

> The damn rat continues to plunder my daughter's doll collec-
> tion. It would be crushing if she found out. The tears would
> never stop flowing. We've tried everything to drive him away,
> but he persists, impervious to our lures and snares. You're

right, maybe we should shoo him out of the house for good
and encourage him to make a permanent home in Heaven.

I handed the letter to Philippa and indicated the paragraph. "He's talking about Bogdan, the rat plundering the doll collection." I chuckled at the ridiculous tone of the note. "It has to be."

"I wonder if this is about the body we found. The rat *continues*." Philippa twisted her lips. "What is this about making a permanent home in Heaven?"

"And shooing him out of the house?"

"If the house is the townhouse in Southwest, then what's Heaven?"

"Death? Deportation?"

"But why say it that way, 'making a permanent home?'" She silently read the note through again. "It's written in a fairly loose code."

"To maintain plausible deniability if discovered: 'We were chatting about a rat infestation. We promise!'"

"Maybe Heaven is a nickname for a place?"

An idea crashed through me, and I dove back into the files, plucking out the deed to Elysium Farm and photos of the property. "Elysium is a kind of Greek heaven—an afterlife for the chosen few, right? Could 'Heaven' be a property that Moira owns?" The portrait of Mr. Closs caught my eye again. The roof of the dreary hermit shack buried deep in the misty rural background bore a striking resemblance to the farmhouse in the photos. "What if that's where Bogdan is? What if he's in Heaven—and Heaven is in Loudoun County?"

Philippa pulled out a notepad and wrote down the address of Elysium Farm. We continued searching the study but didn't find the journal or any photos of us.

"We only have a few minutes left," Philippa said.

"Let's move."

We crept quickly up Moira's grand three-quarters staircase to the second floor, vigilant in case someone stepped out of the shadows.

Again, I was glad Philippa brought her gun. My pulse was drumming at my temples, and a headache was building steam. I wanted to get the hell out of Moira's ridiculous mansion, but I didn't want to leave without the journal and photos. She had no right to them.

At the top, the hall spanned in both directions, with approximately five upstairs bedrooms and several bathrooms. I noticed a glitter of sun through an open door at the north end of the hallway. "There," I said, "I bet that's the master suite."

Philippa nodded, and we traveled silently down the hall, which was papered with dark damask wallpaper and lit with fixtures shaped like gas lanterns. We'd emerged from the Elizabethan era and into the Victorian era. This house was a mongrel, a Frankenstein's monster of grandiose design choices, a combination of Mr. Closs's stern, conservative Protestantism and Moira's flamboyant Anglophilia.

Before entering the master bedroom, we listened at the threshold for movement. A frantic bird twittered in a tree outside, and windows rattled in a gust of wind. I checked with Philippa, and we stepped in. It was bright with sunlight and starkly contrasted the heavy pretension of the house. With sweeping white curtains, faintly pearlescent ivory-colored wallpaper, plush wall-to-wall carpet, and romantic furniture with curved lines and decorative curlicues, it seemed designed to replicate a boudoir from a 1930s Hollywood melodrama. In its center, a king bed was draped in a silk coverlet, piled with frilly pillows, and crowned with a massive, quilted headboard. Under a wide bank of windows—the source of the afternoon light—sat a long dresser, trimmed in gold paint, and a vanity with an ornate mirror and small, silk-topped bench. We made eyes at each other. It seemed indulgent and a little silly, betraying Moira's well-honed chill. I said, "I feel like I should be wrapped in a feather-rimmed dressing gown and getting ready for my close-up, Mr. DeMille."

"This is very . . . glamorous," Philippa said, punching "glamorous" with irony.

Wasting no time, I ordered her to check the side tables by the bed and a small dresser in the corner. I'd search the large dresser and the vanity. Along the top of the dresser's polished surface were family photos in brass and silver frames, many of her son and husband and grandson, but very few of extended family members, and certainly none that connected me to her. It was a collage of Moira's version of events, curated images that reinforced the fantasy of this room, this house, and all of Moira's stylish mise-en-scène.

For a moment, just a flicker, I thought about my father and Alice and all the faces—Negros and homosexuals, the poor and the mad, the truly good and the truly evil, that should've been included in her display for a complete picture of the woman. Hot hatred shot through me again, followed quickly by the surreal vision of shoving Moira into the Tidal Basin. This time I understood something I hadn't before: I didn't hate Moira because she yanked me away from my father and placed me in an orphanage. I hated her because she has never stopped trying to erase me.

Through anger, persistence, and a bit of luck, I transformed from Judy X to Judy Peabody to Judy Nightingale, and the more I reinvented myself, the more she tried to stop me. Now, even though she has the upper hand, I was certain she wouldn't let me go, or for that matter, Philippa. I'd chosen the name Nightingale because a Nightingale is a bird that sings at night, a symbol of beauty despite the darkness and, I believe, because of it. I am somewhere in the gaps between these photos. I am the presence in that darkness.

"I didn't find anything by the bed, but a phonebook, a notepad, and books. Nothing of interest." Philippa said, but I didn't respond. "Judy?" She urged me on. Shaking my reverie, I began rifling through the dresser drawers, but other than her underwear, nightgowns, scarves, gloves, stockings, and sweaters, there was nothing of note. I approached her vanity, hoping that that's where she'd hidden the journal and photos. On its left, she'd clustered a collection of perfume bottles. A mixture of fragrances drifted up, dominated by L'Air du Temps, her signature scent. On the other side was an unlocked jewelry box containing her everyday wear, not the expensive baubles. I searched the drawers; it was just makeup, hairpins, and brushes.

"It's almost time," Philippa said. "We need to go."

My eyes rose to the vanity's ornate beveled mirror. "Just a minute," I said. Reflected in its surface, a wide pocket door was across the room behind me. Now that's where Moira might hide something precious to her. I spun around and went to it. I slid back its double panels, switched on the light, and jumped out of my skin. "Fuck."

Staring at me was, well, me.

The room was a seven-by-eighteen-foot dressing closet lined with floor-to-ceiling mirrored doors with delicate brass knobs. Philippa appeared beside me, and we absorbed our images echoing across the doors, some of which were ajar, causing the panels to catch us at different angles, each warping us a little. "Wow," Philippa said, "she has her very own hall of mirrors. Rita Hayworth would be impressed."

"It's like a fun house," I said, stepping into it. My movements shifted around me, leaping out here and retreating there. At certain angles, it was just the two of us, and at others, we were multitudes, reflected endlessly. I reached for a door and opened it. Inside, hung with care, were many, many dresses. I continued to open doors and more clothes: furs, gowns, racks of shoes, hatboxes, and on and on.

"Judy," Philippa said firmly. "We *must* go."

As if in response, the wind jostled the window casing. Even the gods were putting us on alert.

"We can't risk getting caught." She was coming behind me and, a bit frantically, closing the doors.

I didn't want to leave without what we came for, but who was to say the journal and photos were even here? We didn't have the time to go through Moira's treasure hoard of clothing and accoutrements. We didn't have time to open every hatbox and search every shelf. If we left now, we could return. If we were caught, we'd never return.

I yanked open the door closest to the entrance, and inside, on the closet floor, was a small black Meilinks safe. It must be where she kept her expensive jewels. It also might be where she kept other precious possessions. Noted.

I closed the mirrored door and flicked off the overhead light.

I paused on the walk-in's threshold, silhouetted by the sunlight from the window behind us. I was a shadow, yes, but not a zero. And I had a song to sing.

We'd be back.

○—✦—○

When we entered Allies Lounge again, Roger was craned over an empty beer glass, transfixed, it seemed, by its mysterious lack of beer. His hair was mussed, and his shoulders hunched. Not exactly the tough guy Ray Kane or, for that matter, his creation, P. I. Calvin McKey. He seemed haggard and, perhaps, despondent. Moira had that effect on people. I thought of his collapse at Brentano's and didn't want him to repeat it. We slid onto stools on either side of him. He didn't acknowledge us. He raised his hand to get the bartender's attention and ordered another beer.

"How did it go?" I asked.

Refusing to turn to me, he groaned. "She knew everything about me. *Everything.*"

Philippa raised her eyebrows at me. She seemed to ask: "What do we say?"

"She knows everything about us, too," I said, hoping our misery might be good company for him. "Welcome to the club."

He faced me, scowling. "It's not a club I signed up for."

"What did she say to you?" Philippa asked, her voice gentler than mine.

"She implied that—" he stopped himself. "Women like her, the high society sort, never just come out and say what they mean, do they? They *imply* it. They threaten as they smile and sip tea."

Philippa agreed. Knowing Moira, with time, she'd do more than hint at it.

"Anyway, she *implied* that she knew Lionel and I were together and that she'd make sure I'd lose much more than my job at the State Department if I continued to write about the murdered girls and Bogdan, whose name she wouldn't even whisper. She called him 'my villain,' as if I'd invented him."

The bartender brought another beer. Roger lifted it to his lips greedily.

"I'm sorry," Philippa said, touching Roger's shoulder. She was much better at comforting him than I was. If given the slightest pressure to soothe anxiety, I resisted it—even resented it. What can I say? It's a result of my twisted childhood.

He turned to Philippa. "Get this. At the end of the conversation, she said, 'I've known many writers: political sorts, literary sorts, journalists. One once told me: Be wary of the villains you create. They know you best and are the most dangerous adversaries of all.'" His eyes lingered on the framed photographic war propaganda across the bar's counter. "What a thing to say."

"Sounds like Moira," I said.

"I didn't create this Bogdan fellow." He swung his face to mine. "Those men on the wall, they didn't *create* the Axis. The free world didn't create totalitarianism. Capitalism didn't create communism."

A week ago, McCarthy and Roy Cohn had begun their fight with the army, who, according to these men, were harboring Communists and, although unsaid, homosexuals. Like Moira's threats, it was implied. Everyone was clustered around their TV sets. When I rang yesterday, Edith was watching. All her social engagements were canceled; no one could tear themselves away. "It's all completely absurd," she said, "but you can't look away." I'm sure Philippa's parents were riveted—or at least Bonnie. It would be too distasteful for Philippa's father. I bet Ed and Rich were watching, too. I was glad we couldn't afford a TV. It was all an invention on McCarthy's and Cohn's part, and most people knew it. They were creating villains because they needed them. After all, those villains made them important and gave them leverage, but once you create them, they can turn on you. "If you're writing about Bogdan," I said to Roger, "you're playing a role in creating him, like conjuring a demon."

He sighed heavily. "Lionel and I should've never pursued this story."

"We've *all* created him a little bit," Philippa said, sitting up straighter. "But not more than Moira Closs and the FBI and Bogdan himself."

Edith's comment echoed: "It's all completely absurd."

Like most people, she saw through McCarthy and Cohn. Their witch hunt had been convincing for a time. Not to us, but to many. However, now it was flimsy, poorly conceived, and their baser motives were showing.

"You're right, Philippa," I said and, giving it some thought, added, "We all created him. Now we'll have to uncreate him."

"What does that mean?" Roger said, frowning. "You're talking in riddles."

Philippa stared at me, puzzled.

"We've been trying to get the story of Bogdan's crimes out, and either no one believes us, or they're too frightened to believe us, or they believe us and want to shut us up. It's not working. So, let's tell a different story. One they'll want to believe."

I reached for Roger's beer and took a sip, hoping its crisp carbonation would stir up some idea, some brilliant way to escape this nightmare before our villain materialized.

"Help yourself," he said sarcastically.

I shrugged.

"What story do we tell?" Philippa asked, her eyes blinking, intrigued.

"I don't know," I said. "We need to pay a visit to Heaven first."

"Jesus," Roger said, "more riddles."

"Maybe," I said. "Or a solution to a riddle."

CHAPTER 26

MAY 7, 1954, LIONEL

At the station, I'm escorted to a conference room. The morning light spills through open venetian blinds. Did they choose this room for its cheerfulness? To calm the Raymonds' frayed nerves? Mr., Mrs., and Rose Ellen sit along one side of the table. Mr. Raymond—Noah—offers me a nod. He's a tall, striking man with high cheekbones and hooded eyes, cursing him with a perpetually skeptical look. His thinning gray hair is combed over and slicked down. One strand, an untamable cowlick, has freed itself and is catching the light. Roger has the same cowlick—*had* the same cowlick. I need to get my tenses straight. Mrs. Raymond—Mary—squints at me like I'm out of focus. Is she going to pretend to not recognize me? Finally, though, she says, "Hello, Lionel."

According to Roger, she's put on weight over the years, and her personality dimmed. Once he showed me a photo of her as a young woman laughing uproariously at a church picnic. "This was before she was married," he'd said grimly. On the other hand, Rose Ellen, who I haven't seen in years, has changed. She's no longer pasty, plump, and sausaged into her dresses.

As if in counterpoint to her mother, she's slimmed down, and her relentless scowl, a trait she inherited from her father, has become refined, now more dignified haughtiness than huffy petulance. Her attitude toward me hasn't changed, however. Under her *I Love Lucy*–inspired poodle cut, her eyes glitter with hate.

I sit beside Sergeant Colby, Detective Berg, and Dr. Shipley. Colby begins by introducing himself, Berg, and Shipley and expressing his sympathies. Although he assures them the investigation isn't closed yet, he gives his preliminary opinion of the case: suicide by gas inhalation which, by means unknown (perhaps a short circuit) caused an accidental fire. Colby describes the scene of the crime but says nothing about Roger's ring being on the wrong finger or his missing clothes and service pistol. Shipley takes over to confirm the forensics and then gently tells them that their son and brother has been unintentionally cremated. He is soft and remorseful but offers no apology: "For some unknown reason, a member of our staff concluded that your son and brother was to be cremated. That staff member has since been let go."

As I listen, I watch the Raymonds and wait for Noah to begin yelling or Mary to burst into tears or Rose Ellen to say something biting, but they don't move. No fists slam on the table, no gasps, no tears, no heated blend of anger and grief.

"Mr. Kane, here, was kind enough to identify the body before the autopsy," Shipley says. "Isn't that right, Lionel?"

I glance from Noah's stoic frown to Mary's blurry eyes to Rose Ellen's hateful glare, but I don't say, nod, or do anything. Berg shifts uncomfortably in his seat. Colby sniffs.

"Lionel?" Shipley says.

I recall Colby's threat: "We'll throw you to the fucking wolves" and Berg's proposal to escape scrutiny for lying about Roger's life insurance.

"Lionel?" Shipley says again.

"I—" I mumble.

"Mr. Kane," Colby prods; my name is spoken as if through gritted teeth.

"Look, I can't—"

"I'm sure you're distraught," he cuts me off, his voice soft and edged with sarcasm. "You and Mr. Raymond were very close, after all." He pivots to the Raymonds. "Closer than most roommates. It's unusual." Noah and Mary wince. Rose Ellen's eyes sharpen, scanning her brain for Biblical passages to fling at me like daggers.

"His ring—" I say, anger mounting, a surge of recklessness that feels more like despair than bravery. "It was on the wrong hand when they found him. He would've never taken it off because it's one of a set. The other is on my hand." I hold it up. It's a proclamation: We were lovers and partners, and you know it. You know it!

"That's right," Berg confirms meekly. "It's true."

Ignoring me, Noah's stony gaze shifts slowly to Shipley. "We would like his ashes. We would like to take him home." He glances at his wife and daughter. "That's what we need now."

Mary raises a hand to her mouth to cover a tearful outburst, and Rose Ellen rests her hand on her mother's to comfort her. After a moment, Mary squeaks out, "Must you report that he, he . . ." She melts into tears.

Rose Ellen steps in. "What she's asking is, will it be reported that Roger ended his own life?"

Colby and Shipley glance at each other. "We understand," Colby says. "We can make sure it's reported as an accident."

"We have no desire to bring you more pain," Shipley says, nodding at me. "Isn't that right, Lionel?" Behind his glasses, his eyes threaten: "If you keep this up, we'll take everything from you. If you think you're low now, wait."

I scan the Raymonds' faces searching for something—an ear perked or an eye raised at the possibility that the police are wrong, that there's more to this story. But they don't want to know what happened to Roger. They don't want the truth of his death or the truth of his life. They want to save face. His death is a relief. They no longer have to fear that their friends, neighbors, and fellow churchgoers might discover that their son is a fairy—not only that but a fairy who shacked up with a "half-breed." They don't even have to invent an explanation for why he was fired from the State Department. Colby and Shipley were worried for no reason. The Raymonds want this over. They're not interested in causing a fuss over Roger's body or fretting over evidence suggesting an alternate theory. They want the pain to go away. They want to claim what's left of him as a symbolic gesture: he will be theirs again, and once they possess him, they can tell lies about his life—lies for themselves, lies for posterity. They're morally despicable.

"That's right," I say to Shipley, shaking my head, and then to the Raymonds, "Why should you feel any pain?" I glare at Rose Ellen with as much enmity as she regards me. "Enjoy the ashes. The memories are mine."

⊶

It's impossible to stare down Roger's family and not yearn for my mother as a sort of salve. When I was eleven, my father lost his job as a truck driver for Thompson's Dairy and deserted my mother and me. Mama raised me on her own, working as a seamstress for Woodies. The head tailor at Woodies downtown, Aldous Franklin, took mercy on us and ensured Mama had plenty of work coming her way. He'd often help her if she needed an advance. She loved me intensely but didn't have time to coddle me. Her mantra was: "Hit the books and doors will open. Hit the streets and doors will close." I was predisposed to read and study and often chose to stay in, finish my homework, and read an adventure or thriller tale in *Weird Stories*. The neighborhood boys teased me for my light skin, shyness, and allergy to any activity involving tossing, throwing, or hitting a ball. So, I'd dodge them, head down to the Central Public Library, one of the few unsegregated public buildings, and spend my afternoons with my nose in a book. Sometimes I'd meet Mama on her way home from Woodies. I loved these walks because we'd chat about our days and absorb the sights and sounds of the city. Occasionally, she'd take me to a matinee, and we'd have ice cream for dinner.

I graduated from Dunbar High School and, with financial help from my father, attended Howard University. He'd reappeared when I was sixteen after making decent money in Chicago running a small taxi business and appeased his guilt by paying for my college tuition, but after he paid up, Mama shooed him away, claiming that she'd fallen in love with another man, her boss Aldous Franklin. By this time, I knew I was attracted to boys, and I'd survived several high school crushes. Mama sensed the nature of my desire, I believe, and didn't want my father to catch wind of it and try to stamp it out of me. She was protecting me. We rarely discussed my love life, but she met Roger several times before she died of cancer. I introduced him as my friend, and when he was out of earshot, she told me to "hang on to good friends. They mean everything. They have to me." I thought of Aldous, who although was not her lover like she claimed to my father, had remained her closest friend and confidant for years. And I understood: Aldous is like me.

When she was nearing the end and in a lot of pain, she began imparting wisdom like it was candy. I kidded her about it. I'll never forget her telling me: "Remember, son, don't let emotions build up in you. Emotions should be felt, not stuffed. It takes a strong man to cry. 'Cry hard, fight hard,' that's what my mother told me, so I'm telling you." When she passed, I did just that. Roger was sure I'd lost it. With time, I came to, as I always do.

⊶

After leaving the police station, I walk through the city toward Iris's apartment. A film of gold-green pollen coats the sidewalks and cars. We need a good rain to wash it away. Anger begins to seep out of me. On some level, the Raymonds love Roger, I know, but they refuse to see him for who he is. Their love is incomplete, flawed. Colby's and Shipley's lies wouldn't have gone down their gullets so easily if they accepted him. Although Mama hadn't understood me, she'd protected me. Even if Roger is dead, the Raymonds have failed to protect him. It doesn't make literal sense, but it's true. He would never believe what happened at the station. The underlying meaning is too bleak: they love their lies more than they love him. My heart wants to break, but instead, I remember: his love is greater. *His* love matters, not their lack of it.

Ten or so yards ahead, I spot Iris returning from her night shift at the medical examiner's office. My staggering ambivalence toward her and the girls rushes back. I know Philippa and Judy lied. I suspect they're responsible for sending us the information on the murders. Still, I don't fully understand why. Perhaps I'm misreading them, and they mean well. Who the hell knows? I call to Iris, and she gives me a weary wave. I jog to catch up.

"Lionel," she says, offering me an unconvincing smile. She's getting tired of me. I'll have to find another place to stay soon. "How did things go with the Raymonds?" She knew I was being summoned to play false witness today. "And how's the finger?"

"My finger is feeling better, but the Raymonds were a damn nightmare," I say. "They didn't care. They swallowed Shipley's and Colby's lies like a starving man does food. I didn't need to confirm anything."

"I'm sorry," she says, reaching into her purse for a cigarette.

"Don't be. At least I didn't have to lie."

Iris lights it, takes a puff, and gazes down at me. "I'm so sorry all this has happened to you. It's a terrible thing." I notice a tremor in her dark eyes. An unsteadiness.

"I've been imposing on you for several days," I say. "I should find other accommodations. I can always go to a hotel."

She frowns and her shoulders sink, discouraged. "You can stay with me as long as you like, you hear." She wags her cigarette at me. "It's important to be with others. We'll keep you from going down the self-pity spiral."

"You've been very generous," I say, "but I know this isn't what you signed up for." I chuckle half-heartedly. "Philippa and Judy, maybe. You, no."

She breathes out heavily. She's deeply tired. "What do you know about what I signed up for?"

I detect an emotional wobble in her again. Following a hunch, I ask, "Can you tell me something? Who was the employee at the examiner's office who accidentally sent Roger to be cremated? Shipley told the Raymonds that they let this person go, but he didn't give a name, and the Raymonds didn't ask."

"I don't know." She takes a drag of her cigarette. "Not my department."

"It's not?" The first time I met her the odor of decaying flesh was on her clothes. She works with bodies. "But you would've heard about someone being fired or, at least, moving on."

"Maybe Shipley lied about firing the staff member," she says, taking another puff, pulling on it aggressively. "Maybe he doesn't know who did it." There's that tug-of-war in her eyes again.

She knows something. "I suppose." My mind is spinning, and an idea clicks into place: God, was it her? Did she send Roger's body to the crematorium? Why?

"I'm sorry, honey. I need to lie down." She tosses her partially smoked butt on the pollen-dusted bricks. "I'm beat."

She squeezes my arm lightly, sweetly. As she turns to go inside, a thought blasts through my skull, a near certainty: she knows what happened to Roger.

CHAPTER 27

APRIL 1954, JUDY

The skies had cleared from the rain last night, so we collapsed the roof of the Bel Air. If we were going to Heaven, we might as well go with the wind in our hair. Well, my hair, anyway. Philippa wrapped hers in a peacock-blue scarf and cinched it tightly under her chin to shield her strawberry curls from the open air. The temperature was in the sixties, and the sun was bright. We wore light jackets, slacks, boots, and sunglasses—mine were little black discs; Philippa's were tortoiseshell cat eyes. We took Route 7 to Leesburg and then Route 9 to Hillsboro and eventually veered off onto back roads that traced the property lines of established farms, horse pastures, and rolling countryside. On one side, trees canopied the road. A chartreuse-tinted mist clung to their branches, evidence of new growth. On the other side, the Blue Ridge Mountains rose from the horizon like a wave perpetually cresting. The pleasant odors of lilac and jasmine wafted past us, thwarted here and there by a sneeze-inspiring cloud of pollen. To any onlooker, we were two women heading out of town on a picnic, not two women with a loaded weapon in the glove box.

The air rushing past us made talking impossible, so I leaned back. Philippa steered us from the city into the country, her eyes on the road, her scarf flapping. My love for her had crystalized into something stranger and more perfect: her little idiosyncrasies, whether it was her prissiness about her looks (the scarf!), or her impulsive response to danger (shooting the gun at a shadow!), or her being a touch too sentimental (poor Roger!), had transformed from irritations into, well, *charming* irritations.

She struck me as shallow when we met in high school, but that wasn't true. She was holding on to all these notions of womanhood, these ways of being a woman—the hair, the dresses, the shoes, what you could have conversations about, what you were supposed to read, what sort of movies you were supposed to enjoy—that seemed like a costume she was wearing, a false front. I had to peer around the facade to see the real girl, who I genuinely liked. She'd since sloughed off the most inhibiting affectations, but she was still wearing a costume of sorts—at least, it was a costume *she'd* selected, right? There's a pleasure in knowing she's in control of it and not her father or Stan.

With a chill, I remembered a "notion of womanhood" that she still clung to—motherhood. When she'd thought about the murdered girls, she thought about their mothers' grief, her sympathies aligned with them. It was understandable, but she'd stepped easily into their shoes like it was only natural. Did she want to be a mother? If she did, what would that mean? A battle between love and biology? I didn't want to ask. I didn't want to know.

After passing the turnoff to the farm and backtracking a mile, we followed a narrow tree-lined gravel road sloping down to a rusty metal gate. To the left, wrapped in a vine, was an old wooden sign that read, "Elysium." I got out of the car and opened the gate, which was unlatched.

On the other side, a large, overgrown field spread downhill. A breeze hissed through the grass and wildflowers, insects hummed, and seeds spun, caught the current, and drifted away. The land was a wide bowl of untamed farmland divided by dilapidated fences. The house—its only eyesore—squatted gloomily at its approximate center, its roofline recognizable from the photos and Mr. Closs's portrait. Beyond it, a loose cluster of trees spread along a deep-set creek, running west to east. Farther in the distance, the thin scatter of trees melted into a dense forest that blanketed the mountain behind the property. It was outrageously pastoral, like a movie backdrop from *How Green Was My Valley*.

Philippa guided the Bel Air down the grooved and washed-out dirt road, trying to go easy on the shocks. As we approached the house, a shiver rippled through me like déjà vu, but much more acute, almost overpowering. I tensed in my seat and grabbed the inside of the door. Philippa noticed. "Are you okay?" she asked, but I couldn't answer her, so I offered her a tight smile. She pulled the car into a dusty patch under a gnarled oak tree, where, it was clear, other vehicles had parked. As I gazed up at the house, another tremor of recognition spread through me. Had I been here before?

The house, a two-story Gothic Revival with steep eves, looked abandoned or at least poorly tended to. Paint was peeling off its clapboards in feathery strips, and Virginia creeper had overtaken its front porch and was inching toward the second floor. Deep inside of me, an alarm blared. I did *not* want to go into that house. My insides were curling and twisting. "Run away!" they screeched. "Run, now!"

"Judy," Philippa said, staring at me. "You look like—"

"I've seen a ghost," I said and croaked out a laugh. "I have." I nodded. "This place—I've been here."

Her face spread wide with shock. "Really?"

"Yes." I couldn't conjure a specific memory, but I knew I'd been here before. I was also sure that what had happened here wasn't good.

"How is that possible?"

Anxiety danced along my nerves. "I don't know."

"I can't believe it. You've *really* been here?"

I shoved my exasperation at her: "You know I don't remember portions of my childhood! I'm pretty sure I forgot them because they were goddamn awful."

"I'm sorry," she said, shrinking from me.

"How can you be surprised that my past popped up when I least expected it?"

"I don't know." Her blue-gray eyes searched me and softened. "I'm not sure what to say."

I shook my head. "It's just—why now?"

"What should we do?"

"I don't want to go in that fucking house. I can tell you that."

"Should we head back?"

We sat still for several beats, listening to the tap-tap of the engine cooling and the buzz of insects in the tree above us.

I looked at her. "I'm terrified," I said firmly, like I had a hold of the feeling, "but not of what's in that house or of Bogdan. It's of what I might remember."

She offered me a sympathetic (and annoying) smile. "I know," she said. "We can go. We don't even know if this place has anything to do with Bogdan."

"Let me think," I said, pushing back, feeling pressured. "Just let me think."

I imagined a small bell, like a dinner bell or service bell, dangling from the inside of my skull. Attached to it, a string ran out of my ear and down my arm and over the door of the Bel Air and across the dusty drive and through the high grass and past the creeper and under the splintery bottom of the front door. Deep in the house, an ancient, wrinkled hand, its fingernails long and dirty, and its skin marred with age spots tugged on it gently, its toll far off and, somehow, so, so close. Was it a warning or a summoning? Was this where the cats had been? The dark basement where I was trapped? The odor of cat piss bloomed in my nostrils. It had never left me. Or was this memory some warping of my mind, a symbolic Freudian stand-in? I couldn't turn back. We had to go inside. I'd deal with whatever was there. I opened the glove box and extracted the revolver.

Philippa studied me, confused.

"We're going in," I explained, "but I'm holding the gun."

And so, we crept up the path, the rotten stairs, to the front door. I held the pistol at my side. Philippa hovered close behind, clutching the flashlight. Her Brownie hung with its bulky flash on a strap around her neck. We'd come prepared this time.

I jiggled the loose metal doorknob, and it opened with surprising ease. We stepped into a large entryway with an oval rag rug and hatstand draped with dusty work coats and hats. To the left was a living room, and to the right, a dining room. The furniture and light fixtures were covered in sheets, each room a party of oddly shaped ghosts. I swatted away a childish fear of one of them suddenly coming to life and flying at us. A staircase rose before us, its banisters and risers thick with grime. No one had walked up them in years. A hall ran beside the stairs to the back of the house. I knelt and drew my finger across a floorboard. It was thick with dust. This fact should've been comforting, but I felt the vibrations from the past. Memories didn't leave tracks in the dust.

"No one has been here for ages," Philippa whispered. "Should we go?"

Part of me, the terrified part, wanted to use it as an excuse to turn around and head home, but another part of me, the defiant part, wanted to finish the search. Years ago, Philippa and Iris, at different points, had told me they'd help me remember what I'd forgotten. Of course, they'd assumed I wanted to remember. It's paradoxical, but I wanted to remember and to forget, to feel the satisfaction of knowing the truth and, simultaneously, to banish it. I wanted it both ways, but I had to choose.

I stood up and adjusted my grip on the gun. To my left, I noticed a light switch and flipped it. The sconce in the hall flickered to life. "The electricity is on," I said. "Interesting."

"Moira's still paying the bill."

"We have to finish our search."

I held the pistol in front of me, only mildly confident I could shoot it with accuracy. We crept down the hall to the back of the house. Under the stairs was a cellar door. I knew the detailing of the brass plate around its handle. I'd been through that door. Damn. I noticed something else: the dust had been disturbed on the floor. There was a trail from the cellar to the kitchen, which we followed.

The kitchen table, chairs, and counters weren't draped with sheets. In comparison to the rest of the house, it was relatively clean. The water in the double sink had been run recently, and the refrigerator was humming, and inside it were fresh milk, eggs, meat, and beer. Someone was here or had been recently. The fear of the past and present warred in me again, but now, the present was winning. We could be in danger. My palm pressed firmly against the revolver's grip. I studied the floor again. Footprints crisscrossed the kitchen, split off to the cellar and the back entrance. I parted the sheer curtain that hung over the back door's window and gazed out. Like the front, the back was overgrown. About thirty yards away, an old barn with a collapsed roof leaned into the forest, half consumed by brambles and stuffed with hay bales. Beside it was a dirt path leading from here into the woods.

"Should we go downstairs?" Philippa said, hoping, I think, that I'd say "no."

"Okay," I said, realizing I'd need to go first since I had the gun.

I grabbed the handle and yanked the door wide, expecting the stench of cat piss to waft up and make me gag, but I only smelled dank, musty air. I pulled a cord dangling just inside, and an overhead light bulb lit the wooden stairs dimly. I thought of the imaginary string from my head to the ancient, wrinkled hand: "Beware" or "Come here"? As I entered, I expected to be overwhelmed with flashbacks, but nothing was coming, just the suffocating sense that I'd been here before. We made our way slowly down the stairs. One step had been repaired recently with a new piece of lumber.

At the bottom, Philippa clicked on her flashlight, and we scanned the room. The weeds and grass outside had grown over the small, ground-level windows that I remembered. We could only detect a faint glow from the sun. Behind us, a coal furnace crouched in the shadows. Several walls on the right were lined with shelving, some stacked with supplies and others filled with old preserves in yellowed containers. Next to them stood a long, deeply scored workbench cluttered with tools. It was familiar to me. Above it, I found another string and tugged it for additional light. To its left, gloomy, cobweb-laced steps lead up to the bulkhead door. Beside it sat a large horizontal storage freezer that the Closses—or whoever—must've lowered down through the bulkhead. I didn't remember it. Like the fridge upstairs, it hummed.

"Do you think?" Philippa said, nodding at the freezer.

I knew what she was asking: Was there a body in there? I thought of the girl under the blanket—the flies buzzing, her golden-brown hair. Before Philippa had shot at a shadow, I'd been on the verge of throwing back her shroud to view what remained of her. Then it felt necessary and urgent, but now I no longer had the resolve. Entering this house had become about uncovering the past, about throwing back that shroud and staring it down, and I was exhausted. The hand jingling the bell in my head was a young girl's, not some mummified hand, which wasn't right. Not right at all. *She* is what I'd been summoned to discover, not a missing fragment of my childhood. Emotion swelled in me, pushing out, demanding tears, but I suppressed them. I'd be damned if I'd dissolve into mush.

"Can *you* open it?" I said to Philippa, whose face darkened. "Please," I said. "Do you mind?"

She sensed my distress, my pain. "Okay."

She approached the freezer and grasped its silver handle. For a moment, she collected herself. Its hum seemed to expand to fill the cellar, the entire house. She sighed and yanked on the handle, but it didn't open. She groaned, tried again, and the heavy lid popped up. From the gap, a thin curl of cold mist escaped. She glanced back at me, gathered her courage, and lifted it open. A cloud of frigid air swirled and vanished, and she stared into the chest. She gasped and stepped back from it.

"What is it?" I asked, afraid of the answer.

No response.

"Philippa?"

"A body. It's a body."

I took a step forward but couldn't move another inch. "One of the girls?"

"Maybe," she murmured. "There's a crust of ice. It's hard to make out the features. But I see a knee and an arm . . ." Something drew her attention. "There's writing on her side. I can make out some of the letters. An A and an H."

Philippa was trembling, but she wasn't looking away.

"Take a picture," I said. "Use your camera."

Still in shock, she gripped her camera and raised it to her face. Trying to steady herself, she adjusted the focus and exposure. She charged the flash, its high-pitch whine cutting through the room, and click—evidence on film. The flash, for a moment, revealed every gritty detail of this underworld. She repositioned herself to snap another photo—whine and pop. The room leaped out at me; buried deep in its cracks and corners, the memories embedded there were trying to free themselves. Again, whine and pop. A small metal door caught my notice near the furnace, perhaps the entrance to a coal storage chamber. It tripped a wire in me. The mewling cats, the smell.

The invisible string tied to my skull was no longer just for alarm. It dragged me across the room to the coal chamber like a fish wiggling on a hook. The door was four feet tall, two wide, and slightly raised off the ground. It was significant, but how? Taking a deep breath, I gripped its grimy handle and forced it to unlatch. It squeaked and, scraping against its rusty hinges, eventually gave away. In the twelve-by-seven compartment, mixed with coal fragments, were thousands of bones. Terror slammed through me, and I recoiled. Were those children? Jesus. So many children. No, no, that's not right. The bones were small, delicate, and animal-like. I approached the door again and gazed in, my eyes falling on a small oval-shaped skull with large eye sockets and distinct, fang-like canine teeth. They were the bones of cats.

Behind me, Philippa, who assumed I hadn't left her, was finishing. She slowly, almost reverently, shut the freezer, and I closed the coal chamber door. It hadn't given me answers, and we didn't need more questions.

For now, I'd keep it to myself.

⊶

We knew Bogdan was close, but besides the kitchen, there was no evidence of him living in the house, so we decided to follow the path into the woods. We peeked into the uninhabitable barn, which offered only rotten hay, layers of spider webs, and (we were sure) a nest of snakes. So, into the trees we went like two Little Red Riding Hoods after the wolf, except, unlike Little Red Riding Hood, we had a gun. The trail had been used recently. The fallen branches had been cleared, and the spider webs broken. As we walked, the canopy above us glowed like stained glass, and I was thankful for the fresh air and the cool leafy odors of the forest. After about a quarter mile, we heard the rush of the creek and stepped into a shady clearing.

Across the field, on a small bluff over the creek, stood a rustic stone cabin with red trim and a chipped slate roof. This was more like a hermit's hut and better maintained than the farmhouse. Nearer to us, a sprawling ancient oak shot up from the creek's bank. A children's swing dangled from a low branch, swaying slightly in the still air. Suddenly, a memory emerged: I was a little girl, five or six, and I was on the swing, pumping my legs to go higher and higher, flying out over the creek, the water glittering fifteen feet below. I recalled feeling free. The emotion was crystal clear and unassailable. It's the feeling I'd been pursuing since I could remember. To be free.

As we lingered at the perimeter of the clearing, I leaned into Philippa. "I know this place, too," I said. "I remember that swing. Maybe I lived here at some point." I thought about Crestwood. Alice said I didn't have the scars when I was there. So, had I come here after the orphanage but before being adopted by the Peabodys? Why? Was this some other failed adoption? Why do I remember so little of it?

We crept around the edge of the clearing. Philippa now gripped the revolver, aiming at the cabin. I'd taken the camera in exchange, its strap biting into the back of my neck. A bird squawked and alighted, spooking us and causing an animal to dart through the underbrush. Philippa jumped out of her skin and nearly fired on it. As she lowered the gun, I saw the exhaustion on her face. She was tired of being here, tired of the fear, tired of witnessing horrible things. We gradually drew near the cabin's dull red door, knocked on it, and waited. Perhaps we were in the wrong fairytale: Hansel and Gretel, not Little Red Riding Hood. No movement came from inside. I tried the door, but it was locked.

"Maybe a window?" I shrugged.

We tugged on the casement window in the front, but it was locked, too. I peered in. The cabin was a single room with a small kitchenette, wood stove, table, and chairs. I didn't remember it exactly, but it felt remarkably familiar, like the farmhouse. All around were candles and no electrical appliances. Indeed, it was rustic. Against the far wall was an unmade cast-iron bed above which, fanning out like a peacock's tail, was Bogdan's sick collage of Shirley Temple magazine cutouts. Little Shirley, with her dimples, white smile, and sausage curls, beamed across the den of an unhinged killer.

I searched the ground around me and scooped a stone out of the weeds. I smashed the window, and the brittle glass shattered inward. I didn't warn Philippa, which was stupid, because she gasped and pointed the gun at me. "Whoa!" I said, and she lowered it. If we didn't watch out, we'd kill each other.

I reached in and unlocked the window. We easily crawled through, using a small breakfast table on the other side as a step stool. Although not spotless, the cabin was relatively clean. The sink was piled with dirty dishes, but the table was tidy. Soiled pants and shirts were tossed in the corner, but the dresser on the other side of his bed contained fresh clothes, folded neatly. Bogdan must've lived here, hidden from the world, but stored food—and bodies—at the farmhouse where there was electricity. He was the hermit in the hermit hut, and Moira knew it.

On top of the dresser, he'd lined up various books; some were in Russian—or Ukrainian, where he's from—and some were in English: The Bible, *The Stranger, The Fountainhead*, and a collection of Greek myths. His old guitar rested on a chair next to his bed. We'd seen it in the boathouse. Clearly, he had a sentimental attachment to it.

Philippa stooped at the end of the bed and raised the lid of an old, battered military trunk. She paused, her expression falling, and stood up quickly, her face scrawled with revulsion. "Oh," she muttered. "It's just awful."

Inside, fastidiously folded in rows, were articles of girls' clothing. Calico and gingham dresses, blouses with Peter Pan collars, soft pastel cotton shirts, dungarees, shoes, stockings, and underwear. In a shoebox, also carefully arranged, were bits of girlish jewelry—a wristwatch, a hair bow, a delicate cross on a gold chain. My stomach churned, and bile rose in my throat. "Shit. Goddamn *him*," I growled and slammed the trunk closed.

Somehow this felt more outrageous than the discovery of the body. Perhaps it was because this trunk—Bogdan's little collection—wasn't evidence of their deaths but of their lives. Fury bubbled under my skin. I was angry for these girls, but I was also angry for myself, for having to endure the horror back at the farmhouse, for asking Philippa to take photos of that horror, for being weak, for Bogdan making me feel weak, for how it was all the opposite of freedom. I took a deep breath, wiped my mouth with my sleeve, reined in the emotion, and opened the trunk again. I raised the Brownie to my face, focused it, adjusted the exposure, waited for the flash to warm up, and captured the evidence on film.

Once I emerged from my feverish task, I met Philippa's gaze. She was standing across the bed from me, holding the neck of Bogdan's guitar in her hands, its body slung over her shoulder like a batter about to hit it out of the park. When searching for the spot where Bogdan dumped Betty Hicks's body, she'd become so enraged she'd hoisted a big rock over her head and tossed it into the Rapidan River. She'd needed the frustration to go somewhere, to get it out. I loved that image of her, her righteous rage exploding on the river. I nodded at her as if to give her permission (not that she needed it from me), and she let loose, swinging the guitar like a tennis racket, not a baseball bat. It struck the wall of Shirleys, its brittle body cracking, strings curling, and a strange hollow boing emitting from its core. Unsatisfied—deeply, it seemed—she swung it again. Its body splintered on contact, and a large chunk detached from its neck. Smiling Shirleys drooped sadly, unglued from the wall, and floated to the floor. She swung it again, slamming it into the nightstand, knocking a framed photo to the ground. Her anger and sadness exorcised, she tossed the guitar's remains into the corner of the room, where it struck the wall with a clunk and fell in a heap, Orpheus's lyre now a mess of metal and kindling.

I picked up the photo. It was of Bogdan and his sister Anna somewhere in the Ukraine. It had been lying face down on the nightstand as if he didn't want to look at it but wanted to keep it close. It had a complex meaning for him, and, I was sure, it was his most cherished possession. I carefully extracted it from its mangled frame. It could be useful, very useful. On its back, it read: "Адриан и Анна, 1918." Perhaps he'd loved Anna. Perhaps that's why he kept the photo but didn't look at it. Who knows? Monsters like him follow a warped logic; they believe the universe's rules don't apply to them. I slid the photo into the pocket of my coat.

"It's time to go," I said to Philippa, who was still catching her breath, feeling the elation—or was it exaltation?—from her ounce of revenge.

We left the cabin and began trudging up the path to the farmhouse. Philippa halted in her tracks and held up her hand for me to stop and be quiet. We both heard the crunch of tires on grit and an engine's purr. Silence, then a car door squeaked and closed with a metallic click. "Shit, shit, shit," I said, my heartrate soaring. Philippa shot me a stunned expression. I grabbed her arm, and we veered off the path and into the woods.

"Get out the gun," I whispered to her.

We began pushing through the undergrowth, ducking limbs and circumventing fallen trees. Thin branches and vines lashed our faces, but we pressed on. I have a good sense of direction. We were still headed toward the farmhouse. We paused again and listened. More noises came from the house: a door opening and closing. We kept moving. Philippa white-knuckled the pistol. Adrenaline surged through me. I tried to visualize how we would go from the edge of the woods to the Bel Air. We heard the familiar noise of a screen door snapping into place. He's at the back door. Had he seen our car and then searched the house? Finding no one, did he decide to head to the cabin? It made sense. We pushed on, finally reaching the perimeter of the woods. We were west of the house, and the house was between us and the car. I didn't see Bogdan.

"Okay," I whispered. "We're going to move quickly across the field, creep around the side of the house opposite the woods and beat it to the car."

Philippa shook her head, retreating from me. Red marks shone on her pale skin where the forest had attacked her. She had bits of vegetation in her hair. I imagined I was in a similar shape. "He's in the woods," I said. "This is the only solution. We've got to go."

Still, she didn't move, so I grabbed her arm and forced her out into the open. She snapped to her senses, and we crept quickly across the field, holding our bodies low to the ground like we'd seen soldiers do in newsreels and movies. We kept our eyes on the forest's edge, especially where the path entered the trees. Philippa tucked her elbow close to her hip with the pistol's muzzle pointed out indiscriminately.

We made it to the south side of the house unscathed and followed the foundation through the thick grass and weeds to the front porch. Our gabardine pants were stained with grass, pollen, and dead bugs, but we were so close. A dust-covered dark green Chrysler sedan was parked beside the Bel Air, not a recent vintage. It wasn't the vehicle that had pushed us into traffic on M Street. This car belonged to Bogdan and the other—who knows? An FBI agent?

Neither Moira nor the FBI wanted us to find Bogdan. I didn't understand why they didn't kill him or ship him away. Maybe he was still an asset or had something on them—mutually assured destruction. Knowing he had vacated the townhouse in Southwest, she sent us there to frighten us and, I believe, attempt to satisfy our curiosity. Who knows if she knew about his latest victim? It didn't matter. Philippa had given her cousin Quincy the information on the body, but by the time the police got there, I'd bet good money, it was gone. I wondered if a similar thing would happen here. This time, though, we had photos. What was happening now wasn't part of their plan.

"Are you ready?" I asked Philippa.

"Yes," she said. "Let's go."

We bolted about twenty yards from the edge of the porch to the Bel Air, its blue sheen, a beacon of hope. We flung the doors wide and hurled ourselves in. Philippa held out the grip of the revolver to me. I took it and immediately pointed it at the tree line as if I could strike a target from this distance. She jammed the key in the ignition and started the car, its engine roaring to life, announcing our exit. She threw it in reverse, pulled out, turned the wheel, the rubber grinding dirt, and threw it into gear, and we were off, bouncing and shaking over the grooved and guttered road, the open gate ahead of us, like a mirage on the horizon, the promise of safety.

As we drove away, I gazed back at the edge of the woods with the gun still in my hand, aimed indiscriminately in that direction. After we'd cleared about five hundred feet, a man stepped out from the underbrush where the path rose out of the woods. Although only an outline, I knew it was Bogdan. He lifted something to his shoulder. A rifle? I imagined the heat of his stare, his seething hatred, his icy-blue eyes penetrating us. I aimed at him, but before I could pull the trigger, I heard the crack of gunfire. I dropped into the seat—a bullet whizzed overhead. I quickly sat up, pointed the revolver at the shadow, and fired. The shot rang out. Philippa jumped and cursed, and the Bel Air swerved. She hadn't heard the first shot. The car sped on. When I looked again, he'd vanished.

CHAPTER 28

MAY 8, 1954, LIONEL

The purple dusk presses through our apartment windows. It's so beautiful and mild that it's hard to believe I'm not lounging on the sofa, sipping one of Roger's martinis. Instead, I'm peering out at the skyline from the burnt husk of our lives, like staring out from inside a corpse. I'm not supposed to be here, but after a swig from my flask, I don't give a damn.

Iris knows what happened to Roger's body, and Philippa and Judy know more than they've told me about Adrian Bogdan and their connection to him. When I woke up today, my first impulse was to plunge into a confrontation, but I'd received some intriguing news, and it sent me out into the city on a long, wandering walk. Hell, I wanted to avoid the girls' lying mouths and telling faces anyway. Drawing inspiration from my creation P. I. McKey, who, in one of the novels, tells another character "to let the evidence speak for itself" (I wrote those words, I think), I decided to pick through the wreckage of my life without a cop and a fire inspector standing over me.

My detective work begins at the heart of the fire, the kitchen. The official explanation is that Roger, distraught over losing his job, opened the gas valve and climbed into the oven. Let's face it—the police told me—he's far from the only pansy fired from the State Department to put out his lights. Not Roger, not ever. But let's go along with this brilliant theory: So, before all this melodrama, for some inexplicable reason, he took off his ring, *our* ring, from his right pinky, which he never removed, not even to shower, and jammed it on his left hand. Of course, this isn't the only odd bit of evidence. What happens next is an unlikely series of events: A perfectly good wall socket shorts and sets the kitchen ablaze. Then, thank Jesus, the sprinklers turn on, saving the building. But, shucks, the one in the kitchen fails, even though it was recently inspected. It's like someone wanted to burn Roger (or whomever) and the kitchen to a crisp but spare the rest of the apartment and building. Why? The answer: Conceal the body's identity but ensure that the building doesn't become a towering inferno.

I retrieve a chair that's still sturdy from the dining room. I drag it through the debris in the kitchen and slide it under the fire sprinkler. I stand on it, wobbling a little because of the uneven legs and (maybe) the booze, and gaze up at the sprinkler, hoping the tulip-shaped mechanism might reveal its secrets, but the charred apparatus means nothing to me. The loop of steel and the star-shaped disk attached to its tip appear intact, but I can't tell if someone tampered with it. McKey would be disappointed in me. The odd thing is that it's still here for me to inspect. Wouldn't the fire inspector remove it to analyze it? From the start, the fire department and police have gravitated to a narrative that fits neatly with their assumptions. Why investigate if you're confident you know the story? Or—and this chills me—why investigate if the story has been predetermined? Before I step down, though, I notice a little circular hole in the wall above the kitchen table, behind where a Magritte print, *Nocturne*, once hung. The print's grime-coated frame was on the floor, twisted and ruined. At first, I dismiss the hole, thinking it must be where the hook was anchored in the wall, but in the dim room, I make the hook out a few inches above the half-inch opening. I step down and walk over to it. It recedes deep into the wall and is a perfect circle. I have no idea what it is. I lift my finger to it, to verify it's real and not a result of the bourbon. It's real, all right.

After returning the chair, I move on to our bedroom. The gentle gray light from the window softens the damage in here, almost fooling my eyes, making me believe it's in better shape than it is. Most of it is a loss because of smoke damage. The insurance company promises to hold up their end of the bargain, but I doubt I'll receive fair compensation for my possessions. I'm sure the life insurance is a lost cause. These companies cheat white folks, never mind Negros.

The closet presents another mystery: today, I received the manifest of items the police removed as potential evidence. It's what prompted me to grab my flask and head out. Not listed on it were some items of Roger's clothing, including a pair of nice shoes, one of his better coats, and his dark gray Stetson fedora with a green band I gave him for his birthday several years ago. Most alarming, though, was his missing service pistol, the M1911. Berg wasn't wrong. The police didn't log these things. What happened to them? Who took them? Roger?

More than ever, I dared to believe he was alive. It was a dangerous hope to have. It demanded a new set of questions: If he's alive, why did he fake his death—or did he? Was there another explanation? If he's not the body in the oven, who is it? Someone *is* dead. Someone's body was cremated. And, if he's alive, where is he? Why hasn't he contacted me? Has he abandoned me? Ray Kane? *Us?*

It's also dangerous because I want it to be true. Oh God, do I ever! It's been my experience that wanting something to be this or that way doesn't make it so. Sometimes, especially if it fills a hole in your heart or smooths over uncertainty in your mind, you might be compelled to believe a lie. People do it every day. The fact of me—my love of Roger and who I am—is a truth that some, like the Raymonds, would prefer to wish out of existence.

The layers of uncertainty, not to mention the darkening apartment, make my head throb. I want to be with people—strangers, that is. Not the girls and their lies. I remember Allies Lounge, this crummy place across Taft Bridge we used to go. It mainly catered to servicemen and local joes. It wasn't unusual for two men to be there together, and they never hassled me about my skin color. Amid the other patriotic World War II imagery on its walls, there were a few photos of the Tuskegee Airmen. Not a bad place to have a drink.

As I pass through the living room, I catch the glint of something under one of the chairs. It stands out in the muted gray haze, caught by a random ribbon of light. I crouch to look. It's Roger's mighty shaker. It survived! I extract it and hold it up, its weight still impressive and awkward. I get a flash of Roger, flushed from shaking it. He pours a drink with a flourish and smiles. A crack runs down its side, but it's still whole, its thick crystal impenetrable. I hold it up to the window. Near the origin of the fracture—around the edges of a missing, diamond-shaped chunk of glass—are traces of a crusty brown substance. Blood.

⊶

After two beers at Allies, I'm mildly drunk, but the buzz has dissolved into exhaustion. It's time to go home. I wave down the bartender, a good-looking chatty guy named Eugene. Over the past hour, his crooked smile and deep dimples have been a welcome distraction. I left our cocktail shaker in the apartment. I couldn't carry it around, and I didn't want to risk removing it, especially if it was significant. The blood on it—or whatever it was—bugs me. It *all* bugs me because I can't see how it adds up or why everyone around me seems to know more than I do. I stare at Eugene, hoping he'll sense my urgency and come over. He does, eventually, flashing me a give-me-a-good-tip smile. It's almost a flirt. Has he clocked me? Who knows? I pull out my wallet, pay up, and tip him well.

My back is to the door. I hear it open, a rush of cool air hits my neck, and then I hear it close. A chill, a heightened awareness like a premonition, cascades over me, and startled, I turn, but no one is there, like a ghost. Eugene grabs the money, says, "Thanks," reads my confusion, and nods toward the door. "He was in and out. Must've got the wrong place."

I stand quickly, my vision spinning from the booze, and exit the bar, propelled forward by a sort of sixth sense.

On the sidewalk, I look both directions—up the hill toward Woodley Park and then down toward the Taft Bridge. About forty feet from me, outlined by the glow from the restaurants and passing cars, I spot a man in a distinctive tweed ulster coat, much like one Roger owned, and a gray Stetson hat with that distinctive green band, much like Roger's favorite hat. He was walking away, a cigarette in his hand, smoke trailing. I couldn't see his face, but my heart swelled, and then suddenly, I stopped, my feet freezing to the sidewalk. He'd just stepped in Allies, spotted me, and left. He'd seen me but didn't want to be seen by me. Why? A rush of fear tumbled through me: Roger wasn't dead, but he didn't want me to know because he wanted to escape me. Maybe I'd become too much for him. My skin limited him, my anger, my periods of neuroses, holing up at home, retreating from life, needing pills to sleep. I wasn't easy to live with. Maybe he's faked his death to be free of me. No, I don't believe it. He's not cruel. Maybe he was hiding from me for some reason. Maybe he's in danger, and if I know where he is or why he's in danger—something to do with the dead girls and Bogdan and the FBI—I'll be in danger, too. Maybe this is why Iris, Philippa, and Judy are lying to me. My ignorance ensures my safety. Of course, it doesn't, but that's the reasoning, that's *why*. It makes sense. But I don't care. I don't need to be protected. I'm not a delicate flower, a goddamn jellyfish.

"Roger!" I call out and begin moving toward him, feeling the blood pumping through my veins, stirring up the booze. "Roger, don't walk away from me, damn it!"

He tosses his cigarette and seems to speed up. I walk faster, the world tilting and whirling around me, determined not to let him get away.

CHAPTER 29

APRIL 1954, ROGER

I don't like keeping things from you. After leaving Judy and Philippa at Allies Lounge, the pain of holding it back twists in me. Their talking in riddles amplifies my guilt and apprehension. The urge to sit you down and spell it out, Lyle, is almost irresistible. I want to tell you everything I know about Bogdan, the dead girls, and today's head-to-head with the Closs woman. It's like a plot from one of our novels—maybe one day it will be. But I don't want you to take it poorly. You've been through a lot, the beating, the bigotry. You're not weak, I know, but sometimes, you curl up like a wounded animal. It's understandable, but we can't afford to hunker down and hide out now. We must remain agile, ready to drop everything and go. That's my training.

The lonely thousand-foot expanse of Taft Bridge offers some relief. As I walk, an occasional bloom balances in the breeze and drifts into the lush treetops of Rock Creek Park eighty or so feet below. I almost forget this afternoon, but like a nightmare you can't shake, Moira Closs's pale, powdered face emerges, her lipstick dissolving into the cracks of her puckered lips and her eyes shadowy like pieces of arctic ice. In my mind, she's sitting across that café table, holding a sword of Damocles over us, its hilt dangling between her fingers. After being strapped into a lie detector and interrogated by Scotty McLeod's lackeys at the State Department about our sex life—"Have you ever sodomized another man?"—this woman wouldn't ruffle my feathers. Where McLeod's men were clinical, though, she sneered at me—a look I'd seen before on my sister's face. Such condescension, such hypocrisy. It's provoking coming from Rose Ellen but vile coming from a stranger. If I'd ever truly wanted to murder someone, it was then, but what would that achieve? Nothing—and I'm not a murderer.

I want to get home. Maybe you'll be there, and we can crash into bed. I'll pull you close, feel your limbs in mine, and run my hands over your back and down your legs and over your wiry chest hair, your soft stomach, your cock. Our bodies are reliable and reassuring when nothing else is. Touching you drives out that dull throb the war implanted in me. Right now, brought to a pitch, it buzzes in my ears like a high insect whine.

Out of breath from climbing the hill, I push open the front door to our building. Oddly, the doorman is missing from his post, but I don't give it much thought. I cross the lobby so intent on the elevator that I don't see someone approach me from behind. "Are you Roger Raymond?" a gruff voice asks.

I turn, and two men in suits, colorless ties, and overcoats are glaring at me. Mutt and Jeff, like in the cartoon. One's squat, bald, and muscular. Mutt. The other is tall, has swimmer's shoulders, and a blank slate of a face. Jeff. His dark eyes spark with ill will, made unambiguous by the Model 10 he's gripping. Who are they? McLeod's men? Why are they here? He gestures with its barrel and says, "Let's talk." They escort me down a hall on the right and into a stairwell.

Once inside, Mutt grabs me from behind, slipping his arm under my chin, and shoves me against the wall, flattening my cheek against the cold bricks. I struggle, flailing fruitlessly, and he tightens his hold, and pain shoots through me. My heart slams against my sternum. I bite down to avoid crying out. "You've already kicked me out and ruined me. What more do you want?" I manage to squeeze out, although I had some idea.

Jeff moves close, shoving his lean, pale face in mine. I smell his cigarette breath. "What do we want?" he says mockingly, glancing at his partner. "What do we want?" He snickers.

"We want faggots like you to shut up and go away," Mutt says in a lifeless baritone.

Jeff runs the barrel of his gun up my trousers leg and stops at the seat of my pants. Suddenly, he shoves it between my butt cheeks. I jerk with surprise, groan into the wall, and squirm. Shame fans out in my veins like poison. "You'd like that, wouldn't you?" He jabs it in me several times. "Hard as steel." He stops and cocks the gun.

I think of your lips, your bronze eyes, and your deep brown skin, and how much I want to see you and how much I hope to get the chance. I'm helpless, but I'm not without anger, and that's something. Through gritted teeth, I say, "Fuck off."

"Listen to me, Roger," Jeff says unfazed. "Listen carefully."

Mutt presses my cheek into the wall even harder. My flesh sinks into the grooves between bricks. I whimper. When I'm free, I say to myself, I will hunt them down and put a bullet in each of their skulls.

"Listen," Jeff continues, "you're going to stay away from Moira Closs and FBI business, and you're going to stop your research on the dead girls. You will go upstairs, gather your pet chimp-*pansy*, and find somewhere else to live. If you don't . . ." He removes the barrel from my backside and brings it to my face, pressing its cool muzzle to my exposed cheek. "We'll stick this up Lionel's black bottom and blow his fucking head off." He stands back and lowers the pistol. "Do you understand, Roger?"

I glare hotly at him.

"Do you understand me?"

Mutt flexes, and his thick bicep cuts into my neck. I'm lightheaded. My vision begins to blur at the edges.

He asks again: "Do. You. Understand. Me?"

I nod and blink my eyes.

Jeff lifts his chin, and Mutt releases me. Blood rushes to my head, and I slump to the floor. When I recover, they're gone, and the hall door is closing with a click.

After not sleeping a wink, I roll out of bed and find you in the living room with your nose in *The Post*. You hand me a steaming cup of coffee, and the urge to tell you everything nearly brings me to tears. The Catholic boy in me desperately wants to unburden himself, but I hold my tongue. I'll wait until I speak to Judy and Philippa. We're in this together. I owe them a heads-up.

You squint at the marks on my cheek, and I offer you an explanation. You laugh and say, "You tripped on your way home from Allies? I'm usually the one off-balance after too many drinks. What'd you and the girls chat about anyway?"

I stall here—I'm terrible at lying, even by omission—then I say, "They're just eager for us to write *The Tattoo Artist*. They may be friends, but they're still demanding fans."

You frown and shrug, disappointed with my answer. You don't understand fans since I'm the one who deals with them. I get the glory *and* the pain; you get none of either. There's a fairness to it, I suppose.

"Look at this," you say, holding the folded newspaper out to me and shaking it. "Read about Mr. Lawrence Logan, Jr." It's the obituaries section. Larry Logan was a thirty-nine-year-old bachelor who worked for the State Department and died unexpectedly in his Georgetown home. He's survived by his father, mother, and brother. "It's a euphemism for suicide," you say. "Died unexpectedly at home. Bullshit. These witch-hunting fools strike again. They're killing people. It's vicious."

"You don't know for sure," I say.

You scowl at me.

"But you're probably right."

I hand the paper back to you, rub your shoulders, then bend and kiss your head.

We spend the day together. We go for a long walk, grab lunch, and watch *The Iron Glove* from the balcony of Uptown Theater because of the shirtless Robert Stack on the poster. Home again after dinner, we make love, and you doze off. I slip out of the bedroom, ring Judy and Philippa, and tell them about the men who threatened me. After a day of stuffing my emotion, it was a relief to tell someone: "It's not a good idea to keep Lyle in the dark. He needs to know what's going on."

"Don't tell him," Judy says, her voice tinny. "We have a plan—well, the beginning of one. He shouldn't know for now."

The next afternoon, they arrive once you've left for your doctor's appointment. I make them coffee from the moka pot, and we huddle in the kitchen. If you come home early, they'll pretend they're just stopping by. I lean against the counter, and they position themselves under our Magritte print on either side of your mother's little blue table, which suits them better than it does two men like us.

"So," I ask, "what's this plan?"

She reaches into a small leather knapsack, produces several photographs, and spreads them out on the table, pushing away the coffee cups. "We spent this morning getting these developed. What's in them isn't clear to the untrained eye, or I'm sure the photo studio would've alerted the police."

I stare at them, but I'm unsure what I'm seeing. In one, over an unmade bed, hung an exuberant display of Shirley Temple cutouts. It was bizarre, but I didn't understand what it meant. In another was the interior of a large rustic room, the bed's location. In yet another, the contents of an open storage freezer were obscured by a crust of ice. "Look," Judy says, running her finger along a shape in the photo, and I saw it, "An arm." I scan the other photos of the freezer. I see a leg, the outline of a young face. "It's a body," I mutter stupidly, horrified.

"It's one of the murdered girls. We found her, and we found where Bogdan lives."

I pull out a chair, and they tell me the story of their trip to "Heaven." Any irritation I have from our conversation at Allies burns away. Their nerve impresses me and frightens me. It's clear: the four of us have disturbed a dragon. I ask them again, "Why can't we tell Lyle? Regardless of his nerves, he needs to know he's in danger."

Judy regards me with her dark, marble-like eyes—I feel like a predator is sizing me up—then speaks, "I told you I have a plan." Her statement hangs in the air.

"Yes," I say, "but you haven't told me what it is."

Again, she pauses and examines me. I don't like her superiority, her aloofness. It's unnecessary. "What?" I ask, my frustration evident. "Tell me your plan."

Philippa breaks in, her tone softer. "It's not much of a plan."

"Well, what the hell is it?"

They look at each other, and Judy says, "Kill Bogdan."

They wait for me to react. I assume they expect me to argue or tell them murder is wrong, but I'd be hypocritical. I want to crack the skulls of the goons who humiliated me. I'd do it right now, Lyle. It's the soldier in me. I've been trained to kill. I know how to fight. It's not something you understand, I know. We're different that way. You're a sweet man. You move away from violence, not toward it. Even when we're making love, you're tender and vulnerable. It's a beautiful thing, it's why I love you, but at times like this, it's not useful, which I imagine Judy and Philippa sense. I see it now. The three of us are aligned, as crazy as it sounds. Bogdan is a child murderer. He's not going to stop. So, I say, "That's not a plan. That's an objective."

Judy reaches into her bag and flourishes another photo. It's an old, yellowed, creased black-and-white of a lanky young man with his arm around a dark-blonde girl on a bench. They're sitting in a public courtyard, surrounded by buildings with ornate, old-world facades. Medieval perhaps. Their faces are zapped of expression as if they're petrified to have their picture taken. Judy shows me the back. On it, written neatly, is "Адриан и Анна, 1918."

"This," she explains, "is a lure."

I raise my eyebrow at her. "How so?"

"It's Bogdan's most prized possession." She glances at Philippa. "Yesterday wasn't the first time we've seen it. It's a photograph of him and his sister, the original Eurydice, the inspiration for his crimes—and he'll want it back."

"The good thing about it," Philippa says, "is that he'll come for it, not Moira or the FBI goons who threatened you."

"Especially after you destroyed his Shirley shrine with his guitar," Judy says, smiling deviously at Philippa. "He wants to kill us with his bare hands."

"Gee," I say, my stomach contracting, "you've drawn a big bull's-eye on all of us."

"We were already targets," Judy says, and Philippa nods in agreement. "Think about those FBI creeps the other night. One way or another, they'll try to destroy us. You know it. They've already booted you from your job and assaulted you in your building. They won't stop until they kill you or drive you to kill yourself, their most desirable outcome. No blood gets on their hands. To the world, you're another emotionally disturbed invert."

I think about you shaking the newspaper at me and telling me to read the obits. I think about Larry Logan. I think of your face, your anger. It's true, they want us to kill ourselves, to confirm for the world that we're tragic creatures, that we're weak. They've designed it that way. After I was fired, I considered taking my life. I didn't tell you. It will always be my secret. Even the idea of it would've devastated you. The urge was supplanted with alternating states of numbness and anger, like an ever-spinning Ferris wheel, up into the night, down into the light. Before I snapped out of it, though, I fantasized about how I might end things. I wanted it to be painless for me and not unduly gruesome for you. Oh god, what a dark place that was! It came down to two options: an overdose of sleeping pills or gas. "Died unexpectedly at home," indeed.

A swirl of steam coming from the moka pot on the range top catches my attention, and in that curl, an idea forms out of fire and water. The subconscious doing its work. To the girls, I say, "I have a plan, and it's a bit poetic."

They glance at each other, and Philippa says, "We like poetry."

"You remember *Seeing Red*, right? About the arsonist?"

They glare at me like I'm an idiot. Yes, of course, they remember it.

I go on, "The arsonist, Cyrus Hagan, when committing one of his crimes, switches the power off from outside the house, enters, tampers with an appliance so that it shorts out and sparks when power is regained, and soaks the place with acetone. Once he's safely outside, he flips on the power, and before long, there's a raging fire."

"You want to set Bogdan on fire?" Philippa asks, disbelief in her voice.

"No, I want to set myself on fire."

They squint at me. Either they are baffled or unimpressed with my dramatics.

"Okay, not *exactly* myself."

So, I launch into a rough outline of my plan:

First, I tell them we'll lure Bogdan here with his precious photo. I'll send you away for the day, perhaps to do research. When the villain shows himself, we'll hold him at gunpoint and force him to swallow your sleeping pills. Once he's out, I'll dress him in my clothes, place my wallet on him, and, most importantly, slip my rings on his fingers. The thought of forcing my "wedding" ring on that monster's bloodstained finger turns my stomach, but it'll be necessary. We'll drag him into the kitchen and position him in the oven to suggest he—I mean, I—committed suicide.

Before we do this, before the guest of honor shows up, I'll turn off the electricity, strip a wire in the wall socket nearest the oven so it will short circuit when the current returns, and douse it with paint thinner for an extra kick. My research for *Seeing Red* is coming in handy. I'll also clog the sprinkler nozzle in the kitchen. I'll double-check the other sprinklers in the apartment and the hall. They were inspected recently, but we'll want to be very careful. It's important that the kitchen and only the kitchen is incinerated. We want to conceal Bogdan's identity, not burn down the building. Once the scene's set, we'll loosen the gas valve and head to the utility room in the basement. We'll wait a few minutes, letting the gas fill the room, throw the power switch, and boom.

It's an insane plan, Lyle, but maybe it will be our way to dodge the train barreling down the tracks toward us, stop a murderer, and allow us to escape. It has poetry to it, like one of our plots—the assholes want us to kill ourselves, so let's give them what they want, a story they'll believe, but it won't be my body they bury.

When I'm finished, Judy, listening carefully, leans back and says, "What if they do an autopsy on the body? Lionel will request one, won't he? Or what if someone else, like the FBI, wonders where their psychotic spy has gone and checks dental records? You have records, don't you?"

The gas begins to fizzle out of my plan, like when you would keenly—and annoyingly—punch holes in my plot ideas.

"Iris!" Philippa announces, like it's the solution to everything.

Judy's eyes light up. "Yes."

I know who Iris is, but I've never met her. Judy senses the confusion on my face, but before she speaks, I ask, "How is your half sister going to help us—and why?"

"She works at the medical examiner's office," Judy explains. "She'll ensure the body gets destroyed before an autopsy is ordered."

"Do you think she'll do it?" Philippa asks.

"We'll lay it all out for her," Judy says. "Bogdan, the dead girls, all of it."

"She's not going to like the murdering part," Philippa says.

"She'll get there when we show her the evidence, especially the photos. She understands that sometimes you have to break the law to right a wrong, or in this case, stop child murders. It's a compelling reason to break the rules."

"I'm not comfortable bringing someone else into this," I toss back at them. "We haven't even told Lyle."

Judy leans toward me and places her hand on my arm. Her angular face softens, and her olive skin warms. The gesture has an odd, almost awkward gentleness like she's trying to force intimacy with me. "Lionel must react to all of this believably," she says, pauses, gears turning. "It's key that the police believe the story, and it will be easier for him to sell it if he doesn't have to pretend, if he doesn't have to act."

"I don't like it," I say, shaking my head. "He'll be devastated. He may even crack up." I imagine you twisted into a ball on the floor, fists clutched over your face. It'll be cruel for us to do that to you, to force you to play a role you don't even know is a role in a plot you don't even know is a plot. I'm so, so sorry, Lyle. But they have a point, and your pain will be temporary. I hope you'll forgive me on the other side when we can knit our lives back together.

"We'll watch over him," Philippa says.

"And if it gets too bad," Judy adds, "we'll tell him the truth and bring him to you."

I stand from the table, go to the stove, and prepare more coffee. I think of how you'll see me, if only briefly, as someone who deserted you. Or perhaps you'll see me as a tragic victim of self-interested men who aim to destroy us for political gain. We're the kindling for their fire. Or perhaps, you won't believe the story. You won't buy I'd do such a thing. It's not good for our plan, but all the same, I hope it's what you'll think.

I serve the girls and myself the strong, syrupy coffee, then take a sip, burning my lips.

Judy asks, "Does Lionel have access to your money? He needs to be able to—"

"Yes," I interrupt her. "He'll be fine." I'm relieved we opened a joint checking account at Industrial. It didn't bother a Negro-owned bank that a white man and Negro were "business partners."

"And insurance?"

"Yes, of course. Personal property and life insurance. Unfortunately, not homeowner's. The company wouldn't allow a Negro to benefit from the policy."

"You should withdraw enough cash for several months," she says, "then after we've killed him, take Bogdan's car and head west. They won't be looking for it, at least not at first."

I appreciate her thoroughness, but her pushy commands rattle me. It's a lot to take in. I exhale and say, "Judy, I can handle it." I sip my coffee, which has cooled.

"Where are you going to go?" Philippa asks, her tone open, less demanding.

"I don't know."

"What about San Francisco?" she suggests. "I grew up there. It's lovely. We'll visit you."

The possibility of this unleashes a thought I've been holding at the periphery of my mind: when we do this, when we fake my death, I'll be leaving everything behind. I'm avoiding ruin and a fatal collision with a murderer and his entourage of keepers and protectors, but I'm also burning my life to the ground. Ray Kane will fade from bookstores. In this country, readers will never accept you as Kane; the scandal would be too much anyway. I'll no longer see my family, such as they are, and I'll have to leave DC, a town I love, forever. But I have no choice. To be alive and whole is better than waiting for the train to run us over. My stomach lurches, and I set my coffee on the counter, unable to drink it. Suddenly the plan seems impossible, beyond comprehension, and I steady myself and grab a glass of water. After I clear my throat, I ask vaguely, "What will it be like?"

The girls gaze at me but say nothing. They know I'm asking what it will be like after I'm "dead," but they don't have answers.

To fill the silence, I say, "I've been to San Francisco before."

I visualize the Bay Bridge, the Presidio, the summer fog, and even the first traces of our future there: The two of us sailing on the Bay. The two of us strolling through Chinatown. The two of us under the Redwoods. Will people stare at us? A white man and a Negro?

Maybe, but we'll know what we're capable of then and stare back.

CHAPTER 30

APRIL 1954, JUDY

Iris turned to the last page of the murder book. The final photo of the girl in the freezer, the one with the most detail, not a princess preserved in ice, but a murdered and abandoned girl, met her troubled eyes. She uttered a little soft cry, took the image in, and slowly closed the repurposed photo album. For a minute, she sat with it on her lap. I was behind the sofa, peering over her shoulder, and Philippa was across from her in a chair. The silence in her small living room with its loud, colorful artwork and Ella Fitzgerald beaming from the wall was as heavy as a storm system.

We'd told her everything before showing her the book, which we'd filled out with the new photos. We had to paint a clear picture of Bogdan the monster to persuade her to violate her scruples—no easy task!—and be the final cog in our plan. For the first time, we laid the story out for someone. Based on her response, we achieved the desired effect.

"So," I said, moving around the sofa and sitting beside her. She was still processing everything. Her eyes were distant, and her bottom lip twitched. "We need your help."

She looked at me, eyes blinking. "My help?"

"Yes," I said. "We're going to . . . stop Bogdan."

"What?"

I glanced at Philippa but knew she shouldn't get involved in the conversation. "Since there's no hope he'll be brought to justice," I said, "we're going to bring him to justice."

Iris's eyes narrowed. "How's that?"

"Well," I said, mining my persuasive abilities. "What do you think a man like that deserves?"

"To be locked up and the key thrown away," she said, carefully but quickly moving the book from her lap to the coffee table. She didn't want its poison seeping into her.

"And if he can't be locked up?"

She put her hands on her knees and regarded me skeptically. "What are you saying?"

"We're going to put an end to him."

She stood up from the sofa, her eyes flicking accusatorially at Philippa. "Do you mean what I think you mean?"

"We're going to kill him," I said. "If we don't, he'll kill more girls and, most likely, us. Think of it as preemptive self-defense. Think of it as—"

"It's justice," Philippa piped up. "It's what he deserves." Her voice is clear, certain, loud even, and she's not allowing Iris's deepening scowl to daunt her. "For heaven's sake, we're preventing more deaths by killing the bastard first." She let out an exasperated huff and set her hands on her hips. If I could've, I would've loved her a little more right then.

Strangely, her outburst toppled something in Iris. Perhaps, for a moment, she saw what I saw in Philippa. I don't know. She shook her head and sighed. "Killing a man is a sin," she said, her tone milder. "The gravest of sins. A sin you can't come back from." She was tapping into her religious upbringing, but it didn't matter. We weren't worried about sins; we were worried about our safety.

"I know," I said, "but not stopping this man would be an equal if not greater sin."

She looked me in the eye. "Don't do this, Judy. Please don't do this."

Philippa stepped forward. "Iris," she said sharply. "*If* we don't stop him, he'll kill us. He'll kill Roger and Lionel, and he'll kill more girls."

They stared at each other for ages, intense electricity crackling between them, and then Iris shook her head and left the room. I couldn't tell who'd won the battle, but Philippa took a deep breath and plopped down on the sofa. I plopped beside her, leaned into her, and took in her bright, floral-scented shampoo. "Even if she doesn't get involved," I said, "we have to go through with it."

"What part of 'If you don't help us, we're going to die' didn't she understand?"

I chuckled. "I'm not sure she said no."

"We haven't even told her what we want her to do."

I laced my fingers through hers and pressed my shoulder to her shoulder, absorbing her warmth, knowing that I'd kill to protect her from much less than Bogdan. We remained this way for a few minutes, soaking in the city noises outside the window, then Philippa asked, "The basement at the farm, have you remembered anything else about it?"

I don't answer her immediately. The coal storage full of cat skeletons reverberated through me. I saw the chalky bones poking through black dust like one of the nine circles of Hell. I still haven't told her about it. "No," I said, "but I think it's the place, and I know I was at the farm as a girl. I remember the swing by the creek."

"Do you have any idea why you were there?"

Her persistence annoyed me, but I understood her asking. The truth was, I couldn't place it; that's why her question frustrated me. Although

I was young, I couldn't tell you how long I was there or precisely at what age. Five? Six? I don't recall much from my Crestwood days other than bits and pieces of grim institutional life and Alice's kindness, but at least I could point to it and say: "Those were the Crestwood days." Whatever had happened at Elysium—the cats, the basement, the swing—didn't constitute a period of my life, which made it thorny to think about, drawing into question the reality of it. Would I ever find the key to unlock it?

"I don't know," I said. "Maybe Moira sent me to Elysium to get me out of sight. If that's the case, I don't know why she then brought me back to Crestwood."

Philippa squeezed my hand. "Maybe we'll have to ask her one day."

I laughed. "She'll never give us a straight answer. Ever." I sat up a little and kissed her lightly on the lips. "Speaking of Moira, we need to set things in motion and tell her we have Bogdan's photo and where he can retrieve it."

"What makes you think she'll pass along the message? She doesn't want Bogdan to find us or us, him."

"I still have something Moira wants. The missing pages from the diary."

She considered this. "Are you sure you want to give them to her?"

"Don't worry." I looked at her. "I'll find a way to get them back."

"Will she suspect we're setting a trap for Bogdan?"

"Of course, but I don't think that's how she'll describe it to him."

"She won't warn him?"

"No," I said, "I don't think she will. Although he might still be an asset to the FBI—and that's unlikely—I don't think she wants him around. He's nothing but a threat to her. Even the goons following us and wreaking havoc are just doing damage control. I doubt they're protecting him as much as their reputation."

"Maybe you're right." She pushed herself out of Iris's enveloping sofa. "Should I call her or . . . ?"

"I'll do the honors." I smiled devilishly. "My pleasure."

"Well," she said, straightening her skirt, "I need to return the Bel Air. Dad has been grumbling about it. I'll have to refine my explanation for the damaged bumper."

"Can we keep the gun?"

She raised an eyebrow. "It's a good idea, don't you think?"

"Yes, I do."

Philippa's expression changed, darkening. I turned, and having emerged from her room, Iris was behind me with an inscrutable pout on her face. Her chin was tilted up, causing her prominent cheekbones to stand out. Her hair was tight against her head, and her eyes roamed between us, more uncertain than angry. "So," she said, "this Bogdan guy will continue killing girls."

"That's right," I said, holding my breath, hoping she'd changed her mind.

"And he'll come for you?"

"Yes," Philippa said, not concealing her impatience.

Iris's gaze snapped to her, then back to me.

"Judy," she said like an imperative, her black eyes flashing. "What *exactly* do you need me to do?"

I exhaled and smiled, nodding in thanks.

Philippa spoke. "We need you to make Bogdan's body disappear."

CHAPTER 31

MAY 1, 1954, ROGER

I ask you to go to the Library of Congress for the rest of the afternoon, a relatively safe place. It's also where you'll be noticed. Despite the segregation of the reading rooms, I'm hoping the librarians who broke the rules before in the "whites only" area will help you and be your alibi. Sure, it's an apparent suicide, but we must be careful.

As I push, you once again question the wisdom of us writing our next novel about unsolved child murders. It might be seen as opportunistic, even unsavory, and bring unwanted attention, especially in light of why I was fired from the State Department. How right you are—but I bite my tongue. I need you to leave to avoid the looming danger. So, I talk up the project, saying we'll do it the right way, whatever the hell that means, and urge you out the door. I'd like a little peace and quiet, I say, because I'm feeling inspired to write—"put pen to paper," I say—your usual role in the apparatus of Ray Kane. You give me a warm puzzled look, which is a touch critical and a touch sexy. I embrace you and kiss you harder than I usually do. As you leave, you blow me an exaggerated kiss, a silly gesture I secretly love, and remind me to close the windows you've left open if I get too cold, as if I couldn't figure it out for myself.

Judy and Philippa will be arriving in an hour and, according to Moira, Bogdan will appear close to dinnertime to retrieve his photo and the other evidence they have on him for the astonishing sum of ten thousand dollars. They don't believe he intends to pay or has the resources to do so, but they needed to sell him a convincing motivation for blackmail. They left the photo in question with me. I've hidden it in our office, shuffling it in with our reams of research, but I've kept it easily accessible in case we need to dangle it in front of him to lure him into the apartment.

As planned, I take the stairs to the utility room, switch off the power, ready the wall socket and fire sprinkler, and prep the oven.

Although not part of the plan, I sit at my desk, pull out a pen, and stare down at a blank piece of stationery. I intend to write the perfect suicide note. In my mind, I'll craft just the right phrase or flourish of imagery or appealing rhetorical turn to reassure you. In the subtext, there'll be hints of the truth: "Don't despair, Lyle. I'm alive. Don't tell anyone. We'll be together soon!" But the inspiration falters, and the truth surfaces: only you could write the note; only you would have the right words in the right order. Sure, we made our novels together; the ideas, the concepts, and the characters are an amalgamation of our inspiration and toil, but the words on the page are yours and, ironically—or appropriately—only you could write a fake suicide note to alleviate the pain I'm about to inflict, only *you* could soothe you.

What I hope—and I'm sending this out to you, the future you, the you that's suffering more than you should have to—What I hope is that, on the other side of all this, when we're strolling the streets of San Francisco or wherever, you'll understand that this morbid sleight of hand is our best course of action, that like any hard-won journey to freedom, it requires sacrifice. As a soldier, I understand this, I understand that sometimes you must set your jaw, lower your shoulders, raise your sword, and head into the darkness. I hope you'll understand it, too.

I'm still gazing down at the blank piece of stationery when I hear a knock on the door. Philippa and Judy are early.

CHAPTER 32

MAY 8, 1954, LIONEL

I call to him again: "Roger!" He doesn't turn, but I know he hears me. The dark gray Stetson twitches and his shoulders under his coat tighten and lift. He quickens his pace. I reel from the booze I consumed in Allies and steady myself on a lamppost, its pool of light harsh, even alarming. Thin fibers of dread grow around my heart making me sluggish, as if there's no point in running after him, as if I should sink to the sidewalk and sob like a baby: "Roger has left me! He's deserted me!" I indulge that thought, then brush it away like a spider web. No matter what's happened, no matter what he's done or why, I deserve to understand it.

Spurred on by this resolve, I double my pace to close the widening gap between us. I don't break into a run, though; stirring up the bourbon and beer would topple me over. I lock my eyes on his hat, an outline in the dim light. He dashes across Calvert Street, barely dodging an oncoming car. A horn blares but he doesn't flinch. He keeps heading toward the concrete lions guarding the entrance to the bridge. Although the traffic is thin, a cluster of vehicles stalls me. Their headlights blaze by, and their swoosh cuts through me. Then, I move quickly, abandoning my walk for a run. He's not going to get away. I want my explanation. I want to know why.

Unsurprisingly, I'm unsteady on my feet and trip over an uneven slab of sidewalk. I catch myself, suck in a deep breath, aware of the sharp night air, and continue, undaunted. My legs are aching, and my vision is swimming. The bright headlights and noxious exhaust of vehicles traveling northwest on Connecticut Avenue disorient me, but I'm closing the gap between us.

He stops abruptly beside one of the crouching lions. It looms above him. Its open mouth, fangs, and mane flash in the intermittent light from passing traffic. The effect is ghoulish and unsettling. I pause, unsure why he's halted, then launch ahead. As I run toward him, he seems to grow smaller, more indistinct, his long coat and fedora an abstraction, a shadow, like he's a mirage. It's a bend in my perception, like light waves through a prism, and as I hurl myself forward, it clears. I'm sobering up. He's not far, and I'm closing in, thirty, twenty, ten feet, and, with each yard I gain, I'm more and more aware that something is wrong with him: his wide-legged stance, his height, the way the coat rests on his shoulders. None of it is right, none of it is *him*.

I touch his arm, and he spins, and it's not his face, but a stranger's: He's handsome, fiftyish, square-jawed, and has dazzling blue eyes. But his skin is pasty and sallow and lined, coated with sweat. His expression is blank, but something in the eyes reminds me of the boy from Little Palace Cafeteria, the simmering spite, the barely tethered rage, and the absurdity of it—of such hatred. I'm not sure what to say or do. I'm stunned, paralyzed with confusion. I know the coat is Roger's and the hat is Roger's, and in his hand, held close to his side, is the gun that's Roger's, his Navy issue M1911.

And I see it, the yearning boyish face from the photo, "Адриан и Анна, 1918," but it's now much coarser, harder, reshaped by cruelty.

"Hello, Lionel." Bogdan smiles, exposing his rotten teeth.

CHAPTER 33

MAY 1, 1954, ROGER

Judy and Philippa knock assertively. "Okay, okay," I call out, alarmed by their urgency. Before I open the door, being cautious, I check the peephole, but as I lean in, the door flies open, splintering the edge of its frame and smacking me in the nose. I stumble back, crashing against the hatstand and tumbling to the floor. Pain blooms across my face. Trying to avoid the man charging me, I move backward, pushing my feet and hands off the floor in a frantic crab walk. He looks like an angry, shabby Tyrone Power. He moves quickly, overtaking me. Before I can defend myself, he grits his grimy, twisted teeth, pulls back his arm, and slams his fist into my jaw. White pain shoots through me, and I crumple, flickering in and out of consciousness. He drags me into the living room and foists me into one of the Danish modern chairs. Disoriented and blurry-eyed, I stir and groan—then, with another sudden blast to my jaw, I'm out.

As I come to, I struggle to focus. I hear the phone ringing. It's tinny sound stirring me. The room spins, and my head throbs. The ringing stops. Someone is speaking. I sense movement nearby, rustling noises, the screech of chair legs, and the clatter of metal and glass hitting the floor. As my vision restores, I make out flashes of the blue sky, edging toward dusk. I'm facing the windows. And you're there, stepping into view, gazing out at the late afternoon. "Lyle," I moan. "Help me." Then you turn to me. "Lyle?" I mutter again. You're laughing at what I said like a joke, light bends strangely around you, and you're holding a book—or is it a cocktail? And your smile is. It's . . . It's not you. I'm delirious. The Tyrone look-alike is grinning at me, his teeth little decaying tombstones, and he's holding a pistol, *my* pistol. He holds it to my head, its barrel cold, sobering. The muffled ache in my jaw is brightening and expanding.

"Surprise," he says. "You weren't expecting me so soon, were you?"

His accent is Russian or Ukrainian. He's Adrian Bogdan. Somewhere buried under his middle-aged facade is the young face in the photo. "What, what do you want?"

He studies me, cocking his head. His eyes are blank, predatory.

My heart is racing. "Tell me!"

He leans close. The rank smell of layers of cigarette smoke wafts from him. "I'm here to debug your apartment. I'm your exterminator." He chuckles. "At your service."

"What are you talking about?" I try to move my hands. He's bound my wrists together in front of me with an electrical cord.

He sniffs, raises a finger as if to say, "Wait a minute," and then disappears.

Noises come from the kitchen—or maybe, the dining room. I can't see from where I'm sitting. Then, directly behind me, I hear the clinking of glassware. He's moving the bar cart. I imagine him clawing at our things like a rat. Of course, I was planning to set it all on fire, but that was my choice—a desperate action, yes, but *my* action. I resent him for invading our privacy and doing whatever he's doing. Frustrated, I try to stand but can't. He also wrapped a cord across my chest and bound my ankles together.

After a time, Bogdan appears, holding short lengths of electrical cable. At some point, he set down the gun. On one end of each cable is a little black speaker, and a twist of copper wires on the other. He drops them on the table and says, "Hoover's favorite weapon." He smiles and adds, "You didn't know we were listening in, did you?"

At this moment, Lyle, I understand what will happen to me. He has the upper hand. Maybe he's always had it. The FBI, too. They supplied him with listening devices. He wouldn't have access to that equipment on his own. They've been eavesdropping on us. I wince at the thought of them breaking in and installing bugs. The horror of it begins to trickle down my spine. Where did they hide them? In the bar cart? Or in the kitchen where Judy, Philippa, and I discussed our plans? In the refrigerator? In the coffee pot? Behind the Magritte painting? The horror becomes a steady stream. They may have been listening since we first met Judy and Philippa. Did they know what they were up to before I did? Did they overhear you and me talking casually? Intimately? The horror cascades. Did they listen to us making love? Were they snickering? Did they make a crude joke about it?

They know our plan, and the target of that plan is standing before me, glaring at me with a smug expression. He looks triumphant in his thread-bare jacket and stained trousers. I catch a whiff of his body odor, a blend of fire, smoke, and sweat. I gag, lurching forward in my bindings, stomach acid burning my throat and mouth but not coming out. I'm spared that humiliation.

"So," he sneered, "the faggots thought they could trick me." He crouches and comes close, his ripe breath making me heave again. "I'm not stupid. I'm a god. You can't kill a god. Even the FBI know I'm a god."

"They do?" I mutter.

He grips my chin with his long fingers and shoves his face in mine.

"For many years, I harvested secrets in my homeland and peddled them to Lady Liberty. Then, they liked my secrets so much that they got greedy and wanted to claim me for their own. Like the magic"—he makes a little flourish with his free hand—"I become a US citizen. Now, the US government wants me to stop saving my little Eurydices. For them, it's distasteful, naughty. But they're the ones who gave me my freedom—and now they want to take it away?" Flecks of rust in his blue irises glow uncannily. "So, I had to ensure we were—How do you say it?—'leveling the playing field.' If I die, little gifts, pretty packages tied with bows, arrive in the mailboxes of important newspapermen." He withdraws. I can breathe again. "No one wants your American press to know about me, about my passions. No one wants it out in the open. It would be embarrassing."

"What are you going to do with me?"

"Hmm," he says. "Why change your plans?"

I shake my head, confused.

"Weren't you preparing to end everything this afternoon?" His eyes twinkle; he's enjoying the irony. "Weren't you going to say goodbye to this terrible world with your head in an oven? Ashes to ashes?"

He moves out of my line of sight.

"And then," he says, somewhere behind me, "I'll deal with the dykes and, maybe, your fairy friend. What's his name?"

He reappears again, clutching the photo of you and me hiking in Shenandoah. "Is this him?" he asks.

"His name is Lionel."

Your face in the photo beams at me, and the fear in my chest quiets. Bogdan grunts and tosses it to the side, and it shatters on the floor, but I don't flinch. He continues to talk, believing he's torturing me, the way a sadistic child might play with an insect before smashing it. I don't listen, however. Instead, I see you, your smooth brown face, your skeptical bronze eyes, the light in them when you laugh hard, your toothy smile, your broad shoulders, and thick arms, the slight paunch at your waist, the fuzz around your navel, your pubic hair, your dangling cock, your strong thighs and calves, your large feet. Duck feet, you call them. I see all of you, and I want you—more than ever and right now. I raise my hands impulsively, the Catholic in me turning to prayer, but instead of prayer, I feel the hard certainty of my ring, *our* ring, on my pinky.

Being discreet, I cover one hand with the other as best I can and twist the ring slowly so that Bogdan doesn't notice. It slides off easily; my fingers are slippery with sweat. Bogdan walks away again, moving behind me. I glance down at the ring. On the inside edge, it reads, "R & L FOREVER, 1948." *Forever*, I think, and an idea, perhaps my last, leaps to mind. I slip the ring on my left ring finger, wedging it just below my first knuckle. It doesn't fit properly, of course. If the girls meet the same fate as I do, you'll have a clue, a sign that my death wasn't a suicide. Maybe you'll even believe I'm still alive, hiding out, waiting for you.

Bogdan appears again, clutching my thick glass cocktail shaker, like he's pausing to mix a drink. It *is* about cocktail hour. Ha!

"So, tell me," he says. "Where is the photo?" His voice is flat, impatient. I wonder if he's been asking me about it during his rant, but too wrapped up in my reverie, I didn't hear him. I know what he wants, in any case. To annoy him, I say, "What photo?"

"Idiot. My sister and me."

The bright, unstable glitter in his eyes gives him away. He wants his talisman more than anything. His features may be scrawled with cruelty and his emotions padlocked in his skull, but if you read his face carefully, if you trace the wrinkles and veins and almost imperceptible twitching at the corner of his mouth and the edges of his eyes, you find a map to real pain, deep pain. It's linked to that photo, to whatever it means to him or whatever he's twisted it to mean. But I don't care about his pain. Fuck him. I'm not telling him where it is; I'm not giving it back to him.

Surprised at his vulnerability, he inhales sharply. He must realize he played his cards too soon. He's removed the possibility of hope, so there's no leverage.

I nod at the shaker. "Are you going to fix me one last drink?"

He smiles mirthlessly. "Da." His eyes drain of color, and he says, "Coming right up," and slams the heavy shaker into the side of my head with a swift, powerful motion.

CHAPTER 34

MAY 1-8, 1954, JUDY

After the fire was extinguished, after the firemen left, we escorted Lionel to the police station. Philippa spoke with Quincy, begging him to treat him gently. We sat in the bustling waiting area where Lionel could see us. He was shattered, and to a degree, we felt responsible. What had happened? What had gone wrong? Since we'd arrived at the burning building, we'd been consumed with questions we could only share with each other but without the chance to talk. The most important question: Whose body was hauled out of the wreckage?

In the morning, I'd showed up on Moira's doorstep with a few of the missing journal pages. I'd phoned her the day before, and we'd struck a deal. I'd give her some pages now, and after our rendezvous with Bogdan, I'd give her the rest. I wanted it to ensure she'd contact him. She seemed glad for the exchange, even a little triumphant. After all, what did she have to lose?

When we'd arrived at the apartment, the fire had taken hold. Not part of the plan. We were supposed to be with Roger when Bogdan arrived—Roger armed with his service pistol and the two of us with Philippa's father's revolver. We'd planned to be prepared for the worst, but apparently, we weren't.

Philippa leaned into me. "What do we do now?"

"We need to find out who died in that fire."

"It's . . ." Her voice trembled. "It's not Roger, is it?"

"I don't know. If it's not him, then where is he?"

She drew back, considered my question, and, scooting closer, said, "I scanned the street for Bogdan's green Chrysler. Maybe Roger took it?" She sighed. "Gee. Did Roger even know what the car looked like?"

"I didn't tell him."

Her shoulders drooped. "If it's not Bogdan, then it's Roger," she said, suppressed tears welling behind her eyes. Then, she brightened a little. "But how did Bogdan know to stage it like a suicide? How did he know our scheme?"

"None of it makes sense," I say. "None of it."

"If it *is* Roger," she said, "we're in danger. Bogdan will come for us."

"We need to talk to Iris. Maybe she can confirm details about the body."

After we brought Lionel back and got him situated in Iris's guest bedroom, we spoke in the hall outside her apartment, out of Lionel's earshot. She told us she'd seen the body come in and the damage to the corpse. She couldn't describe him well enough for us to be certain who it was. "Lordy," she said, her face lined with worry. "What should I do?"

She was asking if she should continue as planned and tag and mislabel the corpse for the crematorium. Philippa and I looked at each other. Since we didn't have confirmation of its identity, we had to assume it was

Bogdan. We couldn't take the chance. "Go ahead with it," I said, feeling helpless.

Philippa added, "What else can we do?"

Sunday came and went, then Monday, then Tuesday. Philippa and I discussed and debated whether we should tell Lionel the truth, but we didn't know what the truth was anymore. We were in a limbo of anxiety; Roger hadn't surfaced or communicated with us, but that didn't mean he was dead. Bogdan hadn't come calling, but that didn't mean he was dead. Even Moira hadn't reached out, wanting the remaining journal pages as payment. Could she be behind all of this? We needed to act, but when—and how?

By Tuesday, Lionel had begun to believe that Roger wasn't dead, which was understandable. While it's possible Bogdan stole items from the apartment—the gun, especially—we couldn't explain his ring being on the wrong hand. All the same, before we met up at Croc's, Iris, Philippa, and I had decided it was time to come out with it. Then, just as I was working up to telling him, he showed us Bogdan's precious photo he plucked from the apartment rubble. Seeing the hope on his face and knowing Bogdan hadn't retrieved it threw me off—a tiny part of me had begun to wonder if Roger wasn't alive—so I held my tongue, and the other two followed my lead.

Minutes later, FBI stooges attacked Lionel outside Croc's and took the photo. After tending to his injuries, I was again on the verge of telling him when he snapped at me, lecturing me about pretending to be white and hiding out. It was unfair of him, and he was being hypocritical, and if I'm being honest, he struck a nerve. Suddenly—and yes, spitefully—I was less interested in him knowing the truth—at least not until I could offer it to him in a neat package. Moira, it seemed, was the likely source for answers—the thread that connected Bogdan, the FBI, and us.

Wednesday, Thursday, and Friday passed, and still no word from Roger. Iris and Philippa, so rarely aligned, started pressuring me to tell Lionel.

220JOHN COPENHAVER

Unable to bear the lie much longer, Iris, usually unflappable, hinted that she was involved in the "accidental" cremation.

I'm the only one who's good at keeping a secret. I'm the only one who understands what can be gleaned from withholding. I'm the only one who knows that, sometimes, there's power in silence.

On Saturday morning, I tell Philippa I'll explain everything to Lionel, but only after we confront Moira again.

CHAPTER 35

MAY 8, 1954, JUDY

We rang Moira's doorbell for several minutes and slammed the Green Man door knocker, listening to its hollow echo. Her Cadillac was in the drive—its shiny hood dotted with cherry blossoms—but there was no sign of her chauffeur, Mrs. Streppo, or anyone. I gestured for Philippa to follow me. If no one was home, we'd snoop again.

As we walked around the north side of the house, we passed under the mammoth oak tree that shaded the two-car garage we'd spotted from the rear our last time here. One of its doors was rolled halfway up, revealing the smashed chrome bumper and warped grille of a black Pontiac we knew *very* well. Philippa gasped. "It's the one that tried to plow us into traffic." We approached, cautiously ducking under the door and entering the dark garage. A greasy, metallic odor hung in the air. Inside, glinting in the low light, was the shattered windshield, a web of broken glass with two bullet holes. Bits of glass, like rough diamonds, were sprinkled across the hood. "Well, we now know who was behind scaring us," Philippa said, her tone energized, pleased to have the confirmation. Then she looked at me, "I didn't realize you fired two bullets into the windshield."

I didn't.

The Pontiac's driver's door was open; Philippa investigated, and I followed. A man in a dark suit was slumped forward on the steering wheel. "Oh, God!" She withdrew, startled. I quickly noted the brownish blood splatter above his head on the inside of the windshield, which corresponded with the second of the two bullet holes. A trickle of dried blood ran from his blood-soaked blond hair and stained the collar of his white shirt. "Someone shot him from behind," I said, "seated in the back of the car."

"Who is he?" she said.

"There's only one way to find out." With effort, I pushed his heavy bulk back in the seat, using the doorframe to brace myself for leverage. Eventually, his forehead lifted from the edge of the wheel, the separation of skin and leather making a sticky ripping noise. His right eye was a gory crater, the exit point of the bullet. Philippa yelped and bumped against the workbench behind her. His other eye was open, empty, and his lips were purple and plump. Flustered, I let him face-plant again. His forehead thudded against the wheel.

"It's Moira's chauffeur," I said. "I saw him that day at the Jefferson Memorial."

"Do you think Moira sent him to spook us?" She was trembling.

"Yes," I said, gauging her nerves. "He's not scaring us anymore."

"Who killed him?" she asked.

I shook my head.

"Should we go?"

"No," I said. "I want to know who else isn't at home."

Once again, we found ourselves at the conservatory door, only this time, the loose plate of glass lay on the stone floor just inside, shattered.

I pulled my sleeve down over my hand. We needed to be careful about leaving fingerprints. I reached through and twisted the handle. Philippa's expression tightened. "If Moira discovered it, she would've had it repaired, right?"

"Or at least cleaned up." I opened the door.

Chuckling nervously, she said, "I'm absolutely terrified, but we need to take this chance to search the house." She slipped the revolver out of her coat pocket—it was becoming our go-nowhere-without-it accessory—and held it in front of her. She entered the jungle-like room ahead of me. She'd shaken most of her jitters from the dead chauffeur. Her refreshed confidence impressed me. She wanted to end this Bogdan ordeal. I did, too.

"Why don't we begin where we left off last time," I said.

"Moira's bedroom."

We slowly wound our way through the empty house, the late afternoon sun cutting into the rooms, highlighting dust particles, and deepening the shadows in the nooks and corners of the Franken-mansion. Philippa held the gun steady. We saw no one and heard nothing. On the staircase, we thought we heard footfalls. Philippa stared at me, her eyes bright with fear. "Hello," I called and waited. No response. "Maybe we imagined it?" I said, and she gazed uncertainly at me, but we pressed on.

We found ourselves once again moving slowly down Moira's upstairs hall with its elaborate Victorian sconces and busy wallpaper. Her bedroom door was cracked, and Philippa nudged it open with her shoe. A cloud had passed over the sun, and the room's usually light-drenched walls glowed dimly, giving its cream and pastel hues a pallid tone. Several windows were open, and a breeze stirred pages of a notepad on Moira's vanity, drawing my attention.

On the top page, scrawled quickly, was Roger and Lionel's phone number: Dupont 2-7130. Under the notepad was a Washington Metro directory, which, if I remembered correctly, was by the bedside phone the last time we were here. My eyes drifted up to the vanity's mirror. In its reflection, protruding from the large mirror-lined walk-in closet's entrance, lay two feet clad in expensive-looking patent leather pumps. Attached to them, crumpled in the shadows, was a body.

I gestured to Philippa, who was still at the door, and when she saw it, she uttered, "My God." Then stopped herself. I jerked my chin toward the bathroom on the other side of the room near the bed. We needed to make sure it was clear. Philippa lifted the revolver high, one hand on the trigger and one hand under the grip, her father's instruction coming in handy. I joined her, and we inched to the bathroom. Holding our collective breath, we flung the door open. It was empty—only excessive marble, gaudy gold fixtures, and rows of cosmetics.

We checked the rest of the bedroom and, satisfied we were alone, at least here, we returned to the body. We flipped the switch just inside the closet, and the hall of mirrors exploded with light. Moira's huge open eyes, two dazzling sapphires rimmed with a fine filigree of veins, popped into view, making Philippa gasp and withdraw, a more muted reaction than the one elicited by the chauffeur's bullet hole. Moira lay on her back in a navy charmeuse day dress, her legs twisted at the waist and her feet parted as if mid-step. Dark blood stained her silver bouffant, tangled and misshapen against a patch of blood-saturated carpet. A thin ribbon of blood crossed her forehead and flowed around her ear, glazing a large platinum loop hanging from her right earlobe, conjuring the image of ouroboros, the serpent eating its tail. Even in death, there was something relentless and self-consuming about her.

As I stared at her, I wasn't shocked or revolted. In truth, I couldn't quite believe she was dead. I expected her to blink, untwist herself, sit up, find her feet, smooth down her hair, apply lipstick, lacerate me with a merciless look, and say something cruel or threatening. When you hate someone, they become a part of you, and that part doesn't die when they do. They're always with you, standing behind you, their hands on your shoulders, gripping, squeezing. I was horrified, not by her corpse, not by the loss of life—if I'm nothing else, I'm not a hypocrite—but because she didn't feel dead enough to me, as if there was no getting rid of her, as if she'd always be a part of me.

"Gee," Philippa said, still reeling. "What happened here?"

Above Moira's head, one of the mirrored doors was shattered, an arabesque of fissures fanning out to its edges, shards of glass scattered across the carpet. "Either she fell and hit her head," I said, "or someone pushed her. Hard."

"She didn't fall," Philippa said, leaning toward her, her composure returning. "You usually trip and tilt forward. It looks like she struck the back of her head." She stepped even closer. "Considering the dead chauffeur, it would be quite a coincidence, don't you think?" Her eyes sharpened as she looked at the mirrored door nearest the entrance, which wasn't fully closed. It was the compartment containing Moira's little black safe. She gently tugged on it, its edge grazing Moira's leg as it opened, sending a chill through me. The thought of the woman moving even a fraction of an inch unsettled me. I peered inside. The safe door was ajar but didn't seem tampered with or forced open. Philippa turned to me, her eyebrows high, curious. "You can grab the journal and photos and whatever," she said excitedly. She didn't seem particularly troubled about Moira's fate. Why should either of us be? Moira had threatened to destroy us, and now she was destroyed, a victim of her own machinations, poisoned by her own venom.

Philippa gave me the gun and yanked her sleeve down as she'd seen me do. With her covered hand, she nudged the safe door wide. It squeaked on its hinges. The small compartment inside was empty. No jewelry, no documents, no cash, no journal, and no photos.

"Shit," I said. "Where are they?"

She carefully repositioned the safe door and turned to me. "Is this Bogdan's doing?"

"Maybe he forced her to open the safe—for money or something she had on him—and, in a rush, took all of the contents, even the journal and photos, anything he might be able to use against us or anyone threatening him," I said. "And then he killed her."

Philippa twisted her lips. "It's strange, though."

"Why?" I said, a touch irritated.

"Why wait until now to do this? He could've done it at any time."

"Maybe he figured out she was sending him into a trap."

She wasn't convinced, then her eyes lit up. "Or maybe the FBI was putting pressure on him. The coded note we found in Moira's office from that John creep implied as much. They pushed him hard."

"And he pushed back," I said, nodding at Moira.

"And now he has everything." Her expression fell, worry wrinkling her smooth forehead. "Or maybe we're wrong, and it's still stashed somewhere else in the house."

"I doubt it." I shrugged. "My gut tells me she locked all her most precious keepsakes in her safe. The dragon likes to sleep near its hoard."

She fell quiet in thought, the notepad page rattled again in a light gust from the window. "What was on the notepad?" she asked. "It wasn't there when we snooped last time."

"Roger and Lionel's phone number."

"Hmm," she said, moving across the room and placing a finger on the breeze-whipped page, holding it still. "Why'd she look up their number? She wouldn't have called them, would she?"

I wasn't interested, but I *was* incredibly interested in getting out of the house. I didn't want to tempt fate and get caught standing over Moira's body—or get killed. I was very aware of the pistol I was clutching.

Philippa's eyes suddenly blazed with an idea, then, like a shade being pulled down, almost immediately grew dark, even morose. "Do you think she was planning to warn them? Is that possible?"

"Why would she care?"

"Maybe she knew Bogdan was wise to our scheme, and she tried to warn them but was too late." She breathed out heavily, a glimmer of sadness entering her. "Years ago, she threw her arm over me after Bogdan struck me. Remember? Maybe there was something in her that was at least a little redeemable."

"No," I said sharply. "There wasn't." I huffed, making a show of my impatience. "We need to go."

"I know, I know," she said meekly. Moira's death bothered her; she was trying to stir up emotion for her.

"She was bad. *All* bad. Don't give her an ounce of credit," I snapped at her. "We need to go and find Bogdan and kill him, unless you've decided he's not all bad either." I pressed my palm against the sturdy grip of the revolver, anger tensing my muscles.

Her expression sharpened; her moment of sentimental mush had evaporated. "Let's hope we can do it before he finds us—or Lionel."

"Now," I said, "where the hell do we look?"

CHAPTER 36

MAY 8, 1954, LIONEL

Bogdan gestures with Roger's M1911 for me to take the lead. We're continuing our trek across the bridge, leaving the lion sentinel behind, passing under overhanging tree branches, and walking over Rock Creek Park, roughly eighty feet below. He holds the pistol low at his left hip, away from traffic, which has thinned out. Everyone's home, eating dinner. I'm obeying his orders, but I'm numb and dazed. My senses are muffled as if all my nerve endings have been unplugged. In my mind, the dark gray Stetson twitches and turns, and underneath its brim swims an overlay of faces: Roger, Bogdan, Roger, Bogdan, and, flickering through, the boy from Little Palace. The bridge stretches in front of me, its ornate patinaed lampposts shining dimly and the outline of the Kalorama apartment buildings hovering in the distance. Our building's gargoyles stare into the night, having failed at their job. But, behind all this, in front of me, are those faces: Love, hate, love, hate, love-hate. I'm shattered, I know. I'm devastated, I know. But the pain of Roger's death hasn't reached me. It's as if it's waiting for me on the other side of the bridge, like one of those crouching lions, about to pounce. But I want to make it there, to feel it.

I've known from the beginning. Not the fact of his death—Lord knows, there were many clues to the contrary—but a gut understanding that all this isn't going to end well. If he's here, strolling beside me, he's wringing his hands and worrying that I'll crack up, curl into a ball, and give up. He's probably whispering in my ear: *Don't worry, Lyle. Don't worry. It will be okay, darling. Just keep moving.* Yes, I felt he was gone from the beginning, even as I stared at the windows, watching the smoke pour out. Even then, he was in my ear, reminding me of when he first showed me 2101 Connecticut Ave, and we dreamed about our lives on the ninth floor: "We'll throw parties," he said. "We'll sip martinis and watch DC blink to life in the evenings."

As we walk, Bogdan begins talking to me, telling me the details of Roger's death, clucking about how he and the girls did all the work. But I still don't understand why his ring was on the wrong finger or who was responsible for his convenient cremation. If I'd lied to the Raymonds, ironically, I would've been aligning myself with the truth. What I do understand, though, is that Roger was keeping it from me to protect me, which for a moment, a ridiculous moment, infuriates me. I'm stronger than Roger gives me credit for. *Gave.* He didn't understand that pain must be felt, that it's necessary to really feel it. He loved his manhood too much. But I know that weakness can pose as bravery in our world, and strength can be forged in tears. Mama taught me that. Cry hard and fight hard.

As we continue our crawl over the park, the treetops sway below us in a mild breeze, their leaves fluttering softly. Bogdan begins to lecture me about Greek mythology, casting himself in the role of Orpheus and the girls he brutally murdered in the role of Eurydice. His tone is cheerful, chatty. He explains that "his girls" are waiting to be rescued by him in the underworld.

"But Lion-nail," he says, mispronouncing my name. "I couldn't part with Susannah, so I preserved her on ice. She looked so like Anna—and her name, her *name* has Anna buried in it. It was a sign, so I kept her close." Then his tone darkens, eerily maudlin. "Vera from Clifton, Virginia, never made it to the river. I had to leave her to rot in that house in Southwest. The papers haven't even reported her missing, poor thing." I don't respond; I keep walking, scanning the street and sidewalk for a way out. Suddenly, he tells me to stop and demands I look at him. "You know," he says, wagging Roger's gun at me, "when you think about it, you're like Orpheus."

I stare at him. We're under a streetlamp, and in the shade of his fedora, I see only his deep eye sockets and the contours of his jaw.

"You, too," he nods, agreeing with himself. "You've been trying to access the underworld and bring your lover home."

"I didn't kill him," I say. "You killed those girls. You defiled them."

He falls silent. Just over the three-foot railing, the leaves rustle. "Perhaps it's time for you to go retrieve your lover." He gestures toward the railing with the M1911. "Jump."

"Hell no," I say.

"Do it," he demands gently. "You must."

"No. Fuck you."

"Why?" He's miffed. "You fags love to kill yourselves, don't you?"

A blast of intense, burning rage breaks through me, but I don't respond. I hold on to it—kinetic energy, building and heating. The fog lifts from my mind, and I gain furious clarity, like a camera suddenly sharpening its focus. If I'm going to make it to the other side of the bridge, if I'm going to get the chance to grieve for Roger, to feel that pain, that love, I'm going to have to kill this man. There's no other way.

"What happened to your sister?" I ask.

His face contorts briefly, and he answers, "Our father killed her. Horribly."

"So, you're grieving, too."

For a long moment, he gazes at me with his empty eyes. "I do not grieve," he says, his confidence shaken. "There's no need to. She will no longer be my father's. She'll be mine, bonded to me forever."

"No, she won't," I say. "She's gone."

Fury flashes across his face. "Shut up," he snaps impotently.

"She's gone," I say louder, edged with cruelty. "Just dust."

"You know nothing!" he cries, aiming the gun at my forehead.

"That's the point of that myth, you fool. You can't bring them back."

"Jump," he growls, "or I'll shoot you. Right here."

I lock eyes with him.

"Jump," he repeats, drawing the word out. "Now."

I'm staring at a void.

"Jump!" he demands, shifting his body forward slightly.

And I jump, but not over the bridge—at him. I lunge forward, swatting his hand. A shot fires, vanishing into the night. He recovers, but I catch his hand gripping the pistol as he does. We grapple with it between us, its barrel pointed upward at the stars. I've never been stronger; even my sore finger, nearly broken by the FBI bullies, feels no pain. He squeezes the trigger, and I jerk back, a bullet zipping past my ear and colliding with the light above us, casting us in deeper shadow. He pauses for a split second, confused by what happened—the crack and pop of the lamp—and I shove the M1911 under his jaw and force him to close his finger on the trigger. It fires, sending a bullet through his chin, his head, and the top of his skull. Roger's hat pops off and drifts over the railing. His eyes freeze open in astonishment, the blue flickering out. Blood bubbles at his lips, and his jaw goes slack, exposing his bloody teeth. For an astonishing second, I glimpse the entire horror of the man, all the pain he caused and perhaps all the pain he experienced. Still, it is unknowable to me, like contemplating a black hole, and I can't bear much of it, so I shove him away, his top-heavy body striking the railing, wavering unsteadily. A river of blood pours over his chin, and his eyes, although dead, yearn terribly, like his eyes in that old photo. I shove him again, and his shoulders carry him over the railing, feet briefly in the air, and he falls, vanishing silently through the tops of the trees—but the sound of his body hitting the ground never comes. It's as if the earth swallowed him.

Free now, I scoop up Roger's gun, which fell at our feet, tuck it into my coat, and run to the other side of the bridge, not looking back.

CHAPTER 37

MAY 8, 1954, JUDY

We were in Iris's apartment, processing our discovery of Moira's and her chauffeur's bodies with Iris, wondering if Bogdan was coming for us next. We'd just agreed we should immediately tell Lionel everything when he flung open the door as if we'd summoned him. Startled, Philippa and I shot up from the sofa and Iris from her chair. He stumbled in, breathless, his face scrawled with panic, his bronze eyes glittering with madness. A smear of fresh blood was on his forehead next to his scar and more blood was splattered on the front of his coat. "You!" He growled at us, steadying himself against the doorframe. "All of you are liars, goddamn liars." He yanked a large, blocky pistol from his pocket and wagged its barrel at us.

"You're right," Philippa said, grabbing my arm. She was standing a little behind me. "We lied because Roger asked us to."

"He didn't want to upset you with our plan," I added, blood pounding through my body, sweat dampening my armpits. "Roger told us you were—"

"He told us you'd already been through enough with the Little Palace ordeal," Philippa said. "We're sorry. Terribly sorry. We should've known better."

Keeping him in the dark didn't make me feel good, but his current blend of gun-wielding craziness and righteous anger annoyed me even more than it frightened me. And I wanted to know about what looked to be a substantial amount of blood on him. We'd lied, sure, but he had no right to assume we meant him harm. I remembered him accusing me of pretending to be a white woman—the man who wrote behind a white mask! It was complicated, I'd wanted to explain to him then instead of just biting back. Nothing is black or white. Right now, though, he needed to calm the hell down and listen. "Look," I said, stepping forward and holding my hands up. "We're not part of a grand conspiracy to hurt you or Roger. We love you. We love Ray Kane. The fire was Roger's idea, after all."

His face crinkled, and the muzzle of the pistol dipped.

"We were helping him fake his suicide to avoid a catastrophic confrontation with the federal government, Bogdan, or both." I sighed deeply. "He wasn't supposed to die. It wasn't the fucking plan, Lionel. Why would it be?"

Softening my blunt phrasing, Philippa added, "We don't know what happened."

He raised the pistol and pointed it at us in a sharp gesture. We all flinched. "I do," he said, his voice cracking. "Jesus. I know what happened. I know."

"Please put down the gun, hon," Iris said, maintaining her calm. "We can talk this through." Her tone was warm and compassionate. "You're right. We all have some explaining to do."

"Why are you covered with blood?" I asked. "What happened?"

He seemed confused by my remark.

"Your face, near your scar," I said. "I'm surprised no one stopped you."

With his free hand, he touched his scar and inspected the blood on his fingers, his feverish eyes growing wide and beginning to glaze with tears.

"Are you okay?" Iris asked, moving closer.

He'd lowered the gun to his side. "Bogdan is dead. He tried to kill me, but, like all of you, he underestimated me. I took this from him," he indicated the pistol, "and I shot him through the head and pushed him off Taft Bridge."

Astonishment reverberated through me, and I felt Philippa's hand, still on my arm, squeeze me tightly. "Are you serious?" I said in disbelief. "*You* killed him?"

"Whose blood do you think this is?"

"Oh," Iris uttered. "You poor man."

The tightness in my chest released a little. The euphoria I'd expected when I knew Bogdan was dead or caught didn't flow through me. I felt relief, sure, but the dominant emotion was disappointment. For the longest time, no matter the means, I wanted Philippa and me to stop Bogdan. We'd worked so hard at it. I couldn't help it: *I* wanted to be the one to shoot him in the head and push him off a bridge. The poetic justice of our vengeance was thwarted. Indeed, life is complicated and unexpected, and this conclusion to the Bogdan nightmare was no different.

Without adequate enthusiasm, I said, "That's incredible, Lionel. Incredible."

He glared at me for a long moment, shook his head, and with a tortured smirk, said, "You're jealous."

"I am," I said, startled that I'd said it out loud, half believing I hadn't.

Suddenly something in him melted, and he collapsed against the opened door and slid down. Iris rushed forward, scooped up the gun, which lay loose in his palm, and put an arm around him, softly saying, "I'm so sorry, Lionel. I'm so sorry." She handed the weapon to Philippa, who'd rushed past me to retrieve it. "It must be Roger's," she whispered to me as she held it. "It's like my father's service pistol. Bogdan must've stolen it."

I nodded but didn't say anything. Iris's gentle touch and calming words suddenly broke something open inside Lionel, and he began to sob grotesquely. Terror fluttered in my chest. I didn't like seeing him this way. His shoulders heaved, and his entire body shook and curled in on itself. Iris carefully moved him from the apartment door to the couch. He looked like someone who'd just been punched in the gut.

I stood back, silent and afraid of him. Was grief catching like a disease? It was burrowing into me and clawing at that dark, amorphous thing inside me, the black box of my childhood, what happened at Elysium when I was a girl. No matter how furiously it clawed, no matter how rabid and out of control it was, it wasn't going to get in. I wouldn't let it. No way. I finally understood that what frightened me wasn't the mystery of my black box but that if I solved that mystery, it'd snap me in two.

"Go on home," Iris said to us, nodding toward the door. "Give him space. Once he calms down, we'll talk. I'll take care of him."

I didn't move at first. Philippa took my hand, said, "Let's go," and guided me through the door, gently closing it behind us.

CHAPTER 38

JUNE 12, 1954, JUDY

Philippa and I arrived early to snag a good table. Tonight, Teddie B., a local drag queen and a longstanding act on the Croc's stage, was performing his Marlene Dietrich bit, an act he'd kept alive for a decade. Iris, who had maintained contact with Lionel, convinced him to meet us for a few drinks and, we hoped, clear the air. After we'd left him the night he killed Bogdan, he'd refused to speak to us. The next day, he moved into a hotel, and we hadn't seen him since.

It was 9:00 P.M., and the club was beginning to fill up. With its smoky haze, flickering votives, gingham tablecloths, and strange vault-like ceiling supported by cement pillars, this room was like no other in town. Sitting along the bar, Negros chatted comfortably with whites, laughing, flirting, being served by an oversized Czech named Kasper, who, if he liked you, spoke perfect English. Spread across the space, men and women, no matter their race or sexual inclination, clustered around café tables and leaned toward each other, freed from the social barriers that kept them apart above ground. Soon, the worn velvet curtains on the stage would part slowly and reveal a man refashioned as a movie star standing behind a microphone, aiming for the glamour and talent of the original and missing, but in doing so, he was creating something new, a show that simultaneously mocked and celebrated its source material. Teddie B.'s imperfect Dietrich was a kind of perfection.

Across from me, Philippa sipped her gin fizz. She now had her hair cut chin-length and flipped under, showing off her slender neck. Her eyes glittered in the votive light. Nat King Cole's buttery voice crooned "Pretend" from the Select-o-matic across the club, urging us to pretend to be happy, to be fulfilled, but I didn't need to pretend—well, at least not now. Bogdan was dead, Moira was dead, and we were free. The desire to run my fingers up Philippa's bare arm, place my hand on her cheek, and pull her to me for a kiss was strong. Knowing the others might appear soon, I resisted, but barely. Iris no longer winced at the idea of us as a couple and had become at ease with the denizens of Croc's, but I didn't want to push her, especially after the high anxiety of the past month.

"Do you think Lionel is still angry with us?" Philippa asked, setting down her Collins glass.

I thought about her question but didn't have an immediate answer. Perhaps he'd always be angry with us. He'd continued to meet up with Iris, maintaining that friendship, which puzzled Philippa and hurt me. He was grieving, we understood, but why not include us? We missed Roger, too. His horrible fate would haunt us forever. Bogdan had the upper hand because, however begrudgingly, the FBI protected him. We were reckless to believe we could trick him, and Roger paid the price.

"He's willing to see us," I said. "That's something."

With that, I saw them descending the stairs into the crowd. He wore a tailored suit, crisp white shirt, and burgundy tie, and he was laughing with Iris, who was on his arm. In a slim black pencil skirt, dove gray gloves, and hair in a tight updo, she could've been on the runway at Woodies.

Philippa waved, and Iris spotted us.

"You look amazing, Lionel," Philippa said, rising from her chair and wearing a welcoming smile. "It's so good to see you. May I give you a hug?"

He smiled mildly, thwarting the sadness that hung just behind his expression, and held out his arms. She threw her arms around him. I rose from my chair and extended my hand, not ready for an enthusiastic embrace. I was still leery of him. I couldn't shake our last encounter. The sheer magnitude of his grief had overwhelmed me. And behind that, I still heard his biting assessment of me, especially my pretense of being a white woman. However hypocritical of him, there was truth in it, another tangled thread to unwind—for both of us.

For a beat, he regarded me, his yellow-brown eyes soft, warm, and, yes, still wounded. "Judy," he said, his deep voice calm, resonant. "I come in peace."

I smiled in return, my trepidation easing, and, with mock exasperation, I said, "The crowd is thick tonight, and the waitstaff thin. I'll grab drinks from the source. What will you have?"

They gave me their orders.

When I returned with two hard-won martinis, one dirty, one with a twist, the little group was deep in conversation.

"Well," Iris was saying, "it's something I'll never forgive myself for."

"I understand why it all happened," he said. "And Roger would've chosen cremation. You—*all* of you—were making sense of a terrible situation." His face dimmed slightly. "Remember, I didn't know what the hell was going on. It was a double shock. Instead of Roger, I was confronted with that awful man; I knew Roger was dead, and I knew I might be soon, too. I was angry at all of you because I was confused."

On hearing this, the hum of tension between us softened to a murmur. "Watch out," I said, "martini delivery for the sir and madam," and handed the dirty martini to Iris and the twist to Lionel.

I slipped into my wobbly chair and took a sip of my now-warm beer. "Speaking of Bogdan," I said, "there's still no word of a body in Rock Creek Park."

Philippa and Iris frowned, worry creasing the corners of their eyes, but Lionel shook his head. "He's dead," he said. "*Very* dead."

"The FBI made it go away, I'm sure," Philippa said. "Their ties go deep with the Metro PD."

"And Moira's and her chauffeur's murders have been labeled 'a robbery gone wrong,' citing the missing contents of her safe," I added. "Another cover-up. The case is still open, but they know Bogdan was responsible. They must."

"Damn," Lionel said. "They're good at covering their tracks. I was hoping it would all come out."

"Maybe one day," I said.

The absence of Bogdan's corpse, though, unsettled me. I believed Lionel, of course, but the lack of resolution—the lack of a body—conjured images of Bogdan descending, like his inspiration Orpheus, into the underworld, where he'd torment his victims and force them back into the world. Like Moira, I suppose, he'd always be with me, lurking just behind the veil of my life, scratching at the window and wanting in. All my demons, it seemed, were attendant.

"I want to hear some good news," Iris broke in. "We're supposed to be having fun, you know." She wagged her finger at us. "Come on!"

I appreciated her pivoting us away from the gloom, so I piped up. "This week, I bumped into Ed Davies, one of my bosses at WSDC, and we began chatting. He invited me to return to the station as a writer. He wants my help on their pulpy mystery show 'Dark Secrets.'"

"Cheers!" Lionel said, raising his glass. "You'll have material to inspire you, for sure."

"I'm so excited for her," Philippa said, giving my arm a little squeeze.

"With things pretty bleak for McCarthy and his cronies in the army hearings, Ed and Rich are less timid these days," I said.

"Have you left no sense of decency?" Lionel cried out, parroting the army's council Joseph Welsh, who excoriated McCarthy on national television this Wednesday.

"That's right," Iris said, tipping her glass to him—and the crumbling of Joseph McCarthy.

"Selfishly," Philippa added, "this means I can finish my master's at GW. I thought I would have to pause after last semester to get a job."

I wanted her to finish her master's and teach or write or whatever; it was a future I could imagine for us. Maybe we'd travel. Maybe we'd even collaborate, like Roger and Lionel. Who knows, but it was far away from the things that were a lure for her: suburbs, husbands, and, of course, children.

After more chitchat, Iris and Philippa offered to retrieve another round of drinks before the show started, leaving Lionel and me together at the table. We didn't speak at first. He studied the room, his eyes gliding over the other patrons. Perhaps he was thinking about Roger. Perhaps he's missing him. *Of course*, he's missing him. He turned to me, smiled vaguely, and said, "You know, they still haven't canceled our contract for *The Tattoo Artist*." He lifted his eyebrows. "It doesn't mean they won't."

"Do you want to write it?"

He snickered. "Hell no."

"Do you still want to be a writer?"

His eyes widened, surprised, gleaming a little. "Of course."

"As Ray Kane?"

"Ray Kane is dead. His face, at least."

"Maybe you should write as Lionel Kane, not Ray Kane."

"My dear," he said, reaching for his martini, "no one will read mystery novels written by a mixed-race fairy."

I thought about what it would mean for Lionel to write as Lionel, for what it would mean for his audiences to see his face on the jacket flap. He had a point. His readers wanted to believe Ray Kane was telling them a story, even though they'd already been reading Lionel for years. They wanted the fantasy that Roger's handsome face provided them, the macho white writer writing about macho white things—but the joke was on them. The mirror they thought they were peering into wasn't a mirror at all but an illusion. I wondered, though, why Philippa and I loved Kane's books. Were we, like the others, falling for the same trick, or was there something mingled in with all the P. I. Calvin McKey tough talk and violence, something subtextual, someone peeking out at us from between the lines and calling to us?

"You should try to write as yourself," I said, folding my arms on the table. "Maybe you just need to write something different—a new kind of detective."

He considered it, a curious smile creeping into his lips. "Maybe," he said, his eyes brightening, his brown brow unfurrowing. "What do I have to lose?"

"Nothing," I said.

"And how about you?" He crossed his arms. "What do you have to lose?"

I knew his meaning: When was I going to step out of the shadows and be whatever I'm supposed to be? I'm not a Peabody. I'm not white. I'm certainly not straight. I'm also not a Baker. I'm not a part of the community Iris grew up in. But he was right. Not belonging is no excuse for pretending to belong; it's no excuse for not stepping forward and declaring: "This is who I am. I don't fit in easily. But it's not my problem, and don't make it yours." Of course, I've lived long enough to know I will always be someone's problem. I was Edith's. I was Moira's.

"I have things to lose." I dragged my finger over a thin scar near my elbow. "But, hey, perhaps I have more to gain."

Philippa and Iris emerged from the crowd, weaving their way toward us, holding the drinks high above their shoulders to avoid being jostled and spilling them. It was a balancing act, just as it was to be yourself in this shitty world. But here, in the beautiful muddle of Croc's, we didn't have to balance anything other than our drinks. Soon the stage curtains would part. Teddie B. as Marlene would step up to the mic and, cloaked in sequins and a bad wig, sing, and we'd bask in the glamour of her artifice, which, for us, was a kind of truth.

EPILOGUE

MAY 7, 1954—THE MIRROR

Bogdan and Moira stand just outside the walk-in closet, the door framing them. Beyond them, Moira's vanity sits at a slight angle, and beyond it, her bedroom window divides the early afternoon sky into little gray squares. Moira's dark charmeuse day dress shimmers in the bright closet light, and her platinum hoop earrings dangle, stirring as she speaks. She tells Bogdan she's heading out to a late lunch, a Daughters of the American Revolution function, and doesn't have time for him. She's fidgety and clearly wants him gone. But he's not easily shooed away. After all, he's scaled the trellis at the back of her house and crawled in through an open window to say hello. Something, it seems, he's done before. Not the simplest way in. He's out of breath. He's looming over her; his vile odor must be swirling in her nostrils.

"How did those fucking harpies find me?" he demands more than asks. "Did you tell them about the farm? *Did* you?"

"Of course not!" she says, exasperated. "I told them to hunt you down at the place in Southwest. John told me they'd forced you out of that house, something about urban renewal on the way."

He grunts, annoyed. "I had to leave a girl's body behind. Vera something." He moves in closer to her. "I didn't like that at all. Her soul's deserted. I'll never retrieve her from—"

"Jesus, Adrian," she snaps. "I don't need to know."

He cools, waving his hand at her, like, "You're a fool. Why should I be bothered?"

"I told my chauffeur to follow them and scare the hell out of them."

"You should've told him to kill them."

"I'll leave the killing up to you," she says, wincing slightly at the thought, but not so he notices.

He seethes, black tar bubbling deep in him. "They destroyed my cabin. They smashed my guitar, and they, they took the photo of my . . ." He doesn't finish his sentence, too disturbed by the thought of it.

If you pay close attention to him, you'll note his twitching fingers and the lift and fall of his chest. He misses her, his Anna, and you think, for a moment, that there's some small thing that's redeemable about him: his love for his dead sister.

But, in an instant, the chill returns to his blue eyes, like a door suddenly slamming shut.

Moira regards him warily—no, it's something more profound than wariness; she loathes him. She asks, "What are you going to do?"

"I'm going to kill those girls and their other fag friend."

She's startled, but her horror is contemptible. She knows what he is.

"And," he adds, "I'm going to get back what they took."

"But Judy and Philippa—" she utters awkwardly, trying to hide her alarm. "There's no need to kill them. I'm going to tell the world about their perversion. They'll be ruined."

She desperately wants to believe that she's not a murderer, that she's above such things, that she's not responsible for the monster standing in front of her, blocking her exit from her hall of mirrors, her vanity as interior design. If she was being honest with herself, she'd remember that, for years, she conspired to cover up his sins, that she has the blood of at least nine young girls under her manicured fingernails, that she'd hopped on that train long ago and the doors closed. There's no looking back, and the tunnel is just ahead.

Bogdan glares at her. "That's not enough," he says. "You know it."

"Then why did you come here?" she snaps, not concealing her frustration. "I didn't invite you."

"To find out if I should kill you, too." He suddenly grabs her by the throat with his wide, grimy fingers, lifts her a little, and pushes her into the closet, pressing the back of her head against the mirrored door near the entrance, the one with the safe in it. She's terrified. She's gasping. Her bulging eyes bulge more, like balloons expanding. The mirror rattles behind her. She makes small, sad pleading noises. Her finely groomed bouffant begins to fall apart, bobby pins slipping out and tumbling to the floor.

"After all, I'm curious why you called Raymond's apartment while I was there," he says. "Did you think the girls would be there? Were you warning them?"

She can't respond, but her face is her confession.

He releases her, and she clutches her clavicle with her hand, coughing, and steadies herself against the mirror.

"Don't worry, Moira." He grins. "You won't die today."

After catching her breath, she straightens her shoulders and looks at him. Her eyes, pregnant with tension, sharpen. Her haughty cool arrogance surfaces. "Fine, then get out of my way," she says, gesturing with a dismissive flick.

He steps back, and she leaves the walk-in, vanishing beyond the doorframe.

He's about to turn away but stops suddenly at the threshold. Maybe he heard you. A rustle behind one of the closet doors, something living behind the mirrors, peeking out between the doors. His eyes narrow, their azure irises never brighter. Perhaps he imagined it? He takes a half step forward, then stops. He doesn't like this feeling, the feeling of being watched. The mirrors multiply his reflection—dirty trousers, torn shirt, mussed black hair, lean, unshaven face. The fun-house effect annoys him and undercuts his confidence. You can tell by the way he holds himself. Vulnerable, a little sunken chested. He shakes his head and turns away, but his intuition persists. He swings around. He's being observed; he knows it, damn it. He's being sized up, even judged. A twinge of mortal fear, a foreboding, ripples through him. He steps forward, muscles in his neck tightening, the veins in his temples throbbing. Then something arrests him.

Now it's not himself he sees in the mirrors, but the faces of all the girls he took, his Eurydices, their steady, dark eyes regarding him: Jackie, Carol, Nancy, Betty, Susannah, Maggie, Candy, Melody, and Vera—and somewhere behind them, slipping in and out of the endlessly echoing reflections, Anna. Perhaps they're watching him, taking good measure of him. After all, only they know where to look.

Horror-stricken, he leaves, sliced off by the doorframe.

In the room beyond, Moira recovers from her ordeal, picking up the phone to make an excuse for missing lunch: "I'm sorry, dear, a terrible headache. Yes, yes. Thank you." After a minute, she returns to the closet.

In the mirror, she stares at herself for a long time, taking in the crumbled misery of her current condition: her bouffant a mess, her lipstick smeared, her dress wrinkled, and, tut, a run in her pantyhose. She's exhausted and annoyed—but no trace of fear, no moral qualm. Minutes ago, she subtly pleaded, "But Judy and Philippa, there's no need to kill them." Now, she'd rather mope over having to redo her outfit. There's nothing to her but self-interest. She doesn't see a murderer when she looks at herself; she sees a queen.

What she doesn't see, though, is you looking back at her, creeping behind her reflection. Her chauffeur didn't see you either, his eyes missing you in the rearview mirror as you raised your new go-nowhere-without-it accessory to the back of his head and pulled the trigger. But like the dead girls know Bogdan, you know her, and soon, you'll step through the glass, demand she returns to you what's yours, and, with fury, show her herself.

ACKNOWLEDGMENTS

Hall of Mirrors is a murder mystery on the surface, but it's also an exploration of passing and the complex motivations for concealing your identity during the early 1950s in Washington, DC. What does it mean to be legible as a Black or queer person in this landscape? What does it mean to pass as white or straight during such a socially conservative and oppressive decade? In a time when physical and emotional violence toward LGBTQ+ people and Blacks was accepted as justifiable and institutionally reinforced by the government and much of the dominant culture, the answers for how to express yourself in public were far from cut and dry. Of course, writing characters like Judy Nightingale and Lionel Kane required much thought, research, and reflection, all of which I hope led to fair and multi-layered representation.

To do this work required knowledgeable guidance. So, I'm grateful for a variety of nonfiction resources, including *A Queer Capital: A History of Gay Life in Washington, D. C.* by Genny Beemyn, *Hoover's War on Gays: Exposing the FBI's "Sex Deviates" Program* by Douglas M. Charles, *The Lavender Scare:*

The Cold War Persecution of Gays and Lesbians in the Federal Government by David K. Johnson, *Secret City: The Hidden History of Gay Washington* by James Kirchick, *Indecent Advances: A Hidden History of True Crime and Prejudice Before Stonewall* by James Polchin, and *Images of America: Southwest Washington, D. C.* by Paul K. Williams. I'm also deeply thankful for the brilliant fiction of James Baldwin, Chester Himes, Walter Mosley, Thomas Mallon, and Nella Larson, among others. While research gives a stable framework for historical fiction, the voices of other novelists who have engaged with these issues help me understand the complex humanity of my characters.

A manuscript only becomes a book with a team working together to shape the characters and story and usher it into the world. First and foremost, I'm thankful to my agent, Annie Bomke, who is my first editor and brilliant steward of my career. She continues to embrace Judy and Philippa as they journey from their teenage years to young adulthood. Her belief in me and these characters means the world to me. Likewise, I'm grateful to the team at Pegasus, including my talented and keen-eyed editor, Victoria Wenzel, who helped me refine the manuscript; my publicist, Julia Romero, who tirelessly promoted the novel, and the publicity team at Booksparks, who amplified the coverage; Maria Fernandez for her elegant design of the book's interior; and Derek Thornton for another stunning cover—a book that's on fire but never burns!

I'm profoundly grateful to the mystery reading and writing community, from my dedicated readers to my fellow writers. I also offer a heartfelt thank you to bookstore owners, librarians, festival organizers, bloggers, podcasters, social media pros, and organizations that bolster and celebrate writers, especially Lambda Literary, Sisters in Crime, International Thriller Writers, and Mystery Writers of America. Without your support, it would be impossible for me to share my stories with the world. We depend on organizations like these to protect marginalized writers from censorship.

I'm grateful to my co-organizers of Queer Crime Writers—Kristen Lepionka, Stephanie Gayle, Jeffrey Marks, and Marco Carocari—and my

ACKNOWLEDGMENTS   **323**

many queer crime writer friends—Kelly J. Ford, Robyn Gigl, Greg Herren, Anne Laughlin, Meredith Doench, Cheryl Head, and many others—for coming together to create a loving and supportive community. Additionally, a special thank you to Al Warren, a true crime writer and dynamite radio host, who invited me to be a co-host on the House of Mystery Radio Show in 2020 and has put up with me since—even when my pup, Winky, barks his head off at the UPS man during a show.

To my students and colleagues at Virginia Commonwealth University and the University of Nebraska Omaha MFA program, thank you for your support and mutual love of the written word, especially Jessica Nelson, for your friendship, laughter, and willingness to listen.

To my friends and my family, both blood-related and chosen, I sincerely appreciate your love and support. I don't know where I'd be without you, especially my mother and brothers, who always keep me grounded and focused.

To my husband and ceramic artist extraordinaire, Jeff Herrity, thank you for loving me, being patient with me, and accepting me as I am: a crazy writer person.